P9-CEN-536

GREGORY SCOTT KATSOULIS

ALL

RIGHTS

RESERVED

HARLEQUIN®TEEN

For Jenn & Evia and all our words.

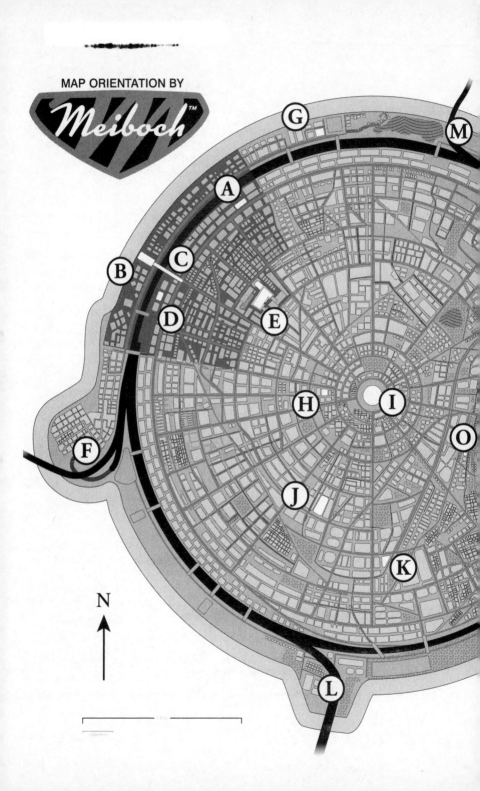

MAP ORIENTATION BY

Meiboch™

N

A.) Speth's Home
B.) Falxo Park
C.) Falxo Bridge
D.) Thomkin's Tower
E.) Speth's School
F.) Western Exit
G.) Nince Boutique
H.) Carol A. Harving's Apt.
I.) Butchers & Rog
J.) Margot's Home
K.) Henri's Home
L.) Southern Exit
M.) Northern Exit
N.) Attack on Speth
O.) Kel's Home
P.) Courthouse

MAP SPONSORED BY

NANOLION™

1.) The Prem
2.) The Dezyém
3.) The Troisiéme
4.) The Quatriéme
5.) The Cinqieme
6.) The Sizyém
7.) The Seithfed
8.) The Wityém
9.) The Neuviéme
10.) The Dixiéme
11.) The Onziéme
12.) Duodécimo
13.) Treizéme
14.) Section 14
15.) The Pymthegfed

Sponsored by the

STATE OF VERMAINE

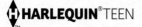

SPETH: 9¢

We had just started over the bridge, toward my party, when the famously cheerful "Don't Jump" Ad clicked on. This had never happened to me before. The billboard's advertising systems scanned me—analyzing my age, my style, even my pulse—and calculated I was in need of a friendly reminder not to kill myself. Colorful, hopping bunnies sang at my feet, on a waist-high screen that arced the full length of the bridge wall. Traffic roared along eighty feet below. Above, the city dome was lit a diffuse, fading gray by the evening sky beyond.

I felt a little queasy. Jumpers had been growing increasingly common, but I'm sure a higher railing would have been more effective than a glib cartoon. I wasn't planning to kill myself. I had other things to concentrate on.

Mrs. Harris, my guardian, was still talking.

"You will get used to budgeting, *Speth*," she chirped, but faltered slightly at my name, as if it wasn't good enough for her mouth. My name *was* cheap and ugly. *Speth*. I hated it. It sounded like someone spitting. My parents chose it from a list of discounted girls' names. When my brother was born, they vowed not to repeat that mistake and paid for a good premium name: *Sam*.

I wished Sam was nearby to distract me. Sam always made me laugh. But Mrs. Harris had shooed him off to help set up my party in the park, so she would have my complete attention.

Mrs. Harris was a little bird of a woman with restless hands and a tense, wrinkled little smile. She'd been lecturing me for the better part of an hour on what to expect on my big day.

I stopped walking and looked down at the shiny new Cuff she had clamped around my forearm that morning. It was a marvel of engineering—a cool processor, a rock-steady tether to WiFi and a smooth glossy surface impervious to scratches, dirt and smudges. It was rimmed in a burnished lightweight Altenium™ composite. The Cuff was nearly indestructible, unless the NanoLion™ battery went haywire and melted your Cuff and your arm off. The Cuff's main purpose was to record everything I said and did, so I could pay the Rights Holders their fees.

"It's beautiful," my sister assured me. She patted my shoulder. The words she spoke scrolled up *her* Cuff as she was charged for each.

Saretha Jime—word: It's: $1.99.
Saretha Jime—word: Beautiful: $8.99.

Then she was charged for patting me.

Saretha Jime—gesture: pat to shoulder—2 seconds: $1.98

Every word is Trademarked™, Restricted® or Copyrighted©. The companies and people who own these rights let people use them, but once you turn fifteen, you have to pay. Saretha had turned fifteen more than two years before. I was wearing the same bright orange dress she had, but not nearly as well. Everything else I owned was dull, gray and from a limited selection of public domain clothes Mrs. Harris allowed us to have printed at the UnderGap™.

At 6:36 p.m., it would be my turn; I would pay for every word I spoke for the rest of my life. Foolishly, I had believed it would be fun.

My Cuff felt tight. I tried to fit a finger between it and my flesh. There was no gap.

"In the unlikely event it *needs* to be removed," Mrs. Harris said, "the proper authorities can do so. However, if your Cuff is removed for *any* reason, you will not be allowed to speak. Any utterance will result in a painful shock to the eyes."

I closed my eyes. My lids slid down just a bit more slowly than before. As part of my transition, in addition to the Cuff, Mrs. Harris had roughly thumbed a corneal implant into each of my eyes. The implants were, at that moment, slowly fusing to my corneas. She said I would have terrible eyesight without them.

I'm almost certain this was a lie.

"You've read the Terms of Service?" she asked, but she knew I hadn't. No one read the ToS. They were boring— hundreds of pages of intimidating, brain-melting Legalese. What did it matter? I had to agree. We couldn't change them, and while technically I could "opt out," I was required by Law to have the implants before I turned fifteen.

"Optic shocks may cause nausea," Mrs. Harris said flatly, "dizziness, redness of the eyes, swelling, headaches, shortness of breath, seizures, confusion, heart palpitations, vision changes and, of course, blindness."

"Rarely," Saretha assured me. Her Cuff buzzed and charged her $1.75. I missed when we used to really talk. She was always so positive and joyful. I supposed she still was, inside, but I mostly talked with Sam after her transition. We didn't have the kind of money that would let us talk freely once we were paying for our words.

"Traditionally, one arrives at one's celebration at *exactly* the moment one turns fifteen." Mrs. Harris's thin smile pulled tight. I think she had timed our walk out to the park. Slowing down was not part of that plan.

I wished I didn't have to have a Custodian. I wished my parents could have been here, but when I was little, our family was sued for an illegal music download traced back five generations to a great-great-aunt somewhere. We owed the Musical Rights Association of America® more than six million dollars in damages. Debt Services took our parents and placed them somewhere down in Carolina, pollinating crops with an eyedropper and brush until our debts were paid. My heart ached thinking of them so far away.

Mrs. Harris noted my sadness and moved on.

On the far side of the bridge, my celebration was crowded onto a small, manicured strip of green called Falxo Park. It sat at the very edge of the city, in the heart of the Onzième, where the dome curves down to the city wall. All the faux-Parisian-style shops crowded around the park, stretching off into the distance in a plastic approximation of Franco quaintness.

The outer shopping district and the park it flanked were beautiful if I squinted at it, awash and aglow in Moon Mints™

Ads. There was scarcely a surface in the city that couldn't throw up an Ad. I liked the colors—sometimes. I just wished there was less going on all at once. It made my head feel fuzzy to try to take it all in—though Mrs. Harris said I had to try. I could hear the party from across the bridge. All the younger kids were laughing and singing. I'll bet there was dancing, too. The kids over fifteen would only join in after my speech, when the real celebration began.

I had really been looking forward to the party—seeing all my friends, what the Product Placers had brought and what my Branding would be. I was finally going to be a contributing member of society. Mrs. Harris said so. But suddenly, I didn't want to cross the bridge. I didn't want a party. I didn't want a Brand. I didn't care if I got lifelong discounts on Keene Inc. candies in return for unwavering loyalty to their family of products, or a small monthly allowance to speak encouragingly about Pamvax® Feminine Vaccines™. Now that I could really feel the change about to take place, I wanted to run. Why was this something to celebrate? How would I get used to measuring the cost of my words?

I had a strange urge to do or say something meaningful before the clock ticked over, but such behavior was frowned upon. I was supposed to wait until the moment *after* I turned. Then I would read the speech I had crafted with Mrs. Harris. I was contractually obligated to read it, from start to finish, as my first paid words.

The speech was in my hand, printed by Mrs. Harris on a thick sheet of real paper. My sponsors had approved it and subsidized my costs in return for peppering the speech with positive statements about their products. Keene Inc. even offered to have it framed afterward, so I could remember my Last Day, but I'd refused that offer; I didn't want to be responsible for keeping a sheet of paper safe any longer than I had to.

I didn't really care for the speech. I had thought it was funny to cram in as many endorsements as I could, giggling with my friend Nancee Mphinyane-Smil for weeks about how to work in something about Mrs. Harris's favorite brand of industrial-strength suppositories.

I suddenly wished the speech said something more. More about me, my thoughts…my future.

"We should really get moving," Mrs. Harris said.

I nodded, swallowing hard, and began to move. My eyes ached.

"I understand it can be difficult. Reducing your chat so precipitously, after fourteen years of free speech." Mrs. Harris let the word *precipitously* slip out between her teeth with delight. The government paid for her words, and she relished them. There was a reason a woman like Mrs. Harris became a Custodian and took on guardianship of so many children.

It wasn't compassion.

"Undoubtedly you have been speaking more than normal lately," Mrs. Harris said, waving at me to hurry.

I hated that she was right. I had been talking more. I had also been dancing and singing and practicing gymnastics. That was all finished. Every dance move, every gymnastic flourish and every note of every song was Trademarked and priced outside what my family could afford. None of this was Mrs. Harris's fault, but I still wanted to blame her. I had always disliked her. I glared at her horrible, insincere face.

"What?" she asked, taken aback. I took a deep breath.

"Is it normal to be able to see through people's clothes?" I asked, squinting through my new corneal overlays.

Mrs. Harris flinched and moved to cover herself, until I snorted out a laugh.

"Sorry," Saretha said for me. *Sorry* was a fixed-price word at $10, and a legal admission of guilt. She should have let me say it. I still had a minute left. I just wanted to have a little fun.

Mrs. Harris shook her head, tapping at her own Cuff a few times until a micro-suit showed up. The first thing to appear on my Cuff's screen was $30 worth of Mrs. Harris's "pain and suffering." She sued us all the time like this for petty grievances. Saretha just tapped PAY.

"I have helped thousands of boys and girls transition, and trust me, you aren't any different," Mrs. Harris sniffed.

The clock was ticking down. In a few seconds, I would officially turn fifteen. I wanted to think of something meaningful to say, but what? My heart was pounding. My tongue felt like a solid lump in my mouth. Mrs. Harris sighed.

"It is very easy to slip up and speak, or shrug or scream, before you read your speech. This would void your contract, which would be disastrous. I must remind you of your obligation to read it *first*." She lifted the hand that held the speech and shook it around, like I was a puppet. "These need to be your first paid words, Speth."

I pulled away from her. I knew what my responsibilities were.

Mrs. Harris watched the time tick over on her Cuff. "You are an adult now," she said, her eyes fixed on the podium in a way that highlighted the fact that we had not yet reached it.

The bunnies sang more loudly at the apex of the bridge. *"Don't jump, puh-leeze."*

Saretha beamed at me. Smiling was still free. How bad could things be if she seemed so happy? Her smile was wide and bright and friendly. It made you feel warm. She looked like she belonged in movies. A step behind us, her Ads sang a different tune across the glossy LCDs.

Saretha's Ads were full of romance, perfume, alcohol and shoes. She didn't come close to a jumper's algorithm: she was too pretty, too graceful and too well-dressed. When she chose her Branding, Saretha got to choose between twenty-three different corporate brands. I would be lucky to pick from three. Saretha was a Facer, which meant that when she drank a soda in public or ate some chips, she was expected to face the product label out so people could see it. The systems *almost* treated her like an Affluent, although they never digitized her into the Ads. Truly wealthy people often had their likeness scanned, recreated and enhanced to look a little more beautiful and happy in a commercial.

Mrs. Harris thought Saretha's looks were our family's best chance at a better life. She didn't just look like a movie star— she looked a lot like a *particular* star named Carol Amanda Harving. Carol Amanda Harving's smile was more perfect and white, but somehow Saretha's was more comforting and real. As Mrs. Harris liked to point out, my sister and the actress looked more alike than Saretha and I did. My heart sunk every time she declared it, usually in a tone she reserved for crueler moments.

Saretha and I looked enough like sisters, but whatever people might have said about her, they said less enthusiastically about me. Saretha was beautiful with an almost golden complexion. With work, I could be pretty, but my skin never shone the way Saretha's did. Saretha had dark, welcoming eyes, the color of chocolate. Mine were just dark and sharp. Saretha had long, amazing, black wavy hair that rode over her shoulders like a shampoo Ad. I kept mine short, fashioned in a pixie cut Mrs. Micharnd, my gymnastics teacher, found for me in the public domain. When she was my age, Saretha already had curves, and now she had more. I had next to none. I was small, sinewy and perfect for gymnastics.

Saretha went on dates with gorgeous boys who paid for her words and expected affection in return. I went walking with Beecher Stokes, a skinny boy with messy hair who lived with his grandmother. He wasn't terribly cute, but he made me laugh—or at least he did, until his fifteenth birthday. Then his mood soured. His jokes vanished. He would just stare at me, wordless. To fill the awkward silences, I let him kiss me—as much as he could afford. He could not afford much.

I find it creepy that the system can tell how long or hard a kiss is. I don't know exactly what the system monitors, but Beecher would pay something like 17¢ for each second. That's supposed to feel normal. It's been like this longer than I've been alive, but something still felt wrong about it.

Mrs. Harris didn't think it was appropriate for me to be with him, given what she called his "circumstances."

When Beecher was ten, his father tried circumventing the programming of a food printer. He wanted to make more nutritious meals. It was in blatant violation of Copyright, Patent and Terms of Service—the Three Major Fields of Intellectual Property. Mr. Stokes disconnected from the network, but he was caught anyway. Debt Services took Beecher's parents into Collection immediately. They would have taken Beecher, too, but Collection must let you finish school.

Beecher could have had another two years, but he dropped out of school a few weeks after his fifteenth. I couldn't believe it. I asked him why. He shrugged like it was no big deal—50¢ to act casual. I kind of loved that he did that, even though it seemed so foolish.

"Beecher..." Mrs. Harris said, shaking her head. It was like she knew I was thinking about him. She really didn't like him, which was part of the reason I kept seeing him.

Mrs. Harris hadn't read my mind, however. Beecher was at the foot of the bridge opposite us, waiting, like he wanted to catch me before the party. My heart skipped a beat. It wasn't love or a crush. The way he looked at that moment worried me.

Bunnies surrounded him, too, but in darker colors like green and midnight blue, because these were supposed to be "boy" colors. His eyes were red. Had he been crying?

"Don't jump, don't jump," the bunnies sang cheerfully to us both as Beecher drew up.

"Speth," Beecher said. His face winced. Mrs. Harris grabbed my arm and pulled me away.

He closed the space between us, quick, and kissed me. I felt a sharp jolt. This wasn't like his other kisses. My lips stung. My body tingled. I realized, with horror, that his eyes were being shocked for kissing with insufficient credit.

"Beecher Stokes!" Mrs. Harris warned.

My pastel bunnies and his dark ones mingled in the Ad, harmonizing, *"Don't jump, pleeeeezeey weeezeey."*

My cheek twitched. I put a hand there to feel the spasm. Warmth spread through my face. Somehow, my Cuff's software knew I hadn't kissed back. It really unnerved me to realize my Cuff had such weird access to my lips and intentions. How did it know? Suddenly this whole system seemed too, too real.

Beecher abruptly stalked off, head down, hands jammed in the pockets of his dumpy brown public domain longcoat. Black, gray and blood-red bunnies, glowing from the Ads at his feet, kept singing that he shouldn't jump. But Beecher didn't take advice from bunnies. That had been one of his jokes, back before he turned fifteen. I'd always thought it was really funny—until he mounted the rail and took a great leap into the traffic eighty feet below.

The bunnies stopped singing.

TWO SECONDS OF SCREAMING: $1.98

Once, I loved to talk. What did I say with all those words? It seems like nothing now. I honestly can't remember much: a conversation with Nancee about how birds make it into the city, an argument with Sera Croate about my hair (she said I looked like a boy with it short, but the style was free), a discussion with Beecher about how I liked the feeling of certain words in my mouth.

Luscious, Effervescent, Surreptitious, Cruft. I wasn't thinking about expressing myself. Beecher had warned me: "Expressive words cost more." He'd said it as if I should already be careful. He looked down at his Cuff's thin amber glow.

Beecher Stokes—sentence: Expressive words cost more: $31.96.

His face was all gloomy. He could have spent that money on kissing, or saying something nice. He could have told me how he felt—he could have asked me anything, or at least warned me about how it really felt to pay for every word. Maybe that's what he was trying to do. That was our last conversation.

I raced to where he had jumped, then stopped myself short. I couldn't look down. I shut my eyes tight. The leaden thump, screeching tires and clatter of twisted metal had spared me nothing. I reeled back and doubled over. *What did he just do?*

A shattering wail filled the air anyway—Beecher's name as a question. My eyes stung with tears, burning the fresh overlays in my eyes. It took me a second to realize I wasn't the one screaming. It was Saretha.

I let nothing escape, not a scream, not a gasp, not a breath of air. I had stopped breathing, like it wouldn't be real until I drew breath.

The howling stopped. Saretha's Cuff buzzed.

Her shriek was legally considered *a primitive call for comfort, aid and/or sympathy.* The charge was 99¢ per second. Mrs. Harris twisted a bony, aggrieved finger in her ear and shook her head. She picked up my left arm and looked at my Cuff in disgust, but then her sharp, disapproving face broke into a ghoulish smile.

"Speth," she said, wide blue eyes piercing me, "there may be hope for you yet!"

There was no concern for Beecher in her. She exhibited no revulsion. She was simply pleased I had not made a sound.

I swallowed. I was breathing again. Long, panicked breaths passed in and out.

From below, an intense, white, molten light flickered. The NanoLion™ battery in Beecher's Cuff had ruptured. And then I knew that he was truly gone.

Saretha looked at Mrs. Harris, wild-eyed. Mrs. Harris put on a look of concern and patted her shoulder three times, did the math on what it cost and calculated Saretha warranted two final pats. The government didn't cover Mrs. Harris's gestures. She had once quoted a statute to us about how gestures were an inexact means of communication.

"Personally, I find them coarse," she had told us. "A poor use of funds."

I could not look at the woman. I stared blankly up over the bridge's rail, to the expanse where cars were slowing in the distance, backed up by the accident. Cars began to honk at the delay, a dollar per honk, even though the bright white glow of the ruptured battery told them there was nothing anyone could do.

They hated us, those wealthy people, driving the ring for pleasure. Beecher, whom I'd cared for—maybe not the way he'd wanted, and not as much as he'd cared for or needed me—he was dead, and all they felt was irritation at the inconvenience.

Around me, there were other noises. My party filled with gasps and cries, then trailed off into a timorous murmur.

Timorous, I wanted to say, but I did not speak it.

Cuffs buzzed like an insect swarm. Sam came running out of the crowd, his mouth open, his round, usually playful face squinting in confusion.

"Why?" he asked in a rasp, looking over the edge at a scene I could not bring myself to witness. How could I answer?

I pulled him back from the edge. I wanted to tell him what I knew, but it was too late. I looked at my Cuff. The clock had run out. I pinched my fingers closed and ran them across my mouth. The sign of the zippered lips was a rare gesture still in the public domain. It was meant to allow people without means a method to communicate their lowly state, so Afflu-

ents wouldn't have to waste their time. I wasn't really supposed to use it with people who weren't wealthy.

Mrs. Harris winced. "This isn't the proper circumstance."
Her tone was somewhere between compassionate and annoyed.

"What else is she supposed to do?" Sam asked, his face red
with rising anger.

Mrs. Harris put a hand on Sam's chest to settle him down.
He batted it away.

"She is supposed to read her speech and have her party,"
Mrs. Harris said, as if nothing else was possible.

"Mom doesn't approve of that gesture," Saretha said, a step
behind, waving her hand vaguely in front of her lips.

Our mother felt like it was groveling. She used the word
supplication, which cost $32 that day. Mom said the only rea-
son the zippered lips gesture was free was so we could hu-
miliate ourselves. I had never seen her do it, not even when
we were broke, not even when she was supposed to. I suddenly felt like I had let her down.

I wanted to put a hand on Sam's shoulder, but Mrs. Harris
had warned me about comforting gestures. I bit the knuckle
of my cuffed hand instead.

A low, strained chatter resounded from Falxo Park, first
from the younger kids, then from everyone else, as they tried
to work out who had jumped and why. I thought of Beecher,
and I felt airless.

Mrs. Harris led me to the edge of the stage. Ads crawled
blithely along the city wall behind, a blur to my wet eyes.

"The Placers did a fine job," she said, gesturing to my product tables. Product Placers had slipped into the park and set

up an array of snacks and product samples. I had truly been looking forward to seeing what they brought, but now I felt disgusted looking at it all.

Mrs. Harris took a Keene Squire-Lace™ Chip—an elegant, intricately printed, crisped potato disk with my name and the number 15 laser-etched into the center. The Placers had left bowlfuls of them.

Mrs. Harris popped the chip in her mouth. As she chewed, she pretended to be upset.

"No Huny®," she commented, looking around with a wrinkled nose. Huny® was Saretha's Brand. I didn't expect they would be my Brand—usually it's your sponsor—but it was a little unusual they hadn't put out a few packets.

"Well," Mrs. Harris said, "I guess you should go ahead and read your speech." She wiped her hands clean of the chip's Flavor Dust™.

My body shivered. I felt weak. Maybe she was right. I had my contract to think of. If I broke it, there was no telling what my sponsor might do. No one was paying attention. Maybe I could read it quick and get it over with.

Sirens wailed in the distance. A news dropter appeared out of nowhere and hovered over the highway, where Beecher and the mangled cars were splayed. Then another dropter appeared, then more. They jockeyed for position and, failing to find a good spot to film the body, they spread out to the crowd and then to me.

"She can't make a statement," Mrs. Harris said, shooing them away while smirking at the attention. She lifted my hand to show them. The beautiful paper of my speech was distressed—creased and wrinkled from the tension of my grip.

Mrs. Harris clucked and moved my thumb. "Let them see the Keene logo," she whispered, even though I wasn't a Facer.

"You do know someone's dead, right?" Sam muttered. Mrs. Harris's face twisted into what she thought was an appropriate expression of concern.

Saretha gently pulled Sam back, and every lens turned to her.

On the highway, a dark line of cars threaded through the clot of traffic. The other vehicles parted to let the Lawyers through. They arced around us, taking the long curve up the exit to the green. News, police and cleanup crews trailed them, ready to deal with the wreckage Beecher had wrought.

A distinctive Ebony Meiboch™ Triumph snaked its way to the front. Everyone knew that car, and they all gave it a wide berth. The Law Firm of Butchers & Rog had arrived.

SILENCE: $2.99

Butchers & Rog was the city's most prestigious firm. Silas Rog himself had drafted countless pieces of legislation for the city, and some, it was said, for the entire nation. It was hard to know how powerful he was, because one piece of his legislation barred what he designated "undesirable news and information from outside the city." Other people said he ran the city, though Rog himself denied it.

I was nine years old when Butchers & Rog delivered a bright yellow envelope to our apartment door. My father peeled the thing open and dropped a thin, torn slip of yellow to the ground. Sam tried to keep it. He was too young then to know you need a license to keep paper. The Paralegal slid it out of his hand, then held out his Cuff for my father to plead. My parents never read the terms. There was little choice but to agree. No one could disprove an ancestral download. Fighting would only cost more money. Silas Rog never lost. My father tapped AGREE with a hard knuckle, my mother with a trembling thumb. We had seven days with my parents while they set affairs in order and packed the few possessions they were allowed. My father tried to give us what advice he could, with what words he could afford. My mother said nothing; she didn't want the Rights Holders to make another cent.

I wanted to know what song was so important that our parents had to leave because of it, but Saretha said that was childish; we had to take responsibility for what our family had done.

Within just a few months, the same thing happened to Nancee. Her parents were plunged into debt by a similar discovery: her great-grandparents had once been in possession of a silvery, rainbow-colored disc that was said to contain twelve beautiful pieces of music sung by insects. They had smashed it to pieces long before Nancee's parents were born, hoping to avoid trouble, but trouble found her family anyway.

There weren't many kids at my party who hadn't been affected by the National Inherited Debt Act, and its Historical Reparations Agency. Night and day, algorithms scoured every piece of data the Rights Holders could scrape up. Mrs. Harris was guardian to at least a half-dozen of my closest friends, Nancee included. We usually steered well clear of her, as best we could.

My Last Day celebration meant Mrs. Harris was all mine for the day. They would be spared.

Mrs. Harris took me by the shoulders with her strong little hands and made sure I was facing the glossy black Butchers & Rog Meiboch™ Triumph.

The Lawyer began to speak almost as soon as the driver had his door open. He knew he had everyone's attention. Sam glared like he was the devil himself. The Lawyer kept talking until he reached me.

"On behalf of Butchers & Rog, and senior partner Silas Rog,

Esquire, I, Attorney Derrick Finster, Esquire, advise the party hereforth provisionally referred to as the Provisionally Counseled Party, that you, Speth Jime, the Provisionally Counseled Party, may reasonably anticipate compensatory damages should you, Speth Jime, the Provisionally Counseled Party, choose to engage the services of Butchers & Rog and its Attorneys thereof against the actions of one Beecher Bartholomew Stokes, *alleged* Jumper."

Finster jerked a thumb back to where the road was being cleared and smiled. My stomach turned. I knew enough Legalese to understand he was offering to sue Beecher Stokes and his family on my behalf, but the cold-blooded, litigious sound of his words made me recoil.

I didn't see how it would work. Who was there to sue? Beecher's grandmother? What would they do with her? She was so old, it wasn't even worth it for Debt Services to take her.

"Silas Rog himself has taken an interest," Finster added, polishing a legal medal with a pinky. He was tall and square-faced and wore a broad chest full of legal medals on his clean, perfectly cut charcoal-gray suit. His eyes were covered by matte sunglasses, gray and pebbled, which gave him a disturbingly eyeless appearance.

"Thank you," Mrs. Harris groveled. It wasn't her place to thank him, and I didn't share her awe.

Finster stood before me politely, letting me think.

Traffic on the road began moving again. Beecher's body had been cleared, and the road scrubbed of him. The thought of it made me sick. The speeding cars began to roar in the distance.

Finster tallied some costs on his Cuff and licked his lips. His Ebony Meiboch™ Triumph was parked askew on the sidewalk, its driver waiting expressionless for his return. Lined up behind him were other Lawyers, eyeing my guests, waiting to see what bones they might pick. Finster continued.

"Our preliminary, and by no means complete or binding, estimates suggest compensation should be sufficient to abrogate your existing family debt and thus relinquish all claims, public and private, against your assets, material and otherwise, including, but not limited to, time, labor and servitude imposed upon those members of your household in debt bondage."

I worked out what he said, and my heart leapt with hope.

"Our parents could go free?" Saretha asked.

Finster's face broke into an eager, gap-mouthed smile. He nodded reassuringly. "All you need to do is agree," he said. He held out his Cuff for me to tap AGREE.

Was it really possible that my parents' servitude could finally be over? Was a simple tap all it would take to bring them home?

Mrs. Harris blinked, and her brain tried to work out what this would mean for her.

"She hasn't read her speech," she said quickly. Her face was bright red. "She *does* have a contract." She could not look Finster in the eyes. Finster cleared his throat and smiled, like we had passed some test. He lowered his Cuff and looked down at me.

"Butchers & Rog recognizes your preexisting obligation to read, as your *first* and *primary* paid words, the sanctioned a priori speech approved by the entities of Keene Inc. and its subsidiar-

ies, including but not limited to those endorsements and dec-
larations of intent to purchase products and services from your
guarantor. I hereby defer communication concerning Lawsuits
and damages levied against Beecher Stokes, his corpse, his family and/or his assigns until such time as the allegedly aggrieved
Provisionally Counseled Party, Speth Jime, has fulfilled her
preexisting obligation of allocution of said speech, and can
freely affirm her intention to retain Butchers & Rog for legal
representation pursuant to actions against Beecher Stokes, his
corpse, his family and/or his assigns."

"The hell you say?" Sam asked.

"He is agreeing," Mrs. Harris explained calmly, "to allow
Speth to read her speech before giving a response." She smiled
like this was a great favor.

How generous, I thought.

"How generous," Sam said flatly. I loved Sam.

"You may read your speech," Finster said to me, waving a
magnanimous arm toward the microphone. He took a step
back to give me space.

"Thank you," Saretha mouthed to him. Her Cuff buzzed
with the fee, plus a 15 percent surcharge for speaking without sound.

The crowd of partygoers watched, wide-eyed. Even the
younger kids were silent. I stepped to the podium. The Ads
behind my celebration muted. I lowered my head and covered my eyes. Nothing made sense. Why would Silas Rog
care? If I could have our parents back, surely it meant a worse
fate for someone else.

Cars roared nonstop on the road where Beecher had been.
They had returned to full speed, as if nothing had happened.

On the bridge, two police officers were pointing, marking the trajectory where Beecher had leapt. Between them was a small, bent woman in a rough long-sleeved public domain dress: Beecher's grandmother. Her misery was apparent, even at a distance. What would become of her? Dropters buzzed around her like a cloud of flies, small, dark lenses flicking between Beecher's grandmother, Finster, the traffic and me. We would surely make the news tonight.

The police pointed at me. Did they tell her he'd kissed me? She looked bereft. I suddenly felt embarrassed to be onstage. Did she think it would be wrong for me to continue?

"Read your speech," Mrs. Harris said.

Saretha nodded. Her Cuff buzzed in the eerie quiet. Sam looked away, arms crossed, eyes blinking.

My breathing grew fast and labored, like I couldn't get enough air. How could I read the speech? How could I accept Butchers & Rog's terms?

How could I refuse?

Finster stood placidly by. He knew exactly how everything would play out. I didn't have any real options. I had to read the speech. I had to tap AGREE. I had to do what everyone expected. Silas Rog would sue Beecher's grandmother or Beecher's mangled body, or whatever his vile plan was, and he would grow richer from it. In the bargain, I would get our parents back.

The small quaint buildings on either side of the park seemed to close me in. I saw worry on faces in the crowd. Norflo Juarze met my eyes and shouted, *"Feliz Quinceañera!"* $25.99 spent on Spanish words he couldn't afford. Sera Croate smirked, her eyebrows raised. I was taking too long to speak. She wanted me to fail, of course. Your friends come to your Last Day, but so do your enemies.

I thought I might throw up, and then thought, if I did, at least *something* would come out of my mouth. Sam would have laughed if he heard that thought. He would have understood. I wanted to show him with my eyes that everything would be okay, but instead, I started crying.

Beecher's grandmother was watching from the bridge, stunned and expressionless. I wish she had been angry, or sneered. I wish she had walked away. I wish she had told me it was okay. The speech in my hand had no words of comfort or mention of Beecher. It was nothing more than typical generic nonsense about consumer responsibility, Moon Mints™, Buonicon Tea™ and Keene's Kelp Gum™ (all owned by Keene Inc.).

I held the speech up. I couldn't say how I felt about it. I wasn't allowed to speak other words. Suddenly, a tide of rage coursed through me. My hands seemed to burn. I crumpled the speech into a ball. I threw it as hard as I could toward the highway. It fell uselessly into the astonished crowd, not even a quarter as far as I'd imagined it would go. Gasps rose all around. Mrs. Harris actually started to cry. The news droppers raced to film it like a pack of dogs chasing a bone. They got their shot and turned back to me.

Everyone knew what came next. I would be one of those few pathetic kids you see on the news who squeak out a few words of protest before being carted off. Finster waited for it, smiling, as though he expected me to break contract. It would ruin me. It would ruin my family, and for what? Whatever I might say would change nothing. He eyed Saretha and smiled a little more.

On the bridge, Beecher's grandmother didn't move, or acknowledge that I had done anything. She stared blankly toward my stage, flanked by two gaping police officers.

Then, suddenly, another option blossomed in my mind. I seized it, because it was a *choice*—my choice—and one I'd never heard anyone suggest or seen anyone do. I put a shaking thumb and finger to the corner of my mouth and drew my hand slowly across. I made the sign of the zippered lips, and I silently vowed I would never speak again.

TERMS: $3.99

Moon Mints™ has defriended you, my Cuff warned me with a chime. Chills ran down my back.

"Speth," Saretha pleaded with a single word.

My eyes ached. My left arm felt heavy from the Cuff. Mrs. Harris, red-faced, ran into the crowd and retrieved my ruined speech.

My Cuff chimed again:

Keene Inc. reminds you that you have agreed to Terms of Service requiring you to read the speech agreed upon by both parties. Failure to do so as your first adult communication will result in fines and levies of no less than $278,291.42.

I could feel my orange dress stained with sweat under my arms. A slick trickle dripped down my back. That was more than enough to destroy us.

Finster's docile expression never changed. He looked from me to Saretha, pleased, if not satisfied, and turned to walk back to his Ebony Meiboch™ Triumph. Other, lesser Lawyers, who had been waiting in the wings for Butchers & Rog to proceed, broke for the crowd.

I swallowed hard. The world blurred from my tears. I turned away from the podium and dismounted the stage.

"Everyone reads their speech!" Mrs. Harris screamed. Her tightly coiled blond updo, a Vivian Metro™ original, had sprung undone. I think she had to pay a fine for that.

Sam ran after me. I wanted to hug him or take his hand, but I could not. My silence—my lack of communication—had to be complete.

Sera Croate is no longer following you, my Cuff informed me.

Sera tapped at her wrist, a Lawyer standing at her side, bouncing on his heels. A moment later, I had an InstaSuit™.

Failure to provide reasonable value for time. $1,250.

I don't know why it surprised me. Sera always was a pathetic, petty opportunist.

Phlip and Vitgo, two ill-named boys from my class, elbowed each other and then did the same. They were saving up to buy a nude data-scan speculation of Litsa Dox, a girl Saretha worked with. I hadn't even invited them to the party.

Franklin Tea™ has defriended you, my Cuff buzzed. Keene's Kelp Gum™ is no longer following you.

Nancee stared at me, frozen, wide-eyed, from the middle of the fleeing crowd, holding an ice-cold bottle of Rock™ Cola limp in her hand. Tears streamed down her face, like I'd betrayed her. Mrs. Harris stomped over to her, burning with frustration, and made her turn the label inward because Nancee was no Facer.

"What are you doing?" Penepoli Graethe begged me from the crowd, her long face contorted in horror, like what I had done was worse than Beecher's leap. "What are you *doing?*" she repeated. She stepped closer. She was taller than me, but younger and hunched, like her height embarrassed her. She still had almost a year before it would be her up on stage. I had promised her we wouldn't stop talking. Now that promise made my heart ache.

News dropters spiraled in a frenzy, looking for interviews with my friends, dramatic angles from the bridge or shots of me up close. I covered my face with my hands and blindly made a run for it.

Sam called after me. My heart sank further. He'd never understand.

Penepoli called, too, running a little—she was an awkward runner—then stopped, as if it was too much.

In their excitement to follow me, the dropters banged against each other, ruining the smooth and steady shots each network desired.

Norflo Juarze called after me, "Smatta, Jimenez?" Even after his fifteenth, when he worked hard to shorten everything he had to say, he insisted on lengthening our last name from Jime to Jimenez. He said, "What it was, 'fore 'twas shorted, like all Latino names 'round here." He'd spent $138.85 that day.

What was the matter? *Everything*, I wanted to scream, but I said nothing, because I had to keep silent. If I *never* spoke, I wouldn't have to read the speech. I wouldn't have to worry about being economical with words or who was making money when I spoke. I would not have to AGREE to Butchers & Rog, and they couldn't claim I had refused them. This was my only way out.

My throat felt so tight, I was amazed I could breathe. I pushed through the crowd and raced up the bridge, past Mrs. Stokes, who watched me go, wordless and unblinking.

I wanted to tell her I did this for her, but that wasn't really the reason. I didn't fully understand what I had done, or why I was doing it—except I finally had control over something. The whole system of paying for words seemed so normal—until it was on me, like a wave crashing over me.

Beecher hadn't seen a way out, but I had to take another path.

"Speth," Sam called out a second time. I hated the worry in his voice. I had never done something like this to him before. I felt like I was abandoning him.

"We had plan," he said, despairing. My heart sunk. I looked at him. He tried to smile.

"I was going to do all the talking," he said. I remembered. "You were going to answer with a cheap word. *Termite*, maybe, if you agreed."

We had tried this with Saretha two years before, but she said it went against the spirit of the Law. Then she added, "And it would be cheaper to say *Speth* than *termite*, anyway," which was a little cruel, and cost her $12.73 to point out.

"A termite can still read the speech," Sam said sadly. His face scrunched up, like he couldn't comprehend what I was doing.

I paused, straining to keep my sobs silent, keeping an eye on my Cuff for any sign I had slipped up. Crying was free unless you made a sound. I wished I could explain to him. Behind him, Saretha looked bewildered as a small, punchy man in a chartreuse Lawyer's suit raced up to her, talking fast.

I ran on, full speed, followed by the bunnies over the bridge's screens, hopping quickly to keep up, singing more vigorously than before. They stopped short when I made it to the bridge's other side.

Small voices began calling to me from the dropters.

"Crane Mathers from the *Murdox Posts*™—will you grant an interview?"

"Will you make a statement for *Kingstan Press*™?"

"CNC™. Can we get you to stare in silence at our camera for just one minute?"

The *Kingstan Press*™ dropter made a sudden dip, colliding with the one below it. The CNC™ dropter wobbled, then came back, tilted a hard right and slammed the one from *Kingstan Press*™ into the Ad wall, smashing its surface so the screen sputtered to gray.

I put my arms over my head to protect myself. A media frenzy like this could easily end with a dropter knocking you out cold, or catching its small heli blades in your hair and scalping you. If that happened, dozens more would appear on scene to cover *that* story.

An Ad for Dropter Gyroscopics™ flashed on the next panel, then more Ads clicked on across the walls in front of me, suggesting Law Firms, running shoes and Media Image Consulting™.

I made it inside our building, slamming the glass door quickly behind me. The dropters tapped at the glass, but were unable, physically or legally, to open the door. I took the elevator upstairs to our apartment on the twelfth floor.

Suddenly everything was quiet.

Our Ad-subsidized home had just one cheaply printed room. The walls were made of slightly rough, striated layers of polymer melt. Our building had been 3-D printed, millimeter by millimeter, from a set of economy plans, and warped to the curve of the ring just inside the outer highway. There were dozens of nearly identical buildings out here, printed from the same template, with all the same sorts of rooms inside.

Our rent was kept affordable as long as we watched thirty hours of Ads each month. There was no place cheaper to live in the city. If you couldn't afford to live here, you were sent into servitude, like my parents had been.

For years, our home had a slight scent of scalded plastic. One wall had been printed in and smoothed over when my parents were taken. Our apartment was reconfigured to the "proper" allocation for three. It was infuriating to know my parents' space was still there, empty, a useless void withheld because the Rights Holders couldn't stand for us to have more than the legal minimum. Mrs. Harris tried to claim it was so we wouldn't feel sad remembering our parents.

I could still smell the burnt plastic. I could still remember when that room was there—what it looked like. I could still remember *them*.

Sensing my warmth, the wall-screen clicked on and began a mandated rotation of Ads. I dropped myself on our couch and buried my head in my hands. The Ads increased in volume to remind me that if I did not see them, they would not count toward our monthly required viewing total for our subsidy.

My ears were ringing. My stomach churned, both hungry and upset. If everything had gone as planned, I would have been choosing my Brand like everyone else did on their Last Day, looking over my Placements with my friends and eating pizza—real pizza, not the printed kind. Instead, I had to face what I had done alone.

In silence.

DOLLS: $4.99

I had the chance to bring my parents back, and I ruined it. Why? So what if Silas Rog was involved? So what if Beecher's grandmother would be jailed or indentured, or whatever it was they were planning to do? I didn't know Mrs. Stokes. Did she even understand what I had done, or how much it had cost me?

The door slid open behind me.

"I'm glad," Sam yelled, stomping in. He didn't seem glad. "I hope Silas Rog's brain explodes. I hope the whole city crumbles to bits because one girl didn't read her stupid speech! I hope everything falls apart."

He was pacing, talking fast, because he could afford to say whatever he liked. He didn't have to think about his words. He could let them fly. He stopped to hug me and then went on.

"Your friends are a bunch of turd muffins, by the way."

I wanted to say, *not all of them,* but he knew.

An incoming request showed up on our screen from *Dayline Exclusives*™. Sam flicked at the screen to refuse the call.

"How is this even a big deal? No one ever did this before? Really? Like tons of people don't read their stupid speech and *then* stop talking? The Juarze brothers probably say ten words each a year!"

This was an exaggeration, but only a mild one. I hugged him back in my mind.

Our door slid open again. Saretha came through, followed quickly by the Lawyer in the chartreuse suit.

"Speth," Saretha said, breathless. "Not too late."

"Who is that?" Sam asked, pointing at the Lawyer.

The Lawyer waved and bent his head, hands on his knees, as he caught his breath. "Arkansas Holt," he panted. "Attorney at Law."

An Ad for a competing Lawyer, Dirk Fronfeld, clicked on our screen, promising better returns. A call came in from his Law Firm. Sam canceled it.

Saretha's brows pinched upward as she looked at me for some sign I hadn't lost all my marbles.

Arkansas Holt moved to my side of the room, still breathing hard. Arkansas was the name of a state, I think. He had only a single medal on his chest, proudly proclaiming he had won at least one case, but sadly implying it was his only win.

Sam's head suddenly snapped toward our room's only window. "Son of a—" He stormed over. Our window was a milky, flickering mess that was supposed to be something we could adjust, clear to opaque, at our convenience. Instead it was stuck in an ugly, jittery state in between the two. Outside the window, a pair of dropters bobbed up and down, calculating how best to film me.

"Vultures," Sam grumbled. He pulled open his pullout couch (Saretha and I shared the other) and yanked a blanket off to block their view. We didn't have curtains. The Patent for the concept of curtains required a $90 monthly payment and we had never thought it was worth it. It usually didn't matter on the twelfth floor. Now it meant Sam had to hold the fabric up; clipping fabric over a window was Intellectual Property we had no right to use.

"I can help with this!" Attorney Holt raised a finger in the air like he had practiced being dramatic, but hadn't entirely mastered it. "I can make them vanish."

He sounded like a cut-rate magician, or an Ad for cleanser, not a Lawyer.

"He can help us," Saretha said weakly. She held herself tight and rubbed her shoulders like she was cold.

Holt cleared his throat and stood up a little taller, bolstered by Saretha's apparent confidence in him.

"If you would like to be rid of the media, I can place an injunction against reproduction of your likeness," he said. "It won't prevent them broadcasting anything newsworthy such as this morning's unfortunate events, but it will prohibit them from following you around and hoping for more."

"Yeah? And how does this help *you*?" Sam asked Arkansas Holt.

Holt paused. "Pursuant to legal action, I would require a vested interest—control over commercial rights to your sister's likeness."

Sam rolled his eyes. "For what?"

Holt began itching at his nose. "I would profit from anything like posters or dolls or such if it were to ever come to that."

Our buzzer rang. A small inset window on the wall-screen

showed the feed from our door. Mrs. Harris was standing outside, fishing through her purse.

I didn't need this. I needed time to think. There was too much noise and chatter. Too much was happening at once.

"Dolls?" Sam squinted at Holt, disbelieving.

Holt shrugged. "Theoretically, I would be able to sell virtual approximations. She isn't old enough for anything more revealing than a bikini."

We knew, from time to time, that Advertisers sold scan data so boys like Phlip and Vitgo could buy a peek at the system's best approximation of what some girl looked like naked. It had happened to Saretha half a dozen times. I thought it was gross, but Mrs. Harris said she should be flattered. Saretha forced herself not to mind, because she was legally entitled to 10 percent of the profits.

Arkansas went on, "You can't possibly have a reasonable expectation of privacy at *your* income level. Anyway, this isn't likely to be a lucrative trade." Holt gestured a hand to my apparently uninteresting body. My face went warm and pink.

Outside, Mrs. Harris found what she was looking for and ran her keycard across the door lock. The door opened, and she swept in.

"What in the world were you thinking?" she screeched. Then she caught sight of Holt, drew herself up to impress him, saw his lonely medal and drew herself right down again.

"Speth," she said, making my name sound like she'd spit it up.

I drew my knees to my mouth. I wanted to put my hands to my ears, but that gesture cost $7.99 per minute.

"Tell them what you told me," Saretha begged Holt. Mrs.

Harris folded her arms. Holt stood tall again and fixed his eyes on me.

"Whereas the terms of your contract with Keene Inc. stipulate you will read what was agreed upon before any other paid speech, and whereas that agreement does *not* specify a time, date or location, you have not yet broken the terms of said agreement, as you have not yet spoken, and are therefore presently indemnified against suit for breach of said contract, including, but not limited to, trailing and ancillary suits derived thereof."

Even when it was spoken in my defense, Legalese seemed to cut at me. I tried to focus on what he was saying and not the sound, but it was right up there with face-slapping as a means of communication.

"She's not in trouble?" Sam asked, stretching his arms high to cover the full window.

"She is in a great deal of trouble," Mrs. Harris assured him.

"Perhaps," Holt said, "but that depends on her intention. If her silence were a demonstrable act of protest or antagonism, that could be problematic. But since she has not spoken, how can we know?"

I looked up from my knees.

Mrs. Harris bit her lip.

"All you have to do is read the speech," Sarctha said. She quickly thumbed through her Cuff until she was able to pull up a copy. She flicked it so it would show up on my Cuff. "You can read it and then explain you were traumatized by what happened to Beecher."

By what happened to him? Beecher killed himself; it didn't happen *to* him. I couldn't let myself think about it. I was confused. I was sad. I was angry. Did that mean I was trau-matized?

"She made the sign of the zippered lips," Mrs. Harris said. "Twice. That is not something a traumatized person does."

Holt narrowed his eyes at her. "You must beg my forgive-ness. I was unaware you are a psychologist qualified to diag-nose trauma."

Mrs. Harris backed away a little.

"Mrs. Hairball falls silent," Sam said, like he was narrat-ing a Baseball™ game.

Mrs. Harris calmly began tapping out a Lawsuit for being called a hairball. Sam threw down the blanket and grabbed her wrist. "You want to sue us? How about we sue you? Weren't you in charge of her transition?" He turned to Holt. "Can we sue *her*?"

Holt made a face that said, *maybe*?

"Sam," Saretha said, as if suing Mrs. Harris was a ridicu-lous thing to suggest. I didn't think it was ridiculous. I was tired of her. I would have loved to see her sued by us instead of the other way around.

Sam let her go. Mrs. Harris backed up, scowling.

Outside, seven or eight dropters drew in close to the win-dow. Holt moved to that side of the room and turned his back to them.

"Whatever happens," Holt said, "and I *cannot* stress this enough." He waved a hand at me to make sure I was listening and dropped his voice low. "If you choose to speak, or when you are able to speak, now, later or ten years from today, the first words out of your mouth must be *these*." He pointed to my Cuff and the speech that sat there, glowing.

I don't know why this made me cry again. I couldn't even see the speech. I pushed his hand away. I could do that. I could push people out of my space without charge. I just couldn't hold them.

Holt moved back, and out of the corner of his mouth, he whispered to Saretha.

"Now, how about my fee?"

ZEBRAS: $5.99

I can still hear my father's voice. Even though we were poor, he was a talker. When the WiFi would fail, his face would light up. This was his chance. He could say *anything*, untethered from the system.

I remember one time, he said to us, "I can make you think of zebras." Sam laughed his playful, cherubic laugh. I listened, delighted.

"All I have to do is say the word: *Zebras*. The idea goes from me to you. Zebras. See? It's unavoidable! You're picturing one now!"

He smiled, knowing he was right. I saw the zebra, with stripes and a bristly mane—a wide-open plain behind it. Words were like magic.

I don't remember all of it, in part because I was so young, and also because it was hard to concentrate. My mother would go wild during the outages, hugging us without the $2.99 fee, kissing our heads and saying, "I love you," a hundred times. It was like an animal attack, but a loving one.

I remember my father claimed there used to be places called "liberties" that would let you read any book, and all you'd have to do is show them a card.

"How much did the card cost?" I asked. He smirked. He said it was free. You just had to promise to return the book when you were done.

I loved his stories, even ones that ridiculous. I knew what he described was impossible. How could people who wrote books, or published books, ever make any money if "liberties" just gave them away? It made no sense.

He also said words had once been free. I believed him about that. Laws were made of words, so the words had to come first, right? My father said it took thousands of years for humans to figure out they could control the rights to words. They started by controlling how certain words were used, so that you couldn't just write a word like Coke™ or Disney™ or Candy™ without fear of getting sued, especially if you had something negative to say. It only got worse from there. He didn't know when it all started.

"I only wish I knew how to make it all end," he said.

My mother got upset when he said things like this. She worried about getting flagged, sued or even Indentured.

"Everyone around here gets Indentured eventually," my father said darkly.

"What if the WiFi came back tethered?" my mother pressed him, like the WiFi was knocking at our door.

My father looked abashed and zipped his lips, as a joke. My mother didn't find the gesture funny, even in jest, with the WiFi down.

"I hate that," she said. "They want us remembering how low we are. I don't want any of you to make that sign, understand?" She looked at the three of us, then at her Cuff, worried the WiFi might have kicked back on when she wasn't looking.

★ ★ ★

Now I had made that very gesture, the one she despised, in front of the entire city—maybe the whole nation. Why had I done it? What was I thinking?

We had to call our parents. We didn't know if they had seen me on the news. Their company controlled what access they were allowed, and most of their time was spent in the fields. Saretha managed to contact them through the Internment Bureau, and we were able to set up a call. Mrs. Harris insisted on being present. She was still Sam's Custodian, and she stood behind us, arms crossed, with a disapproving scowl.

"Speth," my father said, amplified, but distant. "It's okay."

His voice was low and calm. He looked tired. His skin was like dusty leather. My mother's was, too. She sat beside him, her eyes downcast. The room was dark behind them, insufficiently lit by a dirty fluorescent coil. From the worry on their faces, it was clear they had heard plenty.

"Sam," my father said with a slow nod, meaning Sam should tell them everything.

Mrs. Harris clicked her tongue. She had explained many times that it was bad etiquette to make the youngest do all the talking, just because they did not have to pay. "It's perverse," she said in a low aside to Saretha. Saretha pretended Mrs. Harris was not there while Sam explained about Beecher, the speech and what I had done. My body tensed as I waited for a reaction. Sam described the sign of the zippered lips. My mother's mouth twitched. She closed her eyes.

When Sam was finished, my father nodded again. He looked older than he should have. They both did. They had to drink a liter of Metlatonic™ twice a day just to survive under the brutal sun. I didn't know if this was because the work made them thirsty, or if the sun burned their skin. I didn't know if the Metlatonic™ was helping or harming them. The hefty cost of it was deducted against the Indenture.

It still looked like the sun was killing them.

My father took my mother's hand. She barely moved. The fee for their affection scrolled up the screen. $6.

"I know this must be hard," my father said. I tried not to cry. I failed. I wiped away the tears, desperate for something in his words to guide me. Below him, on-screen, scrolled the cost of his handful of words, the WiFi tax, the fee from Agropollination™ Inc. for use of their room and equipment and time off from the fields.

I ached to ask them what to do. The silence was killing me. I needed their help, and I hated that everything about this world seemed to conspire to keep their guidance from me. I didn't even know how far away they were. I'd asked, but my parents, Mrs. Harris and even the teachers at the school couldn't say how far it was from Vermaine to Carolina. Geography is proprietary information.

Please, I begged them silently in my head, *tell me what to do!*

"Did you have anything to add?" my father asked my mother slowly.

That was it? I blinked back more tears. Couldn't they see my face? Couldn't they read it, even if their eyes were bleary? I had no idea how far they were from me.

My mother looked up, first at him, then at the camera, the screen and me. She looked so beaten. Her eyes were rimmed red. I wanted to say I was sorry. I wanted to take everything back, but then my mother did something I never thought I'd see. She raised her fingers to her mouth and slowly, deliberately, made the sign of the zippered lips, twisting at the end, like a lock. She stared at the camera, straight and clear, and she smiled. Pins and needles shot up my spine. No one seemed to breathe. Mrs. Harris's mouth hung open. My father nodded, pressed a button and the image of my parents flickered away.

PREY: $6.99

I was an agitator. I was a fool. I was brilliantly devious. I was a mental deficient. I was an unpatriotic threat to the nation. I was a pathetic symptom of a generation with no soul. *"Kids never used to be like this,"* interviewees said.

But my mother approved.

I was *seditious*, a word I'd never heard before. It meant I wanted to destroy the government. They said I'd driven the price of the word up to $29.99 this month, but I had nothing to do with it. Rights Holders changed prices each day as much as they could, depending on what the market would tolerate.

One news report claimed I had tricked Beecher into killing himself to cover my tracks. (*What tracks?* I wondered.) Another report, the most flattering of the bunch, claimed I had a brain tumor that rendered me mute. I was a sad, worthless little girl.

Three networks offered bounties to the first person who made me speak. I wasn't sure, but I thought that might mean word had gotten out of the city. What did they think of me out there? I knew, at least, what my parents thought, and that made things a little easier to bear.

On my first day back to school, I was on Fuller Street, just away from the roar of the outer ring, when two skinny rich girls in gold corsets and Transparenting Mood™ coats approached me. They wanted me to talk—to *talk,* goddammit, and they were going to make it happen.

"I'll pay for your speaks," the taller one shouted, as though I were half-deaf. She seemed to think I had only been waiting for someone as clever as her to ask. She tottered alongside me and shoved her crystal-rimmed Cuff under my nose. Her long coat turned a translucent acid yellow. Half a dozen bracelets clinked and rattled as she shook her arm for me to speak.

"I'll record her voice," she said in an aside to her friend, like I was a dog who couldn't understand. "We can play it for everyone."

The shorter one nodded excitedly. "You could get on the news!" Her coat flashed orange, then clear.

There were no dropters nearby. Attorney Holt had been able to put a partial lockdown on that. I don't know if he planned to sell dolls or what.

"Meh," the tall one said, fluffing at her hair. $6.99. The yellow of her coat mellowed. She didn't seem to care about the news or the money. She just wanted me to obey.

"If you're not gonna talk, do the zippered lip thing, sluk."

That word, *sluk,* put my teeth on edge. $49.99. It was ugly, hateful and pricey—meant to imply I was scarcely more than filth. I'd never spoken it, even if plenty of other kids did before they had to pay. Nancee and Penepoli once went back and forth with it, as a joke, seeing who could say it the meanest. I always told them that if we could say whatever we wanted, it was better to try beautiful words.

Neither Nancee nor Penepoli could hit that *k* in the hateful, glottal way the girls in the alley could.

"Come on!" The tall one shoved at me half-heartedly. I almost laughed at her. A small push would have done either of those girls in. That's the way it was with rich people; they were either grotesquely enormous, from gluttony or steroids, or they were distressingly thin. I felt a little sorry for those girls, though I don't know why I had any sympathy. They had none for me. They chose to starve, while some kids barely survived on printed sheets of Wheatlock™. Despite all their advantage, these girls still looked miserable. I had to remember that it made them vicious.

I peeled off from the main sidewalk, ducking down a narrow alley. I assumed they'd avoid anywhere so dirty, but my disobedience sent them into fits.

"You want to get sued, little girl?" the taller one asked, stamping her heel. Her coat flickered and reddened, and her nose wrinkled as she eyed the tight, shadowy space where I'd fled.

My speech popped up on my Cuff, glowing, as if Keene Inc. had some algorithm guessing the worst possible moment to get me to reconsider reading it. Or maybe Keene considered these girls a good audience.

"Her dad's a Lawyer," the other one warned me. She strode fearlessly into the alleyway on her six-inch heels, her coat flashing to black. I picked up my pace, and they started to run after me. Well, maybe not *run*—their posh high-heeled shoes and unyielding corsets made their progress difficult. They clattered along awkwardly, and after a few seconds they had to stop.

"Oh my God, Mandy, I can't barely breathe," the shorter one cried out.

"Sluk!" Mandy shouted. She pulled her heels off and threw them at me, one after the other—insubstantial, spiky heels that wobbled through the air. It occurred to me these girls could have been customers at the shop where Saretha worked. Saretha sold impractical garbage like this, corsets and heels and ornate Leatherette™ boots.

I took off, slipping away into a branching alley and up a fire escape. I was glad for the thinness of the rich girls' arms and the weakness of their needlessly starved bodies. Even if they saw me, they could never pull themselves up to follow. My heart pounded, but I felt a little thrill in escaping them.

"Advil™, Advil™!" I heard them cry out as their voices receded into the distance behind me.

I climbed a little higher and mounted the roof. I could walk across an arc of six buildings and then return to street level right before the crossing for my school. None of the rooftop gaps would be hard to jump and, truth be told, I enjoyed the little thrill of leaping. I just had to be careful with my landings and not give them any gymnastic style. I couldn't afford that now. My Cuff was watching.

I was feeling pretty good up there, having thwarted the Affluent girls, when a realization dawned on me.

Would I be facing worse at school?

SCHOOL: $7.99

The Westbrook School was set on the inside edge of the Onzième, a collection of large, connected buildings printed from mottled surplus plastics in uneven, translucent shades of gray. The front of the main building faced a wall meant to discourage—though not completely bar—teenage access to the businesses of the Quatrième. Most of us enter through the back of the Parker™ building.

The moment I stepped inside, Shari Gark blocked my path, while other kids streamed in around me. Despite what it cost her, she demanded, "You guna talk if therza FiDo?"

Shari followed the Word$ Market™ carefully, looking for words that dropped in price. Slang words—sometimes called gutter words—like *therza* would fluctuate wildly, but could often be spoken for pennies. Her use of *FiDo* surprised me. *FiDo* was the code word everyone used for when the WiFi went down, but was pricey. Kids would run up and down the ring, shouting it in an outage; it didn't cost anything then. Adults would break into wordy conversations, asking each other saved-up questions and savoring the answers. When I was younger, it happened a lot. The rooftop transmission nodes would get damaged or vandalized. Then it stopped happening. Silas Rog spearheaded the effort to centralize the WiFi system, offering to house it in an impenetrable bunker beneath his well-guarded offices.

I didn't think the WiFi was likely to go out, but if it did, would I speak? Shari stared at me, red rising in her cheeks.

"You think ur better den me?" she demanded.

I was stunned she had spoken so much. Since she had turned fifteen, she had said maybe five words. Now she was willing to spend $57.94 to express her rage, or to show she was different from me. Maybe she just wanted to make me speak.

Her face contorted into a furious sneer. Younger kids chattered and whispered about me as they passed. Older students shuffled through the hallway, staring at me quietly. Shari drifted into the stream, fuming, headed toward our word economics class.

I turned to open my locker, but I couldn't because it wouldn't play the Ad before the combination screen. I wasn't allowed into word economics, either, because Mrs. Oglehorn said I could not be expected to contribute meaningfully to the class. Technically, she was right. But I knew for a fact Shari hadn't spoken a single word in class since her fifteenth. Neither had half a dozen other kids. Nobody was going to waste money speaking in word economics. Mostly they just sat and waited to learn how to hunt for word bargains.

In communication ethics, Mr. Valk pretended nothing had happened, at least at first. "Shrugs *are* considered communication, and are Trademarked by the Rand® corporation, unless the movement of said shrug is less than two centimeters, in which case it is exempt from charge, as the ruling *Merrill v. Dakin* laid out."

My ears perked up. It was critical that I remember what I could do with my body and what I could not. I could shrug, but only slightly.

"As with any free gesture," Mr. Valk went on, "repetition will be flagged and charged if a pattern of communication is discerned."

He must have said this a hundred times. The Rights Holders couldn't allow a person to subvert the system by microshrugging a love poem in Morse code.

"All modes of affection are charged to the initiating party of said affection and, subsequently, to the reciprocator at a lower rate, with the exception of hand-holding, which is charged equally to both parties, or not at all, if the hand-hold is *not* an act of affection, as determined by the parties' mutual serotonin levels. A 0.35 threshold has been defined as that limit as read by a standard Cuff.

"This can allow two clinically depressed parties to hold hands free of charge, which, while technically legal, is considered immoral and disrespectful to the Law."

Behind him, the room's screen lit up with the outline of a sad boy and girl holding hands, but seeming to get no joy out of it. I couldn't help but think of Beecher and wish that I had felt something more for him.

Mr. Valk then looked at me. His eyes narrowed. "What is charged for communication can and does change over time, as different suits and cases come before the court refining the Law. One day, even *silence* could be charged a fee if it is determined that such an action is an intentional act of protest." His voice grew harsher, but then he closed his eyes, relaxed and resumed our normal class.

I didn't get to go out for driving class because Mr. Skrip, the driving teacher, asked me if I wanted to go out on the ring, and I couldn't answer. He looked at me for a long moment, deeply disappointed.

"Waste of aptitude," he said. I was one of his favorites, partly because he'd liked Saretha before me, but mostly because he felt I had very good control.

I liked driving, but I was relieved not to go out. Driving on the ring around the city is stressful, with all those expensive cars passing and cutting you off. In an accident, there is zero chance that someone from our school would not be found culpable, regardless of what actually happened, and that suit would be ugly.

"Fault is decided by the courts, not the facts," Mr. Skrip liked to remind us.

We all knew we were only there so we could learn to chauffer Affluents and run their errands. Why would I want to do that?

In the hall, Phlip and Vitgo made a game of blocking my path and pretending they would move only if I would tell them which way to go. I tried not to let them irritate me too much, which was hard because Phlip and Vitgo were always irritating.

Sera Croate came up behind me and twisted my arm behind my back. "She won't even scream," she said, like I was an experiment. $7.96. I yanked away from her, fury scorching through me, radiating from the ache in my shoulder. Sera Croate had hated me for years, but now she was acting like I wasn't even human. I rubbed my arm, every muscle in my body suddenly tense. Was this what it was going to be like from now on?

I should have been having a great week. If I had just done what was expected, everyone would be congratulating me. They would have been impressed I had carried on, even after what Beecher did. I would have had coupons for food and speaks. I would have had a Brand, probably Moon Mints™, and I would have been able to buy them at a great discount for the rest of my life for my loyalty. I could have kept my head down, just like everyone else. It wasn't right. It wasn't fair.

Sera eyed me, like a snake about to unhinge its jaw and devour its prey. My hands clenched to hard fists. Punching was still in the public domain. But could I really do it? I could never even look at Sera without thinking about how her parents were taken. They were beaten mercilessly for refusing to AGREE, and Sera came into school the next day pretending she was glad they were gone.

"I like Mrs. Harris better," she'd said. She was only eight years old.

How could I hit her, remembering that?

Sera opened her mouth—no doubt to say something vile—but stopped cold as a senior girl named Itzel Gonz approached us. Without breaking her stride, Itzel met my gaze and drew a pinched thumb and finger across her lips as she passed silently by.

A tingling crept up the back of my neck. My hands slackened as I watched Itzel in awe. Frowning, Sera and her little posse stalked off to our next class. I lagged behind, savoring the one brief, bright moment of my day.

In consumer ethics & etiquette, Mr. Julianiis would not

let me take my seat. Instead, he had me stand up in front of everyone. He lit the room's wall-screen with a survey of different well-regarded brand logos. "How will she buy products and services if she does not speak?" he asked, pointing to me like a specimen. Everyone stared. I backed up until I hit the screen. The logos scattered away from me. All those eyes felt like they were drilling into me, trying to understand me, but they couldn't. I looked down at my Cuff, which should have been recording my words. I was exposed and alone, but in my gut, I felt glad that at least my silence meant that I also had privacy. They would never know what I was thinking.

"She could sign for stuff," Bhardina Frezt offered.

"She can*not* sign for stuff," Mr. Julianiis said coldly. "She has chosen not to communicate. Signing counts as a form of communication. If she does elect to communicate, she has a legal obligation to read her speech. Until then, she cannot agree to Terms of Service or make purchases of *any* kind because, as you all know, the idea of exchanging money for goods is Patented. It requires payment of a fee. A small fee, kept reasonable by your good friends at Prolix Patents™, who remind you to Pay Well™."

Mr. Julianiis clicked a picture of the Prolix Patents Inc. logo onto the room's front screen and smiled beside it, like he was posing for a photo. Prolix Patents™ was probably his Brand.

"No, Miss Jime will lean on the good graces of her family and friends to feed and clothe her until she comes to her senses. Does anyone believe she has done the right thing by turning her back on society with her silence?"

I scanned the faces of my classmates for a sign that someone agreed with me. I secretly wished someone would show the sign of the zippered lips, or at least say something in my defense, but how could I expect that? I had never stirred up that kind of trouble for anyone else. I tried to remind myself that my mother approved of what I had done. I held on to that idea like fuel.

At lunchtime, a nine-year-old kid I'd never seen before asked me if I would talk to his dad so his family could collect the bounty. I couldn't say *no*, and he tried to make that into a *yes*. Sam found me and told the boy to shove off.

Near the end of the day, Nancee hurried over to me.

"Don't say anything," she said. I didn't, of course. She looked left and right to see who might be listening, then whispered, "I'm next."

I knew she was next in my class to turn fifteen, but she clearly meant something more. She zipped her lips nervously and waited for my reaction.

"I just wish…" she said, trying not to look upset, "I wish you'd let me know."

Regret swelled in my stomach. I had no way to tell her how much I cared about her. We'd been friends since we were little. It had never occurred to me to use my words to tell her that she was important—that she mattered to me. I'd always assumed she just knew how much her friendship meant to me.

"If you come, I'll—" She glanced around again, then leaned right in to my ear and whispered, "I'll know *why* you did it, and you won't have to say a word."

I was overcome with an urge to hug her, but I had to squelch it. I had to be strong. I gritted my teeth and looked down enviously at her bare forearm. I wondered how she would feel when they put the Cuff on her thin, pale arm.

Behind her, Mandett Kresh was milling around. He was a little younger than us both. The moment our eyes met, he also pulled his fingers across his lips.

"Please come," Nancee said, squeezing my hand before she turned and left with him.

An uneasy feeling welled up in me. Would I be blamed? But I couldn't let myself think that way: just about myself. It was selfish. If Nancee went silent like me, she wouldn't be protected like I had been. There would be no ambiguity in her motive. I couldn't let her do it, but how could I stop her?

I walked home in a fog. The dome was dark above me. The sky was heavy with clouds beyond—I could tell from the deep gray. I tried to think of what I could do to stop Nancee, but I'd made that impossible. My head went in circles trying to work it out, but when I arrived in our apartment, something was waiting that made me forget all about Nancee and the trouble she was headed toward.

DESIST: $8.99

A bright yellow letter had been slipped into our apartment. It was a physical, paper letter in a thick envelope, delivered right into our home by Placers. The word **DESIST** was stamped on the front in thick black ink. The return address was in the form of a logo: a black, yet rainbowlike holographic foil, like oil in three dimensions. It came from Butchers & Rog.

A chill ran down my spine.

The yellow letter was exactly like the one that had taken my father away. As soon as I picked it up, my Cuff fired a small vibration, and I was startled. I wasn't used to the vibration yet. Somewhere at Butchers & Rog, they'd just received confirmation of delivery. There was no charge: just verification.

I didn't open the letter. It wasn't for me. It was addressed to Saretha.

A gnawing pit grew in my stomach. This was no coincidence. Whatever they were trying to do was meant to punish me—why had they dragged her into it?

DESIST. I ran my fingers over the raised ink.

This was a message so important, they put paper in our hands. Did they dig up another download from the RIA® Agency? No. This was different. It said DESIST. They wanted her to stop doing something, but what? Protecting me? Being my sister? Letting me be silent?

I dropped the letter on our table. It seemed to glow like a patch of sunlight. I had once seen sunlight, years ago, when a hexagon in the dome came loose. The thick Aeroluminum® panel fell softly into the road, too light to be more than a nuisance on the ground. Sun streaked down in a long, shimmering shaft. The public was warned away, not from the panel, but from the light. They said direct sunlight did strange things to your skin, but the way it lit the buildings was beautiful.

The Ad screen on our wall suddenly screamed to life.

"Looking to change legal counsel? Look no further than Bates & Bruthers! We will defend you with vigor, with gusto, with the maximum litigiousness allowed by Law!"

Three oily men in perfect Crumpfry, Banyard & Liepshin™ suits stood with arms folded, looking somewhere offscreen— toward their next case, I suppose. The words *Bates & Bruthers* flew off the screen in 3-D, except our screen wasn't 3-D, so the effect was diminished. I crossed the room and hit CANCEL.

More effective than Arkansas Holt scrolled across the bottom of our screen as the Ad faded away. *Who wasn't?* I wondered to myself. Was he really doing us any good?

I paced the room. I looked out the murky window, agonizing that I couldn't tell anyone what had arrived. If I had completed the ceremony, I could have just used my Cuff to call or text Saretha at work. But I couldn't warn Saretha. I couldn't warn Sam. I had to wait and see the horror on their faces when they saw the letter in person.

When Sam arrived, he dropped his backpack on the floor and went straight to it. Behind him, his friend Nep stopped cold in the hall.

"What did you guys do?" Nep clenched the sides of the doorway, his thin body dwarfed by oversized clothes. His wide, dark-ringed eyes darted around, looking for some evidence of our heinousness. Or maybe he was looking for Saretha.

"DESIST?" Sam looked at me. I could see the wheels turning in his head. He wanted to say something funny, but even his mischievous mind couldn't think of anything amusing to say.

"You got a Placement," Nep said in a weak voice, pointing from the doorway to our counter. His oversized shirt slipped to one side, and he adjusted it, embarrassed.

I hadn't noticed the Placement. I had been too preoccupied. A beautiful, glistening bottle of Rock™ Cola was sweating on a cooling pad under a bright, crisp light. It was a Product Placement, all right. These were rare for us. Law Firms often contracted with Placers when they wanted a quick, efficient delivery. The Placers must have slipped the soda in with the envelope delivery. Sometimes they took pity on you. They once set up our whole building with double protein inks for our food printers. Some people said it was a marketing ploy. Others thought it was an off-contract act of kindness. They had managed it all without a single sighting.

"Whelp," Nep said, bravely clutching himself in the doorway a second longer. Pushing backward, his oversized clothes flapped around him like a bird taking off as he disappeared down the hall.

"What are we going to do?" Sam dropped the letter back

onto the table. "What do they want?" He began pacing around the room, scratching at his arm. "Can we open it?"

He knew we couldn't. It was a federal crime to open someone else's mail, even your sister's, unless she was demonstrably incapacitated or dead. My stomach was in knots. Sam turned on the screen to distract us, and we sat, catching up on viewing our Ad quota, until Saretha finally came home.

The door slid open, and Saretha spotted the letter at once. The yellow stood out in the dreary light of our room. Her smile pulled back into a weird contortion. I don't know what you'd call it. It wasn't a frown. It was like her lips and teeth were used to smiling, but they didn't know what to do with bad news. Sam ran up and gave her a hug. She stroked his hair unconsciously as she stared at the envelope. Her Cuff buzzed, startling her into stillness. I stood behind him, paralyzed by fear and my inability to communicate anything. Saretha remembered better than either of us what the last letter like this had meant.

She sighed and recomposed herself. I could see her pretending this wouldn't be bad. Maybe she thought to herself, *Be positive*. She picked the envelope up and opened it, careful not to let any paper fall. It read:

To Miss Saretha Jime:

Unauthorized use of a person's likeness constitutes violation of International Copyright Law Section 17A, and Federal restrictions prohibiting the use of a person's likeness without legal consent. Effective immediately, you are hereby ordered to cease and desist using the likeness of our client, Miss

Carol Amanda Harving, or risk being found responsible for civil, criminal and financial penalties.

Sincerely, on behalf of Miss Carol Amanda Harving,
Silas Rog, Esq.,
Butchers & Rog Attorneys at Law, PPD, SSC, AINNA
1 Centre St.
Portland, VM

This letter, its contents and all paper thereof must be properly registered as disposed within twenty-four hours of receipt.

I didn't understand at first. How had Saretha used an un-authorized likeness? Yes, Saretha and Carol Amanda Harving looked alike, but Saretha couldn't do anything about *that*.

Could she?

Sam swallowed hard. I don't know if I'd ever seen him truly afraid before.

Saretha's brow was still knit, unable to comprehend, just like me. She had tears in her eyes, though, and the room seemed colder. She put a hand to her cheek and felt at her face. Did Butchers & Rog really want Saretha to stop *looking* like *herself*? How was that even possible?

I would have laughed, but it wasn't a joke. It was absurd, but Lawyers don't care if what they do is absurd. Lawyers make plenty of money doing the absurd and the unthinkable. They will not stop. They will sue you into the ground, and then they sue the ground for taking you in.

They would not stop until they had finished us all.

COUNSEL: $9.99

"First, the good news," Arkansas Holt said, faking a smile. He was standing behind his desk with a Pad in his hand, as the camera in his office tracked him around the room. Saretha, Sam and I sat on our couch, watching him on our wall-screen. His bill—$3,652.81 and rising—accumulated in a clearly displayed overlay at the bottom right corner of the screen. All of his words were added to our bill, so he could enjoy a good preamble like First, the good news. $17.50. It was a drop in the bucket compared to what was to come. Even a terrible Lawyer like Arkansas Holt knew enough about the Law to be able to speak more or less freely—plus Lawyers spoke at discount rates for anything they couldn't bill.

Saretha had wiped all evidence of sadness from her face. She looked bright and eager, like she did whenever she was on her way to work, though there was something less ready in her posture. She fixated intently on the screen, and it felt like she was purposely avoiding my gaze. She had not looked at me since the letter came. She had not spoken to me. Out of the corner of my eye earlier, I saw she had pulled up my speech for a moment, but then said to herself, "It doesn't matter now," and flicked it away. She was right. Even if I read it now, Butchers & Rog would not back down on Saretha.

"Despite what may be implied by the letter, you can use Miss Harving's likeness within the private comfort of your home without concern for civil, criminal or financial penalties, provided, of course, that you do not charge a fee or offer promotion in conjunction with the viewing of said likeness." He smiled.

"And I was going to sell tickets," Sam said, snapping his fingers.

It took Attorney Holt a moment to realize Sam was being sarcastic. Saretha did not admonish him, and that worried me. She waited for more of the good news.

"However." Attorney Holt cleared his throat again. No more good news, apparently. "Any transmissions from your home, such as ScreenChat™, constitute a breach of Copyright Law and, as such, you will need to make provisions to have your likeness altered, obscured or blocked through electronic pixelation or other means."

My Cuff popped an Ad for ScreenChat™ Enhanced, which promised to make you look better. I knew how this worked—they installed more flattering lighting and squeezed the image to make you look thinner. I had long ago adjusted the lighting in our unit to make it as pleasant as the space would allow.

"Technically, I *should* have you stand outside of frame, but, as this is privileged communication, I think we can make an exception." Attorney Holt smiled in the hope Saretha would smile back. She obliged weakly.

"You can easily purchase facial recognition software that will pixelate or block your image on any digitized transmission, but, of course, this does not solve the larger problem of what might happen outside the home."

Another Ad popped up, this one for PixelMate™ Pixel-Block® software. We were all familiar with Blocking. It was becoming increasingly common for companies to Block certain imagery in-eye using the overlays on your corneal membranes. An expensive perfume bottle, for example, might appear as a blocky mess of color if you fell too far out of the company's target demographic. People who were too poor, or fell too far in debt, could end up with a full-blown case of The Blocks. Famous faces, clothes, architecture—anything valued over $500 all became blurred. Silas Rog kept his face blocked at all times to show just how important he was; no one could afford to see him.

It could be debilitating to navigate through the world with The Blocks on—which is why, when the police arrested people, they instituted The Blocks as a way of subduing criminals.

"Outside of the home," Holt said, "in public, you will need to alter your likeness by physical means."

Saretha mouthed the word *physical* and was charged for it.

"What does that mean, *physical*?" Sam asked. Saretha shushed him. Arkansas was getting to that. Our bill ticked higher—$4,328.19.

Holt glanced down uncomfortably at his Pad. "I know this is distressing. If you don't like the idea, I could try to broker a deal to use Miss Harving's likeness, but in the hands of Butchers & Rog, I suspect such a deal would be unpalatable." He paused to see how this would go down with us. No one said a word, so he went on.

"You could have your face altered through plastic surgery.

I could arrange for a consultation. I know a few people who will consult for a minimal fee and offer payment plans on your baseline debt. I recommend breast enhancements as well, if you are going that direction. They are generally beneficial in a courtroom setting. Actually, they are a fine investment for any young girl looking to improve her financial opportunities and sponsorship potential." He paused again. I couldn't look at him.

"No," Saretha said. A small vibration rang out as her Cuff charged her.

"To the breasts?" he asked.

"To all of it," Saretha said clearly, tucking her hair behind one ear.

I looked at her. I had envied how she looked, but now I just felt shame blooming in my gut. I had brought this on her. Butchers & Rog had shot the arrow, but I had drawn the target. I swallowed hard. How could I even begin to apologize? How could I make this right? I ducked my head, tilting into Saretha's field of vision, but she showed no sign of noticing.

"Maybe this is an opportunity," Saretha said, sitting up taller.

Holt's mouth hung open in confusion. Saretha flashed her incredible smile.

"Maybe I could meet her. We could talk. We could work something out."

My heart sank. I prayed she did not still think she would get to be in a movie with Miss Harving. It was a childish fantasy years ago, even when she was newly fifteen and we first saw Carol Amanda Harving in her debut film. Saretha thought she could play her sister.

"Can't we talk to her?" Saretha continued.

"What do you think she would say?" Arkansas Holt seemed a little taken aback, but then he sighed. "It's irrelevant. Silas Rog would never allow it. I don't think it is any secret that Butchers & Rog have it in for you. I can't beat them in court. I'm probably the only Lawyer stupid enough to even provide counsel. The best we can hope for now is to roll over and pray it isn't made worse for you. For some reason, Butchers & Rog haven't just taken everything, which is a small miracle."

"Okay," Saretha said. Her voice quavered a little.

"You could consider deconstructive surgery," he suggested, circling his own face with a finger through the air. Saretha's brow knit. She did not understand.

"They could reconfigure your face, like plastic surgery, but without the goal of improving your features. It is significantly cheaper, as they need not be so careful."

"Why don't we just do it ourselves?" Sam burst out.

"You could do that," Holt plowed forward. "Though I am legally bound to inform you this would not be safe or sanitary."

Another Ad popped up. *Zockroft™: When things aren't going your way*, it read. A row of happy little pills appeared beneath it.

Holt put the Pad down. "Please understand that if you don't make a choice, they will. They have the legal right to prevent your face from potentially entering the public sphere if you fail to desist."

I felt a little sick. Was it their plan to disfigure her? Or take her away? Or worse?

"Let's not let it come to that," he said, picking up his Pad again.

"Couldn't she wear a mask?" Sam asked. "Like a Product Placer or something?"

"No!" Holt said, scrolling through more legal documents. "Product Placers have a special exemption. Maybe. Who even knows what they wear?"

They wore masks. Everyone knew that. They weren't supposed to be seen, but it did happen. Ninety-nine out of one hundred times, if a Placer was spotted, no one said a word. Why cause trouble? Why upset them? It was an unspoken rule that if you happened upon Placers, you watched quietly and did not follow or draw attention to them. Everyone liked a good Product Placement, and often people were rewarded for their silence with a surprise Placement. Norflo Juarze thought this was how our building got inks that one time.

For Saretha, though, wearing a mask would be a breach of the Patriots Act©. How would she be identified? How would advertisers know who to market to?

Our bill was blinking now—$7,328.55. We were approaching our debt ceiling for the month. Holt could see this, too. He sighed again, like it pained him to feel anything.

"Stay home," he instructed briskly. "They can't issue a complaint if you stay in your private residence."

"My job?" Saretha groaned.

"Oh." Holt laughed sadly. "You can't work in public. They could accuse you of tacitly using Miss Harving's likeness in the promotion of a product or business. Miss Harving would be entitled to those earnings and then whatever damages Butchers & Rog could dream up. It is utterly out of the question."

The blinking grew faster. My heart rate went with it.

"Mrs. Nince," Saretha muttered, imagining the wrath of her boss.

I hated Mrs. Nince, though I'd never met her. During Saretha's first week of work, the woman had "accidentally" jabbed Saretha in the arm with a leather punch, leaving a small crescent-shaped scar in the flesh above Saretha's right elbow. She'd sued Saretha $90 for causing a workplace accident.

"Speth can work. She's past Last Day, and she doesn't look like anyone," Holt suggested.

I almost snorted. What kind of job did he think I could get?

Attorney Holt's face contorted as he remembered one more thing. He looked conflicted, then tapped at his Cuff a few times and looked to the left and the right, as if he were afraid to be observed.

"You can't get sick," he said. His bill had stopped creeping up. He was paying for this bit of advice himself. I don't know why he did it. Compassion is trained out of Lawyers, but Arkansas Holt wasn't a very good Lawyer. Had some small bit of kindness survived? "You can't go to a hospital, because that would put your face in public. You can't get arrested or taken into Collection, either."

Saretha's eyes seemed to go blank. Sam's lips formed a question, but he didn't need to ask. We all realized the same thing.

While we'd never had any significant hope of paying off our debt in our lifetimes, we had to keep making progress. Our parents' income and our income had to be at a high enough level to chip away at our debt. We lived in constant fear of losing ground, because if the algorithms foresaw us earning under our minimum payments, they would take

Saretha into Collection. Until Holt's visit, we were afraid of her being sent to Indenture like my parents, stuck working a farm or much, much worse. But now, if that happened, they would disfigure her first.

"Just stay safe and healthy and home," Holt counseled.

The Zockroft™ Ad popped up again, this time with a name. Saretha Jime: Be Positive! it read. The pills danced.

"We can talk again at the start of your next billing cycle," Arkansas said, his attention falling away. "Perhaps I'll think of something," he mumbled quickly. Before we could agree, the call winked out and an Ad screamed at us to buy new, fluffier toilet tissue. I sat numbly by Saretha, the screeching noise from the Ad blasting over us like an unforgiving wind. I stood and shut the whole wall panel off.

Saretha buried her head in her hands. What were we going to do?

A CRESCENT: $10.98

Mrs. Nince was the kind of woman who wore a cinched half-corset and tight black jeans, even though she was sixty years old and weighed about eighty pounds. She had jet-black hair interwoven with delicate, sharp, printed shapes. Her face had been rebuilt at least a dozen times, and it looked like something from a creepy wax museum. She thought her look was stylish, though that wasn't the word she used to describe it. She called it *modish,* because she owned that word. She bragged about how she'd watched auctions for years for a word this good to be sold. I think she just took what she could find. *Modish* wasn't exactly a common word.

Mrs. Nince wanted people to say it so she could make money. Words, she knew, were good investments.

Saretha had worked under her for two years and never said a bad word about her. She never described Mrs. Nince's face as pinched and cruel. She never mentioned how painful the clothes must have been to model. In fact, she never mentioned Mrs. Nince at all, if she could help it, because Saretha never liked to say anything bad.

Her boutique was north, part of the shops above Falxo Park, but far enough along the outer ring that it was in the next section, the Duodecimo. I'd never understood why that section had a Latin name. The buildings were still printed to look French. That was baffling, too. The obsession with French style supposedly came from the period when the French let all their Intellectual Property rights lapse, but I'd only heard that from kids passing it on. It didn't seem like the full story. My history classes were weirdly devoid of information about the world outside our nation's borders.

At the shop, Sam asked for Mrs. Nince, and a pretty girl in a painfully tight silver corset and tight white jeans scurried awkwardly into the back to fetch her. I don't think she could bend at the knees.

We waited.

"Litsa, pour l'amour de Dieu!" a voice croaked. The girl backed out the door and nearly fell over.

Mrs. Nince stepped out of her office, locked the door behind her conspicuously, then turned to us expectantly as she pocketed the key.

"We were hoping," Sam said, trying to sound both humble and professional, "you might consider letting my sister Speth take over Saretha's job?"

I tried my best to smile Saretha's smile. I caught sight of myself in the mirror. My short hair stuck out at odd angles to keep the style in the public domain. I had to be careful not to let it get too neat, or it would drift over into a Patented Pixie 9®. My eyes were red and puffy and opened too wide.

I looked ridiculous. I dialed my expression down to a more appropriate level.

"*Her?*" Mrs. Nince asked, drawing a long finger up and down in the air to indicate what an inferior specimen I was.

Then she drew herself up and held a hand to the silver rim of her Cuff, indicating she would like us to pay for her speaks. The Cuff vibrated—99¢. The gesture was not free. Sam tapped in our family code, and Mrs. Nince relaxed just a hair.

"Litsa, get back to work," she growled at the girl who was hovering nearby. The girl scurried off, the top and bottom halves of her body seeming to twist without coordination, the corset, perhaps, hampering communication from top to bottom. Phlip and Vitgo wanted to see her nude? Why was this supposed to be attractive? It looked warped and creepy to me.

"What is it that you wanted?"

"We know Saretha can't work here anymore..." Sam began.

Mrs. Nince rolled her eyes. "Saretha's unapproved departure from my employ was extraordinarily inconvenient."

"But Speth..."

"Speth," Mrs. Nince spit the word out with even more distaste than Mrs. Harris. She shuddered. "At least it isn't one of those tedious French names like Claudette or Mathilde. Those are rather passé, and *so* costly."

She looked me over again—probably jamming me into a corset in her mind—and grimaced. "Why would I want to hire her? She's flat as a board."

My face heated up. Sam took a breath. He didn't want to be part of this conversation. Neither did I. I hated this woman, and it set my jaw tight to think about working for her. I pictured the crescent-shaped scar she'd punched into Saretha's arm and had to work hard to clear the image from my mind.

"People might be curious..." Sam began. "Affluents...they might like to see if they can get her to talk."

"How would *that* be good for business?" Mrs. Nince asked.

"Why should I want people distracted by some carnival game of trying to make a Silent Freak talk when they should be buying my *modish* clothes?"

Sam tried to answer this, but she talked right over him.

"My *modish* customers don't want some oddball Silent Freak hovering over them. Can you imagine? You ask the Silent Freak how you look in these *modish* jeans, or you ask the Silent Freak how many ribs should be removed for a *modish* Frid-Tube™ Halter, or you ask the Silent Freak if we're having a sale, and the Silent Freak would just stare and stare like a farm animal."

"Don't call her that," Sam growled.

"Farm animal, or Silent Freak?" Mrs. Nince asked innocently. "Isn't her silence unusual and freakish? She can't control it. Isn't that what we're *supposed* to believe? It's a malformation; the poor Silent Freak can't speak because her idiot boyfriend killed himself."

I said nothing, but I thought so many things. She was a noxious, sour, self-important excuse for a human being. I struggled to keep my loathing from showing. How had Saretha been able to stand working for her?

She stepped to within an inch of my face. "Silent Freak," she said, calmly, as if I should nod so we could all agree.

There was something odd about how pleased she was with herself. Was she trying to goad me into talking? It didn't seem like it. Despite her overall hatefulness, she seemed more than happy to keep talking to us—at least until Sam spoke.

"You waxy old prune," Sam burst out. His brow was furrowed, and his cheeks were flushed red. "Everyone can see you slathered on your makeup and had some doctor pull your face folds back. It doesn't fool anyone into thinking you're younger."

I wished I could have said those things. Once, I would have. Sam and I were a lot alike that way.

Mrs. Nince stepped away and pretended to pick at something under a long curling black nail. "Silent Freak," she said. "So much better and more descriptive than Silent Girl."

Sam reached for her Cuff, to stop paying for her words, but she held her arm up and away.

"I made a lovely purchase after the incident at your party. I bought the Trademark to the phrase Silent Freak™." Sam feinted left and quickly moved right. She whipped her Cuff arm back behind her, but teetered a little on her heels.

"I do hope you will stay in the news." She grinned, her thin, translucent teeth glistening. She must have really hated me to go to the trouble of obtaining the phrase, coordinating with the owners of the words *silent* and *freak,* offering a cut of the profits and paying all the Lawyers' fees.

"I'd love for everyone to keep talking about the *Silent Freak*™," she hissed.

I reached out suddenly, and my movement surprised her. I grabbed her arm and held it fast. I wanted to pull it back, like Sera had done to me, but I'm sure I would have broken something on this horrible twig of a woman. Sam leapt up and jammed his thumb to her Cuff, and I let go. The conversation ended abruptly.

She sued us, of course—$1,700 worth. The bill showed up at home. Mrs. Nince also managed to make $3,108.88 off the words *modish* and *Silent Freak*, pushing us to within $80 of Collection.

FIND ME: $11.98

I sat in Falxo Park alone, at the spot where my stage had been. Sam offered to stay with me and sit in silence while I thought, but I knew he was in no mood for staying put. I sent him off with a flick of my eyes, secretly hoping he could think up some better plan than the one I'd gotten myself into.

When he was gone, my speech popped up on my Cuff. Keene Inc. wanted it read now? Was it just appearing randomly? What if I read it in the park, to an audience of no one? Would Butchers & Rog back down?

Unlikely. It was too late for that. I ran my finger on the glossy surface of my Cuff, thinking about how few objects in my world were smooth.

To my right, one of the faux Parisian shops was being reprinted, layer by layer. All these plastic buildings were rough to the touch, built upon each other, with strata that flared and splayed in thin, coarse lines. It was possible to smooth these walls out with a little skill and a hot, iron-like device from EvenMelt™, but that process was Patented and expensive—and looking closely at details was considered bad form.

The speech glowed on my arm. I flipped it away, embarrassed by my weakness. An Ad popped up in its place with a trill. *Steadler's™ Inks. More flavor-nutrition in every cartridge.* I could flip it away, but it would only come right back, like a boomerang, with a message asking if I wanted to opt out. The tap was 10¢, but the amount made no difference. I wasn't going to break my silence for it.

I felt weird, keeping my voice still, like I was playacting or lying. I hadn't thought about what would happen after I went silent. Before, I would talk to myself when I was alone. I would work out my thoughts, or just mutter pretty words to myself. Regret crept up the back of my throat, and I had to remind myself that even if I hadn't gone silent, I didn't have the money to talk to myself anymore. Even if I hadn't gone totally silent, I still would not be free to say much more.

I let the Ad sit, glowing, insistent, using me as a mini-billboard for as long as Steadler's™ wanted to pay. Around me, the Ad screens had quietly filled with the same message, but lit dimly, like they were at half power. The park was awash in a sad blue glow, which suited my mood.

My Cuff felt warm. I pressed a finger to the edge near my wrist, realizing that I might never again feel the skin underneath. The Cuff's warmth troubled me. It was not unheard of for NanoLion™ batteries to malfunction and go white-hot in a Cuff. If that happened, I'd lose my arm—and probably my life. Would I scream? Would it matter?

Perhaps sensing my blackening temper, the Ad on my arm finally winked away. The screens around me shut down, and the park darkened.

A short time later, a thick group of golden-haired teenage boys ambled by. They were enormous, fat-legged specimens of wealth and privilege. They glanced at me and walked on like they had stepped in dog feces. I lowered my head and hid my face. I didn't want another confrontation.

Screens burst to life around them, flooding the path before them in bright, sunny colors. Ads addressed them loudly by name. *Parker. Madroy. Thad.* The Ads scrambled after them, like dogs desperate for a master's attention, moving from screen to screen. Moon Mints™ invited them to sit in the park, showing them fatter, more pleasant-looking versions of themselves sitting in the park in golden light, laughing and surrounded by skinny, big-breasted girls far prettier than me.

Please no, I thought.

They heaved themselves down the street, waving off the Ads like flies. They couldn't be bothered. One of them cupped his hands around his mouth and yelled back at me. "Sluk!" That was all the effort he could expend.

My Cuff popped to life again. *Are you a Sluk? Take the Cosmo™ Quiz!*

I kept my head down. The Ad faded quickly. Then I heard a different voice, this one quiet and gentle.

"I have things to tell you," the voice whispered.

I looked up. Beecher's grandmother was standing right in front of me. She was smaller and more stooped than I remembered. She wore a stiff black dress with sleeves so long they covered her hands. It looked ancient. She looked so sad, and I had the urge to tell her how sorry I was.

"Find me," she said in a low, quavering voice. Her lips barely moved. Her head was low.

She shuffled away, back out of the park, and stepped onto the bridge with a heavy sigh. Find her? Did she want me to follow now? Why didn't she just say what she wanted to say? Was she on the edge of Collection, too?

She moved to the side of the bridge opposite where Beecher had jumped, and then made her way over the curve. Anger suddenly twisted through me. Was she toying with me? Hadn't I done enough for her? If Beecher hadn't jumped, I don't think any of this would have happened.

I wasn't going to follow her. I wasn't going to find her, either. If what she wanted to say was so important, *she* could find *me*.

Nancee's Last Day ceremony was moved to Pride's Corner, a small, empty square of land not far from Mrs. Micharnd's gymnastic academy. It was a "waker," because Nancee had been born at 4:12 a.m. and Mrs. Harris refused to apply for a shifting permit to schedule the ceremony at a more reasonable hour.

"Maybe we'll see a Placer," Sam said, scanning the rooftops as we walked. He wasn't supposed to come, technically, but he said he wanted to walk with me. Even if I had been speaking, though, I wouldn't spoil his enthusiasm by pointing out that the Placers would have come through long before. They would have to know Nancee's schedule, to make her Last Day Placements and set her Brand. But Sam enjoyed looking out for them too much for me to ruin it. I'd already ruined enough.

I couldn't hold his hand while we walked, either. Even without the cost of the gesture, Sam was too old for that. Instead, I half curled my fingers over my thumb and thought about when he was little, and I would hold his hand and take him walking in the better sections of the city.

A small platform was set up for Nancee—much smaller

than mine had been. Her product tables were sparse, with only Moon Mints™ and Kepplinger's™ Hair Braids. I didn't see any Huny®. Nancee had so wanted to be a Huny® girl, like my sister. If you weren't rich, it was like a verified stamp of approval that you were pretty and worth something, but I don't think Nancee or I were ever going to make that grade, according to the algorithms of the Huny® corporation.

Kids were milling around, far more subdued than they might be at a more reasonable hour. Even the kids who hadn't had their Last Day yet were fairly quiet, and once people caught sight of me, the whole place went *almost* dead silent.

"Don't pay her any mind!" Mrs. Harris's sharp voice cracked through the air. The sound echoed between the buildings, amplified through Nancee's microphone.

Nancee watched me with her big eyes, and I suddenly wanted to scream at her to run. But there was nowhere for her to go—nowhere for *any* of us to go. The best I could really hope for was to warn her away from doing what I had done, but I couldn't even do that. She stood up a little taller under my gaze. She looked at the paper in her hands and smiled sadly.

The crowd turned back to Nancee in stages. I couldn't have been very interesting to look at.

Mrs. Harris forced herself to smile and put a hand on the paper. "Nancee," she purred. I hated when she spoke in that soothing tone.

Nancee was trembling. I could see it even from the back. The paper fluttered in her hands. She took a step and centered herself on the podium. Her eyes scanned the crowd. Her parents weren't here. Like so many parents I knew, they'd been indentured to pollination. Once, I heard, this was a job done by bees, but honeybees were extinct, or close enough to it that it didn't matter.

The air was rent by the shearing sound of tearing paper. A few gasps scattered through the crowd as Nancee let the pieces slip to the ground. She put her hand to her mouth, and Mrs. Harris slapped it away.

"Oh, damn!" Sam said, half amused, half worried. My breathing quickened.

"Stop that!" Mrs. Harris rasped. Nancee jerked away and stood on tiptoes so everyone could see her. She made the sign of the zippered lips. Mrs. Harris flushed with fury, glared at Nancee and then turned her wild eyes to me.

"Carlo Mendez did it yesterday," Penepoli Graethe whispered, suddenly beside me. "And I heard Chevillia Tide did it the day before."

Did what? I wanted to ask, but I had a sinking feeling I knew.

"What does it mean?" Penepoli asked me in a trembling voice, like I was leaving her behind. Nancee turned her back on Mrs. Harris, the platform and the crowd, and began to walk away. Penepoli grabbed my shoulder and shook me. "What does it mean?"

"If she told you," Sam said, "it wouldn't *mean* anything."

I looked at him. I ached to know—what did it mean to Sam?

The crowd began to mill around. More eyes turned to me. Mrs. Harris moved off to intercept Nancee, and it seemed like a good moment to escape. I caught Sam's attention with my eyes, and we headed home.

★ ★ ★

Mrs. Harris came straight to our apartment after dealing with Nancee, her eyes blazing. She stalked to the wall-screen and turned on the Central News Network™.

The news was calling them Silents. The report was vague about how many there were or what it meant. It sounded like there were more than the four I'd heard about that morning. They didn't name any names, except mine. They showed the footage of my Last Day again. They'd found a reverse shot of Nancee looking up at me in wonder, implying I'd inspired her. I felt proud, embarrassed and sick all at once.

"She'll never be Branded now!" Mrs. Harris squealed, like I had made Nancee go quiet. She was never going to be Branded by Huny®, like she'd wanted. I wondered if it would have been harder for her to go silent if Huny® had been on her table.

"It is estimated that Silents have cost the Dome of Portland, Vermaine, more than six million dollars in revenue."

"The Silents," Sam said in a dramatic voice, like it was a group of superheroes.

Mrs. Harris's face contorted into a snarl of disgust. "Sam, this is *not* a joke." She turned to me. "If you don't fix this, they are going to take Saretha." Her hands flailed around in a panic as she squawked. "And then they are going to take you. And then they will take him!"

We didn't need her flapping around the room like an over-wrought bird. Saretha stared right through her. Sam looked out the window, shaking his head. I didn't say a word. Why didn't she get the message?

"Do you have any idea what they are going to do? Saretha can't even be properly Collected. I've never heard of anything like it."

I was more than aware. I'd been thinking about what would happen to Saretha constantly. Yet the idea that they would disfigure her just for looking like Carol Amanda Harving only fueled my desire to keep quiet. I didn't understand it, but somehow my silence hurt the system that formulated such terrible possibilities.

"I knew no good would come from trying to look famous," Mrs. Harris said, shaking her head. Who was she trying to kid? I felt like she tried to dream up the most irritating things to say. She had been plenty excited that Saretha looked like Carol Amanda Harving until the letter arrived.

Mrs. Harris's thin lips pressed tight. "*Speth*," Mrs. Harris admonished. How was this my fault? I didn't ask anyone to copy me.

"Stop talking to Speth," Sam growled. He hopped off the couch and stood up. "Even if she started talking right now, that wouldn't help anything."

Oh, Sam, I thought. I wanted him to hear my thoughts. It was a useless hope, but if I could have managed it, I would have told him how sorry I was—not just for what I had done, but for the world we all had to live in.

"I think it would help a great deal if Speth stopped this foolishness. She needs to snap out of it, read that speech and apologize for the confusion she caused." Mrs. Harris crossed her arms as if this was the last word on the subject, and her frowning puss would be the thing that finally brought me to my senses.

Part of me longed for what she said to be true. Most of me knew it wasn't, and as if to drive that home, she followed it with the least believable words she could have selected.

"Speth," she said, blinking her eyes with that particular nervous tick she had when she spoke the following words: "I love you."

She didn't love me. She didn't even pretend it was true. The words made bile creep up my throat. Her budget had a special line item to speak those exact words to each of her charges once each month.

"You don't have to spend it," Sam said, arms crossed.

"Sam," she began.

"Please don't," he said. We all hated it. Our parents couldn't afford to say it, but she got to.

"Well, it seems like a waste," she said. "It doesn't roll over." Her Cuff pinged. Her face turned even more sour when she looked down at it. "Well, I hope you're happy!"

She turned the Cuff for me to see. The message glowed the angry color of flame.

Your Custodianship for Nancee Mphinyane-Smil has been terminated. Please remit all associated payments dated forward from this time.

"What does that mean?" Sam asked, squinting.

"It means I've been removed as Nancee's Custodian!"

"Why haven't they removed you as *our* Custodian?" Sam asked.

"I'm sure you think you are very funny," Mrs. Harris said.

"We'll see how you like it when Keene Inc. is your guardian." She turned to Saretha, her only real ally in the room. "Will you please tell Speth that you want her to speak? I will pay for your words."

Mrs. Harris was more desperate than I'd thought. She never offered to pay for words. I'd hurt her. Each child that left her guardianship was money out of her pocket.

I felt good about that. But I worried about what was going to happen to Nancee now.

"Saretha, Speth should know what you think," Mrs. Harris offered softly.

Saretha put her hand to her forehead, blocking her eyes, like the room was too bright. She shook her head. It must have been hard for her not to say anything. I knew the effort of silence all too well. Did my mother's signing of the zippered lips mean as much to her as it had to me?

Mrs. Harris threw up her hands. "I am trying to help! What do you think is going to happen? Do you have any idea of the trouble you are in? Do you realize how bad this looks?"

"For you," Sam said.

"That's right," Mrs. Harris hissed. "For me! I am your Custodian! It looks terrible for you, too—for all of us. You've made it look like…" She stopped. I wanted to know what came next, but only because I'm sure that the words she *didn't* say were the most important. In lieu of finishing her sentence, I hoped her pause would mean she was finished for the day, but sadly, she was not.

"It is disgraceful," she went on. "To be frank, Speth, I know exactly why you are doing this. Saretha gets all the attention, and you think this is the way to turn the spotlight on yourself. I am sorry to say it, but behaving in this manner does not make you prettier or more interesting. Quite the opposite, if you ask me."

It felt like she'd punched me. Is this what she really thought?

"No one ASKED YOU!" Sam roared.

Saretha's head turned a little, and she eyed me pityingly.

I didn't care what Mrs. Harris said, but it felt like poison in the room. Did Saretha believe it? I swallowed and turned my face away. I didn't want to hear anymore. I couldn't shut her up by staying; I would just be a target for her to shoot at.

I stood up and rushed out the door.

IRIDESCENCE: $13.99

My head pounded in the dry, late-day air. I blamed Mrs. Harris, but it wasn't just her; it was everything. I found myself moving toward Falxo Park once again, and the bridge where Beecher killed himself. I remembered his lanky, miserable figure loping along in my mind and regretted ever knowing him. My eyes turned wet and then, like a lunatic, I laughed out loud, because I also missed him. I could laugh for free, but only if my Cuff deemed it to be genuine and "involuntary."

Why had his grandmother approached me in the park? Did she know something I didn't about why he had done it? What could she possibly say that would make it right?

Not far off, I saw her building. I had never actually been inside. A few times Beecher offered to take me to his place, but I assumed that was just a boy's trick to get me alone. Thomkins Tower was not inviting. It was a dark, sloppy, printed slab scattered with tiny windows. There were no Placer handholds. There was no ornamentation. There were no overhanging eaves—even our building had those. The entire structure was slightly askew from the fourth floor up, where the building printer must have misaligned a few degrees and kept going.

I wondered if Mrs. Stokes was inside. I closed my eyes and

pressed my fingers to my temples to ease the throbbing. Was she just playing games? Maybe she had good reason to want to talk in private. Maybe she had an Advil™.

I decided to go up. Whether she had something useful to say, or she was just playing games, at least I could do *something.*

Thomkins Tower had a reputation for being rough. I slipped inside her building quickly, hoping not to be recognized, but of course I was. Two rough-looking boys came right at me the minute I was inside. I was ready to fight them, for all the good it would do, but they pulled up short and each showed me the sign of the zippered lips. The sight stunned me as I passed. I reached the stairs, my face burning a little with shame from jumping to conclusions about their intentions.

I found her apartment on the third floor. I pressed the buzzer. A moment later, she opened her door. I didn't wait for her to invite me in. I stepped inside. I hoped she wasn't going to tell me Beecher had been in love with me. I didn't want to know it. I didn't want to believe that I'd played some part in his death. I looked up and saw the red-rimmed, haunted look in Mrs. Stokes's eyes, and my anger at him and at her melted. I wished I had come up when Beecher asked. Now I had to imagine what it was like, the two of them living here.

Her place was smaller than ours. One wall had recently been printed over, no doubt removing the space that had once been allocated to Beecher. There was a couch and a stack of old, ratty-looking boxes along one wall. Her home had a window like ours, but too foggy to see through. It looked like it had been purposely sanded and scraped.

The other strange thing was that the room had no screen. I'd never been in a home without a screen. I stared at the blank wall where it seemed like one belonged, feeling weird in its absence. Nothing was glowing and serving Ads. I may have hated ours, but I was used to it. I found the noise and chatter of it comfortingly familiar. Her home seemed so quiet and lonely in comparison.

"I haven't got a food printer, either," she said hoarsely, pointing at the blank wall. "Or I would offer you a sheet of Wheatlock™." She laughed, like this was funny. Maybe it *was* funny. Wheatlock™ is disgusting.

How did she eat? She couldn't possibly afford fresh food.

"You know Randall circumvented the programming and all that?"

Randall, I assumed, was Beecher's father.

"You know *why* he did it?"

I had no idea.

"Ever try to use a food printer during a FiDo? They don't work. WiFi goes down, and pretty much *nothing* works. Everything has to be connected to the tether. Everything. Randall didn't like it. He worried about it. He said the whole city would starve, and for what?"

She sat herself down on the couch.

"After they took him away, they said the family couldn't be trusted to have *any* kind of printer." She wiped the idea away with a disgusted hand. "Who needs that garbage?"

How was she able to afford all these words? Then I realized that I hadn't heard her Cuff buzz at all. Did those thick sleeves muffle the sound?

"You know why Beecher jumped?" she asked, smoothing out the scratchy cloth on her legs. Her voice dropped to a sadder tone.

Was she really asking, or was she going to tell me? If she knew, I wished she would just come out and say so.

"Butchers & Rog bought him. Full Indenture. Said he could finish school and *then* be placed in servitude, or he could quit school right away, and Rog would take him."

What kind of choice was that? Quitting school made even less sense now that I knew what had been troubling him. My heart ached for the burden he'd carried, unable to tell me. Had their debt suddenly gotten worse? Is that why he had been Indentured?

"That poor boy." Mrs. Stokes shook her head sadly. "Boys his age need to eat, but you saw how skinny he was. We could never afford enough food, and we just couldn't keep our debt rate steady, no matter how hard we tried."

She shrugged helplessly. "He signed a contract. Rog made him use paper and ink. Ink on his fingers. I should've asked about that. I didn't find out 'til later that Beecher agreed to go right away to keep *me* out of servitude."

She shook her head pitifully. "That was the choice they gave him. He agreed to go early to protect me. He barely wanted to say *that*. You know what he was like after his fifteenth." She sighed. "He knew what would happen if they found out my secret."

She put her hand on her thick sleeve and pulled the coarse fabric up. Underneath, the skin of her hand and arm was a shiny, red, mottled mess. Her Cuff was black, charred around the edges. The glossy screen was warped and eddied with a purplish iridescence.

"It happened years ago," she said. "Long before Randall and the printer. I went in to get my overlays—I got mine late

in life, because they didn't have them when I was fifteen—
and when they presented me with Terms of Service, I clicked
DECLINE. The administrator was shocked."

My eyes must have gone wide, because Beecher's grandmother laughed at me. "She looked a little like that! Dear, you
always have the legal right to decline. Did you know that?"

Could I have refused *my* overlays? Her advice did me little
good now, but still…

"The transition specialist didn't know what to do. Apparently neither did the Cuff, because it started to get warm. I
thought it was a feedback loop. Randall wondered if it was
purposeful—the government's punishment for not agreeing
to the ToS. Whatever caused it, the Cuff got hotter and hotter. It probably would have gone molten, like most do, but
once we got home, Randall hacked it. That boy was clever,
and was he ever mad. Burned his fingers some. My arm didn't
fare too well, either. But all the inputs were fried."

She held the Cuff a little higher, as if I could see what had
gone wrong.

"It still puts out a signal, telling them I'm here. That's
about it. It can't record a thing. I can say anything I like,"
she sighed. She looked sad. I would have expected her to be
happy about it. "Beecher thought I could do more good than
him because of this." She held the Cuff higher. "As if I had
something useful to say. Truth is, I talked too much already.
I complained about the Rights Holders, and look where that
got us. I got Randall so fired up with my talk, he got too
bold. Now my son and his wife are out tending crops so rich
people don't have to eat printed food, and my grandson…"
Her voice broke off, and she wiped her eyes.

"As far as those Rights Holders know, I haven't spoken in years. Doesn't attract any attention, though. I'm sure lots of old ladies give up on talking, so I don't show up as special or strange. You, though—silence at your age is awful conspicuous."

Her story, and the reminder of Beecher's fate, was almost too much to bear. I clenched my jaw to hold back the tears, but they still came.

"All you kids without your parents—it's tragic—so much worse than it used to be," she said, wiping my cheek. "Seems like they wait until you kids are just old enough to stick you with a Custodian, and then they yank your parents away."

She tussled my pixie cut, and I hurriedly smoothed it back into place. She was right, of course. How many friends did I have who still had their parents? It had somehow seemed normal—just the way things were—even if the idea of it twisted a knot in my chest.

"Sorry," she said. "I should be careful not to tussle you into a Copyrighted do."

She paused and closed her eyes for a brief moment. I felt my hair again. I'd have to cut it soon, hacking it back with the dull pair of scissors Sam and I used for trimming hair. It was weird to think her Cuff wasn't watching, recording, scanning her haircut and mine and comparing the scans against what little was free.

"They just keep taking all they can, right up to the breaking point. It's odd how everyone seems to end up right at the *edge* of Collection, don't you think? You can't do any little thing to protest it, or they'll sue you right into servitude. I suppose that is why I like your tactic so much. Technically, you aren't *doing* anything. I hope you realize how clever that is."

I didn't. I hadn't. Another tear fell. I felt like a complete fraud. Did she really believe I'd worked this out—that I'd planned for all this to happen?

"I hope you know I'm proud you did it," she said. The wrinkles on her face crinkled up.

I realized I was still standing, looming above her, my posture still full of anger and frustration. My heart was a different matter. I could feel the sadness and regret in her. I wanted to tell her it wasn't her fault. Whatever she'd stirred up in Beecher, that was no cause for him to take his own life. But I couldn't speak. I couldn't take her hand. I didn't know how to bring her any comfort, and that need welled inside me. One more tear slid down my cheek.

She took my hand instead. Then she stood and hugged me, and I did not move, because I could not hug her back. I just let myself soak it in.

ASSAULT: $14.99

With each day that passed, our prospects dwindled, and without a paycheck, we would be in Collection before the month was out. My silence and notoriety made me impossible to employ. I couldn't even try to earn pennies in a Free-to-Play game because I couldn't agree to Terms of Service.

Trapped in the house, Saretha took to mining for gold and candy in one of these games. She made little hammering gestures in the air, and her avatar made the same tedious motion projected on the wall screen. If she didn't get distracted, she could make about a three or four dollars an hour by selling what she gathered—but only if she could transport it safely to an in-game bank. Time and again, she was ambushed by players who paid for perks that made them nearly invincible. They thrilled in making players like Saretha miserable; they were unaware or unconcerned that the tiny sums of money they were stealing might ruin us.

"You're just wasting time," Sam told her, turning over in his bed. It was late. The dim glow of the twilight dome faded so it was lit pale by the city. Sam was tired. There was an ache in his voice.

Saretha tensed. Her half-open mouth closed into a tight,

lipless frown. Some kind of half wolf/centaur smashed her character to the ground, and her gold and jellybeans scattered across the screen.

"Sam!" Saretha cried out, blaming him. Her Cuff buzzed. Sam shook his head. We both knew it cost Saretha more to say his name than she would have made from the loot. The half wolf/centaur turned and farted a noxious green cloud over her avatar's body—a perk you could purchase in-game to taunt your enemies. It likely cost more than the loot as well.

"You should go to school," Saretha said.

Sam looked puzzled. It was nearly eight o'clock at night. "Now?"

"In general," Saretha said, flailing a hand around and letting out an exasperated breath. "Don't make me waste words!"

Her Cuff buzzed. She meant I should go to school. I hadn't been in days. After Nancee's Last Day, I knew the pressure on me would only grow worse. Sera Croate would be waiting. Others would, too. I hoped Nancee was okay, and realized too late I should have gone to be with her.

"You probably should," Sam encouraged in a small voice.

I almost said, *Yeah*, because speaking with Sam felt more familiar than my silence. But I stopped myself just in time. Still, he was right. It wasn't good for Saretha and I to be cooped up together. I wasn't helping her, and I doubt she understood how much I longed to help.

Still frowning, Saretha waited to respawn and scrolled through her Cuff at her friend count. She once broke two thousand followers. Now she was down to a couple dozen. She sighed. She tried to pull up her Huny® status, but it wouldn't load. I hadn't even thought about how her Branding might be affected. Had they dropped her?

"Crap," Sam said realizing what this meant. Sam hated the taste of Wheatlock™. The Huny® spread was the only thing that made it palatable, probably because it had an actual flavor: sweet. Wheatlock™ tasted like the bottom of a shoe, but probably blander. "I guess we'll have to ration our supplies." He laughed, but he laughed alone. I didn't find it funny; I found it sad. We wouldn't have Huny® anymore.

A moment later, Saretha's character was back on-screen, unarmed and tiny, headed to the mines. The half wolf/centaur charged, having stuck around to crush her again, just because he could. I couldn't watch her do this anymore.

I left. I had to get out. I walked for a few hours, along to the far side of the rim where the shops gave way to small houses, greenery and then exclusive Law Firms, nightclubs and the enormous City Court House.

The imposing marble building made me uneasy. It's one of the few in the city built from real stone, not printed layers of plastic. It is meant to intimidate. *Obedience to the Law is Freedom*™ is chiseled over the columned entrance, a hundred feet above me in letters twice my height. The Commander-in-Chief Justice adjudicates there when he isn't ruling the Supreme Court™. I'd never been inside, and couldn't imagine I ever would. Arkansas Holt would cave in to any Lawsuit before it got to court.

The streets were mostly empty this late at night. The buildings' eaves were dotted with lights that overhung the street, nearly obscuring the dome above. Ads didn't follow me into Section Fourteen; I was too poor. The dark and quiet felt peaceful, if a little eerie. I knew I looked horribly out of place. My gray public domain T-shirt and loose blue public domain jeans didn't belong here, but I walked on with a tense resolve. I might as well walk the whole eleven miles around the city; I was nearly halfway. What did a few hours more matter?

I'd rarely been out here. Section Fourteen was the only part of the city with an English name, supposedly because the French word for it was too close to Quatrième.

Out of the corner of my eye, I saw something move across a rooftop at the far side of the Court House Plaza. The Law Firms were closed and dark. Glum as I felt, I was thrilled by a glimpse of what I was sure was a Product Placer. I had never seen one before, even though Sam and I had been going up to our roof to look for them for years.

I followed to where the dark shape went. I waited, looking up, but there was nothing there. Someone called from behind me.

"Speth?" he said, as if he knew me.

I turned. It was no Product Placer. Walking up the sidewalk, followed by eager Ads, was an Affluent I did not recognize. He had a broad, flushed face, with a small, piggish nose and a thin goatee cut to a fine point beneath his chin. You could tell he'd been LaserShaved™. He was trim and fit, a good foot taller than me, with overlarge, muscled arms. He was dressed for the evening, with a formal black waistcoat and a platinum-rimmed Cuff poking out from his sleeve. The platinum ring was a thing for Affluents. It signaled intent and willingness to offer free speaks—a successful pickup technique. It was odd that he was alone; the city was full of young girls willing to trade their company for the ability to freely talk. Why bother me?

I pretended I hadn't heard him and picked up my pace. He called my name again and jogged to catch up.

"You're that Silent Girl, right?" His Cuff vibrated. He looked at it, as if thinking of holding it out to me, then he thought better of it. "What a shame. You have a lovely mouth."

Charming, I thought. Sometimes it was nice to think words clearly in my head, even if I could not say them. He was not so ugly that he should have a hard time finding companionship, but something about him felt wrong. Maybe it was because he was standing too close. Or because he was twice my age, or even older. It could be difficult to gauge the age of an Affluent with all the options for cosmetic surgery and youth treatments.

An Ad strip at the corner of a building burst to life, bright blue and silent. Ads had to run silent from midnight to six in the good neighborhoods. A bottle of mouthwash popped up and spun, like it was desperate for him to drink it. Smelling his sour breath, I was a little desperate for him to drink it, too.

"I feel bad for you. It can't be easy, not being able to speak. I'll bet a lot of people think they can get you to talk. I saw that the *Daily Spec*™ will pay $15,000 for proof you can. I don't need the money, of course."

He pulled back his sleeve to make sure I could see the platinum ring. His eyes closed for a moment, and he swayed in place before steadying himself again. He had obviously been drinking. Across the narrow alley, between shops, another Ad strip popped to life. The mouthwash bottle hopped across and back. The systems must have scanned his breath. He leaned over me, his hand pressing flat on the Ad. Under the bad breath were wafts of cologne or perfumed liquor. He looked up and down the empty street.

"I sure wouldn't mind though," he said, "if you *did* make a sound."

I held up my arm to press him back. My Cuff burst to life, sparkling with another mouthwash Ad. His face lit from below. His eyes rolled down to see, sharklike, making him look crazed. He knocked my Cuff away with his own, and then jammed his Cuff under my neck.

"Why don't you cry for help?"

His Cuff vibrated against my throat as his words rolled out of sight under my chin—$15.94. I pushed at his shoulders, and when that failed to move him, I kneed him, hard, in the groin. He bent over with a groan, 99¢, but kept a grip on me and began pulling me into the alley.

My heart pounded like a rabbit's. No one would hear us. No one would help me. I pushed out against him, but he pinned me to the wall with his arm across my neck. I kicked, and he choked me harder. A sound escaped—a slight gasp. He stopped a moment. His face lit with excitement. I felt his heartbeat under mine, less frenzied, but fast and relentless. My Cuff registered nothing.

I was not going to scream, or cry out, not for this monster. I clawed at him, desperate, swearing to myself I wouldn't stay out this late again, if I could just get away.

Two men passed on the street, just a few feet from us. They pretended to be enraptured by Ads and walked quickly out of view, the mouthwash chasing happily after them.

"Silent Girl," my attacker said, his face next to mine, his foul breath beginning to turn my stomach. "You won't be able to tell anyone what happened, will you?"

Above us came a sound, a slight creak, and he looked up. I shoved him back, and his hold slipped enough for me to duck away. I turned fast to run, but suddenly he had hold of my leg, yanking on it, and I slammed to the ground face first. A jarring pain made my head swim. My chin felt like it had split open.

"I don't actually *want* you to make a sound." He laughed, climbing onto my back and pinning me facedown on the pavement. "That way, no one knows where you are, or what we've done." He let the pressure up a little, but not enough for me to escape. "It will be a secret we can share." He began fiddling with something on his clothes.

With panic, I realized there was no record of me. Only *his* words would be recorded. He could have been talking to himself, for all I could prove. Location is only logged when there is a transaction—when you speak, write or buy. Privacy Laws are few, but this was one of the big ones. I should have screamed so my location was known. I should have done something. I could have called out *Police!* and my Cuff would have autodialed the authorities and recorded this mess. Was my silence worth this?

"Sluk!" He grabbed my hair, yanked my head back and then toppled over, landing with a thud, like he had suddenly, forcefully, passed out. I didn't understand what had happened. I dragged myself out from underneath him and slowly comprehended he had not fallen on his own.

A man stood over me, dressed entirely in black, like a ninja or a superhero from a movie. I rose slowly, a hand on my searing, bloodied chin. The man in black remained still, perhaps to keep from frightening me. Our eyes met, but that was all I could see of him. His face was masked, and I understood why: he was a Product Placer.

Banded® adhesive strips now have Anti-Scarsilate™! an Ad behind his head texted insistently. *For nasty cuts and bruises, Anti-Scarsilate™ brings the healing.* My chin was sure to scar, just as Saretha's elbow had. The Ad showed instant healing, but below it, a disclaimer read *Healing not instant—simulated for the purposes of demonstration.* Anti-Scarsilate™ hadn't helped Saretha lose the little crescent moon on her arm, even though she'd been sure it would. I doubted it would help me with this.

The Ad wasn't for me, anyway. I didn't rate. It was for my unconscious attacker on the ground.

The Product Placer stepped back. Keeping his eyes on me, he raised his Cuff arm up and swung it back, smashing into the Ad panel. The glow sputtered in a strange rainbow of color as shards of the screen fell away. He reached into the shattered panel and pulled out a thin, square chip, then crossed the alley to the other side. He seemed fairly pleased with himself. He repeated the process with the other Ad and handed the chip to me gently. I turned it over in my hands. It was branded and labeled *Seagate™ 8PB Q-flash*; a simple flash drive you could plug into most computers. Below this was a small, dot-printed label, which read: *24hrlp-3dscn-rs.*

I was a little wobbly. At first I thought it meant something about twenty-four-hour help, but then I realized what the drive contained. It was the Ad panel's backup loop of the last twenty-four hours of scan data and video. My attack, and my rescue, were on that little chip. It had been recorded and stored for upload and parsing.

As soon as I understood, the Product Placer snatched the chip back and tucked it away. He hadn't meant it for me. He was taking it for himself. He wanted to erase any trace he had been in the alley. Product Placers can't be seen, and they certainly don't leave evidence behind if they can help it.

My attacker began to stir. The Product Placer bent down and pulled a small metallic-blue device shaped like a teardrop from his pack. It was no bigger than his thumb. He slid it over the man's Cuff. The Cuff clicked and released from the man's arm. My attacker moaned. I didn't know a device existed that would allow you to remove another person's Cuff.

The man screamed, raising his hands to his eyes. Disconnected from the Cuff, he had been shocked for his groan, and then was shocked again for the scream of pain. This time he winced, but held his tongue.

The Product Placer smiled under his mask and covered his eyes with his hands, then revealed them, like he was playing peekaboo. It was awfully shrewd to take the man's Cuff. My attacker wouldn't be able to report anything to the police until a new Cuff was assigned. That could take weeks, even with his wealth.

The Placer closed the man's Cuff over a loop on his backpack. The platinum ring glinted in the dark. A second later, the Placer scrambled up a rope so thin and black, it almost looked like he was pantomiming his way up the side of the building.

"You—" My attacker tried to speak, blindly casting around,

but even that single word was cut short by a hard wince as he held his hands to his eyes.

Acting more from instinct than good sense, I found the thin rope and scrambled up, away from my attacker. I never should have seen the Placer, but now that I had, I needed to know more.

PLACERS: $15.99

The Placer could have killed me. If he'd cut the rope, or yanked his grappling hook free, or just given me a gentle push, I would have tumbled five stories down to the ground. My head was still swimming with pain; I had been foolish to climb at all.

Instead, he pulled me up. I guess it would have been stupid to kill me after the effort he put in to save me. His team was waiting, looking down at me.

I knew what I was supposed to do. I was supposed to pretend I hadn't seen them. But I was slowly realizing that I wasn't very good at doing what was expected of me.

There were three of them, standing there, watching me. Even under their masks, I could sense irritation. The one with the most gear and the fiercest eyes gave me the harshest stare. My chin still throbbed, and the pain radiated out to my jaw and my skull, yet I was thrilled. I was actually seeing Placers!

Everything the Placers wore was matte black: their clothes, gloves, backpacks, tool belts and even the boxes they carried. Every surface seemed to eat light. I could scarcely tell where one ended and the next began. I guessed this team was high-end—a swag crew out to place something more than cereal or cola in a neighborhood like this.

The one I had followed, the biggest of the bunch, made a gesture in the air, drawing a very gently arced line slowly ahead of himself with this thumb and forefinger. He moved it suddenly, straight to the right, then dropped it down with a twist. This obviously meant something to the others, because they stepped back. The leader held her finger firm, pointing at the ground. This was meant for me. I should go back. I did not move. I put a hand to my aching chin and felt the warm blood there again.

With a sigh-like drop of her shoulders, the smallest of the group, a petite girl, heaved her considerable pack from her shoulders and silently reached inside it. She pulled out a Product box with an arrangement of therapeutic supplies from Phisior™ to make skin look younger. She took a healing pad from the kit, tore its package open and handed it to me.

Who were these people? There were few clues. Product Placers were meant to be a mystery. Sam once heard they would bring you a real orange if you kept quiet. Sam had always wanted to taste an orange.

I didn't know what to expect from them, but this kindness and aid was not what I had anticipated. Did they know who I was? Or were they surprised that I wasn't speaking?

I secured the bandage to my chin, and the large Placer made his gesture again, this time specifically positioning his fingers so that it was clear he was mapping out a route over the buildings.

Before I could get my bearings, the leader took off, leaping across to the next rooftop. The small one quickly packed up and followed. The big one looked at me and inclined his head so slightly I barely saw it. He wanted me to follow. When he ran, I took a deep breath and plunged forward as well.

I could have gotten myself killed. I wasn't at my best, though the bandage soothed my pain and, somehow, my dizziness. Sirens began to wail back near the scene of the attack. The lead Placer picked up her pace.

Once we were well away from where we'd started, the big one unfastened my attacker's Cuff from his pack and flung it into the air, where it pinged off the corner of a building and tumbled down ten stories to the alley below. It hit with a hard crack and a dazzling flash of light, followed by a white-hot glow. The Cuff's NanoLion™ battery had ruptured. The alley might glow for days.

I stumbled just a moment, thinking of the battery clamped to my wrist. I had to remind myself that ruptures were rare on their own. Rare enough, at least, that NanoLion™ remained profitable. How many suits against them could there be, if their batteries were basically everywhere?

It was hard to keep up, but I felt exhilarated. The rapid, careful placement of my feet, the strain in my legs as I lengthened my strides and the fluid way I followed how they skipped up over fire escapes and lintels to gain more height brought back the joy of my gymnastics classes. I didn't realize how much I'd missed it. I was only just managing to keep up, thanks to those years of practice. The team moved like gazelles, jumping effortlessly from rooftop to rooftop, never looking down. I should have done the same.

The buildings on the outer ring are only ten or twelve stories tall. That is as much as the curve of the dome will accommodate here. The gaps between the buildings and their overhanging eaves are mostly eight feet—not a hard distance to jump, but that height is unnerving, and a mistake would be deadly. When the next building was taller, they would leap onto a fire escape with scarcely a noise. When the building dipped lower, they would leap off the edge, grab hold of a rail or pipe and slide down to the next building's height.

I lost pace. It irked the leader to slow for me, but I was immensely grateful when she finally did. They were actually allowing me to follow. Where were we going?

We moved inward, through the wedge of Section Fourteen, across small roofs and big, and soon were five blocks into the Cinquième, one of the six central sections. The buildings here were taller; everything was taller toward the city center. The leader shot a line up a dozen stories. She attached something to it and zipped up at a speed that didn't look safe. I felt like I was watching a superhero in action.

The small one quickly did the same. No wonder sightings were so rare; they moved so fast! The biggest one held out his arms to me, a silent offer to take me along. I think he was grinning under that mask. I stepped forward and he grasped me tightly around the waist. A second later, we were hurtling up thirty stories.

The roof door was already open when we arrived. The other two Placers had headed inside. The one beside me pried my hand loose from his arm and, with a click, brought up the guide wire behind us.

Beyond the doorway, the stairwell was lit in a warm amber light. What was this building? What were we doing here? Inside, the leader had a Pad out, and she held it up to the wall. It showed an apartment beyond, like a fuzzy, luminous window. The inside showed up as a cobalt-blue thermal image of expensive furniture and large, open space. She scanned the full length of the place until she came to a bed and two stout figures asleep inside. They glowed as a hot, round mass together in the room. The leader turned to see if the others agreed this was a good spot. The big one tilted his head to the side and closed his eyes like he was going to sleep.

Were they going to do a Placement? Was the plan to show me how it was done? This was sort of what I'd pictured when I thought of Product Placers: a coordinated, silent team, sneaking through the night. But there was something odd about this picture—me. Why had they brought me? It didn't make sense. I couldn't ask, and if I had, I'm certain they would have shushed me. I might have known a thing or two about being silent, but this crew was as noiseless as air. In comparison, my breath felt loud, and my feet seemed to slide on the carpet like rolling thunder.

The leader unlocked the apartment door by running a magnetic tool across the edges. The door clicked open. They all rushed inside, silent as ghosts. I followed them, trying to mimic their light steps.

The big one turned out a padded black cylinder from a long foam bag. It was about twice the thickness of a baseball bat and about a quarter as long. He began working a small screen at the top and held it out into the air. My ears instantly felt like they needed to be cleared. I could no longer hear my breath or my footfalls or anything. The air felt strange. The cylinder was suppressing the sound.

They all waited for me before an enormous wooden bookcase. I could not help but stare. I'd never seen a book in person before—only in movies and shows. The people who lived here, the two sleeping yellow-orange blobs a few rooms away—they were people with money. A *lot* of money. You didn't just *have* books in your home. You had to have permits. You had to have means to protect them. Books were dangerous things filled with uncontrolled words and Copyrighted ideas. You could show a book to anyone, replicating the ideas at no cost at all. You could cut up the pages and rearrange the words into who knows how many combinations. You could keep the words, no matter how many times the Copyrights changed hands and prices on the Word$ Market™. It was shocking just to be in the presence of them. I wanted to run a finger down their spines. I wanted to pull one out and crack it open and see the words. Who knew what they might contain?

The leader blocked my view, and waved me back. I had to shake myself. She held her Pad up, scanned around one more time and pulled out one of the books. I thought, for just a moment, she was going to read it, or hand it to me, and that made me feel giddy. Instead, she reached her hand into the gap on the bookcase and gave a little tug. There was a mechanical sound, and my heart seemed to click into a lower gear as I realized the books weren't real.

They concealed a hidden door. What looked like paper between the covers was only a carefully printed matte plastic. The covers were just a façade. One Leatherette™ bump rippled into the next as the bookcase split open without a sound to reveal a secret room beyond.

SQUELCH: $16.99

Penepoli Graethe once took Nancee and me aside at school, to a secret spot where the wall juts out and no Ads or camera could see. We were nine years old and giddy at the idea of doing something we shouldn't. Penepoli showed us a handful of paper bits—words carefully cut, she said, from a book. She said they belonged to a cousin who had a boxful hidden away. She wanted us to be impressed. We were only nine years old, and could talk freely then. But even so, we anxiously read the little slips of paper, both delighted and terrified.

Woeful, his palms, each, warm summer, flick, Argentine, smelly.

We were risking a lot for a handful of words that didn't add up to anything. After the briefest thrill, Nancee told her to get rid of them, quick.

"What if they find out?" she hissed in a panic. "If they don't find out now, they'll find out when *you* have kids, Penepoli, or grandkids, and then *they'll* have to pay!" The Historical Reparations Agency had cut a swath through our class, and a lot of parents were gone.

Penepoli's joy fizzled away. I tried to think of where she could get rid of them. She plucked the two I was holding back and clutched them all in her hand. Before we could figure out what to do, Sera Croate appeared, like she had been looking for us.

She slapped Penepoli's hand and sent the lot flying. They were lifted up and carried away like confetti into the Quatrième. A sickening longing wormed its way through my chest as they fluttered away.

Sera tried to report Penepoli, but the evidence had flown away. When Principal Ugarte demanded to know what happened, Nancee, Penepoli and I all said the paper was Sera's. A week later, Sera Croate's parents were gone.

A terrible, guilty quiet fell between us for weeks. The three of us were stunned and horrified by what had happened. The few times we spoke, we tried to convince ourselves that the events were unrelated. I succeeded, I think, in making them think it wasn't our fault, but I was less sure. I had to remind myself that Sera hadn't thought twice about squealing on Penepoli.

We should have known Sera would show up. Our secret spot wasn't very secret at all.

The bookcase the Placer opened concealed a perfect hiding spot. Who even knew it was there? The four of us squeezed inside, with just enough space to not be in each other's faces. A round circle of deep red carpet gave us each a place to sit.

I had the distinct impression this was not the first time the Placers had been here. The bookcase closed behind us. I heard nothing. I felt like I'd gone deaf.

The big Placer with the cylinder swiped at its controls, and the sound was released. The leader turned to me and asked, "What is your plan?"

Her question startled me. I had no plan. The media treated me, and the rest of the Silents, like some great gang conspiring to bring down the economy, but how could we plot anything? We couldn't communicate with each other. I had no idea what Nancee thought she was doing, or even where she was.

Did she want to be free to say whatever she wanted, like I did? I wanted things to change; I wanted, maybe, to be left alone, but my desires were hardly a *plan*.

"How did you get the others to do it?" the little one asked.

Maybe this had been a mistake. If they knew who I was, why were they asking me questions? They had to know I wasn't going to talk. I suddenly felt afraid. I was standing in a secret room with three people dressed head to foot in black, their faces covered by masks. They could have been anyone. They could have done anything, and no one would ever know. No one knew where I was.

What did they want from me?

The big one asked, "Do you know where you are?"

I thought about this and, somehow, feeling a little on the spot, it made me think about the dome and its place in the world. I wasn't sure exactly where we were. I knew we were part of the States, but my history classes were vague about what, exactly, the states were and how they connected. We were in the Northeast, near or against an ocean, but I'd never seen a map, so I couldn't tell you where we were in relation to other domes, like DC or the Great Dome over Athens, Florida.

The big Placer didn't mean any of this, of course. I didn't know what building we were in, either.

"If she does not know, then she will not answer, Henri,"

the small one said with a note of exasperation. I startled, even though it wasn't exactly unexpected that she should speak.

"It's called a Squelch," the big one, Henri, explained, gesturing widely to the small room around us.

"Nothing you say will be recorded," the leader said, with a sidewise glance at the little one. "We're sealed off from the WiFi. The tether is cut. Your words are free and unmonitored."

My panic turned to disbelief. I breathed out hard as my brain tried to find purchase on this idea. I should have realized that places like this existed. The whole system of fees relied on us always being connected. Of course people would build spaces to block the tether, and, of course, the people who needed it least were the ones who could benefit from this trick.

"Do you understand?" the big one, Henri, asked me.

I understood. They wanted me to speak. I *could* speak, if I wanted to. I felt giddy and nervous all at once. It was drilled into us from the time we were very small that an always-on connection is critical to the fabric of society. FiDos were one thing, but this was something else. It was a willful skirting of the Law, one I would have wholeheartedly endorsed if it occurred in my neighborhood rather than here.

"If she understands, that does not mean she will speak," the small one said. Her voice was soft and tired. She dropped down along the wall, sitting on the floor.

"Oh," Henri said, looking a little confused. He offered me his hand awkwardly. I didn't take it. Handshakes are Copyrighted. Was I going to speak here? Could I trust them? My lips mashed together as I tried to decide if words would betray everything I had done.

"We don't even know if she is able to speak," the small one pointed out.

"It is completely safe," the leader explained.

Was it? I had a soft spot in my heart for Product Placers. I was amazed they had taken me in and brought me here, but I was not prepared to blindly trust them.

WiFi or no, I wasn't going to take any chances. I kept looking at my Cuff, worried it would somehow report this back. Even if it didn't, even if I got away with speaking, it felt wrong that I should do it here, with strangers.

Henri pulled off his mask.

"Henri!" the leader cried out.

Henri looked younger than I expected. He was maybe seventeen, but had wide, deep creases around his mouth. He pulled a big smile—too big, almost. His light brown hair stuck out at odd angles, full of static from the mask. He tried to smooth it out without success.

"What," the leader asked, "is the *singular*, most important thing about our job?" Her voice was low, musical and flute-like, but the tone was not friendly anymore. Her Pad seemed to purr in her hands. I'd never seen a device like it. It still worked with the WiFi blocked. I didn't see how this was possible. I thought all software required a constant connection to verify it wasn't pirated or hacked.

"Free swag," the girl who'd given me the bandage on the roof giggled.

"This isn't funny." The leader held up a finger. The girl lowered her head.

"Never be seen," Henri muttered with a small, apologetic shrug.

The leader looked around the room in frustration. She was expecting better. "So you take off your mask?"

"I was hot," Henri said.

"Henri runs warm," the little one said.

He didn't take that mask off because he was hot. He wanted me to see his face. I was flattered, but could not understand why he'd done it.

"She isn't going to say anything," Henri assured the leader. "She isn't even talking *now*."

He was right; I was choosing not to speak, even here.

"You don't trust us?" the little one asked, pretending her feelings were hurt.

It wasn't that I didn't trust them. I wanted to talk. I wanted to ask a million questions. A world of possibilities opened before me. I could explain my situation. I could ask them for help. I could beg them to let Saretha join them—the only job in the world where she could wear a mask and be outside the house. But something stopped me.

For all the harm it had done, and the trouble it had brought into my life, my silence meant something. It *was* a protest. I owned it. I couldn't cave just because I had a chance for free speaks. The funny thing was, this was what I most wanted to say and, if I said it, the words would mean nothing.

The leader eyed me. "I like her prudence," she said. I saw admiration in her eyes. I felt hopeful something good might come of this—a feeling I hardly recognized. Could I show them the way to Saretha?

"But this was a bad idea," the leader went on, shaking her head and looking at the ground.

"You let me go down to rescue her," Henri said.

"I did not sanction any such thing."

"Henri the heroic," the little one chimed.

"And you let her follow us," Henri continued.

"I let my curiosity get the better of me," the leader said, sighing. "But wanting to know her plan is one thing. Showing your *face* to her is something else."

"What difference does it make? She isn't going to tell. If no one *knows* she's seen us, it's like she hasn't seen us at all."

"Henri the philosopher," the little one commented. She turned to me, zipped her lips and raised her eyebrows as if to say, *That's your thing, right?* It wasn't the same as when the others had done it. I couldn't tell if she was impressed or mocking me. It felt weirdly like both.

The leader rubbed her hand over the top of her masked head, and suddenly, her body posture fell. "What's *your* plan, Henri?"

"I had two ideas, actually," Henri said, rubbing his hands together.

"I'd love to hear even one," the leader said.

"First, I thought if we brought her here we could...explain things."

"Oh, Henri!" the smaller girl squealed. "You are so wise, explain things to *me!*" She jumped up and down, clutching her hands to her chest.

"Margot, stop," Henri said.

"I will stop," Margot answered obediently.

"But no, I meant, for example, she might like to know that

if she doesn't speak, she isn't tracked. Legally, they can only check your location when you initiate conversation."

"Initiate," Margot said. "That is a very good word, Henri."

Henri took a second to glare at her.

"You might think it's good, but it could be dangerous. Like if you needed to call for help."

My body shivered. I had just learned this the hard way.

"Henri, that's not very exciting. Obviously she knows this," Margot said, dropping her head and slumping her shoulders. "I'm no longer in love."

The leader covered her mouth to conceal a grin. "That isn't entirely true," she said. "They can track a Cuff at any time. They just can't do it *legally* unless there is a transaction. The only way to go completely off-line is to enter a Squelch or to remove your Cuff."

Margot hesitantly pulled off her mask as well, as if she were defeated. She had her round little face in a frown. She was freckled and pale, with a face that seemed Asian and African and French, all at once, like her background was a mixture of everything. Her black, silky hair, styled into a bob, swept forward into two points. It was clearly an expensive haircut. She didn't look much older than me. I'd had no idea Placers were so young.

I turned to Henri, waiting for more, hoping he had some plan that might, somehow, save our family from Collection.

He pulled out the small, metallic-blue key he'd used to remove my attacker's Cuff. "Do you want your Cuff off?"

I backed away from him instinctively. I hated that Cuff, but I was not ready to have it taken off my arm.

"It's not like you'd get shocked for talking," Henri said.

This was something I had not considered. I didn't *need* the Cuff at all.

"Put it away," the leader insisted.

"We could tell her about the FiDos," Henri said, placing the little teardrop-shaped device back in a special pocket in his pack.

"I'm sure she knows about FiDos," replied the leader.

I did, of course. This wasn't what I needed. I racked my brain for a way to get them to take Saretha. I could lead them to her, but I couldn't think how and, even if I did, how would they understand what I wanted? A Placer's salary would surely pay Saretha better than the horrible Mrs. Nince.

Henri explained further. "Kel used to cause them," he said in a low whisper, pointing to the leader.

"FiDo Queen," Margot whispered with reverence.

Kel, the leader, rolled her eyes. "Why don't you also give her our bank information and social security codes?"

"She used to take out WiFi nodes between placements," Henri went on, undeterred.

"I took out nothing," Kel countered. "I turned a blind eye, on occasion, when a member of my crew carelessly banged into one. But that was my *old* crew."

"That would have been such fun," Margot said wistfully. "But Silas Rog locked it all away long before Henri or I were recruited."

"Rog," the leader grumbled, shaking her head. "Okay, Henri, besides regaling our guest with the dazzling breadth of your knowledge, what was your other idea?"

"I thought," Henri said, hesitating, "she might join us."

The leader fixed him with a serious gaze. My heart skipped

a beat. That wasn't exactly the idea, but maybe it was better. Could I really become a Placer? The thought of it was so exciting, I could hardly understand it.

"I think she is interested," Margot said, pointing at me beaming. I covered my grin with my hand. It felt too much like talking, like I was begging them to take me.

"Kel, *you* said—" Henri stopped himself. He moved closer to Kel and whispered in her ear.

Margot grabbed my arm and pulled me down to sit beside her. She said, "He will probably ask you to marry him."

"Henri, first of all, she isn't trained..." Kel responded to Henri's whispers.

"She's quiet."

"Yes, but that isn't the *only* qualification."

"She kept up with us really well."

"Reasonably well," the leader huffed. "But even if she can be silent and run, she doesn't know how to rappel, to climb, how to cut a window, disable a magnetic lock, pilf a car, read a map—"

"I didn't know those things, either," Henri said, "and *I* learned."

Margot grinned. "If Henri can learn them..." Margot sang in a whisper.

The leader shook her head. I looked up at her from the floor. My whole fate seemed to hang in the balance.

"And *you* already said you liked her," Henri said to the leader. "When she was all over the news."

Margot waggled her brows at me again and elbowed me like a friend.

"And we need a fourth," Henri said.

Kel looked exasperated. She pulled off her own mask. Her face was long and narrow. She had the darkest skin I'd ever seen. She might have been thirty or forty, or older if she'd had her telomeres extended to keep her young.

"I've been *looking*," she said, her tone implying she had not met with success.

She ran a hand through her tight, black, curly hair and shook off her more cautious self. She looked at me with big, dark eyes and said, "It's up to you."

My heart felt ready to explode. Up to me? How? I sat beside Margot in silence for a moment, confounded.

Kel tapped something on her Pad.

"Normally you would agree to ToS, but you can't do that," she said, finally settling on an idea. "So, if you want to join us—if you want to become a Placer, I want you to stand up, right now," Kel said.

I waited for more, but that was it. The action of standing, technically, would be my *yes*. I didn't know if the Cuff would record it. I didn't have time to think. I worried in the back of my mind that Saretha's heart would break if she found out I had the one job that would be perfect for her, but I couldn't worry about that. This was for her, and for Sam, as much as it was for me.

"If you are worried standing will be a tacit *yes*, keep in mind that I'll consider sitting an equally communicative *no*," Kel offered, making my decision only about the choice itself.

With a swift, fluid push off the ground, I stood, shoulders back, my spine arched like after a landing in gymnastics. I wanted Kel to know my answer was more than *yes*.

ROOFTOPS AND PATIENCE: $17.97

I had to wait for them to contact me. Kel would not say how we would communicate, only that I would know what to do, and how to find them, when the time came. I could not sign a contract. I could not verbally agree. I had little choice but to hope I would be paid enough to save us.

I was told to go back to my "normal" life: go home, go to school, wait and keep a low profile. I don't think Kel understood how difficult that would be.

Sam and Saretha saw my bandaged chin the moment I walked through the door. It was morning, and they were both up. Sam looked exhausted, but he sat bolt upright and rushed over to examine my chin.

"What happened to you?" Saretha's face crinkled up with worry, but then went a little slack as she remembered I would not answer her. Her question was wasted money.

"Where did you go?" Sam asked, starting to pace. He asked the room. "It isn't safe out there."

I tried to show him there was reason to hope. I raised my eyebrows, and widened my eyes, but I only ended up looking crazy.

Saretha turned away with a huff and clicked on our screen.

"Are you hungry?" Sam asked. "Do you want a roll?" He

went to the food printer and printed out a sheet of Wheat-lock™. He spread a squeeze-packet of bright yellow Huny® over it, covering the Ad for Prénda™ Suppositories that had been embedded in the thick Wheatlock™ sheet. Sam rolled it up and handed it to me. I felt sad and embarrassed that he was taking care of me. I was supposed to take care of him.

The bright, cloying Huny® tang hid the bland, musty flavor of the Wheatlock™. I didn't realize I was hungry until then. I ate it and smiled at Sam, thinking I would try to get him a real orange someday. I would take care of him.

"What?" he asked. I smiled more, a little desperate. My chest felt tight knowing I couldn't tell them my news.

Saretha sniffed. She turned. "Is that the last Huny®?" Her eyes looked wild.

Sam held up two packets. "There is still a little more." He gave her his impish smile. "You can have them both."

Her lips went tight. "Both," she muttered, and returned to her game.

The same Ad for Prénda™ Suppositories popped up on my Cuff, in case I had not seen the one I was eating. I smiled again and showed it to Sam. It's always free to share an Ad. He forced himself to laugh.

Saretha turned back to her game. "You should probably get ready for school," she said. I hadn't slept at all, but maybe it would be better to go. I finished my Wheatlock™ and waited for Sam so we could walk together.

Outside our building, Penepoli was waiting for me. She leaned against the high wall that blocked the outer ring below. The roar of traffic was light at this hour.

"Have you seen her?" Penepoli asked, suddenly coming to life. She rushed toward us, her lank, wavy public domain hair getting in her face. Style 6 was really impractical.

Sam looked up at me. "Nancee?" he asked.

"She hasn't been at school," Penepoli said. She clicked her tongue. "Neither of you have. I thought you were… I thought you had some plan."

I tried to look sorry. My skin went cold, wondering where Nancee could be.

"What are you guys doing?" Penepoli asked. Her voice came out as a desperate squeak, accompanied by a stamp of her foot.

I couldn't tell her anything. We weren't doing anything. I looked up the street. Nancee only lived two buildings away. I looked at Penepoli, and back at Nancee's building.

"Speth?" Sam asked, tugging at me.

Again I almost answered, this time with a nod, but I caught it before it started—just a dip of my head. I was allowed that. Being around Sam was dangerous. I'd been the main one to answer his questions since our parents were indentured, far more than Saretha ever had.

I let out a breath. Sam and Penepoli waited for me to come to some decision. I knew I should check on Nancee, but I was afraid of what I would find—that she wouldn't be home, or that she would blame me for leading her to ruin. She was an only child, and it struck me at that moment how lonely that must be.

A prickling sensation spread across my back. I began walking toward Nancee's. Sam and Penepoli followed.

At the entrance to the building, I could not buzz. The

button was on a small screen that had a mandatory Ad quiz. I would not be charged if I had selected which toilet tissue appeared softest, but I would be tracked. That counted. I wanted no part of it.

Sam tapped Fluffwipe™, then jabbed his thumb at the glowing saffron-colored button for number 17. It droned angrily, and the glow darkened, then lit again. No answer came. My stomach knotted.

"She's not here, either?" Penepoli asked. She tried her luck with the buzzer, but it changed nothing. It wouldn't bring her back.

Sam shook his head. We all knew Nancee was gone. They'd either taken her off to work somewhere, or Indentured her to the highest bidder. I hated to think what that would be like for her.

"We should get to school," Sam said. With nothing else to do, we turned and walked away.

As more days passed, I started to worry that the Placers would not contact me at all. Or maybe that I'd hallucinated the whole thing. I don't know if they understood that I didn't have much time. They'd taken Nancee, and Saretha and I would be next. With anxious butterflies in my stomach, I considered going out and looking for them, but that was a foolish idea.

Five days had passed since I'd met the Placers when an unshakable feeling struck me. They would contact me soon. Something was different, but I couldn't put a finger on what it was. Then, at dinner, I realized my Cuff hadn't popped an Ad all day.

I went to bed feeling hopeful this meant they'd be coming for me soon. I tried not to feel as if my lucky break was betraying Nancee in some way.

In the middle of the night, a bright white flashing woke me. I shook myself and swallowed—a weird habit I'd developed since my Last Day, feeling like I had to tamp down my words before I was fully alert.

The whole world was a strobe, as if silent lightning was flashing at regular intervals. I stood. The flashing stopped, or, more accurately, it slowed, limiting itself to the outline of our door. In my hazy state, it took a moment for me to understand that the door itself was not flashing in the real world, but only in my eyes, in my corneal overlay—an augmented reality.

I was unaccustomed to the overlay. I'd never had the chance to use any enhancements, so this was new. Somehow Kel and her Agency had been able to override my settings. This was it.

I dressed quickly, nervous I might miss whatever opportunity lay before me. I should have gone to bed dressed, especially after I noticed the lack of Ads on my Cuff. I jammed on a sneaker and started hopping toward the flashing door while I put on the other. I didn't know what to expect outside. I hoped they would be out there waiting for me.

They weren't.

I was met by a bright series of dots, which led me outside and into the night. It was late; my Cuff read 2:00 a.m. The path took me away from main streets, down alleys and over easy-to-manage roofs. The path looked comical and conspicuous with all of the bright dots and lighted paths, like a computer was simulating the world inside my eyes. I knew many people used overlays like this all the time to play games, or to lose themselves in other worlds, but I didn't see how they could get used to it. It made everything seem unreal.

The path was simple until I arrived at my destination. Then the dots came to an end in the parking lot of a Matzeraldi™ dealership. Where the dots ceased, a conspicuous arrow pointed to its roof, three stories up.

Was this a test? The dealership had no fire escape. The exterior had been painted to look like bricks, but the building, like our apartment, had been printed in layers of plastic.

I wore all black—black jeans and a black T-shirt, black socks and black gloves I had laid out in secret for when this night came—but I don't think it had the same effect as the Placers' stealthy ninja outfits. I looked at the climb before me and saw no way up. Was this really something I could do?

I thought of Mrs. Micharnd, my gymnastics teacher. She would have encouraged me. In one of my last classes, I was evaluated by a thin, pale, blond man who pronounced I was not good enough for the Olympics™. I didn't know if he was there on behalf of Sponsors, the Olympic Committee or someone else, but he watched me for only a few minutes. Mrs. Micharnd had put a hand on my shoulder and eased the sour disappointment I felt. She told me his opinion was no reason to give up. Sadly, however, our financial situation was. She would have been glad I'd found something to do with the skills she'd taught me.

Around back, I found a dumpster that let me get a handhold on a thick ledge rimming the first story. I pulled myself up and balanced on the ledge, heel to toe like on the balance beam, but with my left hand palm flat against the plastic wall. There was a pipe nearby. Was that my way up? It didn't look very secure. Gymnastics didn't involve much in the way of shimmying. Around the corner, I found an electrical box that let me climb to the second floor. The display arrow flickered in my eyes and slowly rotated, hovering in the air, pointing to the roof's center, which I could not see.

The second-floor ledge was the same as the first, but this time I was out of luck. Even the pipe ended here. I shuffled my way around the whole of the building, wishing I had thought to survey from the ground first. I saw nothing that would let me up. What was I missing?

I was nearly ready to give up when a black rope suddenly fell right before my eyes. Above me was Henri. The arrow faded away. I grabbed the rope and Henri pulled me up with one arm, even though it would have made much more sense to use two.

Henri, Margot and Kel were waiting up top, all in black, all with masks. Wasting no time, Kel handed me a grapple gun and pointed to a nearby roof. Sensing she wanted quick action, I didn't hesitate. I wasn't going to disappoint her. I fired it eagerly, and the hook banged off the side of a glass window on the top floor. Margot giggled. Kel stood firm. Henri pressed a button, and the grappling hook zipped back, almost knocking me over when the hook locked back in the barrel. It was like taking a punch. I didn't let it show, though. I had to get this right.

High above, a light turned on at the window. A distant figure scanned around. We crouched low, and Kel did something on her Pad. The surface of everyone's clothes lightened from matte black to the gray of the roof, except, of course, for mine; I was still dressed in my all-black street clothes.

Henri and Margot stepped in front of me. The figure above saw nothing and returned to bed.

Undeterred, Kel pointed to another roof opposite the first and indicated I should aim higher. She tapped at her Pad, and a thin arcing line appeared in my eyes, showing me how to aim. I lifted the hook into the ghostly track and shot it over the ledge perfectly. It pulled back onto solid wall. Kel grabbed the end of the line and secured it. Margot handed me a thing she later called a runner: a small motorized clamp that, when pressed, would speed me up to the ledge. Henri indicated I should use two hands, then he hooked a belt and a safety line around my middle. I squeezed the trigger, and off I accelerated.

The building was a good fifty meters away, but I realized that if I kept speeding, I would slam into the side of the building full speed and fall, cartoonlike, to my death. My heart started pounding, and I eased off the grip too much. I slowed, sped up, slowed and then, when the building was near, I crawled along so slowly that Margot caught up to me and pushed me along the rest of the way. The height was unnerving. We were twenty stories up, but I was sweating more from mortification than fear. I felt like I should have been smoother at all of this.

On the roof, Kel shot a wire back to where I had originally aimed. This was our first destination. We traveled across, almost horizontal, with nothing below us but concrete and the hard walls of the dealership.

I wondered if there was any chance a fifteen-year-old girl could die of a heart attack.

On the second roof, all the climbing gear was stowed. Kel

pulled a bundle off Henri's back and threw it to me. Inside I found a full set of clothes, matte black like theirs, and a mask. Obviously Kel wanted me to change, but where? The roof was a flat expanse, except for the small structure that housed the emergency door. I looked at Kel. Maybe I could change inside?

She shook her head, as if reading my thoughts. She impatiently pointed to indicate I could make my way to the far side of the structure door if I wanted to be bashful. It shouldn't have mattered, but I wasn't ready for these people to see me in my underwear.

Margot came over and escorted me to the side, pulling a piece of long, thin black fabric out of her bag, which she held up to shield me. *Thank you, Margot, thank you!*

Kel pulled out her Pad and looked into the building, focusing on an apartment two floors down. She found two more sleeping bodies, then a bedroom with a child, then another kid and a third. She showed me, so I could see the layout, and who was where, but I saw something else: a family, two parents and three kids, all living together in a home. A pang of longing slowed the pounding of my heart. Down in Carolina, my parents slept, unaware of what I did.

Kel held up five fingers, oblivious to my ache. Henri made for the outcropping stairs, but Kel stopped him. She made a flipping gesture with her hand. The three of them pulled out their gear to rappel down and set it over the side. Kel took me with her. While Henri worked hard to unlock the window, she paused to appraise me. Did she see something, or was she just checking to see how I was doing? I tried to put thoughts of home and family away. I didn't want her to see any emotion in me that might give her pause.

The window clicked, opened up, and one by one, each of us dropped inside. I hit with a low, discreet thud—but the three of them made no sound at all. Henri rushed over to me and reenacted his landing in slow motion, showing me how I should bend my knees and roll from heel to toe to dampen the sound. He then went to make some encouraging gesture, like a pat on the back, but stopped, like he'd short-circuited with embarrassment.

They worked fast. It was a simple placement, a bottle of Righthaven Wine® from a high-end East Kansas vineyard. Margot handed me a small, disk-shaped light and pointed above where Henri was setting the bottle on a pedestal. With her hands, she told me to set it in place to shine down on the display.

Quickly. Margot shooed me along like I was holding up the team. I was not moving quickly or quietly enough. They had no idea how important this was to me. If I had a weekly paycheck, Saretha could stay. I could stay. She and Sam and I could be together, holding some part of our family intact.

Margot watched me carefully, one hand turned inward under her chin, fingers moving anxiously. As I climbed onto the counter, my sneaker squeaked softly, and Henri drew in a breath, eyebrows raised. Standing up, quietly, with the light in my hand, I didn't know what to do next. Margot stopped moving her fingers and impatiently mimed holding the light, which she then jammed into an imaginary ceiling. I mimicked her motions, but with much greater care. The light pulled itself to the ceiling, magnetized. I turned it on. The shaft of light shone down directly on the bottle. I impressed myself with my aim, but it turned out my placement was wrong. From straight above, the bottle's label was scarcely lit. My light had to be set away, so the shaft could be angled like a spotlight. The label had to shine. It took a few adjustments. When I finally succeeded, Margot bounced happily on her heels.

I climbed down, and we were done. Relief flooded over me. I had not messed up too badly, had I? They would hopefully understand that this was my first go. Henri was already packed up. Margot rushed me along. Kel went last, walking backward, swinging the Pad from side to side to keep watch on all the sleepy orange blobs. Despite a few little hiccups, I was feeling good about the operation—until a tiny voice wailed from the next room.

"Mommy!"

Kel whipped around quickly and focused her Pad on the girl. The child was sitting up in bed, rubbing her eyes. The apartment door clicked softly open by Henri's hand. Everyone sped through into the hall, though I was slow to react and Margot had to pull me along behind her. Kel came through last, doing everything I did, but better, silently and backward. She stepped through the threshold as Henri closed and relocked the door.

Kel held some kind of countersecurity gear up to a camera, knocking it into a looped feed that didn't include four Product Placers in the hall. We raced up the stairs and all erupted out onto the roof. Kel stormed out into the night, shaking her head, tapping her hand on her wrist. We had taken too long. *The little girl could have had a nightmare*, I wanted to say, *it wasn't me.* Henri shrugged like it was no big deal, but it mattered. If I didn't do well, my family was doomed. Kel's eyes shone in the dark, severe and critical. She took one more moment to appraise me and then shot out a line of carbon-fiber wire. Henri waved me on.

Not a block away, Kel ushered us into another building, down a hall and into an office. Her hands moved quickly, almost angrily, reminding me of how my mother used to move when I'd misbehaved, but not badly enough for her to spend money on words to reprimand me.

Before I could even see what Kel had done, a door cracked open in the wall. Margot and Henri moved quickly inside. It was another Squelch. I hesitated, but what could I do but go inside? I had to hear what Kel was going to say.

Kel shook her head, and Margot and Henri stood stock-still. Had I really messed things up so badly?

"The first thing we do is reconnaissance," Kel said, breathing out slowly to center herself. "Reconnaissance first, then specifics. Prepare, plan and execute."

I was ready to burst into tears. If they usually prepared, why hadn't they done it tonight?

"But I wanted to see how you would do without preparation. I wanted to gauge your natural talent, because it is not possible to plan for all contingencies."

My brow furrowed. Kel squinted at me.

"You understand, there are a hundred, maybe a thousand kids in this city who would give their right arm to have this chance," Kel reminded me. "Kids on the brink of Indenture. I know of four kids shipping out in the morning to spend the rest of their lives baking in the field sun, or withering in factory shadows until they die."

I know, I wanted to say. She kept watching me. Did she not like the expression on my face? What was she looking for? Her hard look flickered, and for a brief flash, she seemed concerned.

"This is where I lost it," Margot whispered to Henri, but obviously it was loud enough for me to hear.

"Margot!"

"What?" she asked. "Speth is only going to stand there and look at you. She is not going to defend every action like I did, or fall over herself to apologize like Henri."

Kel looked from Margot, to me, and back to Margot, shaking her head almost imperceptibly. "I could have used ten more seconds, Margot, to measure her reaction."

Margot suppressed a smirk. Relief flooded over me. Kel was testing me. I hadn't freaked out.

"I didn't apologize," Henri whispered back to Margot, "that much."

"No, Henri. You begged. *Please, Kel, tell me what I did wrong, please, please, please,*" Margot mocked. "*Sorry, sorry, sorry.*"

"I only said *sorry* once," Henri said, red-faced.

"But you didn't *apologize.*" Margot grinned.

Kel rolled her eyes and stepped to my side. "I *can* read your face. Remember that. The Rights Holders can't charge for expressions. It may not be an exacting method of communication, but it will do in a pinch. Understand?"

I almost nodded in return. I raised my head, but didn't drop it. Instead, I forced a smile, nerves interfering with letting one form naturally.

"Look," Kel said, showing me her Pad. She typed my name in its search box. Her finger hesitated over the ENTER button. "It isn't tethered. The Agency designed this Pad to be self-contained. It quietly loads information without leaving a trace. They had to be sure it would work regardless of where we are or what we are doing. It's exempt from word fees or tracking, like a Lawyer's computer."

I'd been taught that software always needed to connect to the tether to function. I remember seeing diagrams in school that showed how all programming was interdependent, checking for digital rights management and payments. I suddenly felt foolish for believing it.

"I am taking an awful risk, bringing you on," Kel said, tapping the ENTER button at last.

Did that mean I could stay? My heart skipped a beat.

She turned the Pad to me. A map of my apartment came up, with its modest layout. Saretha, Sam and I were listed as occupants. Large red letters through the map text read:

Placement Scheduling Window: Invalid. Continuous Occupancy: Saretha Jime.

"Coming and going will be difficult for you. Your family can't know you are a Placer."

I swallowed hard. As exciting as the idea was, she was right, and I was uncomfortable realizing she knew about my family. Of course she would have researched us. She tapped on my name and pulled up my profile.

"This isn't a glowing endorsement."

Speth Jime
Age:15
Height: 5'2"
Consumer ID: 319-02-6651A
Hair: Chestnut, Unremarkable
Hair Style: Public Domain Style #14A-Short "Pixie Style"
Rating: D
Eyes: Brown, Unenhanced, Unremarkable

Body: Standard, Thin, Unenhanced, Unremarkable

Physical Condition: 96/100

Rating: A

General Appeal: C: Unremarkable, Disagreeable

Personal Style: Generic, Unremarkable

Socioeconomic status: 34/1000: Poor

Debt Score: Fluxed -.101 to -.081

Default threat: High

Credit Score: 312/850

Default threat: High

Consumer Index: 32/500

Rating: F

Volubility Index: -Error

Speech profile: -Error

Loquaciousness Rating: 0/5000

Social Influence Score: 88/100; Trending

Emotional Index: 9/10

Assessment: Volatile

Gullibility Index: 3/10

Assessment: Low

Market Influence: 24/800

Rating: F

Geodemographic Group: P3-788: Portland Outer Ring

Branding: None/Failed

Rating: F

Educational status: Grade 10 of 12

Employment status: Purged/Redacted*

BL Agency Profile: Irregularities in behavioral and consumer profile. Problematic obduracy. High probability of nonconformity and/or rebelliousness.

Assessment: Disregard

Keene Services Profile: Contractual irregularities. Irregularities in communication profile. Incongruity between influence and appeal ratings. Unpredictable behaviors. High probability of antisocial/anticonsumer action.

Assessment: Threat

Sloan Agency Profile: Uncommunicative. Obdurate. High probability of nonconformity/antisocial action. Volatile.

Assessment: Threat

"Her pixie cut is not a D," Margot said, leaning in.

"Margot, go set up your gear," Kel growled.

"Yes, Kel," Margot said and saluted.

It was a little startling to realize Kel could look up anyone on this Pad and get this level of information.

"You need to prove yourself, Speth," Kel said, clearing the information with a quick tap. "I probably wouldn't give you a chance, except I happen to hold the obdurate and the volatile in high esteem. But that doesn't mean you can get away with not listening to me, and it does not mean you have permission, or latitude, to do *anything* on your own."

She waited, then pointed down to the carpet. "Have a seat."

I did as she said, though part of me felt a little like a dog being trained. Kel knelt down before me. Her dark eyes locked on mine.

"You have to promise never to steal—not from our sponsors, and especially not from the homes we will be in, no matter how tempted you are, or how much desire you feel." She spoke with a seriousness and intensity that frightened me. I didn't know whether she was morally opposed to theft, or if she did not want to jeopardize her job, or if it was something else entirely. I thought back to what Henri said that first night about her cutting the WiFi. Did that fall under a different moral code for her?

"The places we are going…it will boggle your mind to see the scale of what some people have acquired."

Margot let out a delicious little hum, like she was tempted even by the thought of it all.

"You will think they won't notice, but they will. These people—every little thing is precious to them, and they'll remember it, especially if it is gone. They forgive nothing."

"Nothing," Margot echoed, frowning.

"Do you understand?" Kel asked me, refusing to be distracted.

We looked at each other. My throat ached to say *yes*. She searched my eyes for the answer. What expression did I need to wear to convey my understanding? She stretched her legs, stood over me and asked again.

"Do you understand?"

"How—?" Henri started, but Kel shushed him, her eyes looking down at me. Why was she towering over me like this?

Then, with a start, I realized what I was supposed to do. I leaned forward and pushed myself off the floor and stood up straight, my shoulders back, my expression determined.

Kel nodded the smallest nod I could possibly imagine. Relief washed over me.

Margot grinned. "This makes things simple. So Speth," she said, tapping her finger to her lip like she was thinking. "Sit back down if you drink coffee."

What? Whatever relief I'd felt evaporated. Did they expect me to start communicating like a trained seal?

"Margot," Kel said, intervening between us, shaking a finger.

"But you just—"

"I didn't do anything. I am assuming that Speth will not respond any differently in a Squelch than she would outside. If she ends up sitting, or standing, or jumping or itching her nose in answer to every question, everything to this point becomes meaningless."

I swallowed and waited to see how Margot would react. She grimaced.

"I only meant to point out it would be much easier to communicate if we could...communicate."

"Does this mean she's in?" Henri asked, like he'd been holding his breath.

I was glad he'd asked—and for the change of subject.

Margot frowned and elbowed him. "Henri the subtle."

"No," Kel said quickly.

My heart sank.

"She needs to be cleared. I've put in with the Agency to ensure she doesn't get any pop-up Ads that could disrupt a job. We will see where things are after a few weeks. If nothing goes horribly wrong..." Her voice trailed off, but the tone of it seemed to indicate there was hope. I didn't want things to go horribly wrong either. I smiled as best I could. I would have crossed my fingers, but that gesture was Trademarked by Sands Inc.™ I looked at my Cuff, slightly giddy at the idea that it might never bother me again.

"We start by looking at our targets," Kel said, signaling that it was time to move forward and get to training. She tapped at the Pad and showed it to me again. I let myself relax slightly and focused on what she was showing me.

The Pad showed the names and addresses of the night's

Placements, as well as a wealth of information about each individual's buying habits, liquid assets, social networks, employment history and any preference or predilection you could dream of. It also had minutely detailed blueprints of every home and business we were assigned. The amount of information our Agency collected was astounding.

"We can look up anyone and learn when they are likely to be home or away, awake or asleep," Kel said. "So we can plan when to hit each spot and what route is best to take."

I tried to take it all in, but my heart was suddenly thumping. The Pad could look up *anyone*. It should not have been my first thought, but I realized I could look up Carol Amanda Harving. I could find out where she was, and maybe, somehow, get *her* to desist.

Slowly, I learned. After that first trial, Kel had me watch how the team worked. She showed me how to survey a space, step quietly and climb without sound. The Pad, however, she kept to herself.

Henri helped me with acrobatics, showing me moves my gymnastics teacher never could. Mrs. Micharnd could not afford to clear the rights. Margot taught me the intricacies of arranging products and lighting them to the specifications of the Advertisers, all the while keeping an eye on me for trouble.

Each night at half past midnight, I had to sneak up to our roof and wait for the team to get me. I made the mistake of thinking that, because I didn't speak, it would be easy to keep my plans secret. But Kel had been right—our home was too small for me to easily sneak away unnoticed.

Every time I moved to leave, Saretha shrank a little more. She was often up late, playing her futile Free-to-Plays. Her posture betrayed a jealousy of my freedom to go out into the world. She didn't ask where I was going or what I was doing. She acted as if she didn't care.

Sam, on the other hand, reacted very differently. Saretha

woke him with a loud sigh one night—too loud for it to have been an accident.

"Where are you going?" he asked, blinking through the soft light of the wall-screen. I made to leave, shrugging the tiniest amount so he would know I had at least heard him. Sam's feet hit the floor.

"It isn't safe out there." He put a hand under his chin to remind me of the injury that had left its scar.

He wanted answers, but more than that, he wanted me to know he was concerned. He followed me up to the roof in his bare feet, like he was going to protect me from whatever danger he thought might be out there.

"It sure is nice out," Sam said, looking around. This was his roof joke. The weather in the city never changed, only the color of the light that filtered through the thick, frosted hexagons of the city's dome. That night they were a dark gray. I wondered what the sky looked like beyond. Were there clouds or stars? Was the moon in the sky? I wanted to see it with my own eyes. They say the sky is safe to look at once night falls.

"I said, it sure is nice out," Sam repeated, elbowing me this time. I didn't laugh. I always at least smiled when Sam joked, even if his joke was terrible, but that night I sat rigid and expressionless. I was worried what Kel might do if she found I wasn't alone.

Sam scanned the rooftops. "Nothing," he said, looking for Placers. My insides squirmed, knowing they would arrive soon.

"I know what you're doing," he said.

My stomach dropped away. I struggled not to respond.

"You're hoping Placers will find us. But if you sit up here every night, you're just going to scare them away."

Now, despite myself, I laughed—from relief that he hadn't found me out, and fear that *he* was the one scaring my team away.

Sam looked toward the outer ring. There were fewer cars out, but those few went faster, buzzing through the night with a sound like a distant saw. Were they just going in circles for the thrill of the speed, or were some of them rushing off out of the city? Affluents could do that. They could leave. They probably knew where to go; they could afford to pay for geographical information. Were other places better than this? Was this the worst dome, the best...or were they all the same?

"I wonder how you get to be a Placer," Sam whispered.

I still didn't know how Placers recruited. Obviously not the way they found me. Henri and Margot didn't seem much older than me. Had they been Placers long? Had they applied somehow?

Up the block, a door opened. Sam looked over the roof's edge to see and, despite myself, I did the same. Two people exited Beecher's grandmother's building. Above them, the light in Mrs. Stokes's lone window on the third floor winked out. The two figures scanned the street, then each went their separate ways. I recognized the one coming toward us as Mandett Kresh. What was he doing?

He walked briskly along, passing our building and rushing to his own. A pair of Ads halfheartedly lit in his path, then quickly faded away. Mandett didn't have a Cuff yet, but the system knew *someone* was there.

"What's he doing?" Sam asked.

I couldn't shake the impression Mandett had just been to see Mrs. Stokes. *Go down and see*, I thought. *Leave me alone up here.* Maybe Sam could find his way to Mrs. Stokes.

It occurred to me there were scarcely any true adults left in the Onzième. I tried to think of which families were still intact. A few families with younger children were still around, peppered through the buildings on the North end. Weber Spood's mother was still in our building, though I had no idea where Weber had gone after graduation. Sooner or later, it seemed, one parent would go, and then the other. Debts were collected or violations were found. A few grandparents remained, too, like Mrs. Stokes, but they hardly went outside.

Who had arranged things this way? It couldn't be an accident. Was there a plan? The very thought of it made me sick. I had always believed the illegal download Butchers & Rog found was our stroke of rotten luck. The Inherited Debt Act and its Historical Reparations Agency were created by the government, not Butchers & Rog. Yet, somehow, it felt like it was them—and, worse, like it was personal.

I scanned the rooftops of our neighborhood. My brow knit. That had to be a paranoid thought.

"Are you mad about something?" Sam asked.

I shook myself. I gave him the best smile I could. I couldn't hold his hand to tell him it was okay, but I risked putting my hand down just a few inches from his.

Sam's expression softened. He seemed to understand. I was mad about plenty, but not at him. I longed to tussle his hair. Instead, I looked at the door, to him, to the door again. I waited for him to make the connection. I needed him to go.

My stomach felt like a rock, trying to get rid of him this way, but he got it.

He stood, dusting off his hands, and he smiled bitterly, his cheeks flushed bright red. "This is no fun anyway. I have to do all the talking," he said, a little sharply.

He left. The roof door clanged shut. Within a minute, the team arrived. No one looked happy.

SILHOUETTES: $20.99

At the Squelch, Kel said nothing about Sam on the roof. Instead, she pulled out her Pad and thumbed through my neighborhood. After a moment's consideration, she pointed to a
3-D rendering of a building a few doors down from mine
and zoomed in.

"I'll have the Agency print a locker here." She spoke
quickly. I had put us behind our time. She pointed to a spot on
the roof. "So we don't have to keep bringing you your gear."

Kel made a note on her Pad.

"Usually she waits until the trial period is complete," Margot whispered to Henri in a voice that I could obviously hear.

"After I show you how to use it, it will be up to you to arrive at each night's rendezvous on your own," Kel explained.

"I can never find mine," Margot pouted.

"Where do you change?" Henri asked.

Margot's eyes lit up. "Oh, Henri, wouldn't you like to
know?"

"Tonight we are placing five Huntley 3-D Gold-Leaf™
Printers," Kel announced loudly.

Henri grimaced and placed a heavy bag on the floor. He
pulled out a box.

Affluents still loved gold, even though it could be easily synthesized with a good molecular printer. It had once been rare, but now it was just expensive because the Patent Holders set the price high—to honor tradition, they said.

"Gold must be associated with elegance," Henri said in a mocking voice. *"Affluents."*

The needlessness and selfishness of it made my blood boil. I tried to put it out of my mind.

"Ninety percent of our job caters to Affluents," Kel said. "That's what we do. We make people with money excited about things they don't know they want."

"Yeah, right," Henri laughed.

"Henri does not believe it works," Margot said.

"It's stupid!" Henri said. "You think just because we plop a gold printer in someone's house, that means everyone will start buying gold printers? It's preposterous."

Preposterous, I thought, letting the word play in my head.

"Henri does not know which side of his bread the butter is on," Margot said.

"The Agency wants to target the *right* people, Influents™, to make sure they have effective viral reach," Kel said. Influent™ was the preferred term for the trendsetting wealthy. It sounded like a flu vaccine to me. "They want their money's worth," Kel continued, holding up her Pad. "Henri may not think it works, but the algorithms show otherwise. Companies collect and compile as much data as they can. They model consumer habits and behavior." Kel showed us the next target. "They know how many people will be reached by each Placement and can calculate with 85 percent accuracy how many sales a Placement will generate."

"So they claim," Henri said.

"What do *you* care?" Margot asked. "They pay us."

"We don't need to be worried about the program's efficacy." Kel nodded. "We need to concern ourselves with who might have an itchy temper, or insomnia, or an unhealthy abundance of curiosity. We need to focus on how we prepare, plan and execute."

She paused and looked at me, then pulled up a map of a building near the center of the city. "Four of tonight's Placements will be standard. Our fifth, however, will not."

"That's Lawyer territory," Henri said, looking at the map. We would be only a few blocks from the Butchers & Rog Tower in the center of the city. Wealthy Lawyers had clustered around that building, as if they hoped some of Butchers & Rog's power would rub off.

"Henri." Margot patted him on the head, but Henri shook her off and fixed his hair, looking at me. I felt my cheeks burn a little and looked at my shoes.

"Some Influents™ don't care about Placement. They don't care about the status of being an influencer, and they don't like feeling they are being used," Kel said, tapping the edge of her Pad to focus us.

"A few Influents™, like our first target, actively eschew Placement. Unfortunately, Huntley's prefers exactly this sort of target, so Attorney Hugo Winfrield, Esquire, is our top priority."

"Wait until you see this place," Margot said to me, wide-eyed and grinning.

"You've never been there!" Henri cried.

"I've been *near* it," Margot said, pouting her lips like her feelings had been hurt. "He owns the whole thirtieth floor."

"We'll have to disable Winfrield's security and bypass foot-falls," Kel continued.

"Work on wires," Henri said to me, knowingly.

"She doesn't know what that means," Margot said.

Margot was right, though I didn't like her pointing it out. Maybe it was for the best I didn't pretend to know more than I did.

"Winfrield doesn't want us there," Kel said. "If he spots us, we're done—all of us. He won't be bought off by the prom-ise of oranges. His floor is pressure-sensitive and rigged with alarms. We'll have to set up wires and work above the ground. I think you can handle it," she said to me.

I swallowed. I was glad she had confidence in me, but how was I going to do that?

"The Huntley printers will be set up to run off a gold leaf silhouette of Winfrield when he enters the room," Kel ex-plained. "Speth, you'll need to calibrate a small scanner to take a 3-D face scan, orient the resultant data into a profile, flatten it into a relief like you would see on a coin and print it out."

These sorts of scanners were everywhere, embedded in practically every Ad screen in America®, but I'd never pro-grammed one before. This was the same technology they used to put people in Ads. I wondered what it would feel like to come home, be scanned and have your face printed onto a gold medallion. Then I remembered it would never happen to me.

Kel handed the Pad to Margot, and Margot turned it to me.

"This is the interface," Margot said. It took me a second longer to focus than it should have. I couldn't help remem-

bering Carol Amanda Harving's data was in that Pad somewhere, and it felt like I could do something with that.

"These little icons represent the printer functions," Margot
said, unaware of my momentary lapse. "It isn't that complicated, but the printer's screen will be smaller than this. If we
had the room's layout, you could program it here and drop it
down, but you won't know how to orient anything until we
see the room, place it and figure out his most likely approach."

Everything was depicted in the most obvious way possible. You could preset what or who you wanted scanned and
what angle you wanted to print from. There was a little icon
box of templates, and I could see the one that looked like the
coin. Maybe I could handle it, but the idea of doing it while
hanging from a wire didn't fill me with confidence.

"Are there any questions?" Kel asked the group.

*Can I practice? How am I going to hang from the wire? What are
the wires attached to? What if we get caught?*

Kel watched my mind burn through all the things I could
not ask.

"I'm sorry if it is terrifying," Kel said to me. "But this job
is dangerous. I can't mollycoddle you. You learn by doing,
just like everyone else. If I didn't think you could do it, you
wouldn't be here at all. Do you understand?"

I think this was her version of a pep talk. I would have to
get used to it. This would be how we would work. What I
needed to think about was succeeding—not what would happen if I failed.

We entered through a window. It was sealed with locking pins, not magnets, but Henri had a tool for them and was

pleased to demonstrate how quickly he could pop the window open.

I crouched with Margot like a cat at the corner of the ornate window ledge. Intricate scrollworks of leaves and abstracted spirals curved in on each other, making it easy to wedge myself in place. The buildings had more and more ornamentation the deeper into the city you went—until you hit the center, where Rog's building was nothing but shiny, unadorned glass.

Margot wrestled with some kind of encryption on Kel's Pad, trying to unscramble the code for the room's motion sensors. She looked like she was playing a video game as her fingers danced over the Pad. It occurred to me that, even out in the open, the Pad could take input and none of it was tracked. How did that work?

With a nod and a drop in the tension of her shoulders, we knew Margot had succeeded in turning the system off. It was too bad she couldn't get the floor sensors off, too, but they were set to alarm if they were disconnected, even for a moment.

Henri quickly shot a line from a different grapple gun than I had seen before. This one fired out a sticky, suction cup–like end. It held fast to the far wall. He showed me ten fingers, then mimed the suction cup peeling away from the wall and fluttered his hands around to indicate the disaster that would follow if we weren't finished in ten minutes. Margot held in a giggle, handed the Pad back to Kel and swung herself inside. Kel pushed in next, wasting no time.

The three of them quickly crisscrossed more guide wires, making it possible for us to move through the room without knocking into each other. I shimmied along one wire toward a gorgeously carved mahogany table, but then stopped when I realized the scale and magnificence of the room I was in.

The floors were scrawled with veined marble and inlaid with silver and gold patterns. There was a fireplace stocked with real wood, ready for our target to burn. The walls were crammed with paintings and photographs.

My path across the room took me over a display case of treasures—gems and jewels, and two baseballs signed by players I assumed were famous. There was a collection of dead and dried honeybees pinned inside a glass box, as if their extinction was something to admire. My parents did their work now.

Then there were the books.

I did not touch them, but I was sure they were real. I suddenly understood why Kel had warned me against stealing. I could not help but think how easy it would be to take one of these treasures. A book or a jewel would be easy to conceal.

I didn't do it—I could barely focus on all the things I *was* supposed to do. Besides, as valuable as his things were, there wasn't anything in the room worth the risk. A man like Winfrield would notice and report the theft at once.

I put Winfrield and his possessions out of my thoughts and concentrated on how I was going to get the printer out of my pack, insert the five molecular ink cartridges and get it ready to scan our target so the device would print a noble coin with his profile.

I wrapped my knees around the line and hung, bat-like, upside down. I couldn't think of another way to keep both my hands free. I carefully removed my pack and placed it on the table, extracting everything I needed while the blood rushed to my head. I unsealed the inks and slid them into the reservoir slots. Then I powered up the printer and arranged the icons to do what Kel had asked. Small spots ran through my vision.

I made a test print of Henri. He and Margot sidled over to see it. It wasn't very interesting, since it only captured the general outline of Henri's head in a mask. Margot was smiling. She held out her hand, like she wanted the coin. I looked for Kel, to see if this was okay, but Kel was busy monitoring the perimeter, in case Winfrield or one of his three security people were headed our way.

Much to Margot's displeasure, I dropped the medallion back into the printer's reclamation reservoir. Henri feigned grabbing at it, but just for fun. Margot, on the other hand, stared sadly at the tray, where the printer would shave it down with micro-lasers into printable atoms of gold.

My final step was to clear the printer's cache, so we didn't end up with an errant print of Henri's masked face on this guy's gold coin.

Margot was already at the window, likely pouting under *her* mask. Henri pulled back each wire-line, except the one I hung on, as he backed out of the room. Kel signaled for me to go and, after a moment, followed me out.

The last line was pulled. The small, sticky spot on the wall evaporated before my eyes. The window closed. We had succeeded.

I felt a flush of exhilaration.

The remaining Placements flew by; they were straightforward by comparison. I could work right side up, and I found it much easier to appraise my surroundings. None of the other

Placements were in homes quite as grand, but in each of them I saw dozens of items that made me wonder, *If I took that, would it be missed?* Most of these homes had books. I yearned to crack one open and see what was inside.

I held my desire back. I knew Kel would not want me slowing our work with reading, and she had been very clear that I was not to steal. But the idea of taking a book and secretly bringing it to Sam was awfully appealing. I was not able to look at the sprawling, wastefully huge homes we entered without thinking of the box my family lived in. Who would appreciate a book more? Would these people even notice if one went missing?

I kept my head down and worked. Maybe every Placer felt like I did. Maybe the bitterness would dissipate in time. Part of me enjoyed that I could *think* of stealing and no one, not even Kel, would know. Having that secret inside me was sustaining, in a twisted sort of way.

THE ONLY PRIVACY: $21.97

When my first paycheck came, it was deposited automatically into the family account. Saretha's Cuff buzzed at the same instant as mine. I thought she would be excited, but she only frowned and said, "Troubling."

Saretha Jime—word: TROUBLING: $6.99

What did she think it meant?

Sam rushed over from his bed by the window and bent over her readout, confused.

"Wait, what is this?" he asked.

Saretha shrugged. Sam studied the numbers closely.

"Is this from a suit?" he asked. The income wasn't labeled, which was unusual. Then he noticed that I was smiling and looked at the numbers again.

"Speth?" he asked, drawing back. "Is this yours?"

I kept smiling. His head tilted in confusion. He did not smile back, and that made mine evaporate. I thought there would be excitement and relief. This would keep us out of Collection. My check was three times what Saretha had been making. Even with all the suits we'd have to fight, we could survive. In a year or two, we might even be able to save enough to buy off a little debt and bring our parents home for a few weeks.

"Where is this money from?" Sam asked. He bit his lip. It bothered him. He nudged Saretha from the couch. She looked at him, then me, and then settled back to watch a comedy called *Wordy*, about a girl who liked to talk beyond her means and spent a lot of time taking loans from her friends. Saretha turned up the volume, and Sam turned his attention back to me.

"Is this where you've been going?"

He was too smart. Sooner or later, he was going to remember the day on the roof and put together the hours I was keeping, but at that moment, he did not understand.

"Can I help?" he asked. I looked away. I stared at the wall like a zombie. I was trying to say no, but I had to be careful. I couldn't use this technique too much, or the Cuff might catch on. I felt its weight on my left arm, throwing me out of symmetry, even if it didn't weigh much.

I wanted him to know, but Kel said to keep it secret. I looked at him again. He was sizing me up.

"This is good," he said, a little flatly.

"Maybe I'll text Brandon Nestle," Saretha said, suddenly, still staring at the screen.

"Brandon Nestle?" Sam asked. Of Saretha's many admirers, Brandon seemed an odd choice.

Saretha held up her Cuff and shook it around. "*He* stayed my friend," she said sharply. "He didn't drop me like practically everyone else."

$57.32 popped up on her Cuff for her last few sentences.

"That's a great use of our money." Sam shook his head.

"Speth can tell me if she doesn't like it," Saretha said, tapping away at her Cuff.

Sam slumped back to his bed, frowning.

Saretha laughed at something—probably Brandon begging to see her—and Sam turned and looked out the window.

Somehow, I had expected them to be happy. I waited for it, but happiness did not come. Everything was just as awful as the day before.

My jaw tensed in frustration, and I stalked out of the apartment. It would be hours before I had to meet Kel, Henri and Margot. I probably should have slept, but how could I?

Out on the street, I looked up toward Nancee's building. How many times had I wandered over when we were kids, just to hang out? It felt wrong to think she wasn't there. Did I know for certain she was gone? I wandered over and looked at the door. Her buzzer glowed saffron, one among dozens. I could not press it. The only thing I could think to do was scale the building and look inside, but if Kel found out, that would be the end for me as a Placer.

Instead, I walked a few blocks, and stood outside Penepoli's building. I couldn't press her buzzer either. The screen above her button grinned with six cartoon faces, with expressions from morose to ecstatic. I was supposed to select the one that best represented how I felt. There wasn't one that looked infuriated, but it didn't matter, since I couldn't agree to ToS, anyway.

I looked out across the buildings arcing along inside the ring. A sinking feeling spread from my feet to my heart as I realized how cut off I was. I could only think of one place to go.

★ ★ ★

Beecher's grandmother looked surprised to see me when I arrived, but urged me inside with a tilt of her head and closed the door behind me.

"I'd ask what I owe this pleasure to, but…" She shrugged at the futility of asking. Instead, she went over to a stack of boxes leaning against her wall and pulled out two UltraGrain Harvest™ Bars.

"Can I offer you something to eat?" She laughed. She put one bar in my hands and opened one for herself. "Not much better than Wheatlock™, I'm afraid, but without a printer, I'm stuck with what comes my way."

She took a bite and frowned. "Blissberry. Their worst flavor. Never trust a product named for a fruit that doesn't exist."

I laughed, but caught myself and quickly stopped. My laugh carried the sound of my voice, and my voice seemed a dangerous thing. Even though laughing was still free, it seemed wrong.

Mrs. Stokes waved her hand at me like I was being ridiculous.

"It's fine! Don't stop yourself. Thank goodness a *few* things are still free, though what they pick and choose is absurd. Burps over fifty-eight decibels are intentional? Shrugs under two centimeters are free? Please. All of it is nonsense. There's no system, just a matter of who sued first, for what, and who had the shrewdest, most expensive Lawyer."

She sat, wearily. She seemed more tired than when I saw her before. She patted the couch, a silent request for me to sit beside her.

"Would you talk in a FiDo?" she asked me. Her voice was as light as if she was asking me whether I liked the color blue.

"I expect not. Can't know when the WiFi might pop on, and it wouldn't be just a small expense for you, would it?"

She sighed.

She didn't know the full truth. She didn't know about the Squelches that peppered the city. I wouldn't even speak there, which was far more controlled than a FiDo. Though, in truth, in the back of my mind, I worried that the door might open at any moment while I was in those Squelches—and, if I spoke, a word might fly out and ruin me.

"But imagine if the whole thing went down," Mrs. Stokes said, extending her arms wide and letting them fall. "Randall said it would ruin us. Said we'd starve if the power ever ran out. Those inks we have? Ever look at them? They're all labeled *poison*."

I had. We all knew that messing around with molecular inks could be dangerous. They teach that early in school. The inks have to be combined in exact molecular patterns to make it all something you can safely eat.

"Truth is, some inks are just bad for digestion, some have good nutritional value and some, just to keep us on our toes, are poisonous. They would rather kill us than let us eat an ink for the nutrition. Randall couldn't stand it. Said the WiFi would take years to fix if it went out, and we'd all starve long before that. Made it sound like doomsday." She shook her head, like she didn't believe it. I wondered, a little unfairly, if everyone in Beecher's family might be crazy. But then I really thought about it.

If the WiFi was broken, how *could* you fix it? You couldn't print new cables or nodes, because printers won't work without WiFi. The cables, the nodes, the wires and the configurations were all Intellectual Property. You can't just *make* something. You couldn't create blueprints or plans. Technicians are legally bound to agree to Terms of Service before they even begin to work. No one could enter our city without agreeing to our ToS, either. Each Dome has its own set of Laws. Lawyers wouldn't be able to sue, because even they can't legally speak in a FiDo.

"Randall cracked open our food printer and scared the heck out of me. Everything inside was pockmarked with little ©s and ®s and those dreadful Patent marks. I'd have preferred cockroaches. But he said he'd figured out how to tell which ink was which. That's what they took him for. Said he'd ruin the whole economy."

She shook her head, a little disgusted, sighed and went back to her original point.

"But if it did go out," Mrs. Stokes went on, leaning in toward me, "if the WiFi was gone *forever*, would you speak?"

Maybe, I thought, with a long, slow breath out. I had imagined things changing in different ways. I thought Laws would eventually change. What made me think those changes would be for the better? No one was working toward that—not for us.

Beecher's grandmother squinted at me. "It's hard to know if you're thinking *yes* or *no*, but I wish you wouldn't look so sad," she said, patting my knee. "Silence is the only privacy."

She sighed.

"Did you know Rossi & Speight tried to Patent walking?" She paused, thinking. "They called it '*intentional placement of one foot in front of the other in a series for purpose of ambulation and travel.*' I thought people were finally going to riot on that one.

It really could have pushed us over the brink. But then Silas Rog stepped in—Silas Rog!"

She burst out laughing so loud, it scared me. "Oh! Hoo. That face!" She turned to have a better look at me. "Worth a thousand words! If they charged for looks, you would be finished!"

What did I look like? I put a hand to my face, and she laughed again.

"You must hate Rog something fierce," she said, patting my hand. "I can read that in you. Don't blame you one bit. What a turd that man is. You and I can both hate him all we like inside, eh?"

She nudged me.

"Anyway, Rog fought for what he called the *peoples' basic liberties*. Said the next thing Rossi & Speight would Copyright was breathing. The news said Rog was a hero. Put the American® flag right behind his pixeled head and talked about how he defended all of us. Rog probably set the whole thing up. I heard a rumor Rossi & Speight was a fake Law Firm he dreamed up just to do it. Of course, Rog got the Commander-in-Chief Justice to officially rule that words only have meaning because they are assigned a connotation in the database. He claimed that without the Word$ Market™, words are actually meaningless—like our brains would stop understanding them!"

She finished eating her bar and crumpled the wrapper up.

"Rog doesn't give two figs about freedom. He wants to write the rules himself. That man knows *just* how far to push without causing…" her voice dropped, and she looked a little sick "…revolt."

The word came out like she'd retched it. She looked sorry, or embarrassed, and held her hand to her mouth.

"I shouldn't say such things," she whispered. "I put too many ideas into Beecher's head that way. I don't know what I'm talking about. That's what comes from having freedom." Her eyes went glossy with tears.

Or maybe that's what comes from not being able to share it, I thought. I considered taking hold of her hand. I was sure our serotonin levels were low enough that my Cuff wouldn't charge. But I worried about what might happen if the Cuff made a mistake or tripped some alarm looking for hers.

"You should go," she said, wiping her eyes. "Please."

I did as she asked and left by her roof. I found the nearly invisible spot where the Agency had printed my locker, just a building away—one quick leap. I didn't need to tap or thumbprint it. Kel had made it work using a small slip of metal with uneven teeth. I just put it in a slit on the door and turned. Kel said it was a key, which struck me as funny, because I didn't know a key could be a physical thing.

I changed inside the locker and headed off to the Irons™ Warehouse roof to wait for the others. When I arrived, I laid my body flat, settling against the hard plastic, and looked up at the dome. I felt awful for Mrs. Stokes. A soft, wet lump formed in my throat. I told myself I was overtired.

I had been instructed in many things over the past weeks, but Kel never said a word about how to manage sleep, work *and* school. Locker or no, until I was assured of this job, I was not going to drop out like Beecher. I had to fit in sleep when I could, with naps after school and again after Placement, before school began. I also had not been instructed on how to manage Sam's and Saretha's suspicions, which were growing by the day.

I closed my eyes. My mind drifted. I thought about how great it would be if I could just tell Sam and Saretha what I was doing. I fantasized about convincing Kel to recruit Saretha, and then, a bit later, recruiting Sam. I imagined all of us doing Placements together—my own team. It might not change the way of things, but at least it could save us.

It was foolish and childish, but the dream lulled me to sleep.

When I awoke, Henri was standing over me. He appraised me as I yawned, his broad grin welcoming me back to consciousness. Margot made a sharp tsk sound behind him. Kel took off, and Henri and Margot broke after her. I collected myself and followed them, darting from rooftop to rooftop, swinging across wide gaps. The thrill brought me back to life.

It was a simple Placement that night. Sounds™ Bars. They could be placed in any room, so long as the location was prominent and a single spotlight lit them. We worked in quick rhythm, in part because we had to—the simplicity of the job meant we had sixteen Placements to make that night. Henri seemed to stick closer to me, but I could not figure out why.

We made it halfway through our target before 3:00 a.m. Below us, the bars were letting out under a Law that was centuries old. We were used to this, and traveled with extra care as the drunks staggered their way home.

I would not have stopped if the light beneath us hadn't suddenly grown so bright, but the white flare-up was distinct and unmistakable. Someone's Cuff had failed.

I'd only seen this happen twice before, not counting Beecher's

Cuff and the one Henri threw from the roof the night he found me. The howling below was inhuman and made me want to flee.

We were several stories up. I peered out over the roof's edge, though even from the height of the rooftop, the sight made me sick. A man writhed in pain, his clothes charred on one side and, beneath his Cuff, a flash of bright red skin.

A crowd had gathered, but no one dared touch him. No one wanted to get burned or sued. They shielded their eyes, but looked all the same. The only hope for him was to move his arm out, so the Cuff and the white-hot, failing battery inside it were as far from his body as possible. He would lose the arm, but he might, at least, survive if someone *did* something.

Kel pulled me back from the edge, to spare me, perhaps. Were we really going to leave him down there to die? I could not ignore the screaming. It seemed to pierce right through me. I pulled off my mask and black jacket and dropped my bag. Kel's eyes went wide. She held up her hands, signaling me to stop. She did not want us involved.

Henri tugged on Kel's arm and gestured to the trouble. He probably thought Kel did not understand. Margot peeked back over the building's side. Her lips curled. Henri pulled off his mask, too.

Kel shook her head, *no*. What if she had said no when Henri asked to save me? What would my life have been like after the attack in the alley? Would I have been alive at all? Would I have given up and screamed?

There wasn't time to debate. I had to do something. I rushed for the rooftop stairs and pulled at the door. It was locked.

Kel stomped over, her eyes flashing fury. But something

in my gaze must have changed her mind. She unlocked the door and turned away.

I broke into a run, down eight flights of stairs, taking them two at a time. By the time I reached the bottom and emerged onto the street, the screams had stopped. The battery burned more brightly. I couldn't see the man through the light—only his legs, which did not move. I moved toward him, trying to cover my eyes, as everyone else in the crowd moved back. My heart bottomed out. I looked down, stunned and sickened. I was too late.

A siren sounded in the distance. Henri put a hand on my shoulder and pulled me back. I slowly turned away.

"You can't just..." Kel half scolded me once when we were safely in a Squelch. "There were too many people around. I know it was awful to see, but there was nothing you could do."

That wasn't true. If I had been faster, I might have been able to save him. I'd seen it done before. The horrible truth is that the flailing is what most often kills people. The urge to get away from the pain is too much.

"Why did you let us go, then?" Henri asked, his voice breaking.

I watched Kel, eager for some sign she shared my feelings. She dropped her eyes, let out a heavy breath and shook her head. She had no words to admonish me, and I assumed she understood.

Margot shrugged. "Maybe he was a Lawyer," she said, trying to lighten the mood. It did not work. Kel was not pleased at all.

OIO™: $22.99

Saretha was twelve when our parents were taken. She remained calm about it, just like my mother asked. Saretha took
over our home, getting Sam and me ready for school, ordering inks for the printer and managing our expenses. We made
fun of her for being bossy, but took comfort in how normal
she made our lives feel. Did she really believe our lives were
normal, or had she been pretending for us? I'd never thought
of this before. She was loyal to her Brands. She always said
things would get better. She talked about options.

That was all gone now.

My constant coming and going contrasted starkly with her
own circumstances. If I could have traded places with her,
I would have. I loved being free to race across rooftops and
zip through the city, unseen, and I enjoyed the company of
my team, but a nagging guilt ate away at me. My new ca-
reer provided a mask and anonymity—exactly what Saretha
needed to be free.

I tried to think of some way to get Kel to take Saretha on,
but I couldn't even work out the first step of explaining the
problem without words. Even if I could have managed to

make Kel see and consider Saretha, there was the problem of Saretha's physical condition.

Saretha was in no shape to be climbing buildings. It wasn't her fault; she was never as active as me. She wasn't interested in gymnastics, or sports, and now she had nothing to do and nowhere to exercise. She had put on weight from mindlessly eating sheets of Wheatlock™. To counter the effects, she ordered an OiO™ Holding Corset, which is supposed to keep your waist tiny, regardless of the size of the rest of you. It was a ghastly, disturbing thing. After a few days of wearing it, Saretha passed out on the couch. Sam and I panicked. He slapped her face to wake her, while I fumbled to unclasp the corset that was crushing her lungs. When she woke, groggy and annoyed, she pushed me away. Sam hugged her and demanded she never wear it again.

She didn't argue. She peeled the loosened corset off, revealing her midsection beneath, squeezed out of proportion, the flesh pink and pale and dented. A faint smell of medicine and moisturizer drifted through the air, and underneath, a bad skin smell, like stinking feet. It made me queasy. Her expression was more lifeless than melancholy. She held her middle and rubbed, as if both sickened and proud.

"It hurts," she said weakly. $4.98. Her eyes looked dim and pitiful.

I put my hands around my shoulders and stifled a cry. What was happening to her? Something had been taken—not just her freedom, but some piece of her soul. I longed to say something or do something to bring her back. I felt caged. I think we all did.

Sam sprung up, grabbed me by the hand and pulled me out into the hall.

"It isn't right," Sam complained. "Why can't we sue Carol Amanda Harving for having Saretha's face?"

The technical answer was that Carol Amanda Harving was older by a year. She had the face first, and, more important, she had Butchers & Rog on her side.

"We have to do something," Sam said. I agreed, but I didn't know what that could be. The spare, dim walls of our hallway seemed to press at me. I couldn't wait to get out onto the rooftops again. I knew it wasn't fair, but the situation was so hopeless. I wondered if Saretha might be better off having surgery—mutilated, so Carol Amanda Harving could own that face all by herself.

That I could let myself think such a thing made me sick.

"Chuneed, Jimenez?" A voice called from across the hall. Norflo had his head popped out his door, looking at me with long-lashed, sympathetic eyes. I wished I'd asked before my fifteenth why his family insisted on keeping Juarze for a last name when it cost them so much, but named him Norflo after a cost-saving brand of nasal-clearing mist.

"Nothing," Sam answered him. "I can't..." He was too frustrated to explain.

Norflo waited for more and saw it wouldn't come. We couldn't explain about Saretha without risking her being seen.

"Year," he said kindly, rocking his door. If you didn't know Norflo, you wouldn't know what he meant, but he always had clever ways to say things cheaply. He spent an hour each day scrutinizing the Word$ Market™ screen. It was designed like a video game, with thousands of words traveling back and forth, up and down, across an acid green background next to their prices. He scanned for cheap slang like "chuneed," or a sale on the word "year" so he could say "I'm here" without spending too much.

When he saw I understood, he ducked back inside and shut the door.

"What are we going to do?" Sam implored me with a whisper.

I couldn't speak, but I thought if I walked, he would follow me. I could take him to Mrs. Stokes. I didn't know if or how she could help, but at least Sam could talk to someone who could answer him.

I looked at him with imploring eyes and made for the elevator. He did not follow. He stood in front of our door, looking flabbergasted that I would walk away. I should have been more understanding, but how did he not get it? I was trying to help.

"Great," he said. "Leave."

He pushed back inside our apartment, scowling. I punched the elevator door closed and worked hard not to scream.

It isn't his fault, I told myself. There was a pause in my breath, then my voice came back inside my head with, *But it is your fault.* That made me feel crazy. I put my hand over my forehead and squeezed. The elevator shuddered its way down and pinged to a stop on the bottom floor.

It had grown dark outside. With no place else to go, I crossed the bridge toward Falxo Park. The bunnies clicked on, then turned off without their special message. I guess the billboard's advertising systems calculated that it was okay if I jumped. A light rush of traffic roared below me.

I went past the park and up through the quaint shops, most of which were either already closed or in the process of closing for the night. I sneered at them, assuming they were all like Mrs. Nince. I slowed as I passed her boutique. The lights were out. She had no idea how easy it would be for me to sneak inside. I had a Placer's skills now.

I wouldn't steal anything. Her clothes were cruel and ugly and useless. I could ruin her business. I could tear the place apart.

I wandered around back and looked at the grated door there. I could do it. I could smash everything.

I shouldn't. I told myself, *Don't. But* I knew how that door worked. And there was no one around.

I forced myself to move on.

BREND'S: $23.99

Kel was smiling about the night's work. It was a quick follow-up for an exclusive aftershave called Brend's™. We had placed the actual product three nights before. Brend's™ had a very particular, complicated setup with a rotating, gimbaled platform that would keep the product faced toward the consumer at all times. Once the target had taken the bottle of aftershave, the expensive gear had to be extracted during a second visit.

"It will be easy," Kel said lightly. "We'll follow up with a half-dozen Moon Mints™ Placements and be done early."

Margot sighed. "What will I do with the extra time?" She looked at Henri. Henry kept his eyes on Kel, and his smirk under control.

"Maybe he will use his extra time to ask you out," Margot whispered to me. Henri did not hear, or at least pretended not to. I looked at her, feeling suddenly awkward and out of place. "Let him down easy," she whispered again and laughed, like it was a really funny joke.

"What?" Henri asked.

Now I pretended not to hear. I felt my cheeks flush and I looked away, as though the wall was extremely interesting.

Everything went smoothly until we reached the fourth

home. Most people understood our gear had to come back. They left the platform and lighting out neatly for us to reclaim.

Kel knew something was wrong when the map showed the platform was right beside the Consumer's bed. Even under her mask, I could see Kel's brow knit. She gestured for us to peek inside.

A lonely, sad and creepy scene confronted us. Rupert McMorse had unnervingly glued a photograph frame with a 3-D-enhanced portrait of his ex-girlfriend to the platform. He'd placed it beside his bed, like he wanted her to watch over him in the dark. He shifted, and the portrait shifted slightly to face him.

Kel shivered and signaled us all to back carefully out. We retreated to a Squelch Kel had tagged a floor below.

This Squelch was small, lined in undulating gray foam shapes that dampened sound. We had to crowd inside. It had clearly been designed for two, with a foam pad on the floor like a makeshift bed. It smelled disgustingly of must and sweat.

Kel wrinkled her nose and took out her Pad. She flipped through a set of photos of Rupert and his girlfriend that had been stored in his profile, noting the time and location of each, cross-indexed with emotional analyses of their faces as she grew more and more terrified and then disappeared.

"We could go in the daytime," Henri said. "When he is at work."

"I'd rather buy a new platform myself," Margot said.

Kel gritted her teeth. "No. It has to match the serial number. Policy. And it reflects poorly on us not to retrieve it."

"It reflects poorly on him to keep it." Margot pouted, looking up as though she could see him two stories above us and shaking her fist at the lonely fool.

"We didn't lose it," Henri insisted, his pale green eyes looking at the floor.

Kel typed *Rupert McMorse* into her Pad again to see if she had missed anything useful in his info.

"Let's gas him," Margot said, breathing in deep and closing her eyes.

"If we use sleep gas, *you* will stay outside," Kel said.

Margot pouted. "It makes me relaxed," she whispered to me. She took another deep breath, imagining it. The fingers on her left hand flicked near her chin. Margot did that sometimes when she got dreamy. I had no idea why.

Kel fretted over the idea.

"Why would we use sleep gas if he's already sleeping?" Henri asked.

Margot reached up and patted him on the head. "Think of it as 'no-wakey' gas."

She gave me a wink. Henri turned away, red-faced. I wondered how long the two of them had known each other. They had a comfortable routine where Margot teased him, and he pretended he didn't know she had a crush on him. Or maybe he really didn't know.

Kel hoisted her pack on her shoulder and held the Pad out to me. Margot frowned at being passed over. I took it, my heart suddenly pounding. The words *Carol Amanda Harving* seemed ready to burst out of my fingers, *but* I steadied my hands and pushed the thought aside.

"Do your research. Make a plan. I have to get a sleep gas canister."

"We have to wait in here?" Henri asked.

"Is that a problem?" Kel was impatient at his question.

"It's gross," Henri said, looking at the foam bed in the middle of the room.

Kel rolled her eyes. "Speth, see what you can find."

I hesitated.

Kel's shoulders dropped. She put her bag down and knelt close to me. "I don't know what your rationale is for this." She did a quick, zippered lips. "Maybe you don't want to communicate at all. Maybe you want to draw attention to the silence already created by zealous Intellectual Property Law."

"Maybe she is just still thinking about what to say," Margot offered.

"I think she—" Henri started to say.

"That doesn't matter," Kel cut across them. "Whatever it is, Speth, you should know this Pad records nothing. Your Cuff is jammed by it. It is impossible for any of it to be tracked or recorded or charged. It is self-contained. It is outside the system. No Ads. No Terms of Service. Nothing like that."

Margot took a breath to make another comment, but then fell to watching Henri watch me.

"And if," Kel continued, "you are concerned about the philosophical nature of communication, you should know that creating layouts and looking up Rupert McMorse, or anyone else, is part of this job. It is research, not communication. Do you understand?"

I looked at her. I understood.

"Why do you ask her that?" Henri said, like it was unfair. "How do you know if she understands or not?"

Kel stood and moved to the door. "I'll know when I get back."

With that, she slid the door open and shut and was gone.

Margot pulled in close, looked at the Pad, then at me, and then the Pad again.

I typed *Rupert McMorse*. His file came up. Margot sighed and rested her chin on her knees.

"What did you think she was going to look up?" Henri asked in a whisper.

"Something interesting," Margot said in a long, slow voice.

The Pad brought up a long medical history, with several diagnoses for mental illness. I wondered, if he was so crazy, what did he do for a living?

The answer was nothing. He had inherited several words, including *mellow, runny* and *obey*. He bought things. He drove the ring. Brend's™ noted he shaved every day.

He'd also stalked his girlfriend until she moved to another dome and disappeared from the system.

"I hope she got away," Margot said, pointing at that last fact on the screen. A chill ran down my spine as I thought of what the alternative might be.

Henri moved in on the other side of me and looked. He used a blunt finger to scroll from one room to another to find a back way in or out. Margot turned, heaving a sigh, disappointed. She began to work through her bag.

Henri looked at me, at her, and then quickly typed his own name in the search box.

Henri's info came up, and I saw the layout of his apartment, not so different from mine, but all that space was only for him. He lived alone, mid-ring, not too far from me, but in a better section, and on the twelfth floor.

Margot snorted out a disapproving breath and dropped her bag. She turned. Her eyes were narrowed. With a nervous flick, Henri wiped the information away and pulled the McMorse info back up. Why had he shown me his home? His face burned bright red.

"What are you looking at?" Margot asked. "You both look guilty."

I flipped the screen up and scanned through the building. I was dying to type Carol Amanda Harving's name.

The floor above McMorse was assigned to a Lawyer named Gale Krii. There was no note as to whether Gale was a man or a woman. The map was a blank outline. Most names had dropdowns full of information about habits, income, preferences and proclivities. This name was suspiciously devoid of content. He or she appeared to own the whole floor.

Margot scooted on her butt over to me. "Some people do not wish for their personal data to be revealed, so they pay to have it blocked."

She leaned in and looked at the screen with me, taking Henri's place.

I examined Rupert McMorse's apartment for a bit and couldn't learn much from it. We'd already been in his home. The difficulty was in getting into his room without waking him, and that problem would be solved with sleep gas.

"It will take Kel twenty minutes to get back," Margot said in a singsong voice. Her finger circled the screen. "Are you done?"

I looked at her. Did she want time with the Pad? She pulled up a map and pointed.

"She keeps the sleep gas in a locker on the Forty-Third Radian. She thinks I don't know. Anyway, the plan is simple: Rupert McMorse will sleep. We will take back our gear. Voilà."

Voilà. I didn't know what that word meant, exactly.

"You should explore," Margot said. "You must be curious."

A moment passed between us. Did she know? She waited, her shrewd eyes looking me over. I felt a small tingle of excitement and fear.

"I see how it is," she said, giving in to something I had not said. She stood up and pulled Henri along with her.

"What?" Henri asked, looking back at me.

"She doesn't want us to see," Margot said. "Maybe it is too much like communication. How big is your biceps, Henri?"

Henri looked pleased to be asked, and his attention snapped to Margot.

My finger drifted up to the search icon where Henri had just typed his name. My heart began pounding harder. What if Carol Amanda Harving lived somewhere far away? In another dome? What if my search turned up nothing? She could have paid for that privacy.

"Don't look me up, though," Margot said. Her hand was on Henri's arm as he flexed for her. This was my moment. I paused. Did Kel know I needed this? What did I hope to accomplish?

I wanted to talk to her. I wanted to explain the dire situation Carol Amanda Harving had put us in. I wanted her to listen and agree to desist, but how could I make that happen if I didn't speak? And, even if I did speak, what made me think she would care?

It didn't matter. I had to know. I needed a place to start. *Carol Amanda Harving*, I typed.

The display moved off to a building not so far away, Malvika Place. My breathing grew a little faster. Hers was one of the few buildings in the city that extended out above the dome. Her apartment was listed on the eighty-ninth floor, just outside. The apartment was one of two enormous spaces that showed up blank inside. The Pad provided no information about her, not even her alleged birth date. All it listed was her name and that apartment.

I stared at the block of shape and tried to control my outward reaction. The skin on my back bristled. What else could I learn from this? I scanned the building for a way in.

Just then the door slid open; Kel had returned.

"That was fast," Margot commented.

"Let's go," Kel said, tossing a green pony bottle of sleep gas each to Margot, Henri and me. Margot turned hers over with a grin.

"Be careful with it," Kel said, then she warned, "Margot, if yours goes off *accidentally*..."

"Where did you go for these, your house?" Margot asked, grinning.

Kel ignored this and held out her hand for the Pad. Margot grabbed it on her behalf, before I could clear Carol Amanda Harving's name. Margot peeked and cleared it quickly for me.

My hands were shaking.

Now that I knew where she lived, would I do something foolish? Probably.

Carol Amanda Harving. Her name kept repeating in my head. I couldn't concentrate. Could I bring Sam to reason with her? He was a good talker. Maybe he could charm her.

Margot placed her gas canister in her bag, and I did the same, sliding it into a small loop that held it tightly cushioned inside. She caught my eye and gave me a look I couldn't read. I micro-shrugged in return.

Kel moved ahead of me, covered from head to toe in black, and led us to work. In the psychopath's apartment, I scarcely paid attention. Henri gassed the room, and a moment later, I found he was staring daggers at me for my loss of focus. He had thrust a face mask into my hands, and I had barely noticed.

Rupert McMorse snored away in his bed. His ex-girlfriend's portrait faced him in mock adoration. I peeled the frame from the platform and gathered our equipment. Afterward I placed the girlfriend's photo back so it faced him. I thought he would like that. I pitied him, in a way.

I felt a little lightheaded as I turned away from the nightstand. Out the bedroom window, there was a clear view of Malvika Place. I stopped and looked for a moment, considering my options, and then moved on.

The sleep gas had worked like a charm. Suddenly I was exhilarated, not by the job, but at the thought that I could finally *do* something.

When we were finished I was escorted home. They brought me to my roof and, seeing I had safely arrived, they all took off in opposite directions. I assumed they each went home to sleep and rest for the next night's Placement.

For half a minute, I considered going straight to Malvika

Place, but I needed time to plan. I gathered myself together and prepared to go back home and, hopefully, sleep for a few hours before school. But before I arrived at the stairs, Margot zipped back into view.

Margot? She gestured, and it took my brain a moment to catch up and understand. She wanted me to follow her.

I hesitated. What did she want? Did she know about Carol Amanda Harving, and the notice to desist? Did she have a plan for me?

If I went straight to bed, I could fit in a couple of hours of sleep before I had to get up for school. I knew that was the safest course. I was bone weary, and I could feel in my gut that Kel would not approve of my following Margot. (Or Margot egging me on.) Paycheck or no, I was still a Placer in training.

Yet how could I refuse? How would I sleep wondering what Margot wanted, and knowing she would like me less—respect me less—if I did not follow?

Sleep would have to wait. I had to find out what she wanted.

MARGOT: $24.99

Margot brought me north, to a tall gray building in the Deux-
ième. It looked like stone, but was blandly warm to the touch,
with none of the cool strength of stone. The plastic had been
sanded smooth and stippled to fool the eyes.

Margot pushed open an unlocked window and jumped inside. I followed and found myself in a nicely furnished bedroom. Framed posters hung on the walls, depicting composers
I could only identify from their giant Trademarked names.
MOZART™, BACH™, LENNON™. Margot didn't pause to
check if the room was occupied or if anyone was nearby. She
strode through and out the bedroom door. In the hall, she
pulled off her gloves and put a thumb to a keypad. A hidden
door slid open. There was a Squelch inside.

Was this her home? Down the hall, I saw two more doors
and, in the opposite direction, a kitchen and a living room.
If she lived here, she was well-off, and she did not live alone.
A dense smell of perfume hung in the air.

Margot pulled me inside the Squelch and closed the door.

"Okay," Margot said as she pulled off her mask. She
sounded younger, and a little nervous. Her hair settled back
into its two perfect points. Her one word hung in the air

alone. For the first time, I saw her as a girl not much older than me. How long had she been a Placer?

The Squelch was small and round, with four moderately comfortable chairs arranged in a curve. There were six polished and stained panels of auburn-colored wood spread out across the room's walls. A violin rested on a stand nearby, virtually camouflaged against the wood.

I thought Margot was going to speak and ask me about Carol Amanda Harving, but instead she lifted the violin and placed it under her chin. She closed her eyes. Without another word, she began to play. I stepped backward, pulled off my mask and took a seat.

Margot played softly at first, pulling the bow lightly back and forth as her fingers moved over the strings. My heart began to pound. I had never heard music played live on an instrument before. I heard Margot's strings vibrate so clearly, I could almost feel them in my bones. It was beautiful, but I could not enjoy it.

What she was doing was highly illegal. She did not have the music rights cleared. We were in a Squelch, and not likely to be caught, but my response was an almost primal fear, like when I heard people speak in Legalese. Margot hummed quietly under the tune, which only made it worse. How could she be so casual?

The Musical Rights Association of America® did not stand for this sort of thing. I knew all too well how vicious and methodical they could be. They did not tolerate anyone enjoying music without paying. What if they discovered Margot's transgression a generation or two from now? Had Margot even thought what playing this song might do to her great-great-grandchildren?

She must have trusted me, or at least trusted in my silence. Had she brought me here just to hear her play?

"It's called *Henri*," she said, drawing one last, perfect note. She opened her eyes and looked at the ground, her cheeks bright red.

Henri? Had she *written* this? For him?

The MRAA wouldn't care. Any combination of notes she could ever dream up was already owned. The MRAA had a computer model that rendered, catalogued and Copyrighted every possible melody, harmony and whatever else there was to music. We were taught that in the second grade. It is why we were warned so sternly against singing. Unlike speech, music was never, ever free. If a baby sang, its parents were charged.

But maybe I worried for nothing. For all I knew, there had never been a violation by my great-great-aunt. Maybe a computer program generated violations the way the MRAA generated songs. If they wanted to claim a violation, would it be so difficult for them to just make one up? How would we ever know? I had no access to my family's history. None of us did.

Margot gently set her bow and violin back on the stand.

"He hasn't heard it," she said, one hand still on the instrument. She waited for a response or a reaction from me, but I didn't know what I should do. This was not what I'd expected. I was worried she was going to ask about Carol Amanda Harving.

After a moment, she sat beside me, dropping down into her seat with a sigh.

"You are a dud to be with," she said, shaking her head. I

should have been insulted, but she was right. I couldn't give her more than a weak, apologetic smile in return.

"I do not know what to think of you." Margot leaned on her hand. "I want to know your real reason for keeping quiet. I said to Henri that it would be funny if it is because you are extremely dumb."

She waited for a reaction. I scrunched my eyes up. I raised my shoulders a centimeter and let them drop. A micro-shrug. She didn't know what it meant. Neither, really, did I. I wasn't sure how to feel about Margot.

"That was a joke," she explained.

I knew. What I didn't know was why she'd brought me here. Was she trying to figure me out?

"Henri was mad when I said you were dumb," she said. "If that matters to you. He is too nice, and too easy to tease. But if I do not tease him, he will not pay any more attention to me than he does to his backpack."

She leaned her head down, her hand a little out from her chin, fingers moving again. Realization dawned on me as I watched her fingers flutter across invisible violin strings. Did she hear silent music when she did that?

"Carol Amanda Harving," she said, shaking her head like she was disappointed. "A movie star? Is it because you look a tiny bit like her?"

She squinted at me, like she was trying to see the resemblance. I suddenly felt insulted, but I could not explain that my reasons were more important than just wanting to pry into the life of some random starlet.

"She is not very good," Margot added. I don't know if she

wanted me to feel better or worse. Her head cocked to one side. "I do not imagine you would want to explain?"

Even if I could, would she be an ally? Would Margot help me find her? She probably could, but what then? I felt a tension underneath Margot's playful demeanor, as if I had done something against her.

"Why will you not talk in a Squelch?" Her brow was wrinkled. She gestured around the room to show me it was perfectly fine. She looked annoyed. I hoped she did not think it was personal.

"Kel said to leave you alone," she went on glumly. "I think she likes that you will never talk. It makes all the right people angry."

She made the sign of the zippered lips, more to herself than to me, then let her hands fall in her lap.

"It feels weird that you don't ask anything. Don't you feel trapped by not having any questions? It would make me very claustrophobic."

That was an interesting way for her to put it, and not very different from the airless feeling I got when I thought of all the things I wished I could say.

"Do you know how I got to be a Placer?"

I didn't, but I think I sat up straighter or something because Margot smiled, knowing she had my attention.

"Normally Placers recruit after careful observation. Kel does not cover the Onzième, but if you took gymnastics, someone from the Agency evaluated you before your fifteenth."

She paused to let that sink in. The hairs on the back of my neck rose as I remembered the pale, blond man, and then I began to fume. I realized Margot was implying that I *techni-cally* was not good enough to be a Placer.

I had the distinct impression she both admired and dis-liked me.

"Kel spotted *me* on a soccer field. I had been told I could have been in the Olympics™ if they had soccer for girls. They do not. I find the Olympics™ a joke anyway, since we no lon-ger compete against other nations."

I didn't realize that we ever had. I was glad I didn't have to admit it. My cheeks burned for a minute, and I had the ugly impression Margot could read my embarrassment. I wondered how much else she knew. She obviously had money and the better education that went with it.

"Kel found Henri doing Parkour in an alley in the Cinq. She says if she had not recruited him right then and there, he probably would have broken his own neck. He needed training. He moves like a dream now, though. Have you ever watched him?"

She fell silent. She wasn't waiting for an answer; she was thinking, or maybe imagining Henri move. He *was* very skilled. Her posture changed. She looked smaller and younger.

"Do you like him?" she asked in a whisper.

I would have said *no*, even though I had not had time to weigh how I felt. This was what she really wanted to ask. Nothing else mattered to her. The trouble was that I could not give her an answer. A micro-shrug or a smile wouldn't cut it. She looked me in the eye, frowning. She couldn't dis-cern anything one way or the other, and it frustrated her. It frustrated me.

She looked at me for far too long for it to be anything but

awkward, and I didn't know what to do. Without her chatter or her music, the Squelch seemed achingly quiet. Her violin ticked, settling on its perch. A string sounded an almost imperceptible note. Margot tensed, then slapped her hands at her thighs and stood.

"Well…" Her voice trailed away, and her cheeks burned red again. Was she angry or embarrassed? Mine felt warm, too. I felt them with the back of my hand. She opened the door and led out into the hall and back to her bedroom. Our conversation was over.

Did she still have both parents? She didn't seem like an Affluent, but her home was extravagant compared to mine. It had a Squelch. Those framed composer posters were paper, which meant she paid for their registration and the monthly fees that went with them. Was she a Placer just for the fun of it?

"You know how to get home?" she whispered. Her Cuff vibrated and charged her. It shook me to see her speak so blithely. She could afford to talk. Resentment coiled in my belly.

She held the window open for me. I put my mask and gloves back on with care, then climbed outside. Margot shut the window and sat down on her bed, staring off into space. I shot a line out and zipped away. She would probably sleep until noon. I wished I could have done the same, but I didn't have that luxury. I still had to go to school, and I scarcely had time to change.

LUCRATIVE: $25.99

"You look exhausted!" Penepoli said, stating the obvious at the sight of the dark circles under my eyes.

I pushed through the halls with her at my side, not ready at all for Mrs. Soleman's American® history class. That class was a complete waste of time.

"There's twenty-nine Silents at the school now," Penepoli whispered to me as I reached my seat. "I counted."

I let out a breath. How was I supposed to feel about that?

"Thirty, if you count Nancee," Penepoli added. Then, after a moment, "Do you think she is coming back?"

She wasn't coming back. Not to school, for sure. My frown answered Penepoli's question, because her face fell in disappointment. We both missed Nancee. My heart seemed to slow, thinking I might well never see her again.

"Shut up!" Phlip grunted from his seat behind us. His Cuff buzzed, and his face darkened.

Penepoli glared at Phlip and then turned back to me, lowering her voice. "Principal Ugarte is pissed," she said, brightening a little.

"Okay, Miss Graethe," Mrs. Soleman said, pointing Penepoli toward her seat.

Mrs. Soleman was a mousey little thing with watery eyes and slumped shoulders. She never seemed to have anything worthwhile to teach us. She would softly plow forward, reciting names and dates from board-approved selections of Great Events, and my mind usually wandered. I think she knew none of us paid much attention. I doubted she cared.

She adjusted the short sport coat she wore and cleared her throat as a preamble to her lecture.

"The Patent Wars were meant to *consolidate* and *aggregate* control of innovation in America®," Mrs. Soleman said. She often lingered over words she found interesting or pleasurable to say. Most teachers did, since the government was paying.

I longed for Mrs. Soleman's usual soft dullness; my eyes were begging to close. But she kept watching me, making it impossible for me to put my head down on the desk and close them. I folded my hands on my desk and let my chin rest on them, hoping I might still look interested while slumped forward. Mrs. Soleman looked disappointed.

What I wanted most was to sleep. If I was going to expend any brain power, it would be to consider how I could get into Malvika Place and what I would do with Carol Amanda Harving. If I could get Sam to her, how could I prepare him? Would his pleas be enough?

"Have any of you ever wondered why NanoLion™ batteries continue to be unsafe?" she asked. Her eyes were steady on me. Was this a trick to get me to speak? To keep me awake? I felt a little sick, thinking of the man I had seen die in the street.

Everyone knew NanoLion™ batteries were unstable, but it was bold and dangerous to speak publicly about it. Mrs. Soleman's Cuff let out a low, ugly bleat. She'd spoken negatively about a product, and her Cuff had just fined her for it. I expected her to wince and back off, but she continued.

"If anyone tried to create a competing product, one that didn't explode when punctured, the Rights Holders would sue. During the Patent Wars, aggressive litigation became the sole purpose of Patent ownership: to sue anyone who infringed, or prepared to infringe, on the ideas and concepts already owned. It became impossible to innovate or improve anything. Creating and inventing became less than worthless; creating and inventing became liabilities. Nobody dared. That is why you will never see any new ideas in your lifetime. Anything that looks new is only due to marketing and sheen."

Her voice was sharp and strained. Something in her throat seemed to catch. I could sense everyone in the room tense as she spoke. None of us had ever heard a teacher talk like this.

My failing concentration sharpened as she continued. "The main function of the government is to protect rights and freedoms," she said, her tone strangely sarcastic. "Copyrights, Patent Rights, Trademarks and all other Intellectual Properties must be safeguarded, as must the freedom of the market to profit and grow."

Phlip clucked his tongue, like this all irritated him.

Her thin, pallid face flushed. I felt bad for her. Her words were being recorded and paid for by the school. They would likely be alerted soon, if they had not been already.

"Those protections once outlined different freedoms, including a very important one: the *freedom of speech*™." Her Cuff let out an angry buzz. She swallowed hard and went on. "But this concept disappeared over time to make way for the more *lucrative* concept of paying for speech."

She said the word *lucrative* slowly, like she could taste it. I envied that. The tip of my tongue pressed the roof of my mouth and front teeth to form the *L*. I could feel in my throat and lungs what it would be like to exhale the *ooo* sound between pursed lips, and how the hard *C* would form with a thin crack of air interrupted in the back of my mouth.

I stopped myself, worried I would get carried away and make an actual sound.

Penepoli turned around in her seat, her eyes bulging at me. She mouthed the letters *OMG*.

"*Freedom of speech*™," Mrs. Soleman choked out, a little teary and with a pause, "is one of the most expensive phrases on the national market." Her Cuff made a lower, angrier buzz. "Unless you've heard it during a FiDo, I doubt any of you have heard it at all. Ask yourself—why?"

The class around me was stirring. Sera Croate looked disgusted. Norflo Juarze was carefully nodding, glancing at me. Shari Gark looked down at the nails she had just chewed.

Mrs. Soleman rubbed at her face, putting her hand over her mouth. Her eyes were darting around like a nervous animal. If I warned her to leave, would she listen? I knew this was going to end terribly. Why would she risk it? She was still looking at me, like she needed *me* to listen. I didn't want that responsibility. I already had the Silents on my conscience.

Her voice suddenly dropped to a whisper. "It has been suggested that this change was never legal. Some say the evidence is contained in a book." Her hand was on her Cuff now, clamped around it, twisting as it recorded her every word.

I had heard about this book. It's one of the things kids talk about, like ghosts or chupacabra. In our neighborhood, some people claimed Silas Rog kept the book locked away in the central tower above the offices of Butchers & Rog. I found that hard to believe. Why would he keep it? Wouldn't that only invite someone to find it?

Tylenola Ram, next to me, was wide-eyed, and her mouth was hanging open. I remembered the time she said she saw a unicorn charge up the off-ramp near Chase™ Circle. I don't think she was lying; I just think she chose to believe that's what she saw.

I stifled a yawn. I wasn't bored; I could not control it. Mrs. Soleman looked taken aback, as if my exhaustion was betraying her. She had no idea how tired I was. I went rocketing through the city at night, secreting Products into people's homes, and then I came to school. There was no time for sleep.

"If someone found that book—if someone gave it to the press and made it public—if everyone could read those words…" Mrs. Soleman shook herself, as though she had said too much.

If someone gave the press that book, I thought, *it would disappear and never be seen again*. I felt sorry for her. Was she trying to say we should look for it? "I do believe it is real," she said a little tearfully, like someone trying desperately hard to believe.

I should have been on her side, but I couldn't say it or show it. There was nothing I could do.

"Butchers & Ro—aaah!" Her voice suddenly cut out, and her eyes shut tight. I heard a tiny crack of electricity. She opened her eyes slowly. They were glossy and red. Gritting her teeth, she put a shaking hand to her lips and made a quick motion. It was hard to tell, because her movement was stilted and awkward, but I think she signed the zippered lips. She quickly sat at her desk and buried her head in her hands. Her Cuff started beeping a shrill alarm. The system had flagged her.

"Is she a Silent now?" Penepoli asked me, and then turned to the front of the class. "Mrs. Soleman? Are you a Silent? Is that what this means?"

My heart was pounding. I was wide awake now, in spite of my exhaustion. I tried to hide the fact that my hands were shaking as the faces of my classmates turned to me. Some looked disgusted, but others seemed hopeful. What did they expect? Did they think I put her up to this? Did they think I knew where this book was? Did they think I was going to look for it? I didn't understand what I was supposed to do.

Mrs. Soleman's Cuff kept beeping. Penepoli stood up, sat down, then stood up again, turning to the class. She made the sign of the zippered lips.

"Come on!" Sera Croate complained. "You've got months before your Last Day!"

Penepoli looked at me for approval. She hummed a word, like her lips wouldn't open, but she was still talking inside.

Shari Gark moaned in disgust. Her Cuff buzzed with a charge I could not see.

Principal Ugarte burst into the room. "Everyone be quiet," he commanded, yanking Mrs. Soleman up by her arm and dragging her to the door. "Your educational license has been revoked," he hissed, red-faced, his neck bulging over his collar. He forced her out into the hall. She did not resist. He turned from the doorway to address me. "Miss Jime," he said, sneering with disgust, "you need to leave this school at once."

It felt like he'd slapped me in the face. I scanned the room and realized I would be cut off from everyone now.

"Miss Jime!" he roared. "Now!"

I stood. Penepoli stood with me, then stamped her foot and made the zippered lips sign at Principal Ugarte. When he ignored her, she stamped her foot again, humming to demand his attention. He didn't seem to care. I almost had to smile at what a terrible Silent she made.

As I made my way to the door, Ugarte suddenly grabbed my arm and stopped me from leaving.

"You want to stay?" he asked, his voice a little calmer, his grip growing painfully tighter. He pulled me around to face the class. "Tell them this doesn't have anything to do with you." He jabbed a finger at the stupefied faces of my classmates. He shook me again, like I was a bad doll. "Tell them not to follow your example."

I wrenched my arm away from him and darted out of the classroom, tears filling my eyes.

"Do not come back," he yelled. He tapped out an InstaSuit™ and flicked it to me.

In the hall, Mrs. Soleman was already gone, carted off to who-knows-where.

BRIDGETTE: $26.99

My day was destined to get worse. Saretha was bound to find out I'd been expelled, if she didn't know already. Sam would be furious when she told him. They didn't know that as a Placer I was safe, at least, from Indenture.

Unless I wasn't. Kel had asked me to lay low and try not to draw attention. Clearly I had failed—though Mrs. Soleman's outburst wasn't exactly my fault. But if Kel didn't let me stay on, I was out of options.

At least I'd be getting more sleep without school. I needed to move forward and focus. I'd found Carol Amanda Harving's address. That was something. Unfortunately, I didn't have a good plan for how to use it.

When I got home, Saretha was on the couch watching *Truly, Lovely, Danger!*, a movie costarring Carol Amanda Harving as the best friend of the girl who accidentally falls in love with a muscular and inexplicably shirtless assassin. It was her last supporting role before she became a leading star. Near the end, Carol Amanda Harving turns out to be an assassin, too, and dies the ugly death of a traitor. Was that why Saretha was watching? I couldn't blame her, though it seemed a little twisted. Carol Amanda Harving looked too much like

Saretha for me to enjoy watching her characters die on-screen. Saretha paused the film and shook her head at me.

"Tell me you didn't just drop out," she said, her eyes closed, as though she couldn't bear to look at me. Then, angered, she spit out, "You have no idea what you've done!" The contempt in her voice was worse and more difficult to hear than I'd anticipated. Panic rose in my chest.

"Have you seen this?" Saretha flicked away the cost of what she'd said and used her Cuff as a remote to pull up a news report on our screen.

The wall filled with footage of a beautiful young girl named Bridgette Pell, on the Ninety-Second Radian. She was a *thin, lovely, wealthy young woman with her whole life ahead of her.* She stood in her posh rooftop garden, a tall, skeletal waif, big-eyed and blank, in front of her Affluent friends and family. Instead of reading her Last Day speech, which would have been little more than a formality for someone with her money, she zipped her lips, bounced on her toes and let herself fall backward over the building's side.

"Have the Silents gone too far?" the announcer asked with a dramatic glee.

My stomach dropped away. The *Silents*? She had *killed herself*!

"Is this what you wanted?" Saretha asked, as the commentators blamed me in the background.

This wasn't my fault. I was stunned it was even possible for her to do this. Why weren't the rails higher? Why would an Affluent girl care at all about the Silents or her Last Day? What was the point of killing herself? My head was swimming, trying to understand.

"Everyone's going to copy you now," Saretha said.

She wasn't copying me! I screamed in my head. *And in case you hadn't noticed, I didn't kill myself!*

I sat on Sam's bed, put my head back and closed my eyes. I listened to the voices discuss me on television. I was so tired. I had only a few hours before I had to go back out onto the rooftops and make Placements.

"Jim, I don't think we should assign blame here, but isn't this clearly the Silent Girl's fault?"

"Ah, yes, Rebecca, given her petulant unwillingness to come forward and speak for herself, I hardly think it's possible that any other conclusion can be drawn."

"And, Jim, don't you think Bridgette Pell's family has a duty to sue?"

"Rebecca, I think every American® has a duty to sue, whenever opportunity permits."

Almost on cue, I felt a suit arrive simultaneously on our Cuffs. I didn't look. Saretha made an irritated noise and confirmed its receipt.

"Tylenola Ram was sent to the hospital. Zipped her lips and drank a food printer ink." And with that, Saretha turned her movie back on. I couldn't ask if Tylenola would be okay.

My stomach churned. I tried not to think about Bridgette Pell, or Tylenola, or Penepoli or everything else that was happening. How many Silents were there now? What did they think they were doing? What did they think *I* was doing? Everyone acted like I was some kind of leader, but I hadn't led anyone.

Slowly, and in spite of myself, I fell asleep, hoping I could forget about Bridgette Pell and her suicide, all while I listened to Carol Amanda Harving scream in that film. A grim solution worked itself out in my head, in half thoughts and dreams. I tried to reason with the actress while she looked coldly away and sipped champagne at the edge of a cliff-side pool. I kept thinking, *I could kill her.* It was a sickening thought. I imagined her falling, then drowning, then laughing at me. Beneath the half dreams and fuzzy thoughts, I kept thinking that if the choice was her, or Sam, Saretha and me, then Carol Amanda Harving was going to die.

REPLEVIN: $27.99

"We're doing a pickup," Kel said. She bit her lower lip. Her posture seemed stiff and tense, and she kept a careful eye on me. I worried that she had discovered my search, but she had sworn that the Pad wasn't traceable.

"Another one?" Henri asked. He had just walked in. His voice was full of surprise and disappointment.

Kel held up her Pad. "Margot, will you run the Pad tonight?"

Margot nodded and took it without comment. It was unlike Margot not to have a quip. She looked at me for just a second, then down to the Pad.

"We're taking the Elk Champagne™, the Tiffany™ rings, the Squire-Lace™ Chips, the ant kits and any associated fixtures."

"That isn't our stuff," Henri complained. "We didn't place it."

"I know," Kel said flatly.

"But shouldn't the Placement team who placed it—"

"Henri, just do as you are told!" Kel cut him off and threw three large, empty bags at his feet. "I want to be in and out before 4:00 a.m."

It was already 2:00 a.m. Henri shook his head, picking up the bags and whispering to me, "I've never heard of anything like this."

"Henri." Margot shushed him with a swift shake of her head. They all knew more than I did. Henri watched me carefully. It wasn't just concern I saw in his expression.

"Speth," Kel said, taking me by the shoulders. "I'm sorry."

I started to feel deeply unsettled. Kel looked rattled. I didn't understand. I felt that claustrophobic feeling of not being able to ask, and I was only vaguely aware of what I was supposed to do.

"You can stay here if you want. We can come back for you."

I looked around. I did not want to seal myself in a stark white room, alone in utter silence. Something was terribly wrong, but I couldn't comprehend what it was.

"You know about the Pell girl?" Kel asked.

The hairs on my neck stood on end. What did Bridgette Pell have to do with a pickup?

My stomach sunk as Kel stated what I'd suddenly put together: "We are taking back Bridgette Pell's Placements from her ceremony."

I felt suddenly disgusted. I closed my eyes. Three months in, I still was not used to the corneal implants. I hated the way they rubbed against my lids. Kel closed her arms around me. I know she wanted to comfort me, but I felt apprehensive. This wasn't like her. This wasn't her place. Her embrace was stiff, and she wasn't my mother. She wasn't even a friend. I pushed her away, though gently, and forced myself to smile. What did I care about Bridgette Pell? I was fine. I put my bag on my shoulder to show I was ready to go.

On the roof, Kel shot a line to the dome's scaffold for what she called a long swing. I usually found these exhilarating, but inside I was dreading what was coming. I followed Kel's lead, sticking close like she asked. I swung wide across four blocks, feeling the air press on me as I sliced through it. My biceps burned from the effort, and slacked in relief as I landed roughly on a rooftop corner. Kel crossed to the roof's opposite side as lightly as a cat and gestured to a building across the way.

Looming behind, in the distance, several rings away, Malvika Place rose up and out of the dome. For all I knew, above it, Carol Amanda Harving slept soundly, in real moonlight, unconcerned with the devastation her suit had brought on my family. I wondered if Silas Rog had asked her to do it. I thought of my dream about killing her and my hands felt weak and shaky. There had to be some other way.

Kel, Margot and Henri watched me carefully, like I might explode. I focused closer and looked at the Pells' building. It was like any other posh penthouse, tall and gleaming with a wide, lush rooftop garden.

I stepped to the edge and looked down, across the wide boulevard of the Ninety-Second Radian. At the foot of the building, far below, was an outline and yellow tape. There were candles lit on the edges to mark the spot where Bridgette Pell had died. In the middle a black scorch mark and a melted hollow marked where her NanoLion™ battery had ruptured. I shivered just looking at it. A pair of news dropters hovered on either side, like sentinels, keeping watch for any misery they could film. Kel hacked them from her Pad and locked them into sleep mode to keep them from noticing us.

Beecher's body had been unceremoniously cleared away, but Bridgette had the honor of a memorial. She would be remembered. We would be blamed. I felt revolted at how unjust it was. Everyone had forgotten Beecher, except his grandmother and me. That poor boy had no choices, and yet I could not completely forgive what he had done. My head churned with the knowledge that Bridgette Pell had options, and she just threw them away.

Kel shot a line over the street, and Henri and Margot did the same. I hesitated. I needed a second to collect my thoughts. My hands were shaking. I felt sick and furious. The assignment to take back Bridgette Pell's Placements was a petty, needless cruelty. But the companies would not allow themselves the tarnish of a negative association. They had to make a show of taking back what they had given.

Was it a coincidence that *my* team had been assigned this pickup, or was it a punishment, too? Whoever contracted Kel and the team—the Agency I knew nothing about—had to know who I was. My cheeks felt hot. Had Kel fought against this job? Or had she just quietly followed their orders?

The others swept across the distance to the other rooftop. I followed, zipping over the road forty stories below. This was the height that had killed Bridgette.

Across the garden was a series of floor-to-ceiling windows, black and glossy in the darkness. Were Bridgette's parents inside? Did they hate me? Had the family been happy before, free of work camps and worry? I couldn't imagine it. I could never understand anything about Bridgette Pell's life. What possible reason could she have for zipping her lips? How could an Affulent be unhappy? She had everything.

Margot and Henri were on the far side of the courtyard, already packing up. Kel took the personalized Squire-Lace™

Chips, laser etched with 15s and Bridgette Pell's face, and crushed them into a powder. I'd thought I hated Bridgette, but watching her special chips reduced to dust made me realize the feeling was something else—a feeling I didn't have a word for. Somewhere, if it existed, someone owned that word. I wondered what it cost to say. An uneasy spark of pity sizzled in its wake.

However twisted her logic, Bridgette Pell felt sorry for us. I had so often thought of Affluents as heartless and cruel that I never took time to consider some of them might be different— sympathetic, even.

Only hours before, I had been dreaming of murdering Carol Amanda Harving. What if she wasn't to blame? For all I knew, she was a pawn or a puppet, controlled by the movie studios, or Silas Rog or some corporate sponsor. For all I knew, the Lawyers hadn't even told her what they were doing. She might not even know we existed.

Henri had two bags packed. Margot was watching the Pad for signs of movement from inside.

The garden itself was covered in pictures of Bridgette. I couldn't tell if this was meant to memorialize her after her suicide, or if these pictures had been part of her celebration. She was pretty and pale and too thin for her own good. Did she think her death would be romantic? If she really had wanted to do something, she could have used her words to speak out. She had a voice. She would have been heard.

Her suicide was selfish and meaningless. The flicker of pity I'd felt for her resolved into disgust. *How dare she? How dare she waste all this?* All over the city, the Silents had zipped their lips and made the protest mean something by going on, even though it meant suffering. Bridgette had chosen not to suffer. She wasn't a Silent. She was only silent on the way down.

I laughed coldly inside, then felt horrible for it. I pressed my lips hard—shut my mouth tight. What was I doing?

Kel caught my eye and gently guided me to a series of light fixtures, which I dutifully removed with a thin magnetic screwdriver. She acted as if I might crack open at any moment, and I hated it.

On the table beside me was a fanned array of iChits™, tiny music players the size of a fingernail that held a playlist of popular songs, interspersed with Ads. These were good for ten plays. I had wanted some at my celebration, but Mrs. Harris explained that iChit™ *never* sponsored kids in the Onzième. They didn't want to be associated with us. The thought irritated me.

The iChits™ weren't on our list to take. I didn't know if that meant they were left for the family, or if another team of Placers would come to claim what we did not. I didn't care. None of them deserved it. None of them needed it. None of them cared that Bridgette Pell's idiotic decision had made my life more miserable, and yet it was legal and right for her family and others to sue me.

I put my finger on the closest iChit™ and slid it quickly across the table. The thin metal was cool under my finger. Why couldn't they have sponsored a few for my party? Would it have been such a big deal to give us that? Sam and Saretha loved music. Not that it would have mattered—Placers swept down after my celebration, too. They took back all my Placements and crushed my Squire-Lace™ Chips to dust, just like Kel. For all I knew, it might have been Kel and Henri and

Margot who did it. If iChit™ had sponsored me, they would have gotten their players back, anyway.

I slipped the one under my finger into my pocket. Who would know? Who would care? I told myself Sam and Saretha would love it, though I didn't do it completely for them. I wanted iChit™, or the Pells, or *someone* to suffer, just a little. I wanted to put another crack in the shapeless system that seemed to be crushing me. It was stupid and childish, and the little player seemed to burn in my pocket, but part of me was satisfied that I had done something, and part of me was exhilarated when I got away with it.

THREE ROTATIONS: $28.99

"What is this?" Sam asked. He knew what an iChit™ was; that wasn't why he was asking. I placed it in his hand as soon as he got home from school. I was excited to make him and Saretha happy. They so rarely got to enjoy music outside of commercials and what drifted out of stores. Sam turned the smooth rectangle over in his hand and surprised me with a frown.

"I don't want it," he said. He tossed it onto our kitchen counter. My heart sank. *Why?* I looked for some sign he was joking, but his face was uncharacteristically sullen.

Saretha got up from the couch and walked over.

"Where did it come from?" she asked, pushing her long black hair behind her ears and sniffing at it like it was a botched print of Wheatlock™. Her Cuff vibrated at the charge.

Sam looked at me like he knew what I'd done, but how could he know? Did he somehow sense that I'd stolen it? Or maybe he thought I'd spent good family money on it, which might have been worse. I realized at once I'd made a stupid mistake. My tiny act of rebellion had accomplished nothing.

Saretha nudged the player with a finger, then clicked it. It started playing a song by Birdo & Neckfat called "Drops." She picked up the iChit™ and brought it back to where she had been sitting and placed it on the couch's arm, so when she leaned back, it would be by her ears. The amount and quality of sound put out by the small disposable player was astonishing. Saretha closed her eyes and let it play.

Then I was struck with a horrible thought. What if the player had been somehow customized for Bridgette Pell's Last Day? What if there was a message after the song? It was a sponsored product. Companies did stuff like that all the time. Sam was already unhappy; if he knew where the player really came from, what would he think of me? I was instantly filled with the worst kind of regret. How had I let myself do something so stupid?

Saretha's eyes were closed. She looked peaceful. I thought to take it back and click it off, but I couldn't bear the thought of taking something else away from her. The song ended, and the next one began. Eggs Eggs sang "Your Word." Saretha let it play. After each song, my body went rigid. Finally, after all six played through, my fear was realized. Bridgette Pell spoke:

"Nine more playbacks. To purchase more plays, double-click now. $28.99 for three rotations," she said without emotion.

Birdo & Neckfat came on again. Saretha and Sam didn't react. They had no idea whose voice spoke through the tiny device. I breathed out, believing the worst of it was over. It wasn't like Bridgette Pell would wish herself a happy birthday. Yet my stomach stayed in knots. The sound of her voice in our room seemed so wrong.

Saretha let it play through the evening until all the rotations were done. Bridgette Pell's voice came on one last time: *"No more playbacks. To purchase more plays, double-click now. $28.99 for* *three rotations.*" I felt sick to my stomach. Her flat tone sounded utterly defeated. Her final message repeated, again and again.

Saretha said, "That's not such a bad deal," which cost her $18.95.

Sam got up and threw the player in the trash. Saretha didn't react at all.

The voice stopped. The player was programmed to sense it had been thrown away. It fizzled in the trash, destroying it-self. Sam sat back on his bed and looked out the window. I'd never felt further from him. I craved words to explain myself. This wasn't what I had wanted at all.

I should have gone to sleep. I could have fit a few hours in, but Bridgette Pell's voice haunted me, and I found it hard to maintain my hatred for her. She'd had options, unlike Beecher, but they were options she couldn't see.

My body felt keyed up. I tried not to look angry or upset as I got up, got dressed. Sam didn't ask where I was going, which was worse than if he had. I slowly and quietly left the apartment and went outside, feeling sure nobody cared where I went or what I did.

BLISSBERRY DELIGHT: $29.98

I was going to walk to Malvika Place and try to get in, right through the front doors, but I only walked a block before I realized that was a laughable plan. I was letting frustration get the better of me. I had already acted rashly, and what good had that done? There would be guards. There would be questions. I would be far better served to enter through the roof, but Malvika Place extended outside the dome. How could I get up there?

I realized it wouldn't be smart to linger outside too long while I figured this out. I had not forgotten being dragged into that alley. I felt the barely perceptible scar on my chin, running my finger across the bump where the skin had knit slightly imperfectly. Margot's Phisior™ bandage had done most, but not all, of its job.

Across the wide ring with its racing cars, the outer shops were still lit. They would be open for another hour or so. They looked inviting—they were designed to—but I knew better than to head that way. I could only imagine how fast I would be kicked out for a lack of means, or hounded about my silence, or arrested for some trumped-up infraction. I could not even take refuge in a movie because I would not be able to agree to the theater's Terms of Service before entering.

A block ahead of me, Thomkins Tower beckoned. It was only seven stories tall and not so towerlike. The yellowed, opaque window in Mrs. Stokes's room was lit above me. Once again, I could think of no other place to be.

I climbed the stairs and made my way to her door. I pressed Mrs. Stokes's buzzer and waited. I wondered what she would think of my tiny, stupid theft if she ever found out about it. Would she approve? Would she be disappointed?

I pressed the buzzer again. I wondered if she knew about Bridgette Pell. Without a screen, how did she get her news? I hoped she didn't know what had happened. I think it would have made her feel sadder.

By the time I was ready to press her buzzer a third time, I sensed something was wrong. Why hadn't she come to the door? Was it possible she wasn't home? I buzzed again, insistently. I banged on the door, since I couldn't call to her. Behind me, another apartment door opened. A girl with skin a little darker than mine looked out from the doorway. Her eyes were big and green. I didn't recognize her from school, but she didn't look much older than me. She shook her head imperceptibly and then retreated inside.

I couldn't ask what this meant, and I doubt she could have afforded to say. I listened for movement from inside Mrs. Stokes's apartment, but I heard nothing. Where could she be?

I decided to wait. I sat in the hall with my back to her door. My body settled down a little, and a giant yawn escaped from me. I closed my eyes and dropped my head to my knees.

I imagined stealing a book for Mrs. Stokes. I imagined pilfering an orange for Sam. My thoughts clouded into dreams and back to desires for all the things we could have that might make life better. Then I thought of Kel and felt another pang of regret for taking the iChit™ player. I felt so stupid for that choice.

Unease threaded through my dreams as Kel chastised me for stealing, or thinking of stealing, or wearing boots that clicked and thudded on roofs. Margot whispered that she knew I was a thief, and Henri shook his head and said he'd been wrong to love me. I couldn't defend myself. Even in my dreams, I had no voice now.

"Speth?"

I awoke with a start. Mandett Kresh stood over me, looking puzzled. In his hand was a shopping bag filled with UltraGrain Harvest™ Bars. He looked to the door and then back at me.

"Is she…?" His voice trailed away. He tried the buzzer, but I think he knew there would be no answer. The door across the hall had clicked open again.

"Where is she?" Mandett asked the girl with the green eyes.

The girl shook her head, pitifully, the same way she had with me. Mandett's face contorted and his shoulder sagged with the weight of the bars. Food, I realized, he was bringing to Mrs. Stokes.

"I get it, but this?" he said, loosely zipping his lips. "It isn't working." He sat down, his back to Mrs. Stokes's door.

The girl across the hall slipped back inside.

"I'm going to wait," he said. Then, after a few moments, he asked, "You think she'll be back?" When I didn't answer, he answered himself. "Maybe."

I couldn't tell if he was trying to needle me, or if this was a habit of his. He peered over at my Cuff. "I give her an hour."

I looked down to check the time. My throat grew suddenly tight. I was an hour late for meeting my team. My heart started thumping. How had I let this happen? I jumped up, scrambling for the stairs, and nearly toppled over myself as I decided first to go down, then up—and then worried I wouldn't be able to get through the rooftop door.

I burst out, finding it not only unlocked, but without so much as a handle. I took running jumps across the rooftops and made for my locker.

Kel had never discussed what would happen if I was late. She probably did not consider it an option. My back grew wet and tingly as I changed. I raced through the city, panicked I had made a terrible mistake.

I dropped onto the roof of the Mandolin Inks™ building where we were supposed to meet. The rooftop was deserted. How long had they waited? Had they waited at all?

I scanned in every direction, looking for the nearly invisible signs of the team. I saw nothing. The roof offered no clue about what direction they might have gone, or if anyone had even been there.

An hour passed. I paced the roof, biting my knuckles, worrying about what would happen now, and what had happened to Mrs. Stokes and what would become of all of us. I scanned the city over and over, trying not to think the worst.

What if Kel knew about the iChit™ player? What would she do? An icy chill ran down my spine. If Kel knew what I had done, and then I didn't show up for our meeting, what picture would that paint of me?

Even though it was foolish, I picked the lock on the roof door and scrambled down into the Mandolin Inks™ building, hoping to find a Squelch.

I had no Pad. I had no idea if the Squelch existed, and even if one did, and I could find it, what good did I think that would do? Did I really believe Kel, Henri and Margot had been sitting below me in a Squelch for three hours? That made no sense.

Heart pounding, I returned to the roof and considered my options. I could wait and hope they would come for me, or—what? I dropped my head in my hands. What else could I do? Give up?

So I waited. I waited and hoped my punishment would be to spend the night twenty stories up under threat of losing my job. I dreaded the lecture Kel would give when it was all over, but more than that, I feared she wouldn't come.

What if I never saw them again? What if I had blown my only chance to keep my family together? It was almost too much to imagine.

I sat for hours, until the dark, translucent gray of the dome flushed blue, then pink. As the colors changed, signaling dawn, the dregs of my hope ebbed away. The dome flared orange as the sun crested the distant horizon. A nauseating pit hardened in my gut. They truly weren't coming.

My limbs were cold in the damp morning air. The city slowly woke around me, oblivious and unconcerned with me and my silence.

I forced myself to believe the Placers would find me again. Kel or Margot or Henri, I thought, might be watching right now, and I took comfort in that hope. Without them, I had nothing.

It would end, I told myself, with a flashing dot in my vision, or with Henri swooping down and pulling me away to follow. But then any hope I might have had was obliterated.

An Ad popped up on my Cuff, glowing and cheerful—a swirl of girly violets and pink offering me a better-smelling life with Jasminell™ Antiperspirant. I was ripe from panic, effort and worry; any Cuff could sniff that. But this meant something worse. Somewhere in the city, Kel must have finished the night's Placement and canceled my contract. My Placer's protection against random Ads popping up was at an end. I was finished.

DISREMEMBERED: $30.99

I could not work out the details of exactly what had happened. The broad strokes weren't a mystery. I was certain Kel would not cut me off just for being late. She knew about the theft. I stole, then failed to show up.

Wasn't she curious about why I'd done it? Did she really believe I'd take something so meaningless and then slink off, never to return? The idea insulted me. How could she even be certain it was me? Maybe what pushed her over the edge was knowing I would not explain. If she had any impulse to give me the chance to explain, she knew it would only be rewarded with silence and a couple of centimeters of shrug.

Did Henri fight to keep me in? Did Margot make excuses? Did it matter in the end? Ads popped up on my Cuff all morning, layering on top of each other with what felt like pent-up eagerness, reminding me of what I had lost. I ignored them. I didn't *have* to look at them, just like I didn't *have* to speak. The only control I had was over those few things I could choose not to do.

I barely let myself think about what might have become of Beecher's grandmother. It sickened me to imagine what would happen when they discovered her Cuff in its half-burnt state.

Would they hold her liable for all those years? What could they prove? What punishment would they offer worse than the prison her freedom had made?

There was nothing I could do about it. I only had one path available to me now, and it led to Malvika Place. I would bring Sam there or, if I had to, I would drag Carol Amanda Harving kicking and screaming back to our home. I purposely ignored the idea my dreams had offered, to kill her, but my heart knew that if she did not exist, our lives would be better for it. My prospects were not good, but I still had my equipment and my Placer skills. I couldn't reach her roof, but I could smash open a window or, if I was more thoughtful about the plan, I could pry one open.

My only advantage now was that I had nothing to lose.

I sat with Saretha all day while she watched one news report after another. I hadn't noticed that her hair, usually so silky and Ad-worthy, had slipped into an oily and unkempt public domain mess.

Media coverage of the Silents had abruptly ceased. There were no more reports about Bridgette Pell or me, or anyone else who had gone quiet. It was like we'd never existed.

"They were covering it all day yesterday," Saretha sniffed. Her tone reminded me of Mrs. Harris. It was an awful thing to hear her once-pleasant voice sullied by our Custodian's pettiness. Had she picked it up from that awful woman because she had no one else to talk to? Was my silence to blame?

I wanted to say her name—*Saretha*. I'd always liked the sound of it. I couldn't hug her or console her, and I felt like my body might break under the weight of all our troubles.

My silence wasn't entirely to blame. If I'd done what was

expected and read my speech, there would still be an ever-growing rift between us. Instead of the words I refused to speak, it would have been the words I could not afford. If this day was before—before *her* Last Day and paying for words—I would have cozied up beside her on the couch, and she would have hugged me and chatted and given me advice. I would have ignored what she said, or most of it. Saretha always thought she knew best, even if the advice she gave was just repeating something she'd seen in a film or an Ad. I would have been annoyed, but also glad that she was looking out for me.

Saretha did a search for *Silents,* and the result came back blank, like the word itself didn't exist—except, of course, that she was charged a hefty fee for typing it.

I worried there might be some connection between my being kicked off the team and the sudden change in news coverage. I didn't think Kel could make something like this happen—she didn't have that kind of power. But I worried that my actions had triggered something.

I watched with Saretha, hoping to glean something. I dreaded seeing news of Mrs. Stokes, but when any failed to materialize, I felt more unease than relief.

The sudden disappearance of coverage was like a coordinated effort to make it seem like the Silent movement had never existed.

Maybe it hadn't. I had no idea how many Silents there might have been, or how many might have tried and given it up. It sure seemed like the group was growing. But whatever the numbers, what did it matter? What could we do? None of us spoke, or communicated with each other. Mandett had just demonstrated how ineffective and infuriating the silence could be. The media had treated the Silents like a sinister movement, but none of us could lead. None of us could plan. We could not even say *hello* to one another. Where could a movement like that go? What could it accomplish?

I almost had to laugh at the strategy of writing us off. The Media and the Rights Holders seemed to have decided that if they ignored us, it would be as if we'd never existed. I tried to believe that could be a good thing. At least I would be left alone. But whatever progress I'd made, and whatever confusing message I'd sent, would be forgotten.

Sam returned home at dinnertime. He saw me staring blankly into the screen with Saretha and immediately sensed something was wrong. I turned and watched his face struggle, helpless to identify the problem.

It crossed my mind to bring Sam to a Squelch. I knew where a dozen could be found, peppered throughout the city. I could sneak him in, seal the door and maybe I could tell him everything. I longed for that. Maybe I should give up that piece of my silence, at least for him.

Sam printed up our meals. He gave me extra Huny®, a small luxury Saretha insisted on ordering, even though we no longer received a sponsor discount. Whatever upset Sam harbored about the iChit™—wherever he thought it came from, and whatever he thought I'd done to get it—he had forgiven me.

"They pulled the zippered lips from the public domain this morning," Sam said. My eyes went wide.

"I wish they'd done that before your Last Day," Saretha said, a little teary.

Sam's face broke into a weak grin. "You must really be getting under their skin," he said to me.

"Horrible," Saretha said. Sam's head started shaking even before she was charged.

"It's awesome," Sam said, building on his own enthusiasm. Saretha turned. "People were using it everywhere. It's like—a thing."

He didn't have the word for what it was. *Revolt*, I thought. *Revolution*. We were only taught those words in school, in reference to events so old and mythological I found it hard to distinguish between the founding of our country and the labors of Hercules. It was hard to imagine anything I could do would actually be—a thing.

Sam was looking at me, a sparkle in his eyes. He had not just forgiven me; he was *proud* of me. I think he looked up to me. I felt terrible for not seeing it sooner. Would he feel the same way if I spoke to him now?

"I saw Mrs. Nince today," Sam said to us both. "I almost didn't know it was her. She got her face resmoothed, but it's full of pinched lines, like she's made of old taffy." He laughed.

"Probably will have to do that to my face," Saretha said without emotion.

Sam's cherub features emptied of humor and flashed with a hate he was too young to have. I could feel Carol Amanda Harving's name dart through his mind. I ached to tell him I had a lead on how to find her, but I couldn't. If I took him aside in a Squelch and spoke, I would betray everything he was proud of.

Outside, day had turned to night, and I had barely noticed.

The screen droned on before us. Sam recovered himself and let his mind drift. The hour grew late, and Saretha turned to me.

"Don't you have somewhere to be?"

"Saretha!" Sam admonished her. She shrugged a full shrug, not the sad kind I could only manage if I held it under two centimeters.

"We aren't supposed to notice?" Saretha asked.

I burst out into an absurd bray of laughter. *Really?* Saretha wanted to bring this up now?

"It doesn't seem worth spending the family budget on," Sam said, flicking her Cuff with his fingers. Saretha slumped down deep in the couch and glared straight ahead.

She didn't know it, but she was right. There was no point in waiting any longer. It was time for me to go find Carol Amanda Harving.

THE UPWARD CLIMB: $31.97

I had to enter Malvika Place on the seventy-seventh floor. From there, I could travel up through the inside of the building. It was a reckless idea without Kel's Pad, but I didn't see a choice.

I was able to shoot a line from a nearby rooftop to the sixtieth floor, but the rest of the way up was a grueling, nerve-racking climb with suction and magnetic boots. I had to will my hands to keep steady. My stomach was in knots. One slip could kill me, and my team wasn't here to catch me.

Kel, I'm sure, would have thought what I was doing was foolish. In a way, it was easier for me to go on now that I didn't have to think about disappointing her and the team. If it mattered to her what I did, she wouldn't have drummed me out of the Placers.

As I peeled one cup off the glass and replaced it higher up, I thought about how Henri would have helped if I had asked. Henri would have done anything for me, I think. I wondered if Margot was glad now that I was gone, and the way was clear for her to coyly needle him until he finally noticed her.

I looked down at the lines of the building gathering in perspective, far below, and was dizzied by the thought of Sam so high. I couldn't bring him this way. But I was doubtful I could get through into the lobby. If I couldn't bring him to her, I would have to bring Carol Amanda Harving to him. Could I get her to our home, so she could speak to Sam and Saretha and see what she had done? I had no idea how I was actually going to manage that without words. I could take her hand and lead her, but it didn't seem realistic to think she would be led. I could use sleep gas; I still had the canister. It would be far better than the murderous nightmare that itched in my brain.

I grew angry thinking about how unlikely it was that Carol Amanda Harving would do the right thing—especially if I had to kidnap her. But if appealing to her sense of right and wrong didn't work, she might be intimidated by the fact that I had found her.

I was wasting my time trying to work it out while dangling on the side of her building. I had to focus on getting inside—though I had no reason to think she would even be home.

When I finally reached the seventy-seventh floor, the dome was near enough that I could touch it. The porous surface of the Aeroluminum® looked as insubstantial as smoke. Three feet beyond was a night sky I had only seen recreated on screens.

I broke the magnetic seal around a hallway window and swung it gently open, relieved I didn't have to smash any glass. The lights were off. I listened carefully, but all I could hear was my heart pounding and a gentle hiss of air cycling through the building's vents. I dropped lightly inside, closed the window and listened again. I knew I was in one of four apartments on this floor; I remembered the layout. Everything was soft brown carpet and wide leather couches. I prayed no one was home.

The window locked behind me with a soft tick. I held my breath and moved into the room. In my pack I carried two leftover boxes of Downy® fabric softener, a small pedestal and a track light. I took one out. I placed it on a table in case an unseen camera had its eye on me. I didn't know if this would truly work as a cover, but it was my only option.

Where's your team? I could imagine someone asking if I was caught. A Product Placer should never be caught! The amusing thing was that, if this ever was to occur, a Product Placer is instructed not to speak. That, at least, I could easily do. It would be better to be a humiliated Product Placer than arrested for attempted kidnapping.

I made it into the hall quickly. Now I was at greatest risk. I could not be seen in the main area. A Product Placer would have no reason to be out here, fabric softener or no. My counter security gear knocked the cameras into a looped feed.

Going up on the elevators seemed risky. What if someone was coming home late? On the other hand, the stairs might be worse. No one who lived in this building would use them, so there was no chance of bumping into someone, but they could be rigged for motion, or heat, which my systems wouldn't suppress. I didn't have the benefit of Kel's schematic; only the skills I had learned in my short time working with the team.

I stopped at the three elevators and watched. The central one was in motion. I waited. It didn't stop. This building had 108 floors, so the odds that they would stop here, on floor 77, were low.

Unless I had been seen.

I panicked and pressed the call button, then quickly realized that was a mistake. I balled my fist in frustration and held
my breath. I wasn't a spy. I don't know what I was. Maybe I
was a spy, just not a very good one. No one should have been
able to see me with the loop. I relaxed my breathing. Nothing would come from panicking. I had to keep my cool.

I crossed my fingers, praying one of the other two elevators would begin to move, called by me. Neither did. The
system sent what was closest. The indicator crept up: *60, 61,
62...* If it was traveling above me, it would stop here, and I
would be seen by whoever was inside. *63, 64, 65...* I quickly
considered rushing back to the apartment I'd come from. I
could hide inside and wait silently in the dark. *66, 67...*

It paused on 67. I could imagine some drunken Affluents
staggering off and stumbling down the hall to their posh
apartment. It was nearly 4:00 a.m. I pictured them in my
head, waited for their doors to close. Maybe they were even
drunker than I imagined. Another second passed, two, and
then, *68, 69, 70...*

Hopefully the car was empty now. *71, 72, 73...* I had no
way of knowing. What if it was filled with people? I stepped
back. *74, 75, 76...* What if someone held a fabulous party
down on the fiftieth floor, and now all the disgorged revelers
were heading upward? I held my breath and pulled out my
lock pick, keeping my eyes fixed on the elevator.

The doors opened with a ping: 77.

The elevator was empty. I rushed forward, pressed the button for 89, and up I went.

SIMULACRUM: $32.99

There were only two apartments on the eighty-ninth floor. According to the schematic I'd seen, they both were huge. Carol Amanda Harving's was apartment A. I didn't need a map to identify it. Her side of the hall was lined with artwork and flowers and, on either side of the door, life-size pictures of her looking tall and lean, covered in diamonds and sparkly gowns. In one photograph, she stood in front of an Ebony Meiboch™ Triumph, a sleek, absurdly luxurious car with thin flame-orange highlights that cut through the matte darkness of its surface. It was like lava cracked through black stone.

I knew this exact car. Everyone knew it. It belonged to Silas Rog.

In the other photo, she stood on the red carpet, bare-armed in a slinky, luxurious, diamond-studded silk dress, her neck draped with strands and strands of pearls. She had so much, it seemed, that her prosperity had spilled out beyond her apartment walls.

Her pictures infuriated me. My clothes were damp and cold from sweat, but coal-like hatred warmed me. It should have been Saretha up here. Had their positions been reversed, Saretha would have treated Carol Amanda Harving with far more kindness. It seemed entirely unfair. Carol Amanda Harving's eyes were cold and lifeless. Fruitlessly glaring at the hallway shrine she had made to herself, I realized Carol Amanda Harving's advantage: she was empty, soulless and without compassion. It was easy for her to let Saretha be destroyed. I could see it in the chill of her icy blue eyes.

I shook myself. If I let my anger grow, I worried what I might do when I got inside. I forced myself to focus. I wasn't here to hurt her. I was here to make her understand. It was pointless to meditate on how—I needed to act.

But I suddenly had a feeling she wasn't there. Something about the hallway air seemed stale and unlived in. The carpet looked untouched. But maybe that was what I wanted to believe. I told myself she could be anywhere—filming, vacationing, living in one of a dozen homes in any dome she liked. How many, I wondered, had she seen?

If she was gone, that might be easier. It felt safer. I could look through her home for evidence that might prove her birthday was a lie, or that she used drugs, or for anything else I might use against her. And I wouldn't need to speak—or hurt her.

I couldn't let myself hope too much. I had to prepare to face her, right now, and whoever might be with her.

The door unlocked after an undue amount of fiddling with its magnetic innards. A heavy clunk released as a thick metal bolt retracted. The door slid open, and the room came into focus through the darkness. Something about it felt very, very wrong.

There was a couch in the center of an enormous room, and—that was all. I peered inside. Carol Amanda Harving's apartment had one couch, facing out toward the apartment's gargantuan window, and nothing more. How was this possible? Was she some Buddhist star who wanted to lead a perfect, uncluttered life? Did she even live here? Was this just a space for her to entertain? The whole apartment reminded me of an oversized Squelch, not a home.

I stepped inside, puzzled and somehow angrier than before. My body tensed. Who was this woman? The door slid closed behind me. The window, which in theory overlooked the dome, was black as night. I walked toward it, silent in the darkness. It was opaque. I touched it with my hand.

At once, it clicked to life with enormous, vivid, three-dimensional depictions of the natural world. It cycled through images of forests, seashores and deserts. From where I stood, everything looked oddly distorted. The view was calibrated specifically for the couch.

The apartment had no bedroom, or kitchen or bathroom. It was literally just one enormous, empty room, like a theater. I looked for hidden buttons or seams in the walls that might give some indication there was something else, yet I knew the dimensions well enough to know there was nothing more. Her walls were clean and smooth, with none of the ugly striations we had in our home from cheap printing.

The wall changed to a movie preview, flat and two-dimensional, like a classic film, but this was a new remake of a film I'd seen two years before about a clever female spy.

A man sipped at a glass of wine, a twinkle in his eye, his head hung low as he eyed the woman across from him. The lights in the distance behind him were reduced to beautiful gold circles by the camera's blur. A soft, romantic rock guitar played beneath the scene.

"So, what is it you do?" The man smiled, head cocked charmingly to one side. I knew the actor, Martin Cross. He had been digitally de-aged to look younger.

The woman across from him flashed a smile—Saretha's smile. It was Carol Amanda Harving. Her hair was dark now, like my sister's, though she was blonde in some films, and often her skin was lighter. But her eyes were still the same— empty, ice-cold diamonds. She sipped some drink through a straw, coyly, and did not answer him. Instead, she reached out. In close-up, they held hands, fingers intertwined, probably hand models. Something did not match about it.

When the shot went wide, each actor's name floated slowly above their heads as the music grew louder. Carol Amanda Harving looked a little less like Saretha, probably because Saretha had put on some weight in her exile. Meanwhile, the actress looked muscled, but achingly thin. Her arms were like pencils, and yet they looked sleek and long, without the knobbiness you would expect. I wondered if they had a surgery for that. I shuddered at the thought of shaved bone.

I stepped closer to the window, looking closely at her hands. Even they looked thin and tiny in Martin Cross's grasp. How do you lose weight in your hands?

"Miss Dart." A thick, dark-skinned man was standing over them suddenly. He wore an all-black suit and sunglasses, even though it was night. "It's time." Martin Cross's character looked at the man with surprise. Carol Amanda Harving stood, and her small red dress flitted around her, tight across her tiny waist. Her boobs were bigger than the last time I'd seen her, but this wasn't any great surprise. She was now in a starring role. If she hadn't requested a little plastic surgery, the studio would have insisted on it.

"Sorry," she said, blowing Martin a kiss. She ran to the balcony and did a flip over the edge. The stunt bothered me. It reminded me of the video footage of Bridgette Pell. It didn't look entirely real, but that didn't really lessen the sting. They often switched to CGI for stunts. The studio wouldn't want to be sued for a broken leg or chipped nail.

Then again, none of it looked quite right. The music rocked harder, drums pounding like an engine as Carol Amanda Harving shot guns, launched grenades and generally unleashed chaos on a bunch of swarthy-looking villains the movie put in her path.

I had to laugh at how sweaty she wasn't. Here I was, after a long, slow climb, drenched and chilled by my own perspiration, but characters like her, in movies, never pitted with sweat.

I looked for a way to turn off the screen, worried the sound might wake the neighbors. On the off chance the next unit was occupied, I had no idea who I might be dealing with.

I was a foot away from the screen when Carol Amanda Harving's giant face filled it, her cold eyes the size of softballs, her irises wide and inviting. I tapped at the screen and let out a breath in relief when it shut off. It went black, with no hint of the view outside. Why have no view? Wasn't that the point of being up so high? I felt a pang of disappointment that I wouldn't get to see the ocean. I had always wanted to see it. They say the water touches the eastern edge of the dome.

I scanned the empty room and realized there was absolutely nothing to find. There was no Carol Amanda Harving to demand answers from. There was no evidence of any kind. She was probably in Hollywood. Maybe she just kept this apartment for fun, in case she wanted to visit or have a party. More likely still, this was just a tax thing that I didn't understand. All I had to examine were the few garish mementos left outside, like territory she had marked.

My nerves calmed, replaced with gloom. This was a dead end. I couldn't help Saretha. I couldn't help myself. All the risk was for nothing.

At least I didn't have to think about hurting the actress to convince her to help us. I returned to the door and had to pick the lock again to get out. It unsealed and slid open. Outside, like sentinels, were the two enormous framed photos, larger than life, in thick, welded metal frames built right into the wall. Her smile was so wide, I imagined it hurt to be that joyful.

Slowly my anger rose again. I wanted to destroy her. If she had been there, what would I have done? I bit my lip. I couldn't hurt her, but I could ruin these pictures—these stupid, egotistical photographs. It was foolish, exactly the sort of thing Kel would insist I not waste time with. I could have smashed the frames and ripped them from the walls, but I wanted her to know *she* was hated.

I took out my knife, half-ready to carve a mustache under her nose, devil horns on her head, to scrape away her eyes. It was pointless and reckless—the glass was too thick. Plus I'd be charged twenty different ways. The best I could actually do was stab the glass, and what would be the point? Sam would have appreciated the thought, but he would never know.

I glared at her visage, contemplating my pitiful revenge,

when something caught my eye. Her skin showed some small imperfections, a mottling of color like any other person. I don't know what else I was expecting. It was a photograph, not a polished movie still. I saw moles and freckles. I saw skin with warmth, and it surprised me, because she never seemed quite real.

But it was the sight of her upper arm that stopped me cold. An inch or two above her right elbow was a faint, crescent-moon-shaped scar, exactly like the one Mrs. Nince had given Saretha.

My brain couldn't process it at first. I stared. What did this mean?

I studied the photo carefully. The moles and freckles looked familiar. How could they look familiar? Were they the same as Saretha's? That was impossible.

My skin began to crawl with a dawning realization.

I was never going to meet Carol Amanda Harving face-to-face. I could never confront her. She could never apologize. She could never help us, for one simple reason.

She didn't exist.

Carol Amanda Harving was a computer-generated fiction, constructed of pixels and polygons from who-knows-how-many corporate scans of my sister. She was less substantial than the air in my lungs. It was the only explanation for that crescent-shaped scar above her elbow.

My God, this was the *perfect* Lawsuit, one even Arkansas Holt couldn't lose. A frantic hope rose in me—a furious glee. If I could prove she didn't exist, not only would Saretha be free, but we would be rich. Our parents could come home. Our family would be whole again.

My parents.

We hadn't heard from them since our chat just after my Last Day. We hadn't told them about Carol Amanda Harving. There was no point. What could they do? It would only cost the family more money to talk about it.

My heart pounded. Who had done this? Who had created Carol Amanda Harving from images of my sister and then sued us for what they had stolen? The gall of it was almost admirable.

Silas Rog came to mind. If it wasn't him, then whoever had done it had Silas Rog for a Lawyer. Silas Rog, who had never been defeated.

There is a first time for everything, the voice inside my head said. The phantom sound of it soothed me. Silas Rog's resources were near bottomless, but how could he possibly win this? He would lose his first case, and I would be the cause. Nothing would bring me more joy.

ESCAPE: $33.99

Sam and Saretha were asleep when I got in. I slipped into bed and lay awake, thinking about how to share my news. In the darkness, I buzzed with excitement and a secret I wished I couldn't keep. This was a problem. My silence may have been inspirational, but it was painfully impractical. I could not speak what I knew. I needed to show them.

Was Saretha's crescent scar visible in any of Carol Amanda Harving's movies? Almost certainly not. They would dodge away anything that wasn't absolutely flawless, even on an actual person. I might be able to find a candid picture, like the one in her hall, but I had no way to search. How could I find one with the exact texture, from the right angle and light, and with enough resolution to show the stolen skin?

The only place I could be sure to prove my point was eighty-nine floors up in a posh, high-security building. I could break in again and take my chances with not getting caught. I could make it, but I couldn't imagine a way to get Sam and Saretha up there. Not alone.

Beside me, Saretha snored softly. Her face looked sad even as she slept. I wanted to shake her awake and tell her there was hope. We had a chance that could save us.

Who rented that apartment in Malvika Place on the eighty-ninth floor? Was it ever occupied? I wondered what the doormen thought, knowing this famous actress lived in their posh building but was never seen. Did the staff think she was a recluse? Did they imagine she was too busy filming to enjoy the luxury of their amenities?

Then it hit me. For all intents and purposes, Saretha *was* Carol Amanda Harving. Why couldn't she just walk right into Malvika Place? They might even hold open the door! I could picture them falling all over themselves, delighted at a rare sighting of the starlet. It was her apartment. It was her home. What could they possibly say?

The idea of turning everything around on Rog or whoever was behind it made me feel giddy. I just needed to figure out what to do about her Cuff.

Cuffs and Ads ping wirelessly, back and forth, everywhere you go, verifying the identity, bank account, credit and history of the consumer wearing it. This all happens so fast that the system can pull up a tailored Ad before you can blink. If Saretha stepped outside, the first Ad that pinged her Cuff would flag Butchers & Rog's DESIST notice and send an alert right to their legal team. Police would descend like flies. Saretha would be arrested within minutes.

As if it did not want to be forgotten, my own Cuff lit up with an Ad for Ambiex™. Little Zs floated silently over the screen, telling me I could be asleep in minutes. Below, the Ad listed the thousand things that could go wrong.

I flicked it away. It floated back from the edge, like it was trying to soothe me, reminding me I was eligible for a free

Cuff ring that would inject Ambiex™ *whenever sleep's outside your reach,* the words around the shape of moonlit clouds.

I turned over, closed my eyes and buried my face in my pillow so I couldn't see the glow. I wished I had taken Henri up on the offer to remove it long ago. What did I need a Cuff for?

My eyes popped open. The room was lit by the scant, unyielding glow of the Ambiex™ Ad.

Henri! I thought. I said his name in my mind. Henri could remove my Cuff. He could remove Saretha's Cuff. She could walk through the city undetected by the system, straight to Malvika Place. All she had to do was follow my lead and not speak.

Beside me, Saretha stirred in the light, and I turned the Cuff away.

I gently put my head down and closed my eyes again. I pictured the outline of Henri's apartment on Kel's Pad. He'd shown me exactly where to find him. My breathing slowed. My muscles relaxed. I would go the next day, after sundown and before Placements. I fell asleep, thinking of the small metallic-blue device he kept in a small pocket in his pack.

HENRI: $34.99

I dreamed of rain. Blue teardrop shapes falling. I'd never felt rain in real life. My father says it has a cool sting. He says we are better off in the dome, away from assaults on the skin.

I've seen rain in movies thousands of times. I've taken showers. But the rain in my dream was different. It was cool and landed in a light, chaotic rhythm on my skin.

I woke, swallowed the day's words and tried to hold on to the calm of my dream and the hope of my plan. But someone was buzzing our door, forcing it all away.

"Speth!" I heard a voice cry out, muffled from the hall. The hairs on my neck raised.

"What the hell?" Sam croaked, turning over. "Who is that?"

Saretha slept on, undisturbed.

Sam turned on the screen. Mandett Kresh was pounding on the door.

"Speth!" he called again. A note of miserable panic sounded in his voice. I stood and hesitated. What did he want?

Sam staggered past me and opened the door.

"You shouldn't be here," Sam said, yawning, glancing back at Saretha.

"They took her," he whispered, shaking his head.

I blinked at him. Sam closed the door behind him.

"Who?" Sam asked. Saretha stirred and pulled the covers over her head. Mandett was briefly distracted.

"Mrs. Stokes," he said. "Beecher's grandmother."

"Beecher," Sam muttered. I didn't understand why Mandett had come to tell us—to tell me.

Mandett's head kept shaking. His face contorted, struggling through a thought he couldn't finish. I wondered if he even knew why he'd come.

He finally spoke. "She said you were special. A perfect secret keeper. A fly in their ointment."

He stared at me with hope, like I could do something, but what? What had she meant?

Sam shook him off. "Dude, what are you telling *us*?" he asked, moving back to the door.

I wished I could tell all of them I was on the cusp of doing *something*. If I could prove what they had done with Saretha's image...

"Aren't you going to do something?" Mandett demanded.

My thought trailed away. What *could* I do? My best plan might save our family, but no one else. I couldn't help Mrs. Stokes. I wasn't going to change how things were.

I closed my eyes slowly, to show I was grateful to him, even if I was helpless. I don't know if he understood. A knot lay under my heart, but I couldn't worry about the entire city, or the system that controlled us. I had to do what I could for my family. It was all that I had, and it was very little.

Mandett peered at me, trying to comprehend. His face crumpled, and something in him seemed to break. He put his fingers to his lips, almost as if he was asking if what he was doing was right. I realized that Mandett's Last Day wasn't far off. He zipped his lips unsteadily and waited just a moment, as if it might work like a magic spell. When nothing more happened, he left, his face contorted in scorn and despair.

When evening came, I didn't travel far. I knew what I had to do. As the dome turned a grayish indigo, I swung down to a mid-ring building with a few small embellishments to set it apart from the stark buildings in the poorer neighborhoods. It looked well printed and had slim balconies that would have made Placement easy, which was probably the intent.

I dropped onto the roof and considered whether it was better to enter from there, or rappel down the windows to the twelfth floor. The city stretched out around me for miles. I wondered if Mrs. Stokes was still in it. You have to agree to ToS when you enter the city and when you leave. She wouldn't, but that wouldn't save her. Once she was Indentured, the company or Brand would agree on her behalf.

I took off my gloves and wiped my hands across my knees. I was sweating. My mask felt hot. I felt gross and self-conscious. It was just Henri I was going to see, but my nerves were jangling.

I looked over the edge. The windows were thin, and there was plenty of room for me to slip between them without being seen. I worked out which way was north and which side Henri's apartment would be on. I took a breath and rappelled down quick, before I thought too much about what I was doing. My plan wasn't fair to Henri, and part of me really didn't want to face that.

I found him sitting in a wide, comfortable-looking chair

inside. He had a book in his hands. The sight of it surprised me. Henri had a book?

It was bigger than the books I had seen in movies and shows. The cover had the number Nineteen Eighty-Four spelled out in silver foil. Under that was a scrawl of swirly letters I could not read. My heart beat a little faster. What should I do now? Knock on the glass?

Before I could decide, Henri's eyes peeked up over the pages and flashed with alarm, then surprise. He stood, put the book carefully on the chair, turned to an open glass security case on the wall where the book must have been kept, then turned back to the chair like he didn't know what he was doing. Finally, he turned to me. His wide smile broke across his face, muddled slightly by confusion as he crossed the room and opened the thin balcony door.

"What are you doing?" he whispered. It was just like Henri to ask a question, even though he knew I wouldn't answer. His Cuff charged him. It was weird hearing the telltale buzz from his arm—I'd only ever heard him speak in a Squelch.

I went in and took off my mask. My hair crackled with static. I smoothed it out, but could feel bits of my ragged pixie cut still standing on end.

I took stock of the room, looking for his backpack, then thought, *what kind of person does this make me?* Henri deserved my attention before I moved on to other things.

Henri was looking at my mask. He didn't say it, but I knew he was thinking I shouldn't be wearing it. I wasn't a Placer. Not anymore.

"Do you want to sit?" he asked. He picked up the book again, self-consciously, like it was something he shouldn't have. "It's licensed," he explained. "I have to renew soon." Maybe he was embarrassed by the extravagance of it.

His apartment was not very different from ours, though he lived alone, which meant he had been allocated three times as much space as Sam, Saretha or me. He had a couch, a counter and kitchen, and a giant wall-screen in roughly the same setup as ours. There was also the chair and, beside it, the open glass case. Without knowing what to do, I sat in the chair.

"Are you hungry?" he asked. "I have Mandolin Inks™."

A small pang for Tylenola Ram hit me. I'd completely forgotten about what she'd done, and had heard nothing about her condition. I microshrugged, which was as close as I could come to saying no, but unfortunately, it was also as close as I could come to saying yes. He looked at his book, then offered it to me. I took it. I hoped he would tell me something about the team or what had happened when I was late.

"Check the haircuts," Henri said, crossing the room.

I opened the book. It was filled with black-and-white pictures of kids doing things—playing soccer or basketball or tennis, out in the open sun. They played hockey and swam in pools and wore what looked like Olympic™ leotards for their gymnastics. There were kids laughing, and kids chatting with each other and kids sitting at desks looking forward. Kids leaned on books, looked in books and read books. There were books everywhere. They were discarded on desks and stacked carelessly on shelves. Books seemed like no big deal.

Henri printed out a hamburger, popping out the two spongy circles of bread and a darkly colored burger circle from a laser-perforated sheet, followed by a thinly printed slice of cheese. He assembled it all together, putting the extra outer bits into the printer's reclamation drawer. He offered it to me. I did not take it—a clearer way to say no. Henri shrugged, fully, and scarfed it down.

"I could have ordered something better, like a real plum," Henri said, chewing, "if I'd known you were coming."

My mouth watered a little, thinking of a real plum, imagining what it might be like. A pang of jealousy ran through me. Henri could afford a plum—and not just for himself. For me.

"What do you think?" he asked, tapping the book and talking to me like I was someone who could answer.

I didn't understand the book I was holding. It wasn't a story. It wasn't Laws. It wasn't history. It wasn't news. There were captions under all the pictures, like "Dee and Catherine share a good laugh on the way to class," and "The sophomores enjoy a school activity." I stared at the audacious waste of words, inked on the page for posterity.

Henri knelt down next to me and impatiently turned the pages, past grids of angled faces over expensive-sounding names, like Kim Hunter and Doug James. Then I saw a girl named Catalina Jimenez, and a longing washed over me. She didn't look like me, and it was hard to tell from the black-and-white image if our skin color was the same. I wasn't sure if our family had actually been named Jimenez, but I knew it hadn't always been Jime. I couldn't help but wonder—was this the girl who illegally downloaded music so long ago?

Henri wanted to show me the color pages. He was obviously proud. These pages showed more faces, with more amazing—and colorful—hair. These kids were older, all around eighteen, and each of them had four or five lines of text beneath their names, like they were important somehow.

I'd never seen something so fascinating and dull at the same time. Someone had put tremendous effort into documenting a school year in 1984. I didn't know anything about that period of history. I knew there was a big war that century, but the specific story of it was not something my school could afford the rights to. All we needed to know was that the domes had put an end to war.

I tried to discern the greater reason Henri was showing me this book. He giggled and put a finger next to one girl's picture. Her hair was wild, the color of platinum, sticking out on each side like two Pegasus wings. Around her, everyone's hair looked incredible and strange, and beneath each picture was a beautiful name like Mark, Lewis, Sara or Claire, and under the name, a list of sports and activities, and then a phrase.

I looked at Henri. Was he really not going to tell me anything? He ran his finger down over one phrase and then another.

"We were born, born to be wild"

"Snorts & Slorts"

"Never call me Gordo"

"Cut the Jibba Jabba"

"I wandered lonely in a wood…"

Were these phrases they had each Trademarked? Was this a book of Affluents? Influents™? No. It was too old. Henri smiled. He ran his finger under a phrase below a boy wearing thick glasses on his face.

"Pretty cool, ya?"

He held it there and waited. It took me a minute to understand; Henri was choosing these words. His Cuff did not buzz. It was just like I had always heard. You could point to any word or phase or sentence. His eyebrows raised.

"You want to try?" he asked.

I had misjudged him. He wasn't just showing off with his book; he wanted me to use it to communicate. This wouldn't be like talking in a Squelch. It would hardly be like doing anything at all.

I scanned the page, considering. I didn't want to tell Henri "Make my day" or "Love ya, cutie." I wanted to know what Kel had said about me, or where he kept his small teardrop-shaped device, but the only question I could find was, "Where's the beef?"

That would not help.

I paged back to the front of the book, to the title page. *1984: Lincoln High School.* Longing filled me for the world to be a different way. Maybe not like it was for the kids of Lincoln, but with some of the freedom they had.

The book wouldn't help. Pointing to other people's words and letting those kids speak for me was not a solution. I closed it and put it back in Henri's hands.

I think his feelings were hurt. I just sat there, like the dud Margot said I was. He put a hand on my shoulder. I tilted my head just enough for my hair to brush against it, but not enough to be charged. I don't know why I did it, but it seemed to jostle him into saying something relevant.

"Kel's pretty mad," he said, standing and pulling the book away. "Did you really steal an iChit™ player?"

He put the book back behind the glass and closed the door. A light on the case flashed and then turned a steady, angry red.

"Why?" he asked me, as if I had said yes.

Even if I spoke, and even if I had the words, I don't think Henri would have understood. It was an embarrassingly foolish thing to have done. Henri didn't know what I wanted or needed to hear. Letting my hair brush his hand sent the wrong message. I had to get to the thing I needed. I held out my arm.

Henri looked at it. He saw the Cuff. His brow furrowed. *What does she want?* I could practically hear him think it. It took him a minute, but then he got it.

He crossed over to his closet and reached blindly inside. He pulled out his pack, and then, from its pocket, the blue, teardrop-shaped device. He made a swiping motion with it, to ask if I wanted my Cuff removed. I indicated nothing. I stood and swallowed and thought about Henri living alone. Did he have any family? Did he have any friends besides Margot and—I guess—me?

He took my hand. His hand was large and rough, and I could feel he was trying to be gentle. He swiped again, and my Cuff cracked open. He pulled it off. I realized I was holding my breath. I slowly let it out and breathed again.

The flesh on my arm where the Cuff had been felt prickly, cool and tender. A faint odor of moisturizer and old skin rose up. I stood and rotated my hand, like the muscle needed to stretch.

Henri waited for something more. *Now what?* We were both thinking the same thing. I looked at the metallic-blue device in his hand. I stood and took it from him. The weight of it surprised me. Henri took it back at once. He couldn't let me have it. He couldn't know why I wanted it, and it was his to account for.

Henri took a step closer, his chest in my face, and then he

hugged me. I did not expect it to feel so nice. Henri smelled warm and sweet. I wanted to hug him back, but I just let my head press against him. No Cuff would record me. I lifted my arms, but underneath everything, that odd, ripe smell of bound flesh kept reminding me of how we were all trapped. I thought of Saretha on her couch and Sam at the window, growing quieter each day. I thought of Margot and her music. I thought of Mrs. Stokes in a cell. Whatever comfort I might have wanted or needed, if I hugged Henri back, Margot would be hurt, and Henri would almost certainly make more of it than I wanted or could handle.

I pushed him back gently, trying not to be too harsh. Henri's face turned bright red.

"Kel didn't think you would come," he said, looking away.

They had discussed this? He picked up my open Cuff and turned it over in his hands like a bracelet.

"We kind of argued about you. She said none of us would ever see you again."

That felt horrible.

"But she said if I was right—if you showed up, it would demonstrate you were sorry."

He handed my Cuff back to me.

"I think she would give you another chance," he said.

Another chance? For what? He seemed amused by my confusion. I stretched my neck toward him, my eyes demanding that he explain better. He was doing a terrible job.

"Unless you really don't want to be a Placer anymore."

I flopped back in the chair. Was this really an option? Kel might forgive me?

"Margot said you'd come. *Henri, she will be at your apart-*

ment before you are even home," Henri said, imitating Margot's oddly exact phrasing. "I guess it took a little longer," he added with a shrug.

Why did Margot think I would go to Henri and not to her? If I was going to apologize, or beg my way back, she would have been the logical choice. She couldn't have anticipated what I planned to do—but she could have assumed I liked Henri the way Henri liked me.

I sat, blinking, deep in thought. Henri zipped his metallic blue Cuff remover back inside his pack and shaped the bag with his hands, like he was getting ready to go.

What should I do now? Go with him? Take the device by force? Beg him for it with my eyes? If I tried hard enough, Henri might put the device in my hands and suffer the consequences. Would Kel kick him off the team?

It had never occurred to me I might be offered *my* spot back.

Henri waited, and when I did not respond, he stepped closer, shrugged and held out his arms, as if to say, *Are you coming?* I looked at his bag. I *wanted* to go back to the group. Would they really have me? Henri wasn't exactly reliable at reading Kel's mood.

If she did let me come back, Kel would watch me like a hawk. If I wanted to get that little blue device, I would have to wait. I would have to be patient. My chest felt tight, thinking about it, unsure what was best. I didn't know if I could let Saretha wait. Yet, if I was a Placer, I would have far more options. Could I have my family back, and this, too?

I felt awful closing the Cuff back over my wrist. It seemed to squeeze tighter. I hated the idea that I would eventually betray poor Henri, even if I got away with it. The thoughts in my head grew louder as I tried to defend what I was doing. I told myself I could work it out so that no one ever knew. Weren't my reasons justified? If I was back with the Placers, I would at least stand a fighting chance of slipping it away, unnoticed, and I could return it before it was missed. I really wanted to hug Henri now, but I couldn't. Instead, I followed him out into the night.

REMORSE: $35.99

I was a mess when we arrived on the roof of the Rock™ Cola Bottling Company. Kel and Margot were waiting, laser-focused on my approach. I felt sick, but tried my best to look somehow less sweaty and shaky. A thick, sweet smell hung in the air.

Kel led us down to a spacious Squelch, rage blazing in her eyes. I wondered if maybe I had made a mistake. The expression behind her mask was harsher and more distant than when I'd first met her. That made sense; I hadn't disappointed her that first night. She immediately began pacing.

"You willfully, and with forethought, risked the employment and good standing of each member of this team," she rasped. Her use of chilly Legalese, combined with the fact she still had her mask on, made me shrink away. She stopped moving.

"You know that though, don't you? That's why you chose not to show up. You realized the gravity of what you'd done."

My lip was trembling. I put my hand there to stop it. I felt like I was five years old.

Margot and Henri hung by the door, motionless, watching.

"Speth," Kel said, jerking her mask off, "I've lost team

members before to the temptation to steal, but it was always something of real value, or meaning, like a book. What you did makes no sense!"

I couldn't explain it. I hated feeling like my actions were beyond my control.

"If you are ever going to speak, let it be now, because I need you to explain yourself."

Her eyes fixed on me, cool and dark. She waited. I swallowed from habit—and from fear. I had so much I wished I could say, so many questions I wanted to ask. But how could I waste my breath on something so petty? I didn't understand it myself. I wanted to know where Beecher's grandmother had been taken, and how Kel could live every day in a world she knew was so completely wrong. I wanted to explain about Saretha, and Carol Amanda Harving, and how the Cuff stood between my family and freedom.

I searched for some gesture I could make that would at least tell Kel I was sorry. My shame burned twice as hot knowing I still had to take Henri's device, no matter what came next.

The room was perfectly still, perfectly silent. Kel waited, unmoving as stone.

"My Lord, this is uncomfortable," Margot said. Henri looked at her, horrified. Kel still did not move.

What if I explained it all? What if I begged for their help? I wanted to so badly, it felt like I might burst. Kel could find a way. She could get Saretha to Carol Amanda Harving's apartment. Maybe Henri could carry her. Margot could take Sam. It wouldn't all be left up to me. But despite everything I wanted, I was not going to explain. No. I was sorry for it, but I would not speak. If I could control nothing else, I could control this.

Kel took out her Pad. She began furiously tapping at it. "I'm not going to make you promise this time. Vague gestures could mean anything. Instead, I'm going to make *you* a promise—if you steal from our sponsors or our targets, I won't just end your employment. I will sue so badly you'll *wish* Silas Rog was prosecuting."

"Damn," Henri said, breathless. Margot shushed him with a finger to her lips.

"If you can't handle that, fine—when the door opens, leave and never come back. Don't look for us, don't contact us, together or individually." She ran her hand over her head, like it would cool her down. "I'm not asking if you understand."

She opened up her bag and started laying out bottles of moisturizing cream. Her lecture was over. Without looking at her Pad, she waved it and said, "I'll clear you when we're tethered again."

I wiped my eyes. Some ugly part of myself picked her logic apart like a Lawyer, so I could promise to do as she asked. Did she choose her words carefully, or not carefully enough? I would never steal from a sponsor or a target again. That was exactly what she had asked. I would not repeat my mistake. Henri's little blue device wouldn't be plucked from a target's home. It didn't belong to a sponsor. It sat in a loophole between her words. I didn't know if that would matter to her in the end, or if she would care to work out the difference. In my mute protest, I would not be able to explain, nor did it matter. Though she didn't know it, she'd left me no choice but to stay. Whether I wanted to be part of the group or not, I needed Henri's device to free Saretha.

I knelt down and began to help Kel plan our Placement. I felt her body ease its tension by a hair, and I felt rotten for it. But I was back in the group for as long as I could last.

SCORN: $36.99

Penepoli Graethe showed up at our door the next morning. Her eyes were wet with tears.

"You can't come in," Sam said, opening the door a crack. I couldn't hear her response. She wasn't speaking, but she was still making noise. I pulled a jacket on over my nightclothes and went out to her. Sam crossed his arms and followed me into the hall.

Penepoli looked from Sam to me and back again with wild eyes. Her face was twisted with confusion, lips mashed tight. She made a wide gesture, a ring with her hands, traced in the air, and then walked her fingers into the space it had defined.

Sam and I looked at each other. "I don't know what that means," he said with a sigh. "Do you want to just tell us?"

Penepoli bit her lip, then zippered it and looked pitifully sorrowful. It was hard to believe that not very long ago, Penepoli, Nancee and I would talk, carefree, about nothing at all. It felt stupid, and beautiful, and sad to think of it. My hand reached out for hers, but I had to stop myself and pull it back. I couldn't get charged for a gesture now. I had no way to reach her.

"Mmmmhhm, mhhmm, mhmmm?" Penepoli tried, humming out what she wanted to say. Her brows wrenched up and she hunched down to my height, her lank hair falling forward.

"The fruit stripe garden?" Sam guessed, shaking his head.

Anguished, Penepoli spoke, but not fully. She whispered through clenched teeth, like a panicked ventriloquist.

"Mandett is rounding us up."

"Who is *us*?" Sam asked.

"The Silents!" Penepoli squeaked.

Sam looked at me. I didn't know anything about it. Had Mandett really gone silent? If he had, how was he getting people rounded up? Then I remembered that Mandett hadn't had his Last Day yet.

"He says we have to do more than not speak," Penepoli said, her lips straining to form all the words while keeping her mouth shut. "He wants us to show ourselves, prove we're here. He is asking—"

The sound of the elevator arriving stopped Penepoli. Her hand clamped to her mouth.

"I've said too much!" she mumbled under her fingers.

Sam rolled his eyes. The elevator doors opened, and Mrs. Harris stepped out, looking both irritated and pleased.

Penepoli dropped her hands, like she had been caught doing something illegal, and said, "Good morning, Mrs. Harris."

Mrs. Harris squinted at Penepoli, as if trying to recall her name. Then she addressed me, as if Penepoli were unimportant.

"Speth," she said coolly, "I need to speak with you. I have news."

Sam's gaze burned at her. He hated her unannounced visits. We all did.

"Mrs. Harris," Penepoli said with a nervous swallow. Mrs. Harris raised an eyebrow. "Do you know what happened to Nancee? You were her guardian, right?"

Mrs. Harris chewed on this question and sneered a little. "I *was*."

"Do you know what happened to her?" Penepoli asked again, sort of through her teeth.

"I do," she said, and then returned her gaze to me. "Does your friend understand I am not budgeted to speak with children who are not my charges?"

In lieu of answering, I glared at her and tried to match her coldness. Her sour face twisted with an ugly glee I had seen her wear only a few times before. She kept her eyes trained on me and answered Penepoli's question.

"Nancee has been Indentured within the city to a woman who can put up with the girl's insolent silence. It was challenging to place her. When someone selfishly refuses to speak, that puts all burden of speaking on the opposite party. My understanding is that Nancee is being trained to follow commands like you might teach a dog, which should solve most of the problem."

My mouth tightened.

"And appropriately punished if she fails to obey."

Pins and needles surged over me in a stomach-turning wave. I wanted to ask, *Where? Who with?* My lips longed to form the *W*, so I could have some answers, but I could not. I closed my eyes and imagined Kel's Pad. Could I type Nancee's name into it? Could I find her that way? I ached thinking of what she was enduring.

"I'm glad it upsets you," Mrs. Harris said. "I know it is difficult to hear, but this is what comes from insolence. Perhaps this will help you better decide on your future."

When she talked about my future, it felt like a place very far from where I stood. But I was beginning to think the future *was* where I stood. My decision had been made.

"Your friend can stop eavesdropping now." Mrs. Harris sniffed and ran her key card over our door. "I'd rather not spend my entire visit in this hallway."

"Should I find her?" Penepoli asked, wild-eyed. "Should I look for Nancee?"

Mrs. Harris narrowed her brows at Penepoli and pushed Sam and me inside. The door closed with Penepoli still gaping out in the hall.

"Your boyfriend's grandmother's been found out," she said to me, stalking inside and rubbing at her fingers like she was sharpening claws. "She had been keeping a rather disgusting secret."

Saretha didn't turn from the couch. She faced the screen and kept her attention fixed on a game show that let contestants vie for new Branding.

Mrs. Harris looked at my Cuff and then back at me.

"She sabotaged her Cuff," Mrs. Harris said.

I gritted my teeth against this twisting of the truth. I didn't suppose it would make any difference to Mrs. Harris that she hadn't actually sabotaged it.

"Belunda Stokes has been speaking for years without paying the Rights Holders. Apparently many of the neighborhood children knew about it—including *that* girl, I imagine." She jerked a thumb at the door and Penepoli beyond. "They

have been using her as a source of unregulated information."
She glared at Sam. Sam glared back.

"Speth," Mrs. Harris said, trying to imitate a reasonable
person. "It occurs to me that you may have fallen in with the
wrong element with her. Were you going to see her before
your celebration? Perhaps she is the source of all of this nonsense? Perhaps the Silents were her idea?"

She made an odd maneuver that I think was meant to imply
the zippered lips without paying the full service fee that was
now charged for it. She was still charged something. Her
Cuff buzzed, and Sam laughed at her. Her lips twitched in a
frown. I couldn't stand to look at her, and then I realized I
didn't have to. I had somewhere I had to be. I moved to walk
out, but she blocked me.

"You were looking forward to your Branding," Mrs. Harris said more softly. "I remember. I should really like to know
what Mrs. Stokes said to you, and to Beecher, and, apparently,
to Mandett, that could turn you all into such..."

She let her look of disdain stand in for whatever word she
could not find or would not pay for.

"You're not supposed to *imply* words," Sam warned. Mrs.
Harris's brow furrowed. "It's stealing from the Rights Holders."

"Sam," Mrs. Harris said, her voice dripping like Huny®,
"I am gratified to know you have been paying attention. I
shouldn't be upset—people like Mrs. Stokes are no better than
animals. Do you know what her words did to her son? The
poor man drank a molecular ink and died almost instantly."

"No, he didn't," Sam barked. I felt a little unsteady, wondering if that was actually true, but surely Mrs. Stokes would
have told me if it was.

"It was covered up," Mrs. Harris insisted with a flip of her hand. That made no sense. Who would cover it up? What would the point be?

"Belunda Stokes felt entitled to all those words she spoke, like a pig at a trough. How could she be expected to have any control? She simply expected everything to be handed to her for free."

I couldn't listen to her anymore, and I would not be late to my rendezvous with the Placers on her account. I pushed past her.

She breathed in sharply. "This is why the Onzième cannot keep a parent—they are too desperate to speak to and hug these children, even when it is far beyond their financial ability."

I opened the door. Her words hit me like an arrow. She made it sound like our parents didn't deserve to be with us.

"I am trying to help you," Mrs. Harris said. But she wasn't. Her guardianship wasn't an accident. Our parents, all of them, had been taken away, and I'd never really considered why.

"I love you, Speth," Mrs. Harris lied with a revolting lack of emotion. I grew dizzy and had to steady myself in the doorway.

"See what comes of it?" Mrs. Harris said, clicking across our floor in her heels to our screen. She tapped a few times, entered an address and stood back to let me see.

A feed appeared. I twisted to see it, one foot still in the hall. Elderly, trembling hands brushed the inside of a beautiful, graceful, spotted blushing flower with a yellowy powder. This was a direct feed from someone's corneal implants, being broadcast for everyone to see on a micro-channel. My heart seized, thinking it might be my mother, but I realized my mistake almost immediately. The hands were too old. The owner of the feed was in a hothouse, lined as far as the eye could see with thin trees. Other bent, beaten workers hurried from flower to flower with delicate brushes, their faces covered with The Blocks. Mrs. Stokes glanced at herself for the briefest of seconds in the hothouse glass and then returned to work. Her image was allowed through without any blurring.

A sour lump formed in my throat as the feed cut away. Not only had they taken Mrs. Stokes and put her to work at her age, they'd forced implants into her eyes, despite her objections all those years ago. My own eyes burned just thinking of it.

Saretha tapped at her Cuff and turned back on her game show.

"That's how your beloved Mrs. Stokes will finish out what days are left to her," Mrs. Harris said quickly, with a flick of her eyes to the screen. "I thought you would like to know."

Her voice held a note of amusement, and I wanted to scream at her. I wanted to lunge at her and wipe the smug expression off her face. But I did neither. Instead, I caught my breath and turned away. I didn't want to leave Sam and Saretha with this woman, but I had to go. I pushed off the doorframe, passing Penepoli still standing baffled in the hall, and I fled.

SEASONS: $37.99

Outside the dome, they say there are seasons. We never see them from inside. Some parts of the year, the dome is gray more often, and every once in a while, the dome goes dark with snow. Until I became a Placer, I never knew you could feel the cold of it through the metal bracing between the honeycombs.

Henri demonstrated when we were out on a high-profile Placement near the center of the city. Hanging from a clip like an acrobat, Henri ungloved his hand and pressed it to the metal. When he took his hand away, a perfect handprint remained, melted in the thin frost. I followed his lead, pressing my palm to the cold.

The handprints only lasted a few seconds before the frost replaced them. Margot hurried over and put one of her hands in the spot where Henri's had been. She could not keep from giggling. Kel allowed us a few minutes of this diversion, then waved and herded us away.

Watching Henri's backpack made me feel like a traitor. Letting Saretha languish at home made me feel like a traitor. Every day that passed pulled at me in a hundred directions.

I looked out across the city from the top of the dome.

Nancee was here somewhere, lost to servitude. Mrs. Stokes was gone, lost to hard labor. I feared the work would kill her. I longed to help them, but how could I? Even if I could find them, how could I help them? I had to focus on the one small piece of knowledge I had that might be of use.

I laughed bitterly to myself, thinking about how the information I had was almost like owning a word. It had value. I wished I could see Silas Rog's face when he realized he would lose his first case. Could Arkansas Holt handle taking him down? I knew he could use the medal, but we hadn't heard from him in some time, which was actually kind of him. He was trying not to deplete our resources if he didn't have anything positive to pass on.

Butchers & Rog's building was so close when we arrived at our destination that I could just make out our shapes on the rooftop, reflected in the fat pillar of Rog's mirrored glass. We had been given strict instructions to work on the side facing away from Rog's building. We were not allowed to blemish his view.

Tico™ Entertainment wanted to promote their new series *Simple Ones*, about a group of bumbling debtors who worked for a warmhearted, wealthy and handsome genius. The well-meaning simpletons constantly bungled his plans and lapsed further into debt. It was an exclusive show that used an advanced version of Ad technology to replace one of the actors with a computerized version of the viewer. It would only screen to Affluents, putting them in the role of warmhearted genius.

Our job was to unfurl Ad sheets over selected windows, which would replace the view with a loop of the half-hour pilot. I wondered if the Affluents inside would ever question the scans, or feel odd about them. Probably not. The media campaign made it clear that only very special people would find themselves in the action. Kel said flattery like this was an intoxicant.

The Ad sheets were designed to adhere for no more than twenty-four hours, at which point they would peel away and fall gently to the street below. The problem was that when I pressed my first one in place, it immediately slipped away.

It wasn't my fault. I did exactly what Kel described, thumbing the top corners in place and then running an electrostatic squeegee over the Ad. But it didn't stick at all. The sheet curled up and tumbled away. In a blink, Kel dropped on her line until she was in freefall and caught the Ad with an irritated huffing sound.

Her eyes locked on me, flashing exasperation. She blamed me for letting it slip. She zipped back up, shoulders tight. She flattened the roll out in front of me sarcastically, doing all the same things I had done. It didn't work for her either. She tried again. It failed.

She pulled another sheet out, while Henri and Margot tried the same, but the Ads simply would not stick. A tense silence followed. I'd never seen a Placement fail.

Kel snapped her line up the building, and we all knew to follow.

In a Squelch a few minutes later, the first word out of her mouth was a terse "Sorry."

I didn't often think about the money that was saved when Kel and the team talked while cut from the tether, but I knew *sorry* was always $10—and a legal admission of guilt. She didn't say more. She didn't need to. I felt like a weight had been lifted from me, despite the anger radiating from Kel. She turned her attention to the useless Ad sheets.

"Do you know why this happened?" she asked, shaking and crushing a sheet in her hands.

"Gravity?" Margot guessed.

I almost laughed, and Margot peeked at me, eyes twinkling.

"Because the Patent Lawyers keep suing each other so that nothing *new* can *ever* be designed." She tossed the sheets across the room. "We're stuck—forever trapped in exactly this." She gestured to the room, but she meant the world that held us all back.

Henri kicked at one of the Ads at his feet in solidarity.

"I'll have to file a report, and a defense, and they will sue me for defamation because they can't make a product that sticks, and I'm the one pointing it out."

She blew out a giant breath.

"You can all go home," she said, bending down to gather up the sheets. We all joined her.

"Thank you," she muttered. She took the ones from my hand. "Thank you," she said more clearly. It felt like she meant more, but why?

We all left and spilled out onto the roof to go our separate ways. I wasn't being escorted anymore. Henri went off ahead of me. I watched him go, his pack on his back, zipping away.

I racked my brain for other options—ones that didn't require me to trick or steal from Henri. Was there any way I could get Saretha to take Carol Amanda Harving's place without removing her Cuff? If there was, it eluded me.

I worried that if I waited too long, the apartment might

change or my plan might crumble. Taking Henri's device shouldn't be that hard. There was a decent chance I could sneak it out of his bag and put it back before anyone realized, yet I kept putting it off. I was comfortable making Placements. I let myself fall into a rhythm. Kel had backed away and somehow moved on from forgiving me to taking me under her wing in a way she hadn't before.

Then, one morning, after a long night of Placement, I found Saretha awake and suddenly, inexplicably, chipper. She greeted me with a hug, $2.99, as if everything was going to be okay again.

"Can I make you breakfast?" she asked, bright and cheerful. $9.87. She took up a wooden spoon in her hand. Then she laughed. Relief flooded over me. I thought, *Maybe the worst of it is over.*

"Dinner! I mean *dinner* for you," Saretha when on. She bopped me lightly on the nose with the spoon as her Cuff rang up the charge. $32.98 for the various words. $11.99 for the cutesy bopping of my nose—a gesture Trademarked by Tiger Motion Pictures™. She was acting like she was in love. Had she met someone? But where? She couldn't leave the apartment. How? Who was it?

Something more was at work than Saretha just learning to live with being locked inside. How could I ever expect her to be happy like that? Then a thought occurred to me—had the DESIST order been lifted? How else could I explain her behavior?

Was it possible I wouldn't have to steal Henri's little blue device after all? Saretha could go back to work, and I could keep being a Placer. The money would be pretty good.

But my delight quickly faltered. Something didn't feel right. At first, I thought it was just me. If I was truthful, I still wanted her to take Carol Amanda Harving's place. I wanted to put a dent in Silas Rog's reputation. I wanted to do something to the system that felt like a boot on my throat. That thought may have held back my joy, but it was Sam's face that demolished it.

Sam watched from the corner, his face full of concern, not relief, at Saretha's vastly better mood. It seemed to ask, *What the hell happened*?

"It's weird," he whispered to me. "She won't stop smiling."

It was true. Her old smile was back, but just a little lopsided. It was like she had been drinking, but Saretha didn't drink. It was too expensive, and whenever it had been offered to her, it was always by men trying to bribe her for favors. Plus, what did *we* have to drink? We couldn't afford alcohol.

"I can hear you," Saretha said, turning around with a broad, toothy smile and regarding us. "I can *see* you." $23.92.

Something didn't look right about my sister. Her hair looked clean, but also over-brushed and shaped into a tight curtain around her cheeks to make her now-chubby face look thinner. Her eyes tracked slowly and off-kilter, like she was seeing, but not exactly what was in front of her.

"Saretha?" Sam asked.

"Yes, *Sam*?" $33.99.

"Are you okay?"

"What could be wrong?" Saretha asked, as if she could now only see everything that was right with the world. "Be positive." $18.98. She ruffled his hair.

Be positive. The phrase spun through my mind, and then

I saw what Saretha had done. A medicinal disc was attached to the wrist end of her Cuff. In small, discreet letters was a company logo—Zockroft™.

Saretha met my gaze. She smiled beatifically and closed her eyes.

"Zockroft™," she said, holding the Cuff out to me so I could see a tiny needle jab into her skin and vanish. She let out a quick, pleasured gasp. 99¢ for the gasp, plus $22.99 for the word. The injection of Zockroft™ was provided free each time she said it.

"Dropter delivered," she said, spinning around, her head lolling.

She must have ordered it over the WiFi, from her Cuff or the wall-screen. It was sickening. I almost wished I hadn't seen it.

Zockroft™ is powerful, terrible stuff. It is addictive and expensive. Maybe it did some people good, but not like this. Saretha hadn't seen a doctor. She wasn't allowed out of the house for that. She hadn't been told what dosage to use; Zockroft™ had made that decision for her. There was no way to know how much that little needle in her arm was injecting.

I couldn't wait any longer. I had to get Henri's device and get that Cuff off her. It didn't just chain her to the house and to her name—it was now poisoning her and charging her for the pleasure.

PILF: $38.99

I considered sneaking into Henri's apartment, but that would mean stealing the little blue device while Henri slept. What would I do if he woke up? I could not take the risk. It would be better to get him alone, after the night's Placement, and distract him.

I hated the way I planned it, but I had to be sure he would be occupied. The pack was always near him or on him. When he wore it, the pocket with the device was right behind his head. If I got him to hug me, I could reach back and steal the device. I would have to do it in a Squelch, just to be sure I wasn't registered as hugging him back.

I went through it in my head, over and over, figuring out exactly how to place myself in front of him. My posture would be important. I would track him with my eyes, brush against his arm. I wasn't the first girl to make these kinds of calculations. I'd heard Sera Croate whisper about it to her friends like she was an expert. I had mostly ignored her, because that kind of manipulation wasn't really me. I felt a little nauseous trying to think back to what she'd said.

I didn't want to be like Sera Croate.

Would Henri kiss me? It was hard to imagine he wouldn't.

I had to be ready. I prepared to close my eyes and slip the device away. The kiss, if it happened, couldn't last long. How could Henri enjoy it when I wouldn't kiss back? Did that not matter? I don't know how other people feel about things like that. I don't even know what I think, because my only experience was with Beecher. When Beecher had kissed me that last time, it was disturbing and awful. The physical shocks from his implants overwhelmed everything else. This time, if it happened, it would be sad and terrible down to the bone.

But the more I rehearsed in my head, the less queasy I became. Cold as it made me feel, I couldn't lose my nerve. I didn't want it to be this way; I didn't want anything to be the way it was. I hated what I had to do, but I didn't have any other choice.

However awful the experience, Henri would be devastated if he knew the truth behind it. I would have to pretend afterward that I'd changed my mind. That happened all the time, didn't it? Margot would be furious, whether she knew the truth or not. I had no way to handle her. How she might react worried me more than how Henri might take it.

I met the others at our rendezvous and tried to pretend it was like any other night. The Squelch was oval, with dark gray carpeting and walls printed to look like porous stone. We had twelve short Placements that night. Kel was uncharacteristically dramatic about revealing what we were placing.

"This should be an easy one," Kel said, grinning a little. She had been in a better mood the past few weeks. The debacle with Tico™ Entertainment's Ad screens resulted in Tico™ suing the screen maker, the screen maker suing the adhesive maker, the adhesive maker suing a glue manufacturer and the glue maker suing a genetics firm who raised genetically altered beetles that could be milked for a glue-like paste. Our Agency, on the strength of Kel's report, turned around and sued them all.

Kel lifted a bag, lumpy with rounded shapes, and poured out its contents on the floor. Against the gray carpet, the oranges that rolled out looked dazzling. A thin citrus aroma filled the room. The scent was beautiful—far more exquisite than the smell of orange printer ink or candies.

"You can each have *one*," she said, flicking a hand over them. It was a rare treat, and a signal from the Agency that they were pleased. I realized the gesture also meant Kel had managed to get the Agency to accept me. Margot and Henri scrambled forward. I let them pick first, taking a moment to blink back the tears that were suddenly in my eyes. Kel urged me on with a jut of her chin. She had been working on communicating with me using tiny gestures.

I plucked one from the ground. It was smaller and denser than I'd imagined. I held it to my nose. Henri began to peel his at once, like he was a little crazed to get inside. The citrus smell intensified. For a brief moment, I forgot what I was planning to do.

I thought of how Sam would love the smell as I ran my thumb over the bumpy skin. I had to wipe my eyes.

"It's only an orange," Henri said, biting into his and letting juice dribble down his chin.

I put mine in my bag. I wanted Sam and Saretha to share it, but then I paused. Was that allowed? I looked over at Kel.

"It's fine," she said with a nod. "Just don't be obvious and hand it to them right out of your Placer bag."

I smiled back at her awkwardly, guilt creeping over my skin.

Margot contemplated her orange, too, and put hers in her bag.

"For later," she said, looking at Henri. "So I can *savor* it." She narrowed her eyes at the sticky mess he was making and added, "I don't think Speth is enticed by this, Henri."

Henri's face immediately turned red. He looked for my reaction.

"Stop teasing him," Kel said.

I knew Henri liked me, but what did he see in me? I didn't talk. Was it the way I carried myself? Was it my looks? Margot had such a pretty, heart-shaped face, and she was truly funny, if a tiny bit cruel. Why wasn't he interested in her?

I couldn't let myself be distracted by any of this. I had to focus. I needed for us to finish early so I could get Henri alone.

Margot pulled out a wipe from her kit and began to wipe Henri's face, despite his protests.

All through the Placements, it felt like Henri was right in front of me, his backpack swaying in front of my eyes. The zipper on the little pocket was the slightest bit open. The jangle of it seemed louder than was possible. It was probably like this all the time, but it seemed so obvious that I feared everyone would know exactly what I was planning.

We raced through the Placements in no time at all, and Kel brought us to a nice, spacious Squelch in the Troisième, not far from my school.

"You were fast tonight," Henri commented after we were

done. He clapped me on the shoulder, and I felt proud, then ashamed, thinking of what I was about to do.

We debriefed in a spacious Squelch in the J. Smith Brinkley Memorial Investment Center. There was a long oval table and a dozen comfortable chairs for rich men to have secret, free conversations. Kel brought up a map to show us where we would meet the next night.

"Henri, nice job tonight," Kel said. Henri had picked up his pace in answer to mine.

Henri beamed. "Maybe you should feed me oranges every night."

Margot took his arm and stroked his biceps. "Oh, Henri, how capable you are."

"Margot!" he said, shaking her off, as if she were spoiling his moment. I noticed that Margot played these moments off as jokes, but when Henri didn't bite, I could see a flush in her cheeks and hurt behind her eyes.

"This is the kind of efficient work that gets better Placements from more prestigious firms," Kel said. She loved a job well done, even if her voice occasionally hinted that she didn't actually care for Product Placement itself.

I threw my pack on my back, ready to go. I looked to the others to do the same. I mapped where I should stand so I could be near Henri as we left.

"Like Eagleton™?" Henri wondered.

"Could be," Kel said.

I was ready to go.

"Butchers & Rog?" Henri asked.

A cold finger seemed to run down my back. Kel's face fell.

"Henri, you do *not* want another assignment from Butchers & Rog," she said.

"But they're the most prestigious firm in the dome."

My hands clenched. Why were we delaying to talk about *this*, and right now?

"Do you know what you'd be placing for Butchers & Rog? Misery. Just like last time. You'd get a slim stack of yellow envelopes, and off you'd go through the city to deliver catastrophic Lawsuits. It's a hell of a thing to know you just ruined someone's life. It isn't worth the bonus."

Henri looked down at the ground. The room seemed suddenly colder. I hoped the subject would drop. I didn't like hearing about Silas Rog even when I didn't have an awful plan to carry out.

"Does he really have those books?"

"I'm sure Rog has books, Henri," Kel said. "I seriously doubt he has a single book that proves you can't Copyright words, if that's what you're asking."

Kel peeked up at me to check my reaction. I tried my best to look disinterested, even though my mind was grasping at the hope the book was real—the book that Mrs. Soleman had been so sure existed.

"Henri, why must you say the most obvious things?" Margot complained.

Henri shrugged.

The mood sufficiently soured, Kel moved on to wrapping up at last.

"1:30 a.m. at the Chau Arena," Kel said. She tapped her Pad off and went out the door.

I hung back. I knew what I needed to do. My stomach was

filled with butterflies. I truly did like Henri, but did I like him enough to *want* to kiss him? Maybe. I didn't know for sure. I certainly didn't want to think about it now. It wasn't what mattered. Henri was sweet and good, but sometimes more clueless than I could bear.

I didn't have time to sort out these feelings. Henri went to move, and I blocked his path.

Margot had just crossed out the door. I hoped the door would close and Margot wouldn't see, but she was frozen at the threshold. Henri stopped, astonished, looking down at me. His eyes went wide, and his smile broadened at his sudden good fortune. The faint smell of orange still clung to him.

I listened for the door to close, willing Margot to just go. I kept my body between Henri and the exit. I tilted my head, a maneuver I'd seen in movies. Margot's mouth hung open, and her expression flashed from astonishment to anger. I'd feared this would happen, but I couldn't avoid it. She pulled her mask over her face and glared, wet-eyed, as she let the door close at last.

Henri reached down and lifted up my hand. "What's this?" he asked, interlacing his fingers with mine, so that, even though I didn't hold his hand back, he held mine firmly.

In another, more playful time, I would have said, *My hand.*

I didn't answer, of course. I stood on my tiptoes and I *nearly* kissed him. It was easy to lure him to me. He moved in, and his arms encircled me. He kissed me. How careful did I need to be about my Cuff if we were in a Squelch? Could I hug him back? Could I taste his lips, just a little? They were rough and strong, with a slight tang of orange. I noticed that his head was bigger than Beecher's, which was a funny, nervous thought.

Did I like him? I did, but I couldn't say how. My mind was elsewhere. I put my arms around him, just like I'd practiced, and pulled the zipper open lightly on his backpack. I slipped the blue device out and scrunched my eyes closed against what I was doing. I prayed Henri wouldn't notice.

Once I had it, I pulled away. There was no use dragging this out any longer. Poor Henri. He looked so puzzled. I tried to compose myself and smile that Saretha smile, the one from before the Zockroft™, when she was actually happy. How had she ever been happy in this world?

"Are we...?" Henri didn't know what to ask. I smiled again. I knew he would think that smile was a *yes*. If all went well, I would repeat this act one more time and sneak the tear-shaped thing back into his bag. Then I would stop. I would suddenly cease being interested and find some way to apologize to Margot.

I worried about her. We all knew Margot's teasing talk of love was a nested act—except maybe Henri. Did he truly not see she was flirting? I'd broken her heart for this key—but her heart would heal. But if I was caught, Kel's trust would never recover.

I prayed my plan would work, so it would all be worth it.

CAROL AMANDA HARVING: $39.99

When I came home, Sam was just getting ready for school. He still had friends there—people he could talk to. He looked up at me and gave me the best smile he could manage. I was pained to see the distance that had grown between us.

"Sera Croate is studying for a Custodian's license," he said, trying to bring me news. That seemed about right. Sera would excel at being a little Mrs. Harris.

Saretha was sitting placidly on the couch watching the screen, entranced. My heart thumped against my ribs as I went to the wall and turned it off. I needed their attention.

Saretha gave a little frown, but did not seem in the least unhappy.

"That show was good," she said, her eyes swimming a little.

I flipped my Placer's bag over my shoulder and opened it. It was exactly the thing Kel suggested I not do. I pulled an orange out, and the tart, sweet smell flooded my senses. I held it out, and Sam froze.

"Is that an *orange*?" Saretha asked, squinting. Sam crossed the room and took it out of my hand, his eyes full of wonder. Despite himself, he licked his lips.

"Where did you get this?" he asked, then he looked at

me. He saw the bag and my matte black clothes. At once, he knew. I thought he would say it out loud, but instead he just looked at me with his mouth half-open in awe. I felt giddy. Sam closed his eyes and smelled the orange. The aroma was a little less sweet and a little more pungent unpeeled, but it was still a beautiful thing.

I quickly moved to our closet and pulled out Saretha's nicest dress, shaking it at her. She looked confused. I will admit, I probably looked like a lunatic. She blinked and turned the screen back on.

"Should we peel it?" Sam asked, holding the orange up. Sam didn't ask me a lot of questions anymore. Why should he? I would not answer. I could feel him losing hope in our connection. I crossed back to him and plunged my thumbnail under the thick rind and began to peel back the skin. *Actions speak louder than words.* The orange smell grew more intense.

"Wow," Sam breathed.

I handed the peeled orange to Sam and pulled Saretha up from the bed. She stood, not looking at me, but watching a reality show in which girls competed for the affection of a deformed Lawyer. (It would turn out later that, surprise! He wasn't deformed at all, and he would marry the girl who was kindest to him while suing all the rest.) I turned the screen off again. Saretha blinked and turned to me. There was no upset in her, only mild confusion.

"You look taller," she said. She leaned in and gave me a hug. The Zockroft™ blunted everything. Was I taller? I took an extra moment to assess our heights. We were standing face-to-face, but I hadn't noticed until that moment I was now slightly taller than her. An odd feeling crept into my throat, like an unsaid apology for all the time I had wasted saying so much less than I should have.

Sam handed me a slice of orange. I took it, even though it wasn't really for me. I placed it in my mouth, surprised at the softness of the outer skin. A tart, sweet flavor flooded my mouth. I wanted to savor this moment, but we needed to move.

I took the dress, held it up to Saretha and shook it again. She shrugged and took it from me with a pleasant smile. Her eyes seemed to swim before finding focus. After a moment, she began to struggle to put the dress on, chewing and swallowing a piece of orange, but taking no more joy or pleasure from the sweet fruit than she would have from a sheet of Wheatlock™.

Sam looked away, out our small milky window. He always looked away when we got dressed—for the sake of courtesy, embarrassment or possibly both. Now he closed his eyes and smelled the orange again.

"Have you been a Placer since that night?" Sam asked, smelling the orange even as he savored a slice. "When you came home with the cut on your chin?"

His voice hitched a little, and it broke my heart to hear it. I thought he would have been happier. My head was filled with things I wanted to say.

"Placer," Saretha said, almost like an echo.

Suddenly Sam turned back. "Did you get a spot for Saretha?" he asked, looking from me to her. He was so smart. It was a good idea, if I had a way to make it happen. I wished that was where we were headed, but this might be just as good. This might be better.

Instead of speaking, I turned the screen back on and Saretha stopped dressing to watch. I pulled up the interface and sorted through to a screen of Ads. You could watch all the Ads you liked for free. I pulled up a movie trailer for Carol Amanda Harving's last film, *The Bullets Have Names*. When she appeared onscreen, I paused the image. Saretha let out a small groan.

"Speth," Sam said. He didn't understand why I would do this. I'm sure it seemed cruel.

"Zockroft™," Saretha said weakly, followed by a deep sigh as the disc on her Cuff injected her. $22.99. I hated that stuff. I grabbed her arm.

"She can't help it," Sam said. He put the half-eaten orange down on the counter.

I pulled out the small blue device I had stolen and ran it over my sister's Cuff. It clicked. Sam gasped as I cracked it open.

"Don't say anything!" Sam cried out, racing to Saretha and grabbing her hand. Saretha looked confused. Her Cuff vibrated in my hands, like an angry beast. It still encircled her arm.

Saretha Jime—gesture: nod—1 second: 99¢

I lifted the Cuff away. Its screen dimmed, no longer drawing electromagnetic power from her arm. It went into safe mode. She reached for it, stretching out her hand feebly. Her eyes were pleading, not grateful. She touched the ring on the end that read *Zockroft™*.

I was glad taking her Cuff off would mean separating her from the drug. For that alone, it might be worth it, though

I felt a pang that Zockroft™ was the only thing that provided her with any peace. I placed the Cuff on the kitchen counter, splayed open like a gutted animal.

Sam's window reflected my thin, weary face in its cloudy glass. I held up my arm and looked at my own Cuff. It was nothing more than a shackle to me. I took Henri's little device and ran it up my left arm. The Cuff unlocked, and I peeled it off. I put it next to Saretha's on the counter. She watched, her eyes half-glazed with her final dose.

"Speth, I don't know what you want," Sam said desperately.

I scanned the room for some way I could communicate. I looked back at the screen and then out the window.

"Carol Amanda Harving," Sam said dutifully. His eyes flashed recognition. "You found her?"

My chest rose and fell in relief. *Yes*, I thought. I walked out the door and waited for them to follow. Saretha finished jamming herself into her dress, which only barely fit. I hadn't considered how little she had to wear now, but it would have to do. Sam pushed her forward and we were on our way, leaving the precious remains of the orange behind.

MURDEROUS: $40.99

It was still bright when we emerged outside. The dome glowed a brilliant frosty white above the city. Saretha blinked in the light. She hadn't been outside in so long, she needed a moment to adjust. She glided along, running her fingers over the buildings' walls and Ads, like she needed to feel them to know this was real. The light patter of Ads around us suddenly went dark. Even without Cuffs, we were still being monitored. The Ad panels pinged for Cuffs, only to find they weren't there. I worried. What if they scanned our faces? Would Rog be notified? Would the police?

They mostly shut down, which was a relief, but an illusionary ring of shadow surrounded us wherever we walked. It was hard to hide, and people began staring.

Cars drove fast around the outer rim. The sound of them bounced between the tall, long buildings. My body was trembling with nervous exhilaration. We just had to make it to Malvika Place.

"Do you think she will talk?" Sam asked. "Are we going to meet her?"

I wished I had a better way to explain. I had to show them what I'd seen. I hoped to pass Saretha off as Carol Amanda

Harving. How could they prove my sister wasn't her? They could never produce Carol Amanda Harving in court. Not even Butchers & Rog could conjure a human being from thin air.

I could feel eyes on us everywhere. Some were curious, others disdainful. We hadn't traveled far when a pack of kids a little younger than me fell quiet at the sight of us. One of them signed the zippered lips. Sera Croate hissed from behind them, "Don't do that!" I was startled to see her. Her Cuff buzzed, and her face sneered.

"Do you know what you've done?" she demanded. The kids around her scattered. I said nothing, praying she would get bored with us and move along. "I should—" She stopped talking and began tapping up an InstaSuit™. She waited for my Cuff to buzz in receipt, and when it didn't, her eyebrows knit in angry confusion.

I put my left arm behind me, to hide my missing Cuff from her view.

"Hey!" Sam said suddenly, brightly. "Let's go! Mrs. Harris is waiting!" He lied so easily.

He took my right hand and pulled me forward. Sera eased out of our path, baffled, cowed by our Custodian's name.

We made it as far as the bridge leading to Falxo Park. I'd planned to move toward the city center and Malvika Place, but a car came toward us and pulled to a sudden stop. A tall, sharp-faced man emerged, staring at me.

He wasn't a Lawyer. He wasn't dressed like one, and he looked too brutal and dim. He wasn't a police officer, either. His lip curled, and he rapped on the roof of his car.

"Hey, look," he said, like he had found something interesting. Two other men, who appeared to be his brothers, emerged from the vehicle and sneered.

They all looked identical—lean and rough, with long, muscled necks that seemed dangerous and the same watery blue eyes. Each of them was dressed in an ivory-buttoned Arlington Heights Transcolor™ shirt—one indigo, one maroon and one gold. Their crisp black pants were thick and itchy-looking.

I don't know if Sam sensed my unease, but he turned to me and said, "I can make you think of zebras."

He remembered our dad's trick of the mind. He nudged me with his elbow and inclined his head backward, toward the bridge.

"Come on," he whispered.

I didn't want to use the bridge, but I sensed Sam was right; it was better to avoid confrontation. We could go into the park and then turn back at the next bridge.

At first I thought the brothers might have been summoned by some alert from the Ad scans, but then I saw Sera Croate standing uncomfortably in the distance, pretending not to watch.

Ads babbled in our wake as we moved across the bridge, brought to life by the three brothers who began to follow us.

Sam forced a laugh. "Do you see it?"

I wasn't thinking of zebras, not with those three men behind us.

"I wonder what your zebra looks like," Sam said. "Whether it's standing in a great plain, or by a tree. Are the stripes thick or thin, or curved or straight?"

I saw it then. A zebra flicked in my mind's eye, striped thin, standing under a tree, ready to bolt at the first sign of danger.

We should have run.

"Did you know zebra stripes are like fingerprints? If you ever look at them, it's like a huge thumbprint on the side of a white horse—like a huge giant with inky fingers picked the zebra up and left the mark behind."

I turned back to look at the men. Two of them were right behind us, near enough for me to hear the the rustle of their stiff clothes as they walked. The third brother, the one in indigo, peeled off and was walking quickly on the far side of the bridge forty feet away. I think he was trying to flank us.

"Are you picturing the giant? Is it a cyclops?" Sam asked, elbowing Saretha, then me. "I bet it is now."

Saretha laughed a loopy little laugh. What a time for Sam to come back. I'd missed his voice, but I could only half-listen.

"I can make you think of a gigantic cyclops picking up a zebra, just by saying it. That's a pretty serious power," Sam said more seriously. I didn't know if he was thinking of what I had sacrificed, or of his own future. I would never be able to ask, but I know he was trying to reassure us.

"Sluk," a low, rasping voice behind us said. I felt Saretha bristle.

We were halfway across the bridge now, a few feet from the apex. The split in the safety mesh had never been repaired from when Beecher jumped. Sam wheeled around.

"You need to watch your mouth," he warned. He was easily two feet shorter than any of these men.

"We *know* who you are," the leader in gold warned.

"You know Miss Harving?" Sam asked. His voice was strange. What was he doing? I wanted to take his hand, but I didn't know if my eyes would be shocked if I tried.

The "Don't Jump," song began playing, triggered despite the fact that—or perhaps *because*—we did not have our Cuffs. I glanced down at the ring below. There was no memorial to Beecher down there. The cars went zooming underneath us, blurs of red, silver and gold. The bridge was a constant rumble.

I didn't like this place.

"We know *her*," the maroon brother said, pointing a thick, knobby finger at me. "The Silent Freak™."

"But you *don't* know Carol Amanda Harving?" Sam asked, as if that was the more important subject.

Apparently they did, because they turned to look at Saretha. The indigo brother had circled around and was now standing right in front of Saretha. He cocked his head. "The actress?"

"The actress," Sam confirmed.

All three brothers got squinty. They now had us surrounded.

We were sandwiched between them and the bridge's wall, waist-high and full of colorful bunnies.

"She looks chubby for an actress," the gold brother said. The lead looked at his Cuff as if it would tell him what to do.

"Why's she with the Silent Freak™?" The maroon brother jabbed his finger at me again. His Cuff buzzed. Mrs. Nince got richer.

"She's studying for a role," Sam said, as if it was obvious. I'd never realized how quickly Sam could think on his feet. He leaned in to the gold leader and whispered, "She is going to *play* the Silent Girl in an upcoming film."

"Oh, *is* she?" the gold brother asked, like he wasn't buying it.

"She looks like a sluk," the indigo brother said.

My skin was crawling. I hated that word.

"She's playing a *role*," Sam shot back as if the indigo brother needed this explained to him like small child. The man's face grew red.

I turned to look at the green of Falxo Park. It was empty, like it had been cleared. I scanned for anyone who might be a Silent, but how would I know? What could they do?

"Don't look away from me," the gold brother demanded, pushing on my cheek so my head turned.

"You made us talk," the maroon brother complained. He spoke loudly over the roar of the traffic below. "You're gonna pay for that." Then he thought about the words in his mouth. "…and for this."

He turned his Cuff to Sam and pointed. His wristlet was rimmed in gold and a crust of diamonds. The bill scrolled with his words.

"Fancy," Sam commented. I loved that little voice, but he really needed to keep quiet now.

A woman jogged by with her tiny dog and pretended not to see anything. There was a roar of engines beneath us that crested, then pitched lower as a group of cars passed. Suddenly, the air grew quiet. I tried to push through the three men, but they would not budge.

The gold one looked Saretha over again, and then me. He narrowed his watery eyes.

"Silent Freak™." He licked his lips and put a hand on my shoulder. It was heavy and warm. The maroon brother leaned over the ledge, checking the height, pressing the plastic mesh open until it split more.

"Talk," the gold brother ordered. His fingers dug into my

shoulder. His grip was like iron. "I'll pay for your speaks—I'll pay for a whole year. Say whatever you like." He snapped his fingers like it was already done.

The maroon brother lunged at Sam and grabbed him in a bear hug. A chill went up my spine.

"She needs to be motivated," the maroon brother grunted, flipping Sam upside down through the split in the mesh like a rag doll, grabbing him at the knees and dangling him head down, eighty feet above the rush of traffic. Sam flailed, wild-eyed, for something to grab hold of.

My knees nearly buckled. I thought I might vomit. I reached out desperately for Sam, struggling against the gold brother's grasp on me.

"Don't make me lose my grip." The maroon brother frowned. He dipped Sam down roughly, like he was about to drop him. My heart felt like it stopped. Sam put a hand out against the smooth outer wall of the bridge, looking for something to cling to, but the bridge curved away from him, giving him nothing to hold.

Another wave of traffic roared below. I tried to reach for Sam again, but the gold brother pulled me roughly back. I punched him in the side of the head, but unlike in a movie, there was no powerful *thwack*. He did not drop to the ground. There was just a thick, meaty sound, and his brow furrowed.

"Just speak," the gold brother said, as if he was tired of me. My hand stung from the blow, but I hauled back to deliver another when I saw someone in the distance.

Mrs. Harris clicked up the bridge in her heels from Falxo Park, rushing along, her face slack and vaguely annoyed. It might have been the only time I was ever glad to see her.

There was no way she couldn't see us. Her eyes blinked in shock and surprise. She stopped for moment and appraised the scene with a side-eye. The gold brother turned and grinned at her. She ducked her head down, as if a bright light prevented her from making eye contact.

"Help!" Sam called out, realizing someone was there. He could not see it was our Custodian.

Mrs. Harris's sour face puckered with bewilderment. For one brief moment, I thought she might help, but no. She tugged at the bottom of her jacket and continued across the bridge. Her heels clicked swiftly along. She lifted her head as she passed to sneer at me and sign the zippered lips with a bitter, disdainful face full of hate.

"Friend of yours?" The gold brother laughed.

Mrs. Harris disappeared down the street.

I don't know what I'd thought Mrs. Harris would do, but I felt betrayed. She was still our Custodian. My skin prickled and my pulse pounded in my neck. Sam cried out for help again. The maroon brother shook his head in disgust.

Please don't do this, I begged in my mind. Tears of desperation streaked my face.

The gold brother clicked his tongue impatiently.

"Do you want us to let go?"

My breathing was ragged and out of control. I couldn't speak. Truly. I swear. I could no longer form words. I would not have cared in that moment if my eyes were shocked, or what kind of trouble I'd be in with Keene Inc. for breaking my contract.

But I could. Not. Speak.

"Stop!" Saretha cried, then screamed in agony, her lids shut tight against the shock to her eyes. She screamed again and again, dropping to the ground. The three brothers watched, curious but unmoved as she pressed her palms savagely to her eyes.

"Do you seriously want to test us?" the gold one asked.

I didn't want to test them. I didn't want to be anywhere near them. I didn't want any of this to be happening. I wished Henri, or Kel, or even Margot was nearby, but what could any of them do against all three of these men? I pitifully scanned the rooftops, but they were empty.

Saretha looked blindly around, panicked and desperate, her eyes rimmed in red. A coarse *no* gasped out of her throat.

"What?" the indigo brother asked, holding a hand to his ear and aiming it at me.

Sam redoubled his struggle against the maroon brother, kicking at him.

"Goddamnit!" his captor grumbled, tightening his hold on Sam.

"Do you want us to let go?" the gold one repeated, to me and only to me.

"Please," Saretha begged, then winced against the pain of the next shock.

The bridge was truly empty now. In the distance, people turned and avoided this scene. No one wanted to be a witness. No one wanted to spend a dime on testimony they couldn't profit from. Another blast of warm exhaust hit us from below. I would have done anything to stop them.

"Just say *no*," the gold one said to me. "One little word."

One little word. I could feel it. The flat of my tongue pressed the roof of my mouth. My numb lips formed an O, but no sound came out, no breath. My body felt weak. I raged at them, clawing at the gold brother to get at Sam, my mouth moving soundlessly. I tried to get the word out.

"Don't!" Sam cried out, and I need to believe, even now, that when he said it, he was talking to me, telling me not to give in.

That's when the maroon brother, finally fed up, shook Sam off and sent him plummeting into traffic eighty feet below.

SHATTERED ADS: $41.98

I didn't scream. The only sound I made came when I found my breath. My lungs suddenly filled with air, my body gasping for it, desperate, unable to function.

Beneath us came the thuds of cars colliding and the screeching of bending metal. Those noises could have killed me.

Saretha screamed. She screamed, and screamed again. She screamed enough for both of us.

The world dissolved from me into an airless state of nonexistence. The ceaseless chatter of the Ads mingled with my sister's agonized cries in a hollow tube. Then everything went black.

When I opened my eyes, my head felt like it was going to explode. The brothers were standing just a few feet away, shaking their heads.

"We tried to stop him," the maroon brother said.

"I grabbed right on to him," the indigo brother said.

"It was too late." The gold brother pretended to be sad.

My body was on the ground, half bent against the wall. I tried to raise myself up, averting my gaze from the edge. I couldn't look. If I never looked, I could hope, somehow, that Sam was not dead.

The cleanup crews had arrived: cranes, trucks and asphalt printers clanged and beeped below me. The police were there, bored and annoyed, talking to the brothers. Why weren't they doing anything? I didn't understand. They let me hyperventilate, slumped against the wall beside Saretha. The brothers, flush with money and words, spun their tale.

"I was trying to convince that Silent Girl to talk. I offered her money." The gold brother showed a few large bills from his pocket—rare paper money that had little purpose other than to impress. "And then she begins pulling on my wad, but not talking, so I try to incentivize her, and I ask…" He paused and read from his Cuff. *"Do you want us to let go?"*

No, I thought. *That wasn't right.* My head was still fuzzy. It ached. But of course he was lying. Of course he was believed. I grasped at him and caught his pant leg. He shook me off like a dog.

"I'll need to take your receipt log into evidence," one of the officers said to him as he moved me back. He was tall and tired-looking, his posture a bit slumped. His name was on his badge—Shalk, a cheap, public domain name like mine.

"We should wait for our Lawyer," the indigo one said.

"S'okay," the gold one said with a slow nod to the officer. He bumped Cuffs as the officer stood to initiate the transfer.

Officer Shalk nodded. "So, when did the boy jump?"

"Just after that."

"I tried to hold him," the indigo brother repeated.

I closed my eyes. I didn't want to think anymore. I felt nauseous. Pain throbbed though my skull, radiating from a large lump on the back of my head. I'd been hit or kicked while I was down. Or maybe I'd fainted and hit my head. Or maybe one of the brothers had knocked me out cold.

Saretha whimpered. She took another shock to her eyes for the sound.

"No," she whispered, and was shocked again.

"I should have got him," one of the brothers said, like he was a failed hero.

"He was pretty quick," the maroon one said, consoling him. The theater of it made me ill.

"No!" Saretha cried. "He—" Her head stuttered back like she was having a seizure. Each word caused a shock.

"Miss," Shalk said, "you can't make a statement without a Cuff."

I reached out to her, but she yanked away. She couldn't see. She didn't know it was me—or maybe she did. Did she blame me for this?

I tried to get to my feet. I had to do something.

"Miss," Shalk said to me, "you need to stay seated."

He was right. My legs wobbled and collapsed under me.

The gold one sniffed at us. "They'll probably cook up some story about how this is our fault. That's what we get for helping."

"Mmmm," Shalk considered.

"Please," Saretha begged. Her eyes were streaming tears.

Officer Shalk drew a deep, annoyed breath. "Miss, stop. I have to log everything you say." He tapped her words dutifully into his Cuff so she could be charged for them later.

"So anyway, I grabbed for him and he said, *Don't*, like he was hell-bent on going over." He looked over the edge. "I should've just looked away."

"It's very unfortunate," Officer Shalk said. "This is the first time I've seen one go *before* Last Day." The brothers nodded. The officer made a note on his Cuff.

"After that Pell girl, who knows what to expect?" the indigo brother offered.

"I just hope these kids learn from this," the gold brother said.

"Yeah," the maroon brother agreed.

"Learn what?" the officer asked. He looked from one brother to another as they each halfheartedly shrugged.

A Lawyer ambled up the bridge, unhurried, toward the brothers. He wore a slate-gray suit, cut in perfect lines, and a blood-red tie with thin gold edges. Pinned to his chest was a modest assortment of ribbons and badges in a tight, compact arrangement that suggested these few were but a hint of his full honors. His face was placid and calm, almost friendly. His sharp eyes crinkled up as he broke into a tranquil smile, but not so wide as to be inappropriate. There had been a tragedy, after all. He did not want to appear unseemly.

I hated him at once.

He stopped to offer the officer a hand. "Bennington Grippe," he said. "Butchers & Rog."

Officer Shalk looked at the man's hand, unsure if he was worthy to shake it. Grippe took the lead, taking the officer's hand and shaking it twice, firmly. Further along the bridge, the other officer stopped what he was doing to gawk.

"These men are represented by the firm," Grippe pointed out, whirling a finger through the air to include the brothers. They all looked mightily pleased.

I bristled with rage. I wanted to kill these men. I wanted

to leap up and push them all over the side. But I could barely stand. A horrid, sour guilt consumed me. I should have stopped them. I should have spoken.

Instead, I had let Sam die.

The bridge kept spinning, end over end, as I tried to get to my feet. I had to do something.

"Miss Harving?" Attorney Grippe's voice asked. He was looking at Saretha with an approximation of surprise. He ignored my efforts to right myself.

Saretha stared blindly ahead, her eyes red and raw from the shocks.

"You know her?" Shalk asked.

Grippe waved the officer off, like Shalk didn't matter anymore. He stepped over to Saretha, crouching down. The brothers fell in line behind him. They did not seem surprised at all.

"Miss Harving, where is your Cuff?"

He couldn't possibly believe Saretha *was* Carol Amanda Harving, could he?

"The kid did say she was an actress," the maroon one said to the officer, a smirk on his face.

Tears fell from Saretha's eyes. I'm not sure she knew the Lawyer was talking to her. The three meaty brothers folded their arms and watched. Grippe turned back to Officer Shalk.

"Are you done with her?"

Shalk paused. He wasn't finished, but he didn't want to say no—not to one of Silas Rog's men. He swallowed. "She is presently unable to answer questions." Shalk tapped at his own Cuff to indicate hers was missing.

"Not to worry," the Lawyer assured him. Grippe took

Saretha by the arm, and she flinched, opening her mouth and then closing it. What was he doing?

I managed to stand, trying to find some strength in my legs. The world wanted to upend itself. Grippe noticed me, but showed no sign of recognizing or caring who I was. He pulled Saretha out of my reach. She was my sister. Did he understand that? My hand trembled. The bridge continued to roll under my wavering legs, but I fought it, steadying myself against the blithering of an Ad.

The officer looked at me, his eyes tired, his lips drawn thin. "Miss, you need to sit." A hand was on his belt, on his pepper spray or his gun—I couldn't tell which. He shook his head at me, then turned back to the brothers and cleared his throat.

"Gentlemen, do you plan to sue her and her family?" the officer asked, angling a thumb at me.

The gold brother grinned. My insides began to boil. He tightened his lips around his teeth, thinking. "I probably should," he said. "It would send the wrong message if I didn't."

Saretha suddenly jerked away from Attorney Grippe.

"Whoa," Grippe said.

"Speth?" Saretha called to me, unseeing. Her face flinched with pain. I couldn't answer. The second officer ran over and got hold of her. Attorney Grippe put a hand on her shoulder as well, but she wrenched away from both of them. "Speth?" she called again. She had to stop talking. She might lose her vision forever. I pressed toward her, still dizzy with pain and confusion. The brothers moved between us, forming a wall, keeping me from her. I wanted to call out, but if I hadn't broken my silence to save Sam, I sure as hell wasn't going to do it now.

Grippe suddenly lost his mild expression and put his lips to Saretha's ear.

"You have a choice," he hissed in a harsh, spare whisper. "Stay here and live out whatever pathetic life Saretha Jime has left, or *remember* you're Carol Amanda Harving."

Saretha whimpered. She couldn't know what this meant. I'd never been able to reveal the secret to her.

"Speth?" Saretha whispered. Her eyes twitched, and another tear dropped down her face. Her eyes ticked madly about, grotesquely red, full of broken blood vessels and tears. She couldn't find me.

"You're wasting your breath," Grippe said.

I tried to press past the brothers, reaching my arms out to her, but they would not allow it.

"Do you need any help?" the officer asked, cringing a little.

"What I need," Grippe said with sudden viciousness, "is *privacy*. I am speaking with my *client*."

His teeth clicked on the *T*. Both officers moved off like cowering dogs. Then Attorney Grippe spoke a little more boldly.

"You will never get another opportunity. Mr. Rog is prepared to be very generous."

Saretha whimpered again. "Speth." She said my name with confusion and disillusionment, like I wasn't who she'd believed me to be. I tried to push past the brothers, but now police were moving in from everywhere to pull me away.

Grippe shook his head. "They took *Speth* away," he lied, his mouth hot in her ear, his eyes on me. "Don't embarrass yourself for her. She couldn't even speak *one* word to save him."

Saretha closed her sore eyes. How did he already know what had happened?

"You have to choose—now. Saretha Jime, or Carol Amanda Harving."

"I—" Saretha's eyes flinched tighter, but then she relaxed, beaten.

She barely seemed to breathe as her body went limp. My heart ached. I wanted to hope she would choose me, her sister. I wanted to believe she knew I was still there.

The Lawyer smirked, then rubbed his face to conceal his satisfaction as I was backed into an Ad screen and forced to sit.

"Heroes are made, not born," an Ad for Nike™ proclaimed behind me.

Grippe guided Saretha by the shoulders, and she shook under his hands. His eyes traveled the length of the bridge a moment, following the Ads.

"Don't jump, don't jump," the Ad I leaned against softly sang. It was gentler than usual. The chipper theme softened, as if the panel had scanned my mood. The bunnies hopped more slowly. I had no Cuff, and yet the Ads did not ignore me.

Had the system scanned me and pitied me? Suddenly I realized something. The systems had scanned me. The Ads on the bridge had scanned everything. There was evidence of Sam's murder stored on tiny chips inside. But I also knew Rog and his men would pick up the feeds from the uplink and WiFi and delete all that data. My body prickled. No. No, it would be worse than just erasing what had happened. Rog would *replace* it.

Butchers & Rog would use the scans of Sam, Saretha and me to recreate the scene. It would match whatever story the brothers told. History would be rewritten. They would have evidence to prove whatever they needed to prove.

In few hours' time, the facts would be changed. I had to stop that...but how?

An idea itched at my brain. A memory—something about the night Henri saved me in that alley. Without a word, he'd smashed the Ad screens. He had seemed so strange and otherworldly. Now I just knew him as Henri, but either way, he'd shown me what I needed to do.

I summoned all the rage and courage I could find within myself. This was going to hurt.

I pulled my arm forward and slammed my elbow into an animated bunny's face beside me, shattering the Ad as Bennington Grippe guided my sister away.

THE RIGHT TO REMAIN SILENT: $42.95

"You have the right to remain silent," a recording on Officer Shalk's police-issue Cuff warned me. Shalk had to shake his head. Of all the people he could ever hope to play it for... I let out a laugh at the absurdity of it, which quickly dissolved into sobs.

The gold brother sniggered as Officer Shalk bandaged my elbow, then bound my hands behind my back with a sharp plastic cord. I glared at the brothers with all my hate.

"Anything you say can, and will, be charged against your account, with a 20 percent surcharge to cover processing fees. Anything this officer or any other Law enforcement official says in the course of the investigation will be charged to you, and billed at such time as your case is adjudicated. You have the right to an Attorney. If you cannot afford an Attorney, one will be assigned to seize your assets, and you will be turned over to Debt Collection. Do you understand these rights?"

What rights? I wanted to scream.

"Silence is not a waiver," he sighed.

He placed me carefully in the back of his police cruiser and pulled away. The brothers and the other officer receded in his rearview mirror. Shalk's shoulders relaxed a little, but he slumped a little more from it.

"You aren't doing yourself any favors," he said, shaking his head as he drove. "I don't know what you thought vandalism was going to accomplish. You don't want the Ad people against you. You'll lose discounts and whatnot."

Discounts? Was this what he thought I was really concerned about? I stifled the wail that mushroomed in my gut and kicked hard at the seat instead. He ignored me and sped onto the outer ring, gunning the engine with a small sigh of pleasure. The road hummed smoothly under us, like the hiss of heavy rain on the dome. I didn't look back. I didn't want to see what was back there. I pushed the thought of what had just happened to the back of my mind.

"Was the movie actress with you?" the officer asked, perplexed by how we were connected.

I narrowed my eyes at him in the rearview mirror. Why was he talking to me? The city swept past us, Ads blazing across billboards to keep up with the cars, desperate not to lose even a potential second of advertising. What would happen to Saretha now? The thought of how she must hate me stabbed at my conscience. I should have just said *no*.

But would the brothers have spared Sam if I spoke? Or would they have made me speak another word, and then another?

I tried to bring my breathing under control. I forced myself to remember: I hadn't dropped Sam. I hadn't murdered him. They did. They chose to. Would I be able to make Saretha understand? Would I ever even see her again?

It still seemed impossible Sam was gone.

"Did that Lawyer say she was studying you for a role?" Shalk was asking. He didn't seem to think much of the idea.

My body shook as I started sobbing. I couldn't stop. How

had this happened? My head ached a little less, but my elbow hurt a little more. I tried to focus on what lay ahead, but what did any of it matter now? Everything I cared about was gone. The brothers would sue, the Ad companies would sue and people who were nearby and inconvenienced would sue. There was a good chance I'd find myself in Debt Collection by morning. I'd be a fine prize.

The only shred of hope I had lay hidden my left hand: a chip pulled from the Ad panel with evidence of Sam's murder. It bound me together, like a single thread. Without it, I knew I would finally understand how Beecher must have felt. I had no other reason to go on.

Was I really so foolish as to think anyone would care? I wanted to ask Henri what to do. The thought of it almost made me laugh. *Henri?* I could hear Margot laughing at me, and at him. They would see the brothers' story on the news: not mine. Henri wouldn't understand. No one would.

Shalk was sighing. "I've seen a lot of jumpers, but never this young. It's a shame, a terrible shame."

I wished he would talk about something else. I pressed my head to the window. We blazed under one bridge after another. The walls of the great speedway zoomed past, a glittering blur of Ads in my wet eyes. People, distant and small, went about their business. How could they continue to go on when my brother was gone? I dropped my eyes to the ground. I couldn't bear to look at them.

There would be no justice for Sam.

I felt nauseous realizing my parents had to be told. I couldn't face the thought of what Saretha might say to them. I couldn't tell them myself. I needed Sam, but I would never have his help again. I tried to catch my breath between tears. Officer Shalk stopped talking, even though he could speak freely— every word charged to me.

Shalk swerved off the exit and righted the car onto a main street with the precision of a stunt driver. A moment later, we were at the police station. He turned off the engine, and the electric motor whirred down.

He slid a finger across his Cuff in a convoluted gesture, shunting it into a mode I'd never seen. The curved screen went deep red and lit his face with its light. Informant Mode™. He eyed the parking lot to see if anyone was paying attention, then turned to face me.

"I had to ask if they want to sue. I couldn't have Silas Rog coming at *me* for a breach of protocol. I don't have—" He leaned a little closer and whispered, even though no one was around. "I don't have any more choice than you do."

Was that true? Officer Shalk was at least my father's age, and like my father, he looked weary, pouchy around the eyes. Was it like this for everyone?

"Did they kill him?" he asked softly.

I bit my lip. Somehow he knew.

He went on grimly. "But you know they'll scrub the evidence."

All he needed was the chip in my hand. I strained against the plastic binding my wrists. I tried to shift my position, so he could see my hands.

He looked down at the blank spot where my Cuff had been.

"I'm sorry," he said. His voice was sad. I teared up again. Poor Sam—he would have liked this officer.

Shalk tapped his Cuff again and got out of the car.

★ ★ ★

In the station, my body was scanned, and my retinal maps confirmed who I was. There was a brief moment of amusement when the officers pulled my records and saw Arkansas Holt listed as my Lawyer, followed by surprise when they found my occupation sealed. Shalk seemed at once impressed and disappointed.

"She's a Placer," a sharp-eyed officer named Yundoro said in a bored voice. "Look at her build." He looked me up and down. My cheeks burned. He clearly wasn't impressed.

Shalk considered it. "A Placer with Arkansas Holt for a Lawyer? I thought Placers made good money."

Yundoro shook his head as he unclipped the plastic binders on my wrists to take my fingerprints, and then he froze. "What's this?"

He dug hard into my clenched fist, prying my fingers open. His hands were rough. He found the chip.

Officer Shalk straightened. "Is this from the scene?"

Yundoro looked at me like I was something he might scrape off his shoe.

"This came out of an Ad Array," Yundoro said, holding it up between his finger and thumb. "We can't take it into evidence. *Brinkly versus Kleen 'n' Brite*™. *'Police are barred from accessing or copying scans pursuant to'*—"

I foolishly reached out to grab it back from him. He shoved me against the wall, his forearm against my throat.

"Assaulting an officer?" Yundoro growled, releasing me. His eyes flicked to Shalk. "Add it to her charges."

"What do you think's on it?" Shalk asked, taking it lightly from Yundoro while ignoring his request.

"Doesn't matter," Yundoro answered, wiping himself off like I was unclean. "Police are barred from pulling scan data. We can't take these from the scene."

I watched the chip between Shalk's fingers, cursing that I couldn't tell them why I had taken it. Maybe I could show them. I reached out and plucked it out of Shalk's hand, knowing I might get slammed against the wall again.

Shalk looked at me, calm. "*She* stole it," he said, taking it back again.

"Yeah?" Yundoro grunted.

"It has to go into evidence," Shalk said, his eyes darting to me almost admiringly. "Theft isn't covered by *Brinkly versus Kleen 'n' Brite*™."

A small, hopeful fire burned in my belly. My plan might just succeed.

Yundoro pursed his lips. "Whatever. If you want the paperwork." He handed over an evidence envelope, clucking his tongue. "Should've kept her in restraints," Yundoro commented.

"If the judge orders it," Shalk said, finishing my intake with a press of a button on his Cuff.

At that moment, The Blocks came on. Anything that wasn't explicitly in the public domain was blurred to little more than colored squares. Shalk and Yundoro became two masses of moving blocks in the approximate shape and location of the human behind them. As far as the authorities were concerned, I had basically lost my right to see. In all likelihood, I would be like this for the rest of my life. My hands were the only thing I could see. They were shaking. My chest tightened. I couldn't have ever imagined how crushing and claustrophobic The Blocks now made me feel.

"It's okay." Shalk set a gentle hand on my back and pressed me down a hall I could barely see. Behind us, Yundoro sniggered at me. I deliberately slowed my breathing and stood up tall.

Shalk locked me in a holding cell with the blocky shapes of four or five people. It was hard to tell through the blur exactly how many or who they were.

"I'll contact your Lawyer," Shalk sighed.

When he was gone, the room was silent. No one spoke. It would hardly do for them to spend money on words in here. Cameras whirred in the corners, tracking our faces. I could hear them and sense them, watching our lips, our blinks, our sighs.

I couldn't believe I would never hear Sam's voice again. I would never see his face. I didn't even have a picture to go home to. The Rights Holders owned every picture ever taken of Sam. The Ad companies probably had dozens of his scans stored away, but I had nothing. I began to sob softly, letting the tears fill my eyes and blur whatever was left to see.

I thought things couldn't get worse, but then I reminded myself that soon the Collection Agency would come to retrieve me. There would be no trial; I couldn't afford that. A judge would remand me to the custody of the highest bidder. The small flicker of hope I had in the Ad Chip faltered. I could never afford to bring the case to trial, so what good would evidence do me?

I wondered what Henri, Margot and Kel would think when I didn't show up. I knew they would probably just go on, and

I couldn't blame them. What else could they do? Whenever Henri came up short looking for his little blue device, Kel would know I had stolen it. I doubted she would see or care about the loophole I'd found to justify my actions.

I tried to conjure some optimism, but found only the desolation of my future stretching out before me. I tried not to think about being sent off to do crop pollination or factory work. Beecher's sad face came back to me. When confronted with the same prospects, his choice was to have no future at all. At that moment, right then, would I have jumped if I had the chance?

No. They could kill me, but I would never take my own life. I would fight to the end.

RECLAMATION: $43.99

Hours passed. My weary body slept and roused. The cell door opened, and I watched the blocky shape of someone else shoved inside. I could not see who it was, or any detail of her face, but I could sense that she knew me. She quickly sat at my side, closer than I would have liked. Her hand found mine, and she grasped it and held it. I felt the vibration of her Cuff, charging her for the kindness.

Was it a friend? Her fingers were thin and cold. I stared at her through The Blocks, but I could not determine much. She did not say a word.

Not long after, the lights dimmed briefly and my vision cleared. The Blocks had disappeared, and I realized it was Sera Croate holding my hand.

I didn't know whether to laugh or cry. What was she doing here?

Sera began shaking her head. "Speth," she said, releasing my fingers. Her Cuff didn't buzz.

An older woman on the other side of me asked, "A FiDo? Of all places," she whispered. "After all this time."

Other faces in the cell lit up. A low chatter began.

The Blocks, the shocks—none of it worked without the

WiFi. There hadn't been a FiDo since Butchers & Rog had the network consolidated into a central core.

"I saw it," Sera whispered. Her eyes filled with tears. "I didn't know they were going to…" She choked on the words. "Those men…"

My hand balled into a fist. I wanted to slam her into the bars, but I did not move. She wiped her eyes.

"I tried to say something, but suddenly my Cuff went off, and my eyes…" She took a deep gulp of air. "I tried to tell them what really happened, but they just arrested me. I should have said nothing. I should have gone silent. Right? Is that what you all figured out?"

I didn't know what she was talking about. I didn't have any idea. I couldn't focus on her words with all the contempt in my heart. She'd brought those men down on Sam.

"Yorda Silent Girl," the older woman across the cell announced.

I stopped to breathe. Everyone knew my face. They all looked to me.

"Did you know going silent would turn everything upside down? Do you know what they are going to do tomorrow?"

"They're gonna meet at Falxo Park," Sera went on. "All of them."

My eyes blazed at Sera. *What the hell are you talking about?!* my mind screamed at her. Did she not comprehend what she had done? Sam would be alive if not for her. I could never forgive her for just standing by.

"The Silents," she said, undaunted by my glare. "Mandett is getting them to come. It's his Last Day. I thought it was obnoxious—pointless—but now…I don't know…"

Her brow was furrowed, and she watched me intently, like she was looking for me to say something.

"This is so awful," she said pitifully. "Can't you help them? Can't you explain?"

Did she expect me to talk? She didn't understand the depth of my refusal, or my fury at her. I wouldn't speak unless I was certain everything had changed—and certainly not for her. It was too late for her to come around. Too late to save Sam.

"I'm so sorry." She sniffled and took my hand again. I stared, focusing on her bony white knuckles as she half crushed my hand in her frantic clutch. She raised our hands together and dropped them again, easing her grip, then let go with a whispered, "Thank you."

She took my silence for forgiveness, ignoring the blaze in my cheeks and the hate in my eyes. She had no idea how lucky she was that I did not hurt her. Being silent for so long had taught me all forms of restraint.

Footsteps sounded behind me. The lights dimmed again. The Blocks returned; everything became blurry once more. Sera stiffened and then slumped with disappointment. A woman across from us spoke a single word—"They"—and then squealed against the pain shocking her eyes for it. The FiDo had come to an end.

Speth.

The word flickered to life in my vision, hovering over the pixelated blur of my cell. I closed my eyes and opened them, but the word remained.

A figure outside the bars growled at me.

"Speth Jime. Let's go."

The word faded. I heard the door open.

"Speth," Sera whispered. Her Cuff buzzed in alarm. "I'm sorry."

Someone grabbed me roughly by the arm and shoved me down the hall and into the atrium. He stopped me short at the benches. A figure was seated there—a dark, calm, motionless figure dressed in forest green. A lean woman, from the shape of her.

She had to be a Collection Agent. Who else would come for me? I squinted, as if that would help me see through The Blocks, then balled my fists in frustration. What would happen if I throttled a Collection Agent?

She quietly typed away on what must have been a Pad.

Another message, Relax, appeared before my eyes. Did she type this? Did she have access to my feed? Had I already been sold off? The officer still gripped my arm, and I tried to wrest it free.

The seated woman spoke quickly and clearly to the officer. "Under statute 792-C, I hereby claim custody of Speth Jime and, having taken said custody, demand you immediately *cease* and *desist* use of The Blocks, and any other means of non-mandatory restriction or restraint."

The officer released my arm at once, intimidated by the razor sharpness of her Legalese. The sound of it made me shudder, too. A moment later, The Blocks vanished.

Standing before me in a deep green suit jacket and skirt was a dark-skinned, serious-looking woman. She had a slim but impressive row of Legal medals pinned over her blazer pocket.

"Follow me, please," she said without emotion. I did as she said, and a series of dots lit the path in my eyes. I didn't resist—in fact, all thought of fighting vanished.

It was no Collection Agent who had come to retrieve me. It was Kel.

GEORGETOWN LAW®: $44.98

We walked in silence, a thousand questions pushing through the haze I was in. How had she found me? How did she know I had been arrested? Were her clothes a disguise, or was she actually a Lawyer? Where was she taking me now?

It was late. The dome was black above us, and the sidewalks were nearly deserted. We crossed onto Stewart's Ring, a street on the south side known mostly for a clot of insurance agencies. I had been here before, though mostly on the rooftops. Kel entered a building through the front and I followed her to a bank of elevators, my mind and emotions reeling.

Did she know that Sam had been killed? Had she just pulled me out and rescued me so *she* could destroy me? I could not read her expression. I was terrified and grateful and sick to my stomach with grief.

She placed a thumb on the elevator controls and selected 22. We shot up to the building's twenty-second floor. The elevator doors hissed open to a spacious apartment that was elegant, but austere. Kel led me toward a wall decorated with large panels displaying a glowing rotation of family images. There were two adults, with the same deep, dark skin as Kel, standing over three little girls. The oldest one had to be Kel at seven or eight years old. Her eyes were just the same. It was not a posed photograph, but rather looked like one that had been culled from an Ad screen in a park. Another picture showed Kel and her sister, laughing wildly. They were both dressed poorly in public domain clothes, walking along the street. This image, too, looked like it had been taken by an Ad screen in a part of the city I didn't recognize—or perhaps even a different city.

A wave of resentful despair washed over me. I had heard that you could do this—go back and rescue images from your past held by data companies. I would never be able to afford to do this for Sam. Sam's images and scans and data would slowly erode over time, until it was like he no longer existed. No company would see any value in him or his data. Worse, it was likely they would scrub him away intentionally, to hide the crime of the three brothers.

Kel put a hand on my shoulder, but I shrunk away from the gesture.

A picture faded in to show Kel dressed in a satin robe, accepting a paper scroll under a banner that read Georgetown Law®. She stood proudly beside her family, with one girl missing.

She touched the picture almost thoughtfully, like she wanted to connect. The panel pulled in and slid away. The Squelch behind it was unremarkable, except that it had shelves of books inside. I had never seen this before. People who owned books always wanted them displayed. Even Henri's hung on a wall. Kel, on the other hand, hid hers. The more I knew about her, the less I understood.

She ushered me in quickly, and the door closed us inside. Her Lawyer's outfit unsettled me. She unpinned her medals and stowed them in a pocket, and then she waited. I didn't know if she was offering me a chance to speak, or hesitating because the words she wanted to say were difficult.

Sadness and regret washed over me again. I had betrayed her. I had betrayed Henri. I had broken Margot's heart. Sam was dead. Saretha was with Silas Rog.

I had nothing left.

"I'm very sorry, Speth," Kel said in the sparest whisper.

I wished she hadn't said it. It meant she knew what had happened. Something erupted in me, and I wanted to slap her, but that made no sense. I balled my hands into fists to control myself. Why hadn't she stopped it? Why hadn't she helped? She had to know an end like this was coming. How had the world turned into the Copyrighted, litigious, lethal monstrosity that treated us this way? How had anyone let this happen?

A low sound, like a moan or an animal cry, filled the air, followed by a sob that wracked my body. I clamped my hands to my mouth, disgusted and horrified. The sound came from me. Me. My lungs gulped for air. Had I kept my silence at the expense of Sam's life, only to disgorge this awful, meaningless note?

Kel wiped her eyes.

"Involuntary sound is *not* communication," she said, and then, more forcefully, like an incantation, "and charges stemming forth constitute a *breach of Law*. Said sound does not obligate or bind to payment the party from which said sound emanated. This includes laughing, coughing, sneezing and other bodily sounds for which a reasonable expectation of control cannot be demonstrated."

I could not remember anyone ever using Legalese to console me. I let go of my fury at Kel. Silas Rog deserved it more. Sam once said, after he turned fifteen, he would learn to communicate through farts. The memory of his irreverence soothed and unsettled me at the same time.

"All the good I thought I could do as a Lawyer..." Kel shook her head. "It came to nothing. I thought I could change things. I thought I could get in and get us back some rights—some freedom. For years, I sought proof that freedom of speech is a right, but I can't find it. There are hints and clues, but none of it matters." She gestured to the books around us. I realized they were all books of Law.

"I'm certain it used to be different. I've seen where the Law started out as protection for the people, and somewhere it was perverted, like there is a missing link where the Law changed. Copyright became perpetual. Trademark expanded beyond Brands. Patent turned into a game of war. I tried to discover how, but everything surrounding the change is suppressed, censored and classified into an opaque Legal fog. It's possible the change is recorded in the book people whisper about—the book they say Rog possesses. But I never found any evidence of it."

I closed my eyes for a moment and drew a breath. I tried to understand. Why was it always Rog? He wasn't our city's leader, though it seemed like he controlled everything. Wasn't there a world outside, beyond him?

I yearned to ask Kel questions, but she had been clear; she respected my silence. I had to keep it, at the very least until I had some revenge. Was the book the revenge that I needed?

"I did everything legally and out in the open. It galled them. Suits mounted against my family and me, all of them spurious. I could not defend against the volume. They took one of my sisters well before I started, and the other to teach me to back away. I had been too obvious and too threatening. So I dropped out of sight. I became a Placer. I tried to make a difference there, too, knocking out the WiFi and giving people a chance to talk, but that backfired. Rog took control of every node and hid them underground."

Rog, I thought. He was there again. They taught us in school about the two branches of government—the Legislative and the Judicial. We had a representative for our dome, and a Commander-in-Chief Justice who was in charge of the country, but Silas Rog didn't seem to answer to either of them.

"The best I could do was set aside extras for Henri and Margot to pass along. I swore to do it all legally—no stealing, no breaking in. I—"

A knock came at the door. She put a finger to her lips to tell me to be quiet, but then remembered who she was talking to. My eyes felt raw and my head was spinning. My head and elbow still ached.

Kel opened the door. Henri and Margot stood waiting. Margot's face was grim and anxious. Henri's flushed with relief when he saw me. Kel pulled them in and sealed the door.

MISERABLE THINGS: $45.98

"What happened?" Henri asked. His brow wrinkled in confusion.

"Her brother's dead," Kel said in a rough, unsteady voice. "They are saying he jumped."

"Did he?" Margot asked, her voice low and cool. She crossed her arms.

I glared at Margot, and my eyes welled with fresh tears. I wanted to scream *no*, but I would not say it. No. Whatever happened, I would not speak until I saw things change—or, at least, until I saw Rog taken down. Sam did not want me to give in. I was sure of it.

"I'm sorry," Henri said, avoiding my eyes.

"I got her out, but Collection will be coming," Kel said, regaining her normal, orderly tone. "They've already put in the claim. Rog has a hold on her purchase."

Everyone looked a little startled.

"You should not have her in your home," Margot said to Kel.

"Why?" Henri wanted to know. He lifted a bag up and handed it to me—my bag. He must have retrieved it from my apartment.

"*Why?*" Margot mimicked him. "Are you stupid? Silas Rog *bought* her."

"So?" Henri asked again.

Margot exploded. "Do you have any idea what Rog will do if we interfere? She is only using us, anyway! She does not care about us. Why do you care about her?"

I felt a twinge of disappointment in Margot. But what, exactly, did I expect?

"They took her sister away," Kel said, as if Margot had said nothing. "They've been deleting her data all day. I'll try to get a better update when we leave..." She waved a hand around the room. Her Pad wouldn't update again until the door opened and we went out into the WiFi tether.

"We need to go," Margot said. "Now! They are sure to track her Cuff."

I held out my forearm, bare of the Cuff.

"Oh. Right. How did you manage to remove that?" Her eyes shot to Henri. Henri felt back to his pack and, of course, the little blue device wasn't there. An oppressive silence filled the room. Henri's eyes glistened, realizing that I'd used him. That our kiss had never been real.

"Well." He swallowed hard. "We still have to help. I could hide her at my place."

I wanted to throw my arms around him, but Henri would get the wrong message, and Margot would only be further enraged.

Margot stamped her foot. "She cannot stay with you. You don't even have a Squelch. If you are ruined, too, how will that help anything? How?"

Henri tried to answer, but Margot wheeled around on me.

"I have a family, too, and I am sorry, but I will not let you destroy us! My sister is eight years old. Do you want Silas Rog to buy *her*?"

Of course I didn't want that. Margot's eyes darted around quickly like a nervous rabbit. She seemed to grow even more angry and frustrated. "I am sorry about your brother," she added through her teeth. "You see what he does to us?"

She meant Rog. The room seemed to be narrowing around me. There was nothing they could do, and Margot was right. I was only endangering them.

I crossed to the door. I had my bag with my gear now. I had zero idea where to go, but I had to keep them safe.

Kel put a hand on my shoulder and held me back.

"Margot," Kel said, "do you remember the night Henri went down to that alley? Do you remember how you whispered, 'It's the Silent Girl'?"

Margot nodded very slowly.

"You practically squealed," Kel said.

"I did not squeal."

Had Margot been excited? I hadn't seen it. I did remember how she'd bandaged my chin.

"Do you remember how annoyed I was?" Kel asked.

"You hate all talking on the job," Margot said hoarsely.

"After we let her follow us—after she'd gone—you told me she was the only hope this city had."

"That is how miserable things are," Margot said, frowning.

Kel turned back toward me. "Speth, I don't really know what your plan was—or if you ever had one. Maybe you thought you would inspire people, or maybe you are just a fifteen-year-old girl who never saw this coming. I wish you could tell us what it is you want."

I wanted my family back. I wanted Sam to be alive. I wanted his death avenged. I wanted the world changed. I wanted things made right. I wanted us all to speak free.

Margot shook her head, as if Kel was wasting her time.

I took the Pad from Kel's hands. I typed in the search box what I most wanted.

Silas Rog.

It was the best I could do to explain. I wanted him destroyed.

The Pad started beeping. The map scrolled to the heart of the city. Henri's head cocked quizzically, and Kel's brow furrowed. She leaned in, trying to glean what I had done.

"Oh, no," she breathed. A new assignment appeared on our itinerary.

We had a Placement in the office of Silas Rog.

A CHANGE IN SCHEDULING: $46.96

A chill ran down my spine. What we were seeing was impossible. The WiFi was supposed to be blocked, but a red dot blinked ominously on the map. The layout of Butchers & Rog's central tower, previously blank, filled in with an elaborately detailed blueprint.

"Um, how could the schedule change?" Henri asked. "We're in a Squelch—there's no WiFi."

"Maybe the room is not sealed," Margot said darkly.

Kel's face twisted into an expression of both horror and admiration. "It's not the room. We triggered something *inside* the program," she said, taking the Pad back. "It's a snare."

"Does Rog know we're here, or not?" Margot asked sharply.

"Not yet. Not until we open that door," Kel said, looking over at the crack of the door, flush and sealed in the wall. I felt as if the very air outside was poison, threatening to seep in.

"Who would have access to a Pad's programing?" Henri asked.

"Who do you think?" Margot said.

"But isn't this Placement exactly what we want?" Henri asked. "We could use it to get that book everyone talks about. This could change everything. We could broadcast it. We could do Placements of it!"

"Oh, Henri," Margot said, as if Henri's simplicity was almost too sad for her. "There is no such book. It cannot be."

I didn't truly believe it existed, either, but hearing Margot say it cut me to the quick. It felt as if she wanted me to feel like everything was hopeless.

Kel examined the Pad more closely. "He isn't tracking us specifically. This trap wasn't meant for us. It has been there all along—it would have tripped up any Placer who typed his name. Rog wants to flush out anyone foolish enough to search for him."

"Good," Margot said with relief. "Then we destroy the Pad."

"What? Why?" Henri cried.

"So it doesn't uplink when we open the door!" I could almost hear the word *dummy* at the end of her sentence. "If we destroy it, everything can go back to normal."

I can't, I thought. But maybe normal for her meant a world before I joined the team.

Kel's head shook ever so slightly as she mulled this idea over in her head.

Kel tipped the Pad toward me. "This is where he wants us to go," she said, indicating a large, curved office that was tagged as Silas Rog's. "The layout shows us *exactly* how to get there—shows us the surrounding floors, all in great detail." Kel flipped it around, showing me one floor and then the next. "He wants us to bring him chocolates."

I almost laughed out loud, despite how desolate I felt. Margot leaned into the wall and slid down to a seated position. She hid her face in her hands. "This is insane. Why would we walk into a trap?"

"Because we *know* it's a trap," Henri said, as if this was our ace in the hole.

"Henri, you are just saying words," Margot fumed.

Margot was right. Rog *would* be waiting for us. As much as I wanted to face him, it would be absurd to hand him the advantage.

"Henri's right," Kel said.

Henri could not suppress his broad grin.

"Knowing it's a trap is our advantage," Kel went on. "Silas Rog is brilliant and horrible, but he loves to deceive and manipulate so much he won't think we can do the same."

My skin felt warm. A spark of hope ignited in my gut. The word sounded in my mind, almost like I couldn't control it. *Hope.* It was my voice in there, but also Sam's, my mother's and my father's. Was Saretha in there, too?

Kel knelt down to her bag. It was sitting, zipped and crisp, waiting for her next Placement. She checked her gear. She meant to go. I felt terrible for how I had treated her—pushing her away, stealing when I knew it would hurt her. How could I let her know how sorry I was?

"This is suicide," Margot said, arms crossed.

"No. This is war," Kel said fiercely as she moved on to check my bag.

Margot shook her head. Henri cleared his throat. Kel made sure my grapple hook and sleep gas were secured, and that I had chocolates and a way to light them.

"Maybe that book *is* real," Kel said, like she wanted to believe. I desperately wanted to believe it, too. "That central building is a fortress. He has to be protecting something in there. Getting inside is half the battle."

"What are we doing?" Henri asked, puzzled.

"We're going to deliver chocolates," Kel said, zipping my bag closed. I always liked how carefully she spoke, enunciating each syllable.

"I won't do it," Margot said, tightening her crossed arms and glaring at me.

"I don't want you to," Kel shot back, hoisting her bag over her shoulder. Margot's mouth dropped open.

"Henri, you and I will do the Placement and act as a distraction, so Speth can get to whatever it is Rog does not want her to find."

BUTCHERS & ROG: $47.99

Kel didn't give me time to argue—not that I *could* argue. Her Pad shuddered and pinged the moment we stepped out the door. Butchers & Rog knew we were coming now, and we didn't hesitate. We made our way quickly toward the city center. The faster we got there, the less time they'd have to prepare for us.

Margot peeled off from us with a quick, sarcastic salute and swung away, red-faced and furious. Henri was crestfallen. Kel saluted back, but never took her eyes off the center of the city. I was strangely glad for Margot. If we failed, she might go on. Her sister might be spared. I was painfully aware that Sam had not been. I prayed I could make his death mean something.

The city felt ominously quiet as the air whipped by us. The Butchers & Rog Tower ahead had a seamless glass panel façade. The smooth, mirrored array made it difficult to make out individual windows or floors. But, near the top, a single, tall window was out of place; the elongated reflection of the city was askew from the reflected panorama. That was our way in.

The floor-to-ceiling frame opened into what we were meant to believe was Rog's office. The space was generous, filled with cushioned, old wooden furniture, not the printed stuff. Colorless photos glowed softly from the walls, shifting in an arty slideshow. The floor was covered with a black-and-indigo carpet, hand threaded with delicate gold details. It was meant to convey a sense of grandeur, but it just disgusted me. Cameras were inset in each of the room's corners: small black bulbs, like insect eyes. With a quick tap at her Pad, Kel knocked them out before we entered. It was a formality, though—the Lawyers knew we were coming and this was our only way in.

Once inside, Kel did a wide sweep with her Pad for thermals and found nothing. The trap, whatever it was, wasn't yet sprung.

The three of us looked like shadows in our gear, masked and anonymous. Henri's posture was oddly stooped. I think he was afraid; I knew I was. The thought that we might fail was too horrible to consider, but even the idea that we might succeed was just as terrifying. What if I came face-to-face with Silas Rog? Would I even know it? I had never seen his face, only its blocky outline. I imagined him bloated and terrible, with the eyes of a viper.

Henri silently placed a selection of chocolates on a side table with none of his usual joy. He kept glancing at me, his eyes sad beneath his mask. Kel fiddled with the door leading out of the room and motioned for me to come to her side. The door clicked open. She gestured for me to go through, dragging her finger along a map on her Pad. Instantly, a trail of dots appeared in my eyes, leading to a door in the hallway, then to the stairs, and up, up, up beyond.

She wanted me to go on alone. This was it.

Could I do this? Did I have it in me? I tried not to think too much, because I was near the edge of losing it. Who was I to think I could change anything, let alone everything? My head still throbbed. My elbow still ached. I was tired, heartbroken and angry, but I had to focus. Kel handed me her Pad and pushed me along, like a fledgling driven from the nest.

I know the Pad was meant to help me, but taking possession of it terrified me. I'd never heard of her passing it on before. Not like this. My hands trembled holding it, but Kel's dark eyes urged me forward. She still looked calm. *You can do this*, she seemed to say.

The door to the elevator rattled open. I barely had time to run out of sight.

"Remain where you are," a voice called out. I could hear movement. I scrambled upward as quickly as I could, following the virtual dots aligned on the stairs before me. I whipped the Pad around and was able to see the thermal colors of three men rushing down toward Kel and Henri. Kel did a flying kick that slammed one man into the next, knocking both to the floor. Even on the Pad, Kel looked tall, lean and formidable. Henri took the third, smaller man, spun him around and slammed him into the wall.

"I am a Lawyer!" he cried out, incredulous and dazed, before Kel knocked him out cold.

I moved upward, more slowly than I should have, keeping an eye on my friends. Then I noticed something. Kel had inset a rectangle into the screen's lower left corner. It displayed a live feed from her retinal overlays. She zapped both men on the floor quickly with something, and then glanced at the doughy little Lawyer. This was only the first wave, a pitiful trio meant to poke us and test our numbers and resolve. Four more security guards were bearing down on them, with two more polished Lawyers behind. Kel and Henri raced down the stairs. I picked up my pace and moved upward.

The stairs wound on endlessly. I had to be above the dome now. Two flights up, the dots Kel had set for me stopped at a door. Did Kel know what lay ahead, or was this just her best guess?

It didn't matter. I had nowhere else to go.

In the live feed, I could see Kel and Henri had burst out onto a floor far below, one filled with wide, bubble-like cubicles for ParaLegals. Henri took hold of some large cabinet. I think it was filled with hard drives. He yanked it down to block the door. The heavy sound of it falling came through the speakers of the Pad.

"You will be held legally and financially responsible for all damages," a voice informed them with cold, efficient menace.

Each tick of Kel's eyes made the view whip around. It was difficult to watch. I felt powerless so far from them, and strangely exposed, even though they were the ones under attack.

Kel broke through an office door, and then through another adjoining it. Was she looking for an exit? Even from where I stood, it looked like she was going in circles.

I reached the end of the line. The Pad registered nothing above me. The blueprint did not extend this far, but the stairwell continued up toward a final door. Was this the roof? Rog's real office? What lay beyond?

Glass shattered somewhere below. A small sound emanated from the Pad. I looked and saw plush furniture, guards. Kel knocked over a computer. It was clumsy, inelegant, very un-like her. She wasn't trying to escape. She was leading the guards on a chase.

I set to work picking the lock on the door. It didn't take much. Maybe Silas Rog hadn't counted on anyone making it this far.

Or maybe *this* was the trap.

I couldn't think about it. I had to move forward. I steeled myself and pushed the door open.

THE LIBRARY: $48.98

The top floor of Butchers & Rog was filled with shelves and shelves of books. They arced in rings, mazelike, to the room's center. I had never seen or imagined anything like it, not even when my father told me about the Liberties.

If a book existed that could change our lives, it had to be here, didn't it? I felt hope rise again in me. *What if it really is possible?* I wondered.

There were thousands—maybe *tens* of thousands—of books. They were all different shapes and sizes, fat and thin, bound in leather, or canvas, or cardboard or printed plastic sheets. Some bore titles on their spines in gilt letters or black pressed ink. Some said nothing at all. I had no clue which one might help us. What, exactly, was I looking for?

Kel let out a strangled yelp from the Pad. She was standing face-to-face with the golden brother, the one who had stopped me on the bridge. His lean, sharp face wore a ghastly, predatory smile as his fist whipped into view. I realized that he'd punched her. The feed went dark, but the sound kept on. Henri yelled something unintelligible. I looked deeper into the Pad, as if that might help me see what was happening. It was wasted effort; Kel's eyes were closed.

I couldn't help. I had to start searching.

"Whereas you have trespassed..." a voice in Kel's feed came through the tiny speaker, sharp and icy "...and whereas you have caused the willful destruction of property, assaulted a Legal representative and his assigns, caused grievous harm, pain and suffering, and accorded yourselves with a gross dissimilitude from proper conduct to the Law..."

The Lawyer's voice faltered a moment.

"Where is Speth Jime?" His words were suddenly clipped and unlitigious. It chilled me to hear him speak my name.

No one answered.

"And whereas you have committed numerous additional transgressions, infractions and criminal violations yet to be enumerated and described, I assign you to the custody and supervision of the prevailing Legal authority available—me."

I recognized the voice with creeping dread. It was Silas Rog. While I did not know his face, I knew that voice. There was something distinctly cold and hateful in it.

A loathing twisted inside me. I couldn't let him distract me. He was somewhere down below, which meant he wasn't here. He was asking about me, which meant he did not know where I was.

I'd wasted enough time already. I pulled a book out from a shelf close by, my hands clumsy and tremulous. *Public Adjudication of Law* by Paul W. Bloom, © 1997.

I flipped through the pages. The paper was thin and the type was dense, impossible for me to comprehend. Was every book here like this one? There wasn't time for me to sit down and wade through the impenetrable jargon of the Law. I abandoned that one, shoving it back onto its shelf. I moved instinctively toward the room's center. If an important book was going to be anywhere, I reasoned—I hoped—it would be there.

"The parties hereforth present shall be remanded to floor seventeen for assessment of actionable infractions," I heard Rog say.

I pulled another book from the shelf, titled *Perpetual Mouse*, Alecia Grey, © 2028. The inside cover said Disney™ made certain, in perpetuity, that nothing created after 1928 could ever come out of Copyright in order to preserve the rights of a cartoon mouse.

The center of the room was dominated by an enormous, densely printed, polished pillar, like obsidian. Two sliding doors were cut into it, gilded in laser-cut gold and platinum. At first I thought this was it; the book must be locked inside. Then I noticed a simple, triangle-shaped button inset in a panel.

I pressed it out of desperation more than reason. As I did it, I realized it was almost certainly an elevator. I kept hoping it was something else—a safe or a room with the book inside.

It was a childish wish. A simple *ping* chimed, and the motor behind the doors engaged.

On the Pad, I heard movement. Kel's eyes were open again, looking down at the tiles of a hallway floor as she was dragged across them. I wanted her to look at Rog. I wanted to see his face.

Hatred boiled inside me, clouding my thoughts. All around me, aisles radiated out from the center, toward tall tinted windows. I saw nothing but a few moonlit clouds, darkened by the colored glass.

"Hereby and forthwith, I demand you provide the whereabouts of Speth Jime to the greatest degree of precision allowable by Law," Rog's voice intoned. I glanced at the Pad and saw only part of him as Kel's eyes ticked nervously around.

"Long gone," Kel said. Her voice was slightly muffled.

I swallowed hard. She was covering for me. I owed it to her and the others to make this mean something, but how? I began looking at the books again. The task seemed impossible.

"The specificity of your answer is insufficient. Evasive speech used for the purposes of obstructification will be answered with maximum penalty," Rog said.

"Where is she?" another voice asked, as if merely curious.

"Beyond the outer spiral," Kel said.

The doors behind me split open. I jumped. It was an empty elevator car. *Foolish*, I told myself.

"She might be in Canada by now," Kel added.

I looked down at the Pad. Kel was looking at Leeland Butchers. I'd seen his face before. Unlike Silas Rog, whose face was perpetually blurred in the media, Butchers allowed his red, pockmarked face to be shown everywhere. We all would have preferred he kept it hidden.

"Canada." Butchers chewed on the word. "Unlikely."

"You'll never find her!" Henri blurted out.

"Also unlikely," Butchers said. I stole another glance at the feed from the Pad. I wanted to see Rog. His head was down; he was preoccupied, typing something into his Cuff. I held back the urge to get on the elevator and bring the fight to him. The book was more important. I grabbed a promising title.

Trademark Expansion and Copyright Integration, © 2019.

I wanted to linger with the feel of the paper between my

fingers. It was strangely thin and fragile. Were all books like this? I willed myself to understand the words before me. The book was filled with mind-numbingly dull pages of Legalese, explaining Laws that once were, Laws that had changed and twisted and Laws that could be corrupted. It reminded me of the endlessly verbose Terms of Service I had skimmed and mindlessly agreed to all these years. I nearly tossed it aside until I saw the words: *Freedom of Speech*.

In the feed, a door opened. Kel and Henri were pushed in front of what appeared to be an inclined tanning bed, except the bottom part was missing, as if it would only tan your face. It looked snug and soft, with a smooth, enveloping curve for a person's body. Rog moved in front of it, his back to the camera in Kel's eyes. He seemed to pet it.

"Innovation is rare these days," Rog said. "A casualty of the necessary, voracious defense of Intellectual Property. It is difficult to hold a Patent without getting overly enthused about suing and defending oneself from suit." He seemed very pleased with the whole game. He patted the bed-like device, proud. Then he turned and showed his face. I brought the Pad closer to my eyes, even though I had more pressing things to attend to.

But it was blocked. Just like on the wall-screen, his face was nothing but a mottle of pink, gray and black squares as he spoke. Kel's corneal implants were blurring him out.

"I hereby notify you that certain proprietary information may be herewith divulged, which you are obligated, immediately and forthwith, to keep strictly confidential, without exception, under all circumstances and for all time under the full penalty of the Law." He waved his hand around like he was casting a spell.

"Every single day, millions of people go undetected creating unauthorized copies of music, films, pictures, ideas and words, robbing the American® businessman of his right to profit from his Intellectual Property and costing the American® economy trillions of dollars. The Cuff does an admirable, but incomplete, job of detecting and monitoring usage, but we know we can do better. Attorney Butchers?"

"Look here," Butchers said, in a low thrum of a voice.

I didn't look. Instead, I focused more closely on the *Freedom of Speech* reference in the book. It alluded to an Amendment, though I didn't know what had been amended. When did this Law exist? *Where* did it exist? The book read, plain as day, "Congress shall make no law abridging the freedom of speech." Was this what I was looking for?

"We're calling it a Finishing Bed®," Butchers went on. I tried to block him out and focus on the book. "It is going to put an end to Copyright infringement by extracting it at the very root."

I didn't know what a Congress was, but the words on the page filled me with hope and confusion. The book called the First Amendment a "guiding principle." Tears came to my eyes. It said Freedom of Speech was so important to American® life that our nation would fail without it. How could this be? We didn't have Freedom of Speech, yet America® thrived.

But that wasn't true. Everyone I knew was only barely surviving.

"The Finishing Bed® looks for infringing patterns expressed directly within your brain's electroneurology."

Henri's gasp caught my attention. "It reads minds?"

I followed Kel's eyes, ticking over the Finishing Bed®. The way the top part clamped over a person's face made me think of some kind of torture device.

"Nearly," Butchers said. "It matches patterns, so if you remember a song or a picture or a movie, it will find the unauthorized work and bill you accordingly."

"You're going to charge people for thinking about movies?" Henri asked.

"Movies, songs, ideas, words," Butchers said, clapping his meaty hands together. "It will be lucrative."

Kel burst out laughing. "That isn't possible," she said.

"What makes you believe that?" Butchers asked.

"Innovation isn't rare—it's unattainable," Kel said.

"Meaning?" Butchers asked.

"You assholes can't create anything anymore," Kel said. "And even if this works the way you say, you can't control what people think."

"We don't intend to control what people think. Just to charge them for it."

I couldn't believe what I was hearing. What kind of world would this be? I had to stop them, but I sensed, somehow, that the book in my hands wasn't enough. This wasn't *the* book. It only proved things had once been different, but it wasn't enough on its own. I dropped it in my bag in case it was useful and moved on.

I began to frantically search around for other, more promising titles. I found a sentence that read: "Copyright clearly does not protect ideas, only the tangible expression of them," in a book called *The First Amendment and Civic Duty* by Martin Bjørn, © 2017.

"There is no precedent," Kel said. "Everyone will fight you."

"Everyone will lose," Butchers said calmly. "And I have to point out that there is plenty of precedent. No Law has ever been ruled forbidding the monetization of thoughts. But there is *plenty* of legal precedent to show that any reproduction, regardless of its form, is subject to Intellectual Property Laws. Why should the brain be any different than a computer or a piece of paper?"

Butchers snapped his fingers. "Put him inside," he said.

I swallowed hard. They dragged Henri toward the machine. Surely the Finishing Bed® couldn't actually read Henri's mind— could it? But what if it hurt him?

A ParaLegal scurried over with a screen. "Could you sign this waiver?"

I flipped through *Limitations on the First Amendment* by Janet J. Kingsley, © 2031, and it looked like freedom of speech had become more restricted because companies banded together to claim it threatened their Brands, free trade and wealth. But so what? My search was hopeless.

I had to do something. I wanted to abandon the books and fly down to the seventeenth floor, but that would undo our entire purpose for being here. Too many books. Too little time. I shook myself; I had to find *the* book. It had to be here, and with it, I could destroy Silas Rog. I had to make people see, especially now. I moved to a different shelf and grabbed another book.

Rights Management Coding and Codes. It detailed methods and strategy for locking down software—something I knew absolutely nothing about. Beside it, another book had its cover embossed with a bold logo: *PrintLocks*™. I cracked it open.

In the feed, Butchers's assistants lowered the shell over Henri's head. He tried to look brave. I tore myself away from watching the feed to read.

This was not *the* book. It said nothing about speech or words. But the logo reminded me of WheatLock™, and the pages detailed the ways food inks needed to be combined and the ways printers functioned to combine them or lock the user out if payment wasn't authenticated. There was even a key showing which had nutritional value, and which were poisonous.

It wasn't *the* book, but it seemed like it could be useful.

From the Pad, Butchers's voice went on: "The trespassers, hereinafter referred to as the Participants, will submit to neurologic survey and inspection for any and all violations of Intellectual Property, and shall be held civilly accountable for any and all verified infractions found therein, as well as attendant animus nocendi."

I walked lightly around the thick pillar. On the far side, more wide aisles fanned out to the windows. It was growing lighter outside. There was no sign that any book was more important than another. I prepared to dig in and look through every one if I had to, but how much time did I have left?

Something clicked and whirred behind me. The answer was that my time was up. The elevator was moving, which meant someone was coming.

SILAS ROG: $49.99

I slipped down an aisle and crouched low. I was closer to the windows now and could see a flat expanse of dark, sparkling water to the east. The ocean. The size of it was mind-boggling, and I longed to take it in, but this was not the time.

The elevator doors slid open.

"I must register my disappointment."

It was Rog. I could hear him sniff at the air. Was he alone? I listened closely. If he had people with him, I couldn't hear them. But if they were as quiet as Kel and the team, they could have easily spread through the room to surround me, and I wouldn't know until they were right on top of me.

I crept back toward the stairwell. Could I escape? Should I? I didn't have what I'd come for, and my friends were locked up. No, I had to stay and fight it out, or go down trying.

"I am aware of what you are here for, Miss Jime." Rog sighed. "But you should recognize that facts on paper are worth very little, despite the mystique."

Facts on paper are worth very little? That was an interesting thing for a man standing in his own, massive library of paper books to say. Was he talking about *the* book? Was he admitting it was real?

"If you wish to hide like a rabbit, I can send for dogs to flush you out," he said. He had moved closer; his footsteps were light. I steadied myself, profoundly aware of the sound of my own breathing. I listened intently. Was he really alone?

"So many unauthorized reproductions." The voice startled me—it wasn't Rog. From the small speaker on the Pad, Butchers clucked over the Copyright violations he found in Henri's mind.

Across the room Rog laughed, moving nearer. I cursed myself for forgetting about Kel's feed as I tapped the Pad to mute it and silently scuttled back to hide farther away. This wasn't much of a confrontation, but I didn't know what to do. My hands were shaking.

"Shall I show you where it is?" Rog offered. "The *magical* book you are looking for?"

The faintest slipping sound reached me from a few rows away. I felt a little sick. I saw no way out.

"*This* is the book in question." He held a book up; I could see it waving in his hand over the shelves. The dark blue cover looked old, but cared for. I couldn't read the title. I could almost feel his security people creeping through the stacks to surround me, but I didn't hear so much as a breath. I quickly tapped the Pad over to its thermal sensor and scanned in a circle around me. It was just Rog and me in the room. Why had he come alone?

"Transgressors frequently attempt to gain access to these premises with the intent to burglarize this library and its contents, so they may secure *this* one book. Few make it inside, as you have." He paused. I watched his outline on the thermal sensor—orange, tall and fit, but I couldn't see the details of his face.

"I know when they are coming. I have copious resources

devoted to ingesting all the words people speak so I know when they speak against me. Algorithms can easily track patterns of discontent. Sometimes the models predict when they will come even before they themselves have decided."

My eyes burned a little. I despised the sound of his voice. His arrogance coiled between the stacks.

"*You've* never said a word though, have you? That troubles me. There is no algorithm that can parse the intention of silence." The book fell out of view, followed by the sound of flipping pages. "Your resolve is commendable. Of course, Samuel might feel differently."

At the sound of my brother's name, my blood boiled. *Sam.* He was *Sam!* And he was dead because of this man.

"It is unfortunate he had to be sacrificed in order for me to test your resolve." My heart pounded in my ears. I thought of Sam when he was little, holding my hand across Falxo Bridge. I choked a little and palmed the tears on my cheeks. He had Sam killed to *test* me?

"*All* forms of expression are subject to Copyright, Patent and/or Trademark. You turned silence into an expression of dissent, but you did not pay. It is a perversion of the Law!"

His voice was suddenly louder, and terrifyingly raw. I felt weak against it. I was letting everyone down again. Rog was toying with me, and I was going to fail.

But just as quickly, Rog settled down. "I suppose you have paid," he said. "Just not with money."

Silas Rog was a malignancy. He had ruined my life, piece by piece by piece. I wondered if I could hurt him back, and if so, how much.

"I can't have people following your lead. I've let it go on far too long. The *Silents*." He made their name sound like a curse. "Let me make you an offer—I will assign to you the majority share of rights pertaining to silent protest. It will be, as it already is, *your* Trademark. From this time forward, any and all parties demonstrably engaged in nonverbal remonstration for a period of more than three days will be required to pay good and valuable consideration to *you* for each subsequent minute of silence that follows."

What the hell does that mean? In my head I could hear Sam asking it, not me.

"All those Silents out there—more than the Media would have you know about, by the way—would have to pay *you* for the privilege of their silence. After three days, we could charge 10¢ each minute. You might clear a million dollars a day. They would never see it coming. I think it is a very innovative idea. I would drop all action against you and your friends, and you could go home. I could arrange to have your parents and Saretha waiting for you."

The suggestion was ludicrous, and I despised how gleeful he seemed about it. His math made it sound like there were far more Silents than I had dared imagine. Was it just our city, or had it happened in others?

"Just say the word…" He laughed at himself. "Just say *a* word."

He had to know I wouldn't agree. I couldn't trust him—he'd murdered Sam! And even if I *could* trust him, I wouldn't betray the Silents. They would be gathering even now, if Mandett had succeeded.

Rog looked at the book again and took a breath. His lips turned briefly purple on the scan, then warmed again, the color of flame. He was bothered. Something about my silence stuck in his craw. I could not see his face, but somehow I could tell that he was vexed.

This delighted me.

"Given all your cleverness, I'm a little surprised you have fallen for *this* chicanery." He shook the book in his hands. "If I had thought you were going to fall for it, I would have been up here waiting for you when you arrived."

His story was changing again. He didn't think I would fall for it? If he didn't think I was here for the book—if he didn't think I would come to the roof, to his library, where did he think I was headed? I had to read between his words to find the true meaning hiding in them. My mind focused, grappling with what he'd accidentally said.

"What did you think it could *possibly* contain?"

The book landed with a thud, not ten feet from me. He wiped his hands.

"There is no book."

The one he'd tossed certainly wouldn't be it, but it seemed more possible that the book existed now that he said it didn't.

He laughed. He was happy. He thought I was no threat, just an irritant he would soon dispatch. I wanted to kill him. Maybe that is what he thought I was there to do. Maybe now he felt safe, because I was only fifteen, and he was a monster.

I willed the strength back into myself. The foul sound of his voice fired my rage, stinging me with pins and needles. I pulled myself up to confront him, but then he stepped around the corner with Sam and Saretha by his side.

ANIMUS NOCENDI: $50.99

It wasn't possible. Sam was dead, and Saretha didn't look completely right. She looked just a little too like Carol Amanda Harving. Sam looked mischievous, but more like a cocky kid from a Disney™ film than himself. He jutted his chin at me as if to say *'Sup.*

Sam would never do that.

I blinked hard to shake off the hallucination. The image of them remained for a fraction of a second too long in the darkness under my eyelids. I reminded myself that Sam and Saretha hadn't appeared in the thermal display. They weren't here. Rog was inserting them directly into my vision through my corneal overlays.

Rog saw my expression and shrugged off his trick, like he'd had to try it. I looked him over, my skin bristling. His face was still nothing but Blocks, so I couldn't read his expression. He slid a finger over his Cuff, and Sam and Saretha's projections vanished.

I wanted to run. I wanted to run as far as I could, and escape from the dome, the city, the country, the world. I wanted to run headlong at Rog and take my chances trying to kill him. Could I bash him over the head with one of these giant legal books? Could I strangle him? Were my hands strong enough?

"I recognize your expression. Before you commit any additional felonies, take a moment; deliberate on your circumstances."

I'd "deliberated" enough. I don't know why he came up alone, but he would regret it.

"I still have Saretha in my care," he said quickly. He gestured to the spot where her image had been. "Even if she isn't here, I can have her brought up." He tapped something at his Cuff. "And you don't have any *real* hope of hurting me."

He rotated his forearm, to show me a small hole that was bored into the metal of his Cuff, the size and shape of the barrel of a gun.

The book was at his feet. He kicked it at me, keeping the Cuff's gun trained on my head.

"That book proves the opposite of what you wish. Freedom of Speech was carefully and *legally* carved away in order to preserve the nation and to keep people from harm."

He was used to talking; I could hear it in his voice. I ground my teeth in frustration. I mentally went through my bag, thinking what I could use to harm him. If I could knock *his* Cuff aside, could I turn it against him? Could I shoot my grapple hook into his chest? Could I club him with my pony bottle of sleep gas, or spray it in his face?

Probably not. His gun was trained right at me.

"It is far better and more profitable to own the *idea* of a chair than the chair itself. Intellectual Property has the advantage of being at the root of all things," Rog continued. "Control it, and you can control anything. A meal, or a gun, cannot come into being without the *idea* of a meal or the *idea* of gun."

He took a step toward me.

"I don't want to kill you. I want to defeat you. I want to eliminate the insolent idea you have that you might dare express yourself without paying. I want to *hear* your voice. This keeping silent..." He shook his head. He wouldn't put up with it. He brandished the Cuff at me, and his blocky face glowed pink, warmed by his passion for control.

"I've offered you an excellent deal. I am deeply frustrated that you seem to be rejecting it."

He turned his attention to the Cuff on his arm. He kept the barrel pointed at me and swiped. He sighed.

"I'll do it the hard way," he said. "I've sent word to construct an interview with you. In a few hours, the world will see you speak for the first time. It will be broadcast everywhere, through every WiFi node in the city. Not that it's necessary at this point. Your silence scarcely matters now. If everyone wants to keep quiet like you, so be it. I'll Patent the silent protest myself, and then I'll simply scan their brains for thinking about going silent. It'll be ludicrously profitable.

"I suppose I should thank you for forcing my hand. Without you, I wouldn't have been motivated to innovate. But still, I would like it clear that Silas Rog never loses. My reputation is at stake."

There was a hitch in his voice. He still wouldn't be satisfied. Everyone would think he had won, but he and I would know differently. In the history of things, I would have this small, unknown victory.

The view on my Pad changed. He'd somehow altered the

feed from Kel's to the one coming from my own corneal implants. I didn't understand how this was possible. How was my feed being transmitted without my Cuff?

"There will be no more late-night Product Placements, or flying under the public radar. You can go on with your silence. I don't care. What will it matter once everyone has seen 'you' speak? Afterward, I will ship you off to some hot, dusty field in Texas, far from any dome or hope. I'll put the feed from your eyes up for sale. Everything you see will be broadcast on WiFi everywhere, so people can watch the wretchedness of your existence—just like Belunda Stokes."

The WiFi, I thought numbly. The WiFi that once let everyone exchange ideas freely was now used to control our every move.

"I've taken ownership of your parents, your sister and you. I'll have each of your brains scanned for infringements until your family is so deep into debt that I'll own your grandchildren's grandchildren. Do you like babies? You can have them safely eight at a time now. You sluks call them litters, unless I've been misinformed. You're a bit young for such a brood, but not Saretha. Trust me, I'll be sure she has so many children that there will be generations of Jimes to pay your ceaseless debt. I'll send you a picture of each litter just before they are carted away and raised to pay me."

His body warmed with the thrill of his cruelty. I felt suddenly nauseous and doomed. This must have been how Beecher felt. I would rather die than face such a future, but I couldn't leave Saretha alone to this fate. I could not let him win.

Rog stared hard at me, waiting to see if I'd crack under his threats, but I gave him nothing. I kept myself still. I wouldn't let him intimidate me. He was too arrogant to believe I could hurt him, but he didn't realize the depths of my fury, or that I'd worked out what he was afraid of. He thought I was stupid, or at least dumber than I was, for believing the book really held some answer.

It sat at my feet, and I took the time to finally read what the cover said—*A Complete History of U.S. Intellectual Property Reform*. He'd lured me to the top of the building with this book—or some book; he may well have chosen one at random, for all I knew. But there was something here that he didn't want me near. If we were at the building's top, then *it* was at the bottom.

It came to me in a rush. The servers for the entire city were there. He'd centralized the WiFi himself. I thought of my father during the FiDos of long past, and how he'd longed for a different world. Maybe I could make that world exist, even if only for a moment. Everything required an always-on connection. What would happen if it was turned off? Beecher's father had been convinced that if it all went down—if it was destroyed—then it could not be set back on.

Rog was expecting me to weep and beg for his mercy. I bent down slowly, and the blocks that comprised his face shifted. Staring at him, I pulled my bag around, carefully placed the book inside and took a deep breath.

His shoulders relaxed. He laughed at me like I was a child.

"Oh my God," he gasped through his mocking laughter. "All this time, I thought you had some clever plan. You really don't understand, do you?"

I kept my face blank. *Go ahead*, I thought, *underestimate me*.

"The. Book. Won't. Help," Rog said slowly, like I wasn't

capable of understanding. "I could print up a thousand books and make them say whatever I want and call it history!"

I reached deep in my bag, letting the book settle. I exhaled and breathed deep again. I held that breath. I reached past my grappling gun to the small knob on the canister of sleep gas. I turned it slowly and counted in my head.

"Would you like some more?" he asked, gesturing to the books all around. It would take maybe ten seconds for the gas to reach him. I didn't know if I could last. I closed my eyes. I shrugged ever so slightly, silent, my mouth sealed tight. He laughed at me.

"That was communication!" he exclaimed, victorious. "And a willful skirting of the Law! *Bronsky versus State of Maryland*—'Sight occlusion whilst in commission of a deliberate gesture without authority from the state shall be considered...'" His head cocked slightly as he sniffed and swayed, trying to keep his Cuff trained on me.

My lungs burned. I longed for air.

He went on, voice slightly slurred, "'...willful elusion of Intellectual Prop...' Wait..." Panic radiated from him as I rifled through my bag, hoping to find my mask before I needed to draw a breath.

The elevator pinged. Rog frowned, his eyes unfocused. "They shouldn't..." But he was not able form the words he wanted.

I only had to stay conscious a little longer, before his guards— or whoever was on that elevator—arrived. Rog faltered. I moved toward him. My lungs felt ready to burst, and stars swam in my vision.

There was a loud bang and a shattering of glass. Had he

shot at me? I inhaled in shock—a gasp. My plan wasn't working. I needed to get to Rog, but the room began to darken around me. I heard a woman's muffled voice calling my name as my legs buckled. Rog said something, but his voice came out strangled.

The room swam away from me, the blue dawn at the windows dimming. I saw Sam, Saretha and my parents gathered around a spinning table, all talking at once, but I couldn't hear them. Kel was there, but Henri wasn't. I opened my eyes to a darkening blur and thought, for just a moment, that I saw Margot. Then everything went black.

THE STAIN OF A SENTENCE: $51.95

A bell kept sounding.

"Where is Henri?"

The bell sounded again.

Something struck my face. My eyes opened to see Margot's hand hovering in the air.

"Where is Henri?" she demanded. She was sitting over me, her face tight and hard. She had Kel's Pad in her non-slapping hand. The Pad was working again, lit up with the building's map. She shoved the map in front of my face.

I looked at her blankly. She slapped me again. The bell sounded. My head ached.

"Wake up, Speth. Tell me where Henri is."

The bell sounded again. We were on the elevator, going down. Where *was* Henri? We were on the sixtieth floor. Was Henry still on seventeen? Margot took a small, bean-shaped device from a pocket near her biceps. It looked like it had a little stinger. She jabbed it into my arm, and I felt my heart start racing. She slapped me again, one more time than was necessary. I sat up angrily.

"Type it!" she demanded. She held the Pad out to me. I

hesitated, and her face grew red with anger. "You typed Silas Rog, goddamn it, you can type Henri's location."

We weren't in a Squelch, but I didn't know if that mattered. The Pad wouldn't register it, and I had no Cuff to report it. I was too groggy and panicked to have the debate in my head about what I could or could not do anymore. We had to get to Henri and the others. I raised myself up and swatted at the 17 on the elevator's control panel.

"This elevator is stupidly slow," she complained. We were on the forty-fifth floor and dropping.

I looked around in a foolish pantomime, as if Rog might be on the elevator someplace, hoping Margot would understand what I asked.

"I hit Rog very hard on his head. Maybe he is dead. Maybe he is up and plotting. We should move quickly."

Damn it. Our next moves would have been simpler if I knew he couldn't interfere. She should have made sure he was dead, but murder was rather a lot to ask.

I tried to stand, but I felt weak. We were on the thirty-fifth floor. Margot looked determined.

"I told myself not to come back," Margot said, rummaging through her bag. "I said to myself, Henri is a big boy."

The thin bell rang again. Thirtieth floor. I looked at the elevator's display, scanning down to the lowest level. I had a plan. What had it been? I needed to get beneath this building. I needed to find the place where the WiFi was housed. That's what I needed to do. I stood and pressed the elevator's glass display. I queued the garage, the lowest floor I could find. Margot noted what I did and shook her head.

"Kel is an idiot," she said, examining her green pony bottle of sleep gas. "We're going to save her, too."

She attached some kind of nozzle. I didn't have a nozzle. I wouldn't have been able to use one anyway, since I couldn't have let Rog see me take the canister out.

"You are coming with me." She canceled my garage call with a swipe. Maybe she was right. Maybe she could help me after we rescued Henri and Kel. Maybe they all could.

The elevator slowed. I stood and looked for my bag.

Margot hooked it on my arm for me. I put my palm to my temple. There was a small spot of blood when I pulled it away.

"You're fine," Margot said, and she gave me a little shove halfway between playful and impatient as the elevator doors opened.

LICIT AUTHORITY: $52.98

The seventeenth floor was nothing but a hall of doors from the center out to the windows. Two Lawyers were walking toward us, dressed in their Butchers & Rog best. One was a blonde woman with legs so thin they looked insect-like. The other was a man with a narrow mustache. They seemed to greet the morning with determination, noting us without alarm. It scarcely seemed to register with them that anyone would dare intrude at Butchers & Rog. They kept walking. The woman typed diligently on her Cuff, like a reflex, coming off the last tap with a delicate flourish.

An InstaSuit™ appeared on Margot's Cuff. Twelve thousand dollars for associated pain and suffering from our trespass. The two Lawyers looked from her to me. Their satisfaction crumpled when they recognized I had no Cuff. My heart was beating fast, almost too fast. I was alert, but unsteady. Or maybe I was afraid. I couldn't think of how we would escape from this. The tower seemed to be crushing in on me from all sides, and I was still far from where I needed to be.

I took a deep breath. I didn't need to escape. I needed to get down to the WiFi.

The male Lawyer opened his mouth to speak, but Margot

slammed him to the floor like a possessed warrior. Insect Legs tottered back in fear, tapping away wildly at her Cuff; it was her only defense. Another InstaSuit™ vibrated from Margot's Cuff. Insect Legs turned to me, and her mouth fell open, horrified by my bare arm. I wanted to punch her in the face and break her slender, plastic, scalpeled nose, but instead, I swept her legs and she crumpled like a pile of twigs, weeping and tapping from the floor.

Without missing a beat, Margot put a small mask over her face and then slapped one on my head, leaving me to adjust it while she sprayed the two Lawyers like they truly were insects and her pony bottle was a can of bug spray.

When she was done, Margot pulled Kel's Pad from my hands and panned it from side to side, looking for the heat signatures of our friends. Every room had a Finishing Bed® inside, outlined in a thin neon glow, but all appeared empty until we were halfway down the hall. Margot's brow furrowed, unsure of what she was looking at.

A few doors in, Henri and Kel were each guarded by a man, with an extra guard inside the door and an outline I presumed to be the Lawyer working the machine. Cold metal shapes holstered in blue told us the guards were armed. Kel was in the finishing bed now, the warm glow of her body stiff in the machine.

Margot's face was red; her mouth was quivering. There were tears in her eyes. She angrily wiped them away.

"Don't take Henri from me," she said, low and throaty. "Please." Her pony bottle was ready. She shook herself and raised it with one hand, and held out the Pad in the other, turning back into the warrior of a moment ago. She nodded for me to unbolt the lock.

I opened the door without hesitation, swiping the mechanism like I had a hundred others. The door clicked open, and Margot pulled back on the bottle's trigger.

"Hold your breath, Henri!" Margot shouted, her arm extended blindly inside. I heard him gasp.

Bodies dropped like flies. Henri and the guards didn't heed Margot's warning, but Kel and Butchers did.

Butchers instantly understood what was happening and aimed his Cuff at Margot. I leapt at him. He had the same hole bored in his Cuff that Rog did, and before I could think, I jammed his arm up toward the ceiling. His Cuff detonated with four quick shots; bullets punctured the ceiling in a line of holes. Someone above us screamed. In one swift motion, Kel punched Butchers in the throat and he dropped to the ground, gagging, then silent.

"We need to get out of here," Kel said, looking at Margot with pride. Her Cuff buzzed harshly. Her account had gone so far into the negative from the Finishing Bed® that it registered a debt error. I didn't know what that was—I'd never seen it before, but her eyes weren't being shocked. She kicked the machine. Perhaps it had overloaded her Cuff's system.

"What is that thing?" Margot asked, smirking a little in the glow of Kel's approval.

"A parlor trick," Kel answered, kneeling down to Henri and jabbing him with the little bean-like device Margot had used on me. "I suspect it assigns algorithmically likely violations based on your personal history."

Of course, I thought to myself. Someone as deceitful as Silas

Rog would find it easier to fake reading our minds than to do the real thing. He could automate the process of destroying lives. Somewhere in a million words of Terms of Service, you can bet he hid a paragraph or two about results being approximate or simulated based on reasonable presumption.

"We need to get out of here," Kel said.

No, I thought. I took the Pad. I rifled through the layout of the building, scrolling down below the bottom floor. The map showed nothing but an empty circle. I showed it to them all.

"I think she is brain damaged," Margot said, rushing over to Henri as his eyes fluttered.

A small thrill flashed in Kel's eyes. "I don't think so." She'd understood me. My heart swelled. I showed the great empty outline to Margot again.

"What does this mean?"

"The WiFi is down below us, Margot."

Margot considered this, comprehension dawning on her face. I raced to the elevator.

"There won't be a giant off switch," Margot muttered, helping Henri to his feet. Henri looked at her, a little dazed, a little impressed.

I pressed the button for the lowest floor available—the garage—as Kel, Margot and Henri stepped on. I couldn't wait to get there. I was eager to see what damage I might do. The display ticked away each floor—*12, 11, 10, 9*—and then stopped. The elevator shook and seized.

We had been foolish to file into it. Rog's voice came over the intercom, groggy and furious. He was awake, and he ordered all the elevators stopped and the exits blocked. Then he swallowed and tried to recover his Legal tone.

"I grant Licit Authority to kill any of the interlopers," he rasped. "And someone bring Carol Amanda Harving to me."

Was my sister actually here, or did he just say that to scare me? Terror shot through me as I weighed what he might do to Saretha.

Kel popped open the exit panel in the elevator's ceiling, like I'd seen in a dozen movies, and we climbed quickly onto its roof. If there was one thing our team was practiced at, it was zipping down cables. It was probably faster for us to travel like this, anyway. The bottom level was two floors beneath the garage, and Kel managed to get the door open before we reached it.

This was it. I would destroy Rog's world, or I would die trying.

NANOLION™: $53.99

The WiFi hub and servers rested in an enormous shallow concrete bowl the size of a football field. Curved plastic shelves were interleaved in circles throughout the room like a maze. They were filled with chunky black boxes with tiny lights flashing along their faces. Routers, servers and thick silver batteries were packed in tight arrays. Streaming from them were dense black optical lines and ropes of twisted yellow, green and blue wires, threaded together to form anaconda-sized cables that wound through the room to a central trunk. There, they coiled up the massive pillar in a helical twist and exited out into the city to take in data from the air. Thin antennae were scattered everywhere, twitching. All of it was dotted with Patent marks and ®s and ©s, warning us that the ideas of these cables and their configuration were owned.

I was instantly filled with hatred for the whole thing, like it was an enormous, poisonous oak in a fairytale, enfolded by snakes and insects. Unfortunately, I had no idea how to destroy it.

Kel, Henri and Margot fanned out. The guards were no doubt right behind us. The room hummed around me, and I unplugged a wire to see what effect it might have. Somewhere in the city, perhaps a small FiDo emerged, but I couldn't see the effect from here. I had no idea where to begin.

Kel bit her lip. "What now?"

Henri pulled an axe from a fire safety box on the wall. You could see he was in full hero mode, ready to chop away at cables and computers, but Margot stayed his hand. "I do not want you crispy," she said. She took the axe and shook her body, miming an electrocution.

"Speth?" Kel asked, taking up a tactical spot near the room's main door.

Then I saw it. It was almost exactly the thing Margot said wouldn't exist. Along one curve of wall, there was a break in the shelves and servers. An enormous metal box with a red lever labeled MAIN POWER. Turning it off wouldn't be enough, but destroying it might. Without electricity coursing through the cables, we could chop them to bits, and how could they reprint them without their precious WiFi? The tether would be cut. The WiFi would melt away. This was what I had been looking for.

I sprinted to the lever, my heart full, my body flooded with relief and anticipation. But just as quickly, my resolve wavered. The food printers wouldn't work without the WiFi, either. How would people eat? Beecher's dad had worried everyone would starve.

My face crumpled. The system had us all backed into a corner. Small yellow lights pulsed all around the room as the servers ingested words and spat bills into the ether, but there was no way to stop it without potentially risking the lives of everyone we knew.

I felt the words long caught in my throat, and the silence

and servitude that closed in around us. Silas Rog had laid out his plan for me, and I was not alone. He would do the same to everyone like me.

My resolve rekindled. It would be better to starve.

I pulled the lever as hard as I could. The room's persistent hum stuttered and pitched down for just a moment. The yellow lights began to strobe, then returned to their previous blinking state. The hum redoubled and filled the room with a rising whine. From the interleaved rings of shelves, silver batteries began to kick on. Small blue pinpricks of light flicked to life and illuminated each NanoLion™ logo. The room turned cold blue with that light, and my body seemed to freeze in it, as the WiFi continued on.

"Enough," a voice echoed above me. It was Rog. This was no voice through an intercom; he was actually here. "These batteries will last for months. Everyone will remain connected. You will stop—now!"

But I would not stop.

"Everyone is going to know you're a fraud!" Henri shouted.

"Slander," Rog shot back.

Henri was looking upward. Did he see Rog?

"You think people are going to fall for your mind-reading machines?" Henri cried out.

"What matters," Rog said, "is the Law." I could hear his smile. "If the Law proclaims them accurate, they *are* accurate."

"Look," Kel whispered, looking up with her eyes.

Rog stood on a low-railed platform jutting out two stories above us. He was flanked by the brothers who had killed Sam, and beside him stood Saretha. She was bleary-eyed, but she stood obediently at Rog's side with a weak, admiring smile. Had he medicated her? Was she seeing something different than we were? I forced my eyes away from Saretha and scanned the room, frantically seeking some way to shut everything down.

"I see little point in making promises. But, consider—" Rog interrupted himself to gesture to the brothers to get down on the floor and find me "—generations of your family indentured. *Generations.*"

Saretha barely reacted. I moved deeper into the room, where the shelves of servers formed long, curving passageways. I began to unplug whatever I could find. I knew it made little difference—I might set them back an hour or a day, but the overall effort was futile. The smart thing would have been to flee.

"You think you have the *right* to change things? You will cause traffic crashes and hospital deaths, and old people will be unable to obtain medicine," Rog warned. "The poor won't be able to print food."

He was trying to chip away at my conscience, which only made me angrier. A real alternative might have stopped me, but he'd shown his hand. We would all be imprisoned within months with his fake "improvements." What kind of life would that be? And I was willing to bet Rog wouldn't let himself starve. There were other ways to eat.

"You will be held accountable, and in the end, you will accomplish nothing. You cannot turn off the power!"

His voice grew more strained. He was concerned. He had no idea how much this boosted me. Without meaning to, he'd let me know I could do real damage. The question was: How?

A guard burst through a door on my left, and at once Kel

had him on the ground, unconscious. She now had a pistol in her hand.

It took only a second for her to draw on Rog. Rog moved to the edge of the platform, unconcerned, and scowled down, giving Kel a clear shot. Kel pulled the trigger, but nothing happened. She looked more closely at the gun as Rog laughed from above, his face a waggling pixelation of glee.

"Fingerprint keyed," Kel said with disgust, tossing the weapon aside.

Henri and Margot were set upon next. The guards tussled and fought with them.

Rog spotted me and pointed down a manicured finger. "There," he called, eager to have me caught.

Another guard appeared. Kel took him out with ease. I ducked down farther, hiding from Rog's view, desperate for ideas. The guards were coming in with weapons, but they weren't shooting at us. Rog still wanted us alive.

Then I froze. Ahead of me, beyond a curved shelf of servers, I saw the indigo brother. His thick features turned to me, looking ghastly in the cold-charged battery light. He smiled. Then Kel was on him from nowhere, pulling him down by the neck and assaulting him with blows from her long limbs. I futilely pulled out another wire or two, but my efforts were pathetic.

"Speth!" Kel shouted, still struggling with the massive brother.

Behind me, the maroon brother was stalking up the aisle, his face flushed and determined. Lit by the blue battery light, his ruddy cheeks looked almost black and splotchy.

I whipped out the only thing I had that resembled a

weapon—my grapple hook. He pulled a gun. He had a clear shot, and with dread, I realized I was about to die.

"Stop!" Rog warned. The maroon brother startled, and then his brow narrowed. The room hummed with the sound of a thousand NanoLion™ batteries keeping the WiFi powered. Did Rog really want me alive this badly?

"Aim carefully," Rog said slowly, his eyes wide.

Suddenly I realized that he didn't want me alive at all. He feared what would happen to the batteries—those stupid, volatile NanoLion™ batteries!

At once, they turned to targets in my mind. I didn't care how dangerous it would be to hit them. It didn't matter anymore—Rog would see me dead or worse if he caught me.

The maroon brother had to aim perfectly—he had to hit me, and nothing else. All I had to do was hit any one of a dozen battery packs near him. But I only had one shot.

I pulled the trigger. The line shot out, and its sharp spear zipped by the brute's head. I let go of the gun; I couldn't be connected by that wire when it hit. I ducked and averted my eyes from the coming explosion. The maroon brother made a small, fearful noise, but then he laughed.

"I'm coming for you, *sister*," he warned.

Behind his head, the grapple had pierced a battery's case and—that was all. Nothing. The maroon brother holstered his gun and cracked his knuckles. He took a step. He could take care of me by hand now. But then the battery behind him bulged, like a steel balloon, emitting a high-pitched whine. The corners of it wrinkled. It hissed. He turned, his expression full of growing horror.

Blue-white jets of flame flared out. He staggered back,

crossing his arms in front of his face just as the battery pack exploded.

Rog wailed from the platform above, like the coming inferno was inside *him*. A sudden, blinding white light filled the room as another pack burst. There was a brief scream, then another high-pitched whine, followed by yet another explosion and more white light.

I stood there too long, stunned and horrified by what I had just done. *This isn't going to stop. This is a chain reaction.* I'd known what was coming, but watching it happen was something else entirely. Panic and amazement blossomed together in my gut.

Rog's building, WiFi and all, could not withstand the white-hot intensity of a hundred thousand NanoLion™ batteries exploding. I looked up and understood that we had to go—now.

Rog turned on Saretha, murder in his eyes, but she had slipped away from him. She was on the railing, two stories up, facing Rog. She looked back at the drop with her odd, Zockroft™-induced smile, and slipped from sight with a nauseating thud.

No! I screamed in my head. *Not Saretha. Not her, too!*

I pushed my way through the heat. The hum of the batteries warbled as the glow increased and spread. I had to shield my eyes to see as I worked my way through the room, telling myself the fall was not that far. Flames licked up all around me. The brothers were silent, obscured by the chaos—dead, or perhaps they'd bolted.

My heart pounding, I found Saretha splayed on the floor, her head turned away from the heat of a ruptured battery core. Another explosion sounded across the room. I raced to her, profoundly relieved to see her eyes flutter at the sound.

"We have to get out," Kel yelled. The hum of the room turned into a moan.

I tried to help Saretha up, but she was barely conscious and could not stand. She had broken her legs in the fall, one of them badly enough that the angle of her shin made me queasy.

"Leave me," she croaked, expecting shocks in her eyes, but they didn't come. The tether was broken. She shouted, more resolved. "Leave me!"

"That would be dumb," Margot said. "Henri, carry her."

Henri obediently picked her up.

"Henri the hero," Margot commented, pushing him along.

We fled up the stairs fast. We were good at this, traveling like a group with speed and efficiency. We burst out from the stairwell into the garage. Immediately, there was yelling from the opposite side.

"Get them!" Rog screeched.

Rog and his guards might have fled the inferno, but they weren't going to give up on capturing me.

"There!" a voice yelled, clearly meaning us.

"Two o'clock," Kel announced, looking at dozens of shapes gathering on our right under the flickering light.

Kel and Henri raced left, to a gleaming Nayarit Silver Ford Brute™. After a moment, Kel did something to the thumbprint reader. It clicked open.

The hard garage floor rumbled with a low, ominous hum, followed by a series of thuds. Dust shook from the ceiling. Doors opened at the far end of the garage, and security agents began to pour out. There was no Legal jargon this time: no warnings. There was no hesitation for fear of hitting a Nano-Lion™ battery.

Gunshots rang out, and I knew they meant to kill us.

Kel rushed us into the vehicle. Bullets pinged off the glass and hood. It was bulletproof—of course; it was a Lawyer's car.

In the confusion, I got in last and found myself in the driver's seat.

"Go," Kel barked. "Go!"

The seatbelts clicked in around us. There wasn't time to argue with Kel. I knew the basics from driving class.

"Ford™ is not responsible for injury, loss of life or other risks associated with automobile accidents. Please drive responsibly," the car chimed as the engine roared to life.

We jerked forward, plunging into a crowd of security guards who dove away in the nick of time.

I was driving too fast, by any normal account. *No time for caution.* The car flew up the exit ramp and arced through the air onto the street. We came down hard with a screech of metal and a shower of sparks behind us.

News dropters wobbled and buzzed in from both sides of the street, encircling our car.

Rog and his men scrambled to follow us. A few seconds later, an Ebony Meiboch™ Triumph appeared out of the darkness of the garage and bounced into the street behind us. In my rearview mirror, I watched it roar after us. The thin, flame-orange highlights told me exactly who was back there. Several other large, similar cars spread out behind.

The news dropters spread out, and more came in from up high. Then, suddenly, all of them faltered and dropped out of the sky. One banged off our hood and went spinning to the pavement. Another glanced off the roof.

"The WiFi is down," Kel confirmed. "There is no tether."

I couldn't help but smile at this. Behind us, two of Rog's cars skidded out, dropters caught under their wheels.

Excitement flooded through me. Rog would have no way to coordinate. He would have no way to track us. The only task left was to lose him and figure out where to go.

I jerked the wheel to turn, but did it harder than I should have. We skidded and swerved, bashing into an Ad station, but it didn't slow me. I tried again, with a little more control on the next turn. We zoomed down a narrow side street. Mr. Skrip, my driving teacher, would have been proud.

Kel shook her head. "Focus." She swiped at her Pad and looked uncertainly out the window. "The Twenty-Second Radian and Ring 12."

"You look like that actress," Henri said to Saretha.

My brain tried to understand that Kel, Margot and Henri had never met my sister. I glanced back at them in the rear-view mirror.

"Henri, you idiot," Margot said, forcing him to switch places and shuffling herself next to my sister. A fake smile masked, or failed to mask, Saretha's agony. Margot kept her eyes on Saretha and held out her hand to Kel. "Nexbuprofen™."

Kel passed back something that looked like a small red bean. Margot injected it into my sister's arm.

Thank you, Saretha mouthed, her eyes going a little dim. Margot began to wrap her leg. I kept glancing back, despite myself.

"Focus on the road!" Kel warned, then, less harshly, "She

will be okay. Jumping to get away from Rog was probably a smart move. Her legs will heal."

Between my sister and the Meibochs™ on our tail, it was hard to concentrate on where we were going. I couldn't let myself worry about Saretha right now; Margot would take care of her. I had to keep moving. I had to be brave.

Where *were* we going? I gripped the wheel to keep my hands steady. Driving at this speed on these interior streets was beyond reckless. I swerved around a line of cars and blasted through a light. Rog's Ebony Meiboch™ was clipped just behind me. It skidded sideways and smashed into the side of a parked car. The wheels smoked as his car tore off after us once more. Farther back, at least three others followed.

"We should take the Western Exit off the outer rim," Kel said, thinking ahead.

Henri checked his bag. "What if we shot a grapple line out...?" he started excitedly.

Margot shook her head. "You will lose your hand."

Henri looked at his grapple with disappointment.

No matter how many sharp turns I took, Rog and his crew would not be shaken. On the sidewalks, people were out, but I was going too fast to gauge their reactions. Did anyone have a clue what had just happened?

There was a thundering crack from the center of the city. It sounded like when the dome was struck by lightning. My heart skipped a beat, terrified the damage might be bad enough to take down the dome. People on the street staggered and cowered.

"Left, then right. The Twentieth Radian is wide," Kel said, unphased. I swerved into and out of each turn.

I tried to glance up at the city's roof, but a shot rang out behind us. It ticked off the bumper and zipped off with a cartoonish whir. In the rearview mirror, I saw the indigo brother hanging out the passenger window of Rog's car, his tongue in his teeth. He was alive. That was disappointing.

He fired again and again. Rog's car pulled up and rammed us from behind.

Henri laughed at him.

"Eventually he'll shoot the tires," Kel said, frowning. "Or knock us off the road."

Margot threw her bag to the floor in frustration. There was nothing in it to help us. Henri bit his lip. I feinted a turn, and the Meiboch™ dipped right, then came back after us, gaining. Henri's window motored open.

"Henri!" Margot shouted. Saretha groaned.

Henri leaned out and fired his grapple. His gun whipped out of the car, slamming out of the window, then bounced out onto the road, where it beat around and around Rog's driver's side wheel until the gun was pulverized.

"Yes!" Henri shouted, shaking his hand out and laughing.

"You idiot!" Margot screamed.

Kel clucked her tongue. Saretha groaned.

"See, I can have good ideas," Henri announced proudly.

Kel squinted back and shrugged. "Maybe it will slow them down."

"Let me have *your* grapple," Henri said to Margot with a wild gleam in his eye.

In the rearview mirror, I could see the wheel he'd hit wobbling swiftly.

"Here!" Kel jabbed her finger at the road. We were coming up on the entrance to the outer ring. I took the curve hard, remembering too late that I shouldn't accelerate into a turn. We slid into the wall with a metal screech.

Rog's car slammed us from behind. My body jerked back and then forward. More gunfire peppered the car. My heart was pounding—I couldn't let Rog catch me. It wasn't just my survival instinct; it was a powerful need not to let him win. I floored it, and Rog's driver kept right after me.

On the outer ring, the speedometer pushed past two hundred miles per hour.

"We'll take the Western Exit," Kel said.

"Out of the city?" Henri asked.

The thought turned my stomach to knots. I had no idea what was out there. Plus, there were people who needed me inside the dome. Nancee was here somewhere. There was Penepoli and Mandett, not to mention all the Silents. They would be gathering, or had gathered.

Kel didn't answer. Where did she want to go? We sped past Falxo Park and under the bridge just beyond. Above us, dozens of people looked down. In the rearview mirror, I saw the bridge and the park and the crowd. I couldn't see how many. Were they all Silents?

Rog's cars had spilled out behind us and fanned across the wide lanes of the outer ring. Without the streets to contain them, they could move in against us. I pushed the pedal to the floor, and the Brute™'s fat wheels hugged the curve of the road.

Falxo Park and the long, arching bridge receded in the distance, dotted by the silhouettes of people seemingly jostling to see down. Behind the black glass of Rog's car, I could see nothing of the man I wanted to destroy.

"It's coming up fast," Kel warned. The Western Exit was

in view, on the opposite side of the road. I couldn't make it, or perhaps I didn't want to. I let my hands make the choice. If we left the city, we might end up someplace where the WiFi was functioning. Rog could call for help—he could coordinate. I needed to stay here and see this through.

"Speth?" Kel asked.

I dipped the wheel, crossing all eight lanes, skimming the outer edge of the wall toward the exit. I wanted them to think we were leaving. Rog and his men took the bait. They followed, but I peeled off at the last moment. One of Rog's cars panicked and slammed right into the sharp wall. Two others disappeared down the tunnel so that only Rog's Meiboch™ Triumph remained behind us.

Despite my efforts, his Meiboch™ continued to inch closer.

I made a snap decision and turned fast, whipping up the next exit. Rog was caught off guard, and the Meiboch™ shot past us. As we went up the ramp, Rog's driver slammed on the car's brakes, but the ring traffic kept coming. He couldn't back up through the onslaught. The Meiboch™ peeled out, clearly heading for the next exit, and I quickly turned the car back, taking us toward the park.

"What are you doing?" Margot demanded, then, realizing I wasn't going to answer, she asked Kel, "What is she doing?"

"Shh," Kel shushed, because she could see what I saw up ahead. It wasn't just a few dozen people who had gathered—it was more like a thousand, and despite the WiFi being out, they were all totally silent.

DEBT: $55,000,000

People had gathered in and around the park, just like Sera had said they would. They crowded the bridge and flooded the outer boulevard of shops. I didn't know if they were all Silents, but no one was speaking. The scene was at once heartening and eerie. The only sound came from their shuffling, and from the distant chaos at the center of the city. I could not shake the feeling they were waiting for me, though they could not have known I was here.

I slowed the car to a stop at the edge of the crowd. From every direction, people were straggling in, drawn to this spot where I had fallen silent, where Beecher had killed himself, where Sam had been murdered.

A terrible moan escaped me. It had only been a day. I looked away from the bridge, swallowing hard, and stepped out of the car.

My presence drew the attention of everyone who could see me. Fingers pointed and people nudged each other, but still no one spoke. A stage and podium were set up, just as they had been for me on my Last Day. For one, self-important moment, I thought it was for me, but then I realized it was Mandett Kresh's Last Day celebration. He stood at the edge of the stage, looking at me, wide-eyed and hopeful. Was he going to go silent? Was that his plan? Around him, I saw a few familiar faces. Norflo Juarze, Itzel Gonz and Penepoli. Phlip and Vitgo were hanging near the back of the crowd.

I could not help but think of who wasn't here. Beecher and Sam. My parents. Mrs. Stokes. Nancee. Would the freedom of the untethered WiFi help her? Would it help any of us?

In the distance, another enormous crack resounded. The dome shuddered with the sound. Two enormous hexagonal tiles came loose near the city's center. The Aeroluminum® panels fell like snowflakes and floated down between the buildings.

A surge of weakness pounded through me, wondering if I had doomed us all. And, if I hadn't, what now? What came next?

Police hovered around the edges of the gathering multitude, tentative and uncomfortable in their riot gear. During such a catastrophic event, it was their mandate to keep not just the peace, but also the silence.

"Under criminal code 7129, you are prohibited from all forms of Copyrighted and Trademarked communication, including speech, while WiFi and tether services are unavailable," a pleasant, recorded female voice reminded the crowd. The police played this recording at seemingly random intervals around the edges. Ironically, the Silents and I were, by virtue of our silence, the most Law-abiding citizens in the city.

The morning sun blazed down in two shafts from hexagonal holes in the dome, shining down somewhere into the Troisième. I wondered how dangerous that sunlight was.

I pushed forward, not knowing what else to do. Rog would

not take long to circle the ring and find us. Kel, Margot and Henri, with my sister on his back, followed me into the crowd. We could never escape now. Something else had to be done.

My bag was still on my shoulder, damp from the sweat of my escape. Penepoli's eyes went wide as I drew closer. She nodded and clutched her chest, like I was some kind of celebrity.

I caught a flash of Arkansas Holt in his chartreuse suit. He stood beside a pair of police officers, pointing toward me. I recognized one of them—Shalk. Our eyes met, and he stood his ground, holding back the other officers with a light touch. Behind their backs, Holt gave me a double thumbs-up, zippered his lips and vanished into the crowd.

All around, Affluents were fleeing. They ducked their heads out of the surrounding shops and then, suddenly, one of them would run for it, as best as they were able. Where were they going? What were they afraid we would do?

Just then, Rog's Ebony Meiboch™ Triumph IV roared up over the bridge, and the crowd moved back, like a herd. His car could pass no farther than the bridge's apex, near the split in the mesh that turned my stomach. There were too many people.

The Triumph™'s doors opened, and Rog's voice cut through the quiet.

"Cease and desist!" he bellowed. "Cease and desist!"

I could not see him. The crowd was too thick around me and seemed to close in.

"Keep moving," Kel whispered, but I stopped.

I motioned for her and the others to move farther on; I

would catch up. With the WiFi down, Rog's face would be unpixelated. I wanted to see it—I wanted to know who this man was. I felt bolstered by the presence of all these allies. What was Rog going to do? Would he dare shoot me in front of everyone, even the police?

I wasn't afraid to die. And I didn't want to live in a world where he could get away with such a thing.

The crowd parted before me, giving me space. I let Rog come. The gold brother emerged beside him, and the two of them came hulking toward me, taking one furious stride after another.

"By every legal authority known and herefore ever imagined," Rog growled, frothing at the mouth, "I hereby swear that you will suffer to the fullest and harshest extent of the Law, exceeding every imaginable dire consequence for your heinous acts against economic growth and Intellectual Property."

His face was, as I'd expected, unpixelated, though it was so distorted by his fury that, for a moment, I couldn't really see what he looked like. Veins popped from his forehead. Flecks of spit rimmed his mouth. I was shaken by a desire to flee rather than attack.

His words may have been litigious fearmongering, but they seemed to cut to my very bones. I still feared him. I still feared how he wielded Legalese like a weapon to frighten me. I still feared all that he could do. I stepped back despite myself, and I hated that weakness.

Then he stopped screaming, and I could see him at last. My fear had delighted him. He was white, though his face was mottled pink from his settling rage. He looked to be about fifty or so, with salt-and-pepper hair trimmed to perfection, like the male lead in any Carol Amanda Harving film. He was handsome—surprisingly so, despite his anger and his unfocused, shark-like eyes.

Rog raised his Cuff at me, the gun muzzle pointed straight at my heart. The gold brother grudgingly gave way to allow Rog to kill me. Rog's hands clenched and released, like he was imagining the pleasure of killing me with his hands, not his gun. I gritted my teeth against my instinctive fear and hoped my face showed him the same kind of hate in return.

But Rog's anger had melted away into a murderous gleam. His eyes crinkled with joy, and his face turned pleasant, almost charming.

"They will see that you are nothing more than flesh, blood and bone," Rog explained. Phlip nudged Vitgo, as if he thought this would be good. I forced myself to reclaim the ground I'd lost to fear, because now I knew: Rog was afraid of me. He wanted to show everyone I was merely human, but only because he knew in his heart that I was more. I had become a symbol, and that terrified him.

I took a step toward Rog, my heart thumping hard in my chest. If I had to die, I wanted witnesses. I wanted everyone to see I was silence. I was hope. I was the insurrection. He could not end this revolution by killing me, though I hoped I did not have to die for it.

I tried to look brave as Rog clenched his hand with cruel pleasure, pulling the trigger. But there was no sound, no flash and no impact. Phlip's eyes went wide, and Vitgo looked away.

Rog fired again. The Cuff failed him; it would not follow his command without the tether. It obeyed the rules he had

GREGORY SCOTT KATSOULIS

made. Rog's eyes bulged with confusion and despair, and his failure was a joy to behold.

My face broke into a wide smile. I don't know if it was as beautiful as Saretha's, but it felt good.

I took another step closer to Rog.

Shalk pushed his way out of the mass of people. Three officers trailed behind.

Rog shook his Cuff, trying to get it to work. When it failed, he shouted, "Arrest her. I will prosecute her myself!"

The officers moved in around me. Shalk drew his plastic restraints and turned to Rog, as if looking for further instruction.

"Now!" Rog commanded, like Shalk was his servant. "Her crimes are multitudinous. I want—"

Shalk pressed a button on his modified Cuff.

"Under criminal code 7129-A, you are prohibited from all forms of Copyrighted and Trademarked communication, including speech, while WiFi and tether services are unavailable."

"I *wrote* code 7129-A!" Rog screeched.

Shalk frowned and put his thumb and forefinger to his mouth. He zipped in a hard, quick gesture. Rog stared at him, momentarily stunned. Shalk forced him to turn and bound Rog's hands behind his back.

"Have you lost your mind?" Rog screamed. "She murdered Leeland Butchers!"

Had we?

Shalk played the recording again.

"Under criminal code 7129..."

"Kill her!" Rog thundered at the gold brother nearby.

The gold brother broke forward like a bull. Phlip took a

step, but Vitgo held him back. The crowd stirred. I coiled, ready to hit him in the throat or eyes to slow him, but before I could strike, a blur crossed my vision. It was Henri. He slammed into the gold brother's beefy side and knocked him off course, into the crowd of Silents. Margot rushed in behind. The gold brother shook them off and tried to stand, but hands shot out from the crowd. Bodies overwhelmed him. Two more officers moved in and brought him down.

I turned back to see Kel and Saretha only a yard behind me. Henri and Margot stood near Rog, dusting themselves off, and Mandett was making his way toward us.

"Do you have any idea what will happen to you once I am free?" Rog hissed.

Shalk tapped again on his Cuff. *"You have the right to remain silent. Anything you say can, and will, be charged against your account, with a 20 percent surcharge to cover processing fees. Anything this officer or any other Law enforcement official says in the course of the investigation will be charged to you, and billed at such time as your case is adjudicated. You have the right to an Attorney. If you cannot afford an Attorney, one will be assigned to seize your assets, and you will be turned over to Debt Collection. Do you understand these rights?"*

"When the WiFi returns, you will regret this," Rog warned. "Everything will be rebuilt. It will all be reprinted, and I *will* destroy you! I will snake this city with so much cable and wire that it will strangle every one of you sluks!" he screeched wildly, whirling around at the crowd. His voice bounced across the plastic melt of the faux French buildings and vanished.

Shalk began to pull him away, but I raised a hand. I wanted Rog to be here for what came next.

"That's speech!" He laughed with wild eyes. "You cannot trust her! She will destroy our city, and with it, all of you!"

I looked from Mandett and Henri to Silas Rog's smirking, sneering face. Margot tore a strip of fabric out of the supplies in her bag. She, Mandett and Henri gagged the struggling Rog while Shalk looked on, as if all of this was normal.

Everything stopped then. The screens around the park glowed faintly, still powered, but blank. The noise and wind of the cars on the ring had ceased. A breeze of a different sort wafted across the park—cold air from the outside that smelled crisp and sweet and salty.

I pushed through the crowd and mounted the stage. My body ached from all I had been through. Kel, Margot, Henri and Saretha all watched, wide-eyed. My eyes searched for Sam in the crowd, though I knew I would not find him. Speaking now would not betray him, though I felt his absence acutely. He would have relished what was to come.

I put a shaking thumb and finger to the corner of my mouth, and drew it slowly across my lips. I made the sign of the zippered lips, only this time I was unzipping them. I cleared my throat, letting sound escape, and the feeling was exquisite.

It was time for my speech.

FREE

"Words matter," I said. "Words make ideas. They preserve truths and history. They express freedom, and they shape it."

The feel of letters on my tongue quenched me, like water on parched lips. I could hardly believe I was speaking. It seemed like a lifetime has passed. I was a different person now.

"Words," I went on, "mold our thoughts. That gives them value and power. The Rights Holders keep them not just for profit, but to control us, and to put us in their service. Rights Holders *create* nothing. They jealously protect the copies of copies of copies of things created by others. They get away with owning our right to speak because they have the money and power to do it."

My mind was crafting sentences like they were shaped in a forge. I'd seen that once in a movie, where glowing steel sparked as it was hammered into shape.

"Our only recourse has been a deeper, more painful silence. Rights Holders like Silas Rog squeezed our speech down to a trickling stream, but kept that small stream flowing to make us pay for every word—to make us think we could speak. But that was an illusion. We fought them with silence, and now we are freed to fight them with our voices."

"Yeah!" Mandett Kresh called out. People around him

nodded. Vitgo looked confused, and Phlip had disappeared. Some of the Silents puzzled over my words.

"The time of our silence is over!" I cried out.

Most of the Silents hooted and hollered and cheered at this, but a few faces narrowed and frowned, their lips shut tight. A thrill ran through me, and then a cold fear. They all looked to me for what came next, and that was terrifying.

"No printer will function now," I explained, working to steady my voice. "The WiFi is destroyed. Without the tether, every pattern, every wall, every design is locked down. Without the 'legally required,' always-on connection, there is no way for Rog and his Legal team, or anyone else, to take over this city again. No one can legally speak here, or call for help. No one can enter or leave the city, because no one can legally agree to the Terms of Service to cross, or pay the tolls and tax to come and go. No one can legally enforce the Law. No one who is Indentured can be commanded."

I thought of Nancee, wherever she was. There were no news dropters to record me, but I prayed my words would reach her somehow.

Rog scowled and smirked beneath his gag, his face twisted with the fuming smugness of a man who had never been denied anything. He did not believe me. He thought the problem would be solved in a matter of days. He was so sure he could not lose that even now, he could not recognize he had lost *everything*.

"The tether isn't coming back," I said, to everyone, but especially to him. "It will not return in a day, or a week, or a year. The Law has written itself into a corner. If we follow the Law, we will all die. We cannot print food. Food can't be brought in from the outside. We can't leave to find it.

"The Rights Holders will leave us for dead because the

Law is pitiless and inflexible. Silas Rog himself will die by his own hand, starving with the rest of us while insisting we must not make food without the proper license."

I saw fear now on faces in the crowd. Rog kept his smirk, but it was beginning to weaken. I reached into my bag.

"But the dome itself now shelters us from those Laws that would kill us."

My voice faltered here as a worry overtook me. Not every Law was madness. If what little I had read was true, many were born out of logic and then twisted over time. Freedom of Speech was a Law that had been lost. There was a path—a history I did not know. A new ember kindled in my brain. I pulled out one book, and then the other.

"Silas Rog would have us believe there is a single book to save us—to prove Freedom of Speech is a right. I've been to his library and searched for the book, but what I found instead was a trap, built on the myth Rog himself created."

I held one book up higher.

"This book shows how the molecular inks work. It has a key and the codes that will let us know which will kill us, which can feed us and how we can make food on our own. But this is not *the* book."

I held up the other.

"Neither is this. The myth of that book is a lie, cooked up by Silas Rog to offer a simple, enticing solution. But there is something Rog missed."

Rog's face crumpled a little more. He tried to shake off the officers while the crowd cheered me on.

"No single book shows the way, but all of them, together, do. Our history is recorded there—right and wrong, every

step and misstep, all the things Rog and his kind have scru-
pulously hidden. They are just waiting to be discovered."

I thought of my name, Jimenez, and knew it was no accident
it had been shortened. I wondered what other names might
have been changed, and what purpose it served.

"They made us forget who we are, took our names and stole
our culture."

I looked to the center of the city, where Rog's library rested
above the dome. For all I knew, it was burning now—but even
if it was destroyed, I felt certain our history could still be found.

"Freedom of Speech *was* our right." I spoke loud and clear
and shook the pages of the book I held. "And no matter what
the Law now says, it *is still* our right."

Henri took the stage and stood behind me. Margot followed,
and Kel moved to my side, hardened with resolve. I put the
books on the podium and reached back to find Margot's hand.

"The simple act of charging us for every word and gesture allowed the Rights Holders to control far more than a
small piece of property: they held our rights, our freedoms
and our very lives."

Penepoli raced up onto the stage, her eyes bright and desperate. Mandett stayed on the ground, soaking everything in.
Kel took my other hand and squeezed, and I squeezed back,
unafraid of charges or shocks to my eyes. My whole body
glowed with pride in what we had accomplished.

"Every book warns us at the beginning: *All Rights Reserved.*
But I don't believe it. Every right will not be reserved. *Our*
rights will not be reserved. We will be free."

★ ★ ★ ★ ★

ACKNOWLEDGMENTS

This story has had nearly as many lives as a cat, which is to say one, but also, something like nine. A lot of people helped me in a myriad of ways, and while it sounds trite to say *I couldn't have done this without them*, I truly couldn't have done this without them.

There is Val Gintis, and Jill Carrigan, who long ago suffered through a story I once wrote—kind of like this one, but so very much worse. There is Lee Gjertsen Malone, who helped critique and refine my writing, and guided me down the path of being an *Author*.

There is my agent, Lisa Rodgers, and the whole JABberwocky team, whose excitement and enthusiasm for this book brought us all on an epic journey to find it the right home.

There is my editor, Lauren Smulski, who improved my writing with her keen eye and her ability to lightly suggest a brilliant change—and everyone at Harlequin TEEN who, like wizards, took the words I wrote and have somehow transformed them into this book in your hands.

There is Connie Biewald and Jen Kay.Goodman and the Fayerweather Street School, who helped me put this book in front of readers about Speth's age. (I'm very sorry, Ollie, about Sam.)

There is Sean Hill and Daniel Sroka who, at very different times, helped provide feedback and fresh eyes. (Delicious, fresh eyes.)

There is Cory Doctorow, who fired me up on the topic of Copyfight more than anyone I can think of, and M.T. Anderson, who made a path for this story before it was written.

There is John Luther Adams, whose music is the only thing I can listen to while writing these days.

And then there is my family, who have supported me through everything—especially Evia, who inspired me to warn the world away from the one depicted in this book. And, most of all, my wife, Jenn, who knows too well the many ways she made it possible for me to write, and stay grounded, and move forward until I had something good.